Chan Ling Yap's third novel has all the assurance of her first two successes – and more. A strong story line, deftly rendered in brief and readable instalments, takes us from the turbulence of a China unmercifully exploited with opium by the western powers in Victorian times, to the race and clan rivalries of an emerging Singapore and Malaya. The beautiful and tragic figure of Hua might serve as a metaphor for the suffering sub-continent; and that of her husband Ngao for the resilience of the Chinese themselves.

The refinement and the thuggery of China alike, the bustle of Singapore and the tropical potential of Malaya in those days are all made to feel familiar rather than foreign, the high emotions to be shared rather than differentiate us. The characters are entirely believable, the degree of background 'colour' is perfectly judged, and the pace seductive: don't be surprised if you find you read this book at a sitting.

—Bill Jackson,

Editor of *The Corporal and the Celestials*

Reviews for *Sweet Offerings* and *Bitter-Sweet Harvest*:

Bitter-Sweet Harvest is one of "4 Books you Won't Want to Put Down". A controversial page-turner ... heart breaking and thought provoking.

—Review from *Cosmopolitan* (Singapore, January 2012)

Bitter-Sweet Harvest is a love story beautifully and engagingly told. It reflects the complex ethnic, religious and social tensions of Malaysia and beyond—all made vivid through the experience of characters, movingly depicted, and the exciting action, which carries the reader briskly from page to page.

—Dato' (Dr) Erik Jensen,
Author of *Where Hornbills Fly*

Tautly written, Chan Ling Yap's second novel is a powerful story of the problems of intercultural marriage that can arise from family interference. With a superbly woven plot, *Bitter-Sweet Harvest* leads the reader through a minefield of cultural, ethnic and religious conflicts. Compelling and gripping, I found I could not put down this tragic saga of missed opportunities for the lovers. A poignant love story that is highly recommended!

—Professor Bill Edeson,
Professorial Fellow, University of Wollongong

Sweet Offerings is a great read with real emotion and such detail as one can almost smell the atmosphere coming from the pages. Also I cannot recall ever reading a book where the very last word carried so much meaning for the future.

—Chris Allen

NEW
BEGINNINGS

CHAN LING YAP

Marshall Cavendish
Editions

Published by Marshall Cavendish Editions
An imprint of Marshall Cavendish International (Asia) Pte Ltd
1 New Industrial Road, Singapore 536196

The publisher makes no representation or warranties with respect to the contents
of this book, and specifically disclaims any implied warranties or merchantability or
fitness for any particular purpose, and shall in no events be liable for any loss of profit
or any other commercial damage, including but not limited to special, incidental,
consequential, or other damages.

This is a work of fiction. Although references have been made to real historical figures,
the events and acts surrounding them are a product of the author's imagination.

Other Marshall Cavendish Offices:
Marshall Cavendish Corporation. 99 White Plains Road, Tarrytown NY 10591-
9001, USA • Marshall Cavendish International (Thailand) Co Ltd. 253 Asoke,
12th Flr, Sukhumvit 21 Road, Klongtoey Nua, Wattana, Bangkok 10110, Thailand
• Marshall Cavendish (Malaysia) Sdn Bhd, Times Subang, Lot 46, Subang Hi-Tech
Industrial Park, Batu Tiga, 40000 Shah Alam, Selangor Darul Ehsan, Malaysia

Marshall Cavendish is a trademark of Times Publishing Limited

National Library Board Singapore Cataloguing in Publication Data
Yap, Chan Ling.
New beginnings / Chan Ling Yap. – Singapore : Marshall Cavendish Editions, 2014.
pages cm
ISBN : 978-981-4408-61-5 (paperback)

1. Chinese – Malaysia – Malaya – Fiction. 2. Malaya – History – Fiction. 3. Opium
abuse – Fiction. I. Title.

PR6125
823.92 – dc23   OCN849881434

Printed in Singapore by Fabulous Printers Pte Ltd

Dedication

In honour of the men and women pioneers
who gave so much to the foundation
of what is now Singapore and Malaysia
and not least to my husband
for his support and encouragement.

Acknowledgements

I drew upon numerous sources of information in the preparation of the book. I am greatly indebted to all of them, but I would like to mention in particular:

- *Kongsi* NetWorks, *The History of Yap Ah Loy: Kapitan Cina of Kuala Lumpur and Klang (1867–1885)*, 2000, for the wonderful insight into the turbulent times of the Selangor civil war and the life of Yap Ah Loy;
- C.M. Turnbill, *A History of Singapore 1819–1975*, Oxford University Press, 1980;
- Barbara Watson Andaya and Leonard Y. Andaya, *A History of Malaysia*, Palgrave, 2001; and
- Julia Lovell, *The Opium War*, Picador, 2011.

I would also like to thank my husband, Tony, for his patience, encouragement, and support throughout my writing of the book. Thanks also go to my children, Lee and Hsu Min, and to Bill Jackson and Marian Gosling for reading and commenting on my draft manuscript.

A note on Chinese names

In writing the book, I toyed with the idea of changing the names of the main characters to a form that would be easy to remember for people unfamiliar with Chinese names. I decided against it, because I believe this would only serve to perpetuate a difficulty that in reality need not be a problem at all. After all a Chinese name has only one or two syllables.

Chinese words are generally arranged in order of their importance. Hence as far as names are' concerned, this means that the family name comes first, followed by a person's given name.

Chinese given names can consist of one or two characters (words). When a person's given name has two characters, the first one is generally the generation name. This name is shared by all family members of the same generation. The second character gives the personal identity of the person. When generation names are used, it is inappropriate to refer to a person by the first character of the given name.

Take, for example, my name. Living in the West I followed the style of putting my family name 'Yap' after my given name 'Chan Ling' so I am known as and write under the name 'Chan Ling Yap'. If I were to follow Chinese practice, my name would be written 'Yap Chan Ling'. 'Chan' is the name shared amongst the girls in my generation and together with the second Chinese character, 'Ling', is my complete given name. I am called 'Chan Ling' (for simplification, think of it as equivalent to *Ma-ry*).

In the book I have used the traditional Chinese way of presenting names, that is placing the surname first. So in the case of the character called 'Ong Wan Fook', 'Ong' is his surname, 'Wan' is his generation name and 'Fook' is his given personal identity. He would be called 'Wan Fook'.

There are variations to the above general example. Some given names do not have a 'generation' name and consist of only one character.

For example, Ngao, the main character in the novel, has only one character to his name. Various reasons have been given for the use of one character names. It is said that for a period under Han rule, the use of two character personal names was forbidden and so the use of one character given names might be a result of this. The use of one character name is also common in rural and farming communities. In such cases, it is not uncommon for people to attach the prefix 'Ah-' in front of the first character. So 'Ngao' would sometimes be called 'Ah Ngao', where the prefix 'Ah' has no meaning. It is only used to soften the sound.

In rural communities, it is not uncommon for people to name their children after farm animals reflecting their perceived characteristics. For example, 'Ngao' means 'bull' (strength). 'Hua' means 'flower'. Generally masculine names are strong sounding names while feminine names relate to beauty or feminine softness.

Today many Chinese people have joined the two characters that form their given name into one to bring Chinese names more into conformity with western practices. For example, 'Mao Ze Dong' used to be written in three separate words to reflect three characters in Chinese writing. Now, it is often written as 'Mao Zedong'. 'Mao' is the surname; 'Ze Dong' or 'Zedong' is his given name.

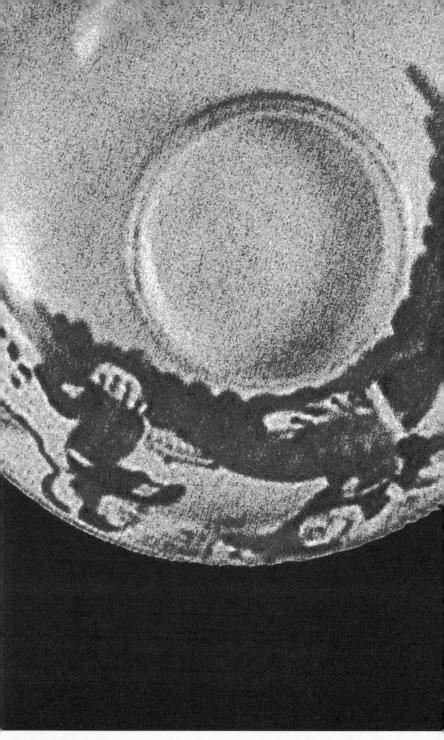

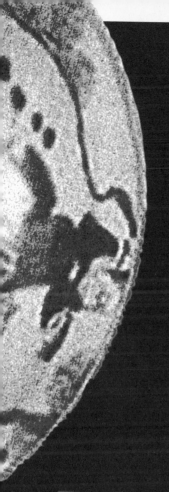

Part
One

Yuzhou, Guangxi Province
Southern China

1856

Chapter 1

SPIRALS OF SMOKE rose into the air. It spread like a dirty fog blanketing almost the entire city. From the hill above, all that could be seen were sporadic patches of grimy crimson rooftops amidst a sea of grey smog.

Gunshots rang out. The little girl clutched her ears, pushing her pigtails, two little bunches of tightly braided hair, away from the sides of her face. The pigtails pointed upwards and outwards; they bobbed violently as she held her ears and ducked at the sound of the gunshots coming from the city. She squeezed her eyes tight and kept her head low, crouching beside the goat tethered next to her. Her bottom barely skimmed the ground. Minutes passed. The gunshots gave way to a crescendo of different noises. The clamour reached where she crouched, muted only by distance.

After a while, the little girl stood up and tiptoed towards a ledge on the edge of the slope. She lay flat on her stomach and looked down at the sprawling city of Beiliu below. Slowly the fog dispersed. She could see movements; distant figures no bigger than dots moving en masse like ants but with none of their organisation. They were people, running, pushing and fleeing the city. She imagined pounding feet and creaking cartwheels. She had overheard her father telling her mother about the chaos in the city, of people getting trampled to death, of the indiscriminate killings.

Ordinary Chinese, proud of their Han ancestry, were rising in revolt against the oppression of their foreign Manchu rulers. Led by Hong Xiu Quan, they refused to shave their heads and grow long queues – symbols of their subjugation to the Manchu. Instead they grew their hair long, earning the nickname '*chang mao*'. Her father spoke of the reprisals. The Qing emperor's army had marched on the city to destroy the long-haired rebels. Day after day, carnage followed. Shao Peng had listened in awe. Though she did not understand all that was said, she was fascinated. She had never been to the city. She had never even left the hill.

She leaned further over the ledge to get a better view down the hillside. Tier upon tier of paddy fields stretched out beneath her. The fields looked strange – straggly tufts of yellow paddy dotted the ground, their stalks and leaves shrivelled by the drought that had hit the country. Along the bunds separating the fields, banana trees stood like sentinels, their large palm-like leaves ragged, torn by strong thermal winds. Everywhere she saw the destruction caused by the drought and the ravages of hungry men and women who had fled the city. Yes, people were fleeing from the city, yet today, her father had chosen to do just the opposite. He had gone there in search of work. There was no food to be eked out of the parched soil of the farm.

She turned around quickly to look at the goat tethered to a fallen tree trunk. We have little to eat except for my goat, she thought. Tears welled up in her eyes at the prospect that the goat might have to be killed for food. Scrambling to her feet, she quickly went over to untie it. She had heard her parents discussing the possibility in hushed whispers, as she lay huddled in the corner of the plank bed that she shared with them.

"Shao Peng! Shao Peng! Where are you?" Her mother's voice rang out from behind the copse of trees set well back from the rise of the hill. "Come back, come back at once!"

The little girl gathered up the rope and coaxed the goat forward. "*Lai lai!* Come, come! We have to go." The goat remained stubbornly still, ignoring her commands. She pulled and then ran forward half dragging the resisting animal. The movement disturbed birds roosting on the tree; squawking they took flight. Suddenly the goat seemed to sense the urgency and trotted meekly by her side. "Come, come," she coaxed breaking into a run. "Father might be back."

❀ ❀ ❀

NGAO PICKED HIS way through the debris in the street and headed for the eastern side of Beiliu. From there, he would walk beyond the city walls to the clay mines. His search for work in the city had been a failure. He hitched up the much-patched cloth bag slung over his shoulder. It contained his lunch, a boiled sweet potato and a leather flask of water. He looked around him. The street was quiet. Yet just a few hours earlier, it had been milling with people. People with crazed looks; people brandishing knives, cleavers, anything that might offer a vestige of protection from the approaching army. Women with children toted on their hips scrambled through doorways and windows. Their screams resounded long after they had fled.

Caught up in this heaving crush of bodies, Ngao too had run and pushed. Several times, he fell and was almost trampled underfoot. He saw an open door that led into a courtyard. Quickly he hid behind it and squatted next to a huge urn. He saw others doing the same. Doors opened and slammed shut. Then almost like magic, the street was empty.

Hours passed. Word came through that the army had marched on by. The gunshots that had been gaining ground on the fleeing crowd had veered to the western side of the city. It was safe once more in this quarter. The army claimed that they had no quarrel with the ordinary people. They were only looking for the *chang mao*. People knew, however, that it would take only one rebel to be found in their midst, for a whole family to be decapitated. One disgruntled suspicious soldier could send dozens of them to prison. Yet life had to go on. Slowly people came out of hiding and returned to their homes. Others continued their flight into the surrounding hills. This had been the pattern of life in the city ever since the start of the Taiping rebellion. Seeming calm followed by disruption and violence, and then a return to normality. The tension was always there: in people's faces, in their furtive movements, and in the mistrust between families and clans.

Ngao had come to the city to look for his uncle. He had hoped to find work in his pottery. It was a final attempt before he left for the clay mines. He was skilled, having been apprenticed at the age of eight to the master potter in his uncle's establishment. He had only left the pottery when he got married.

His uncle had shaken his head when he saw him earlier that morning. "*Zou!* Go! Try your luck at the clay mines. Clay is still needed to make pottery, but no one wants the fine porcelain we used to make in the old days. People are buying less and less. Even the imperial court is not buying. The country is suffering from the demands of foreign powers and incessant squabbling among the people." His uncle's face grimaced with disgust at the array of brightly coloured jars on a shelf. "Look at what we have to produce now: inferior stuff for export, exports that earn little to nothing. Can you remember the beautiful vases and tea bowls we used to produce from that kiln? Their translucence! *Aaah!* Those were the days!"

His eyes took on a dreamy look, but not for long. "Go!" he shouted, his long wispy beard shaking with anger, "perhaps you will have better luck in the mines. If you don't you should think about going overseas. People are already leaving in droves."

"*Wo de jia ren hui ze me yang?* What would happen to my family, uncle, if I did that?" Ngao was shocked by the suggestion.

His uncle shrugged his shoulders, rolling his eyes up to the heavens. "They will survive like other families have survived. You will make your fortune and return. The short-term ill for the long-term good," his uncle had replied sagely. "I would go if I were younger."

"No, I can't leave. I will try the mines."

His uncle shook his head again. A sneer appeared on his face. "I have given you my opinion. Do what you think is for the best. You are well named *Ngao*, an ox! Born to work and slave. Stubborn! Like your father, my brother! That was why he was poor. That is why, like him, you will always be poor."

NGAO FROWNED AT the memory of his uncle's words. It is the clay mines or nothing, he thought. He looked at the devastation around him. He would find no work here. And there was almost no food left on the farm. He had been forced to plunder the seed store and few vegetables remained in the ground. He hitched his cloth satchel once more on his back and gingerly stepped out from behind the urn. Looking left and right, he ran down the main street. He jumped deftly over the debris on the ground, carefully avoiding over-turned carts and the bodies of people cut down by the soldiers and already putrefying in the heat. A little boy sat howling in a corner, his legs splayed out in front of him, his face smudged with dirt. Ngao hesitated, unsure if he should pick him up. A woman appeared from behind him. She shoved him roughly aside and ran towards the little boy, her arms out-stretched. Ngao heaved a sigh of relief. He did not wish to be involved and had no desire to stay in the city. He had to reach the clay mines.

Chapter 2

SHAO PENG THREADED the rope round the tree stump and secured it with a knot. The goat bucked in protest. She put her arms around its neck and whispered. "Be still, be quiet. I have to go in. You stay. Eat this." She grabbed handfuls of hay from the trough next to the lean-to and scattered it on the ground. "Be good," she added, nuzzling her head against its neck.

Hua stood by the doorway of the farmhouse looking at her daughter. She tugged at her worn cotton top, crushing the cloth at its seams in her agitation. She wondered how to broach the subject of the goat with her daughter. Ngao said that they might have to slaughter it if he failed to bring back any food supplies. She had scoured the backyard, digging up every little root in sight. She had found only two clumps of turnips and one sweet potato. With the leaves of the sweet potato plant, she would make a stew; it should be sufficient to give the goat another day of reprieve. After that ... she sighed, expelling the air in one loud breath. They would have to take each day as it came.

Shao Peng heard her mother. She turned and smiled revealing little white pearly teeth and two dimples. "Mama," she said, going to Hua and clasping her mother's waist, "is father home?"

"No! I called because I was worried. You must not go out on your own. It is not safe out on the hill anymore. Come in and clean up." With that, she turned and went into the house.

Shao Peng dutifully followed and went straight to the large clay pot by the charcoal stove. Squatting down onto the dirt floor, she scooped a ladle of water into a basin and washed. Then carefully, holding the basin with both hands, she rose and carried it out to the small vegetable plot some ten yards away. Bending over, she dribbled water round the base of each young plant. Barely the height of a man's hand, they were already wilting under the hot sun. Water was scarce; not a drop could be wasted, she had been told over and over again. She stood for a moment to look at the dark stain of water seeping into the bleached dry ground. Insects hummed and a long line of ants retreated in haste from the wet patch of soil.

Hua came up behind Shao Peng and placed her hands on her shoulders. She could feel the thin blade of her shoulder bones underneath the cotton blouse. She turned her daughter around to face her. "I almost forgot," she said with a wry apologetic smile, "we need water for the drinking jar and for preserving vegetables. I need you to come with me to the well. I checked this morning. It has still not run dry. You can help me hold the bucket to stop any water from spilling out."

"You mean these vegetables? Are they big enough?" Shao Peng asked pointing to the wilting plants. She had never seen her mother preserve vegetables with such thin stems. "Have we no pickled vegetables left?" she asked, thinking of the pickling jar that stood by the cooking stove.

"Hardly any. What remains will be packed for your father to take to work. He has gone to look for a job in the city kilns. He will not be able to afford the food there." Turning her gaze to the young seedlings, she said, "You are right. They are too small. But I worry that they might not survive. If we do pickle them, at least, we might have a little something to eat later. Come," she said.

They walked towards the backyard. Hua held on tightly to her daughter's hand. The distant rumbling of gunfire could still be heard. Hua could feel the tension in her neck even as she looked down and smiled at her daughter. Shao Peng had begun to recite a rhyme and was doing it quickly and loudly to block out the sounds of gunshots from the city. Hua squeezed her little hand reassuringly. "Father will be back soon. He'll take care of us," she consoled, aware that Shao Peng was looking at her anxiously.

Without warning a wind picked up from the west; it grew in force whipping up an eddy of dust from the parched earth round them. Dried leaves blew and twirled. Dropping her pail, Hua stopped to shield her eyes with one hand and those of her daughter with the other. She ran towards an outcrop of boulders for shelter, dragging her daughter with her. They spluttered and choked. Then, suddenly, they heard the crunching of footsteps. Hua dropped down on her knees and drew her daughter close to her shielding her with her body. Slowly she opened her eyes a fraction. She could discern shadowy figures emerging from the cloud of dust. There were three of them! Men with scarves tied around their necks and mouths.

"Stay quiet," Hua whispered. Shao Peng could feel her mother's hot moist breath on her cheeks and hear the panic in her voice.

"Did you hear that? Coughing!" one of the men asked. "Do you think they are out here?"

"I can't hear a thing for the howling of the wind. They must be in the house. Her man is still out in the city or the mines. Let's hurry. We don't want to be around when he returns."

Peering once more from behind the boulder, Hua saw one of them draw out a sword; its blade glinted in the cloud of sand that still swirled around them. She gasped!

The man came to an abrupt halt. Raising his sword with one hand, he jutted his head forward to look closer at his surroundings, his eyes squeezed into two slits. With his other hand he signalled his two companions to spread out. He nodded towards the boulder. Then, just as fast as it had risen, the wind dropped. It was as though it had never been. A complete silence followed and, like magic, images that had been blurred came into focus.

The man spied the pail lying on its side and smiled. He waved his companions forward towards the boulder. Hua heard them. She broke into a run, dragging Shao Peng with her. The men sprinted after them and within minutes had them surrounded. They closed in, grinning, their lips drawn back in glee. She could smell them; a stench of sweat mingled with an odour she could not define.

"That was easy," said the man with the sword. "Tie them up and bring them back to the house. Don't touch them. They want them both intact, unspoiled. So if you are tempted, just forget it. I will kill you with my own hands. You can spend your rewards from this later in the flower house. There are plenty of women there." He led the way, striding back to the house.

Hua struggled, her feet skidding on the ground as she tried to stop her captor from dragging her along. He had both her hands pinned together with a rope tied tightly around her wrists. Shao Peng screamed. Without turning, the man with the sword yelled, "There is no point in struggling and screaming. No one can hear you."

"This is a wild cat," the man holding Hua gasped. He lurched to one side as she tried to kick him.

"So is this little one," said the other, holding Shao Peng as she twisted and tried to wrench herself free.

"Right! Both of you wait here. It's easier than dragging them around," said the leader as he sheathed his sword. "I'll go in the house and search for food. Farmers always have something tucked away even when they say they have nothing. Then we will get going. We don't have much time."

Chapter 3

NGAO MADE HIS way up the rough path that clung close to the hill slope. The soil was dry, so dry that the bushes and plants lining the path were parched and their branches snapped easily. He had never seen it like this before. He paused for a moment. Breaking off a twig from a bush he rolled it between his fingers. It crumbled into dust. It should not be like this. Yuzhou was always green, a tropical paradise, people said. Its forests were called jade forests because of their lushness, so why this, he wondered. He was tired and despondent. He had no good news to bring home to Hua. The drought had changed the clay soil at the mines into a mosaic of hard slabs. He was told that it was too expensive to take on more workers to mine the clay when demand for porcelain was so low. Like the hundreds of workers who had turned up that day, he was sent away.

He renewed his climb up the hill. Every sinew in his legs protested. He had been walking for almost two days, with little food and water. On his way back he had stopped once more at his uncle's pottery. Again his uncle told him to leave China. Surrounded by his friends and drunk, his uncle had become expansive. Perhaps expansive was too moderate a word; he had ridiculed him.

"You! *Ahhh*! You cannot bear to leave your wife," his uncle had said with a smirk. "That is why you can't leave even when everything indicates that is what you should do; the only way out of your present poverty. And do you know why?" he asked turning round to address the people gathered around them. "It is because of his beautiful wife and daughter. Perhaps I too would be reluctant if I had such beautiful women in the house. She is not called Hua for nothing, a beautiful flower ripe for plucking, or re-plucking in this case." His laugh was coarse as he winked at his friends, a motley group who Ngao did not know. He had never seen his uncle like this. He decided to bring the discussion to an immediate end.

"*Wo zou le*. I will take my leave Uncle," he said brusquely. This was not the uncle he knew. If he had stayed, he would have felt obliged to answer back and he did not wish to be disrespectful. Abruptly, he turned and walked out; his ears ringing with the sniggering and laughter that he left behind.

His aunt Heong Yook had waylaid him just as he was leaving the moon-gate in front of the house. She was upset. "Forgive him," she pleaded. "He has lost most of his business and his new associates, those men you see in there, are not what I would call honourable men. They encourage him. After a few cups of rice wine he becomes unseemly. He is not always like this. You saw him yesterday morning. He did not behave badly did he?"

"No Aunty! He was sober and rational. Who are they?" Even as he asked he saw three of them hurrying out of the house.

She had followed his gaze before turning to look at him with eyes that spoke of deep sorrow. "Be careful!" was all she said before entreating him to stay a while and eat and talk with her.

Ngao wondered what she meant. He always knew his uncle thought Hua was pretty. He had said so many a times. Ngao had thought nothing of it; his remarks were those of an uncle praising the pretty wife of his nephew. Today's insinuations bore little resemblance to the light-hearted comments of the past; at best they were coarse. They left a sour taste in his mouth.

He quickened his pace, breathing hard as the climb steepened. Finally he reached the plateau; he saw his house ahead. The doorway was unbarred. Surprised, he looked around for the goat that normally would be tethered near the lean-to. No sign of it. The place was quiet. Even the birds, it seemed, had no song left in them. Unease filled him. He hurried towards the house, his anxiety heightening with each step.

"Hua! Hua! Shao Peng! Shao Peng!" he shouted.

He went in. There was no one, just wreckage strewn everywhere. The water jug was broken. The pickling urn was rolled empty on its side. He looked to the far corner where the bed was. The bedding was unrolled and the grass mat on the wooden bed dragged askew. The cupboard by the side of the bed stood with its doors opened, it's meagre contents scattered on the ground. The doors creaked softly as they swung gently on their hinges. On the dirt floor, the wooden box that Hua inherited from her mother lay face up, gone were the hairpins that Hua treasured. The whole place had been ransacked.

He hurried out of the house in search of his wife and daughter. A mocking silence greeted him. Foot tracks and signs of struggle marked the ground to the rear of it. He could not be sure how many people had been there. He imagined the worst. He swallowed hard; his mouth was completely dry. He could not still the wild beating of his heart or stem the rush of blood to his head. His hands were cold, numb. He ran from one end of the farm to the other, to the outhouse, to the well and then back. He saw the pail discarded on the ground.

He shouted their names, hollering to an empty sky. Then like an ill omen, the light waned. The sun that had earlier shone with such intensity disappeared. Darkness enveloped him.

HUA STRUGGLED, TWISTING her head from side to side. She screamed and kicked as her captor dragged her into the bedroom. "Shao Peng! Shao Peng!" she cried as the door slammed shut. They had taken her daughter.

"*Wo jiu sha ni*, I'll kill you if you dare to kick me again. I will tie up your feet as well as your hands for all the trouble you give me. So what good is it to protest?" Roughly her captor caught hold of her ankles and bound them tightly together with a coarse rope. Pulling a rag cloth out of his jacket, he tied it around her mouth.

Hua tried to plead but her voice came out muffled and incomprehensible. With a snarl, he pulled her hair back so that her face tilted towards him. He placed his face close to hers and with his other hand he pushed her down on to the bed. "It is no use, your screams, kicks, and attempts to flail at me. I would have given you a beating had I not been cautioned against it. I would have really enjoyed that," he leered, eyeing her breasts.

Instinctively, Hua drew up her knees clamping them together, ready to ward him off with a kick.

"*Huh!*" he exclaimed, forcefully pushing her knees down. She felt her body twist to one side and her long loose blouse ride up until her midriff was exposed. He leaned over her, his body almost touching hers, his face barely an inch away until she could feel his breath and smell him "Don't think I am not tempted. Only I can find pleasure aplenty with the money I have been promised for you. So keep your virtue," he laughed, drawing his fingers down her body, lingering midway at her navel. "You are safe, at least for the moment." Abruptly he left, slamming the door behind him.

Hua lay in the middle of the bed. For a fleeting moment, she was stunned to find herself alone for the first time since she and Shao Peng had been taken. She struggled to a sitting position. She felt the rope cutting into her wrists. Her eyes darted from side to side like a wild animal's. Dirt and tears smudged her face and strands of hair clung wet to her cheeks.

She wriggled to the edge of the bed and stood up, almost toppling over with the effort. She hopped to the door. She took a deep breath and then bashed her head over and over against it. The noise reverberated through the corridor beyond. She heard people running towards the room. She hopped back, just in time to avoid being knocked over by the door opening. A woman, with her face powdered almost white and with dark painted eyebrows plucked to a thin line, strode into the room, crashing the door shut behind her.

Her lips, painted crimson and drawn into a cupid bow, opened to let out an enraged roar. "Are you mad? Do you wish to disfigure yourself? Look what you have done to your forehead! *Aiyah!* You have only yourself to blame. If you'd cooperated, then you would not be gagged and tied."

The woman turned away and shouted through the door, "Mui, come here to help me." Then turning once more to Hua, she screeched, "My job is to prepare you like a fat juicy chicken for the table, not turn you into some bloodied and scarred fowl! You will leave tomorrow and I have only hours to prepare you. I won't stand for it if you behave like this."

Hua fell to her knees. She looked up. She wanted to beg this woman. Surely she would listen. She is a woman. "I have a child, a daughter," she wanted to say. "Where is she?" she wanted to ask. To no avail, the rag choked her and her attempts to speak just came out like the whimpering of an animal.

The woman stared at Hua, at the tears streaming down her face. Momentarily nonplussed, she reached up to pat her hair, lacquered into a black top notch. Hairpins with gemstones protruded from it and their hanging tassels swung when she nodded.

"Alright, alright. My husband always said that I am too soft hearted. Bless his soul! May he rest in peace! I will untie your gag. Believe me the moment you scream I will have it tied back again, even tighter. You understand? Make sure you address me as Madam Yeong. I own this house. And I paid good money for you."

With great care, the woman went behind Hua and untied the rag around her mouth. Hua spun around on her knees immediately.

"Please, please," she cried, her voice hoarse, "where is Shao

Peng? What have they done with my daughter?" She clutched at Madam Yeong's long tunic. "She is my only child. Help me! Let me see her."

"I *am* helping you. She will be well taken care of. Is that not sufficient? She will remain with me and I will look after her. I will dress and feed her well and she will learn the art of singing and entertaining. I will make sure that she will be well prized. What would she have in that hole you call a home, up in the hills? *Aiyah!* You ungrateful wretch!"

"But ... but you said I have to leave tomorrow. Where? Won't Shao Peng go with me?"

Madam Yeong narrowed her eyes and looked at Hua with scorn and incredulity. "You do not wish that for your daughter, do you?" she asked. "You would not want her to go with you, surely! Look, just rest and stay in this room." She was bored with Hua's tears and was fast losing her patience.

She waved to the maid who had come in. "Ah Mui, stay and untie her. Bring her some food and then clean her up. I will come later to supervise her preparation."

"And you," she turned again to Hua, pointing her finger, "you behave and do as you are told or I'll get that dog of a man, Ah Kow, back into this room and you will have him to face rather than me or Ah Mui." So saying, she flounced out of the room, fanning herself with an ivory fan that she had fished out from the waistband of her wide black silk trousers.

LONG AFTER MADAM Yeong's departure, Hua remained huddled on the floor. The maid tried to go to her. Each time she approached, Hua screamed.

"Please, if you scream, I will get into trouble and it will do you no good," Ah Mui said. "Let me help you. At least let me clean you up and give you some food. What good will it do if you starve? If you eat, you will be able to deal with the situation better."

Hua pushed with her feet, sliding on her bottom, until her back was against the wall, distancing herself from the maid. Every bit of her body was tensed. "Where is Shao Peng? Take me to her. She must be frightened. She is only a little girl. She is of no threat to anyone."

"*Shhh!* Hush! Keep your voice down. She'll be all right. Madam always looks after her young charges well."

"What did she mean when she said she will make sure that my daughter is well prized?"

Ah Mui looked away. What harm was there in telling this ignorant woman, she wondered. On the other hand, what good would it do if she knew? She debated with herself. It would just cause her more pain. Far better that she remained ignorant. She often wondered how people could be so innocent. She stopped; her hand reached out to touch her own face. She chided herself. How could she forget that she herself was just as naïve when she first arrived in this house? Away, in her father's home in the countryside, she too had no idea that such places existed. So how could she blame this poor woman who was going to have a worst fate than even her? The woman's beauty would prove her curse, while she, Ah Mui, was saved by her own ugliness. She touched her pock-marked face and gave a silent prayer of thanks.

"Tell me," Hua persisted. "Please!"

"Madam will tell you herself. All will be fine. Your daughter will be well looked after. Let me bathe you and dress the wound on your forehead," she coaxed gently, all the while inching closer to Hua.

"Don't come any nearer. I'll scream. Promise me that no harm will come to Shao Peng."

Ah Mui nodded. A smile spread over her face and her voice was affable and gentle. "Madam loves children, especially pretty girls. She spoils them. She has no children of her own so she adopts little girls every year. They become her family. Shao Peng will be treated like her own daughter."

She looked at Hua with genuine sympathy. Fate has brought this woman to this situation, she thought and you cannot fight fate. You just have to accept it. So why make it harder for the woman by stirring up unrest. Truth is what you want it to be.

Hua's shoulders relaxed. Reassured by Mui's explanations and sympathy she felt the tension in her body drain away and with it a sudden fatigue came over her. She was glad that Shao Peng would be well treated. She did not mind her own sufferings as long as her daughter was well. Perhaps if she did what they asked of her, she would not be separated from her daughter.

Ah Mui could see the changing emotions flitting across Hua's face, the slump in her shoulders and the resignation in her body. She sensed it was the right time. She approached Hua and, gently, solicitously, helped her to rise. "Come, let me help you wash and change out of these clothes."

"What does Madam mean when she says that I will be sent away? Where? Why? Why can't my daughter come with me?"

"So many questions," said Ah Mui, her voice soothing and soft. "You will have the answers soon enough. In fact, the faster you let me attend to you, the sooner you will know. Come," she persuaded with a kind smile on her face.

❀ ❀ ❀

NGAO SLID AND half ran down the path scuffing the loose soil and sending dislodged stones riochetting down the hill. It was dark. The only light came from the moon. It cast long shadows around him. Branches swayed and their dry leaves chafed in the wind. They sent a ripple of crackling sounds down the hillside. Ngao ran almost without stopping until he reached the city walls. Then with great caution he entered the city gate.

He heard a gong strike in the distance. The night watchman on his rounds! It was almost dawn. He sprinted towards the front of a building and slipped behind a pillar. He did not wish to confront the Qing army nor did he wish to be embroiled with the activities of the *chang mao*. He would have to wait until people came on to the streets so that he could mingle with them before going to his uncle. The Qing soldiers would take him if they found him walking alone at this hour. More haste did not mean more speed.

He sank onto his haunches, his knees hugged tightly to his chest. His head lolled back to rest on the pillar. He closed his eyes. He was utterly exhausted. His feet were sore. His shoes had worn through and stones and pebbles had cut into the soles of his feet until they bled. He pictured his wife and daughter. They must have struggled ferociously. His tiredness vanished in a flash. If only he could do something, anything but this waiting. Yet he had no choice other than to be patient. He closed his eyes again and forced himself to rest. Images of Hua and Shao Peng continued to interrupt his thoughts. He tried not to dwell on what might have happened to them.

Who could have come all the way up the hill in search of his family? Where were they?

And so he sat crouched against the pillar waiting, waiting for the city to awaken.

HEONG YOOK WOKE with a start. It was barely dawn. She turned and saw that the bed was empty. Her husband had not come to bed. It had been like that for weeks or even months. She threw her bedclothes aside and sat up, undecided about what to do. She did not wish to confront him; she feared going to the study and not finding him there. She did not want to discover that he had been out the whole night and not, as he professed whenever she asked, working at his desk. In any case, he had left instructions that no one was to disturb him. She went to her dressing table and sat down.

Heong Yook stared at her image. The mirror only confirmed what she already knew. Her cheeks no longer embraced the sheen of youth. Her eyes that had delighted her husband so much that he had waxed lyrical in their praise were beginning to dull. Perhaps, it was her mood that made them look so, she thought. She blinked and tried to brighten her expression. She shook her head. No, the change was there. She winced at the sight of the fine lines radiating from her eyes. She peered closer at the mirror and sighed. Instinctively, she reached up and with both hands pulled her cheeks upwards to tighten her jaw line. "Age!" she murmured. "I no longer look like *perfumed jade*, my given name, the woman my husband married. No wonder he is speaking of Hua in such a way." The hurt pierced her like a knife.

"*Bu ti mian!* Unseemly!" she blurted out loud when she recalled her husband's behaviour. Yet what could she do with all those uncouth men around him? What could she, as a woman, do in the face of her husband's change in affection? What could she do other than seek out Ngao to apologise for her husband and warn him?

She got up from the dressing table and walked slowly to the window and looked out to the little courtyard. It was always more difficult to move with any speed in the morning. She swayed and held on to the wall.

When she married her husband, Ong Wan Fook, at the age of fifteen, the house of Ong was one of wealth and stature. The Ongs were famous for their kilns and the pottery they produced. They owned even the mines that supplied the clay. Her husband was the elder son and, when his father died, he inherited the entire estate. He had one brother, Wan Kwang. He though was not interested in the family business. Against the wishes of his father, Wan Kwang married a poor village girl. His father disowned him and Wan Kwang left with his wife vowing never to return. He was never heard of again, until that fateful day when a little boy was left at their doorstep.

Heong Yook remembered that day vividly. She stared into space hardly noticing the roof and skyline. The boy, just eight years old, had one thing on him, other than his clothes: a paper pasted on his chest with the words, written in an ink dried the colour of rust, "This is Ngao, my son, your nephew. His father has died. Please give him a home."

She learned later that the words were written in blood, Ngao's mother's blood. She had not written the note. She had no learning at all. Instead she had begged the village's only letter writer to take the boy and pen those words on her behalf, cutting her arm to give him the 'ink' for the letters. Destitute, alone and grief stricken at the loss of her husband, she later took her own life.

Heong Yook remembered the child. He had not looked down when he stood before them. He had stared dry-eyed and defiant at his uncle and aunt. Evidence of the tears that he had shed lay in congealed streaks of dirt and grime on his cheeks. Her heart had gone out to him that day and from then on she tried to protect him.

Her husband had not wanted to take Ngao in. Wan Fook did not wish to be reminded of his brother, a brother who might still have been alive if he had put in a good word for him. He did not wish to be reminded of his own guilt. He only agreed to put the boy to work as an apprentice potter because she had begged him. Eventually, however, even her husband was won over by Ngao's diligence and skill, his instinctive ability to model from clay and his growing mastery of the art.

Like his father, Ngao proved to have a mind of his own when it came to matrimonial matters. He refused to be guided by his elders in his choice of a wife. This did not particularly trouble his uncle. Wan Fook never intended for Ngao to inherit from the Ong family. His own son would take over the entire family estate.

Heong Yook walked slowly away from the window, her gait hesitant and laboured. The family estate! Not much left now. The bankruptcy of China was echoed in the poverty of its populace. And all because of opium! In the early days, her husband had ranted about the injustice of it all. How China exported porcelain, tea, silk and spices to Britain and got in return opium, addictive, soul destroying opium. The Qing Government's attempt to prevent its import and make opium illegal had proved futile, as the amounts brought into the country grew ever larger.

Wan Fook had read to her the open letter published in Canton in 1839 by the Imperial Commissioner, Lin Zexu, to Queen Victoria. With quivering indignation he had related Lin's thesis on the immorality of the opium trade. Opium that had been forced on China following successive treaties imposed by Britain and the west. Opium that had resulted in a steady drain of silver out of China as the balance of payments tipped in favour of foreign traders. Opium that had led to the collapse of his own business as demand for his porcelain waned within China.

Heong Yook emitted a sigh. "And now, to cap it all," she cried aloud, "we have a civil war. The Taiping uprising is the last thing we need in this impoverished country. How can we defend ourselves against the incessant demands of the West for territorial concessions and ports, when we are plagued with internal conflict? I blame the Qing regime. Like a rotting apple, it will cause all of us to rot with it."

She sighed again, this time letting the air come out in a prolonged sound: *hhah … hahh!* It was an expression of her frustration, a release of pent up emotions. She was an educated woman; one of the few women in her generation who had learned to read and write. Her mother had insisted on it. Yes, her mother, despite all her conservatism, had allowed her daughter education. She did not give credence to the belief that 'stupidity in a woman is a virtue.' At least I am not confined to needlework, Heong Yook thought.

Yet for all her learning, Heong Yook was imprisoned in a code of silence imposed on her as a wife. She could hardly bear it. Her husband, after years of anger and righteous behaviour, had joined forces with the rest of the mob. While he did not use opium, he consorted with those who did, and he drank taking out his anger on those around him. Perhaps that was the reason why Ngao left to start a new life in the hills. He wished to protect his family from the evils of the city: from the opium dens that had sprung up everywhere – the dens that had claimed her own son.

Heong Yook heard voices in the courtyard. She went once more to the window and peered out. It was Ngao. She hurried down as best as she could, but he was already in the house by the time she had descended the stairs. He ran to her. She was shocked to see the state of him.

"Aunty Yook! Help me! They have taken Hua and Shao Peng!"

She stopped in her tracks. "Who? Who has? Who would do such a thing?"

"I don't know. All I know is that they have been forcefully taken. Help me!" He then told her what he had found when he reached home the previous evening.

Heong Yook sat very still until he finished his story. Her face changed from shock to one of worry. Her brow creased into a thousand lines. "Sit here!" she said. "I'll speak to your uncle."

She left the room without waiting for Ngao's reply and went to the study. She prayed that her husband would be there. She threw open the door. A smell of liquor permeated the air. She found him slumped on his desk, his face to one side, his arms hung slack on either side of him. A small dribble of saliva seeped from the corner of his mouth on to the desk.

"Wan Fook!" she called out loud. She shook him. He grunted and turned his face over to the other side. "Wake up!"

She shook him again, this time harder, thumping his back, venting her anger and disgust. She lost all sense of propriety, of her duty as a wife, of the need to be compliant and respectful at all times to her husband.

❀ ❀ ❀

IN A BIG rambling house in a tiny street in Beiliu, Hua sat lifeless as Mui combed and dressed her hair, turning her long shiny tresses into coils and pinning them back with hairpins. But when Mui tried to draw her eyebrows and paint her cheeks, she came to life. She whipped her head round each time the maid came near her with the pot of paint. "No!" she protested, pushing Mui away.

"Leave her! Let her be," intervened Madam Yeong.

She had entered the room and stood in a corner to observe Mui's ministrations. She was very satisfied. They had not lied. Hua was beautiful. Perhaps, leaving her unpainted and natural would make her stand out even more. She looked at Hua's unbound feet. She would fetch a good price, perhaps not here, but certainly in the foreign concessions where virginity and bound feet were not important issues. Perhaps, someone might even pay a retainer to keep her for himself. She made a sign to Mui and then left the room.

Mui placed her brushes and paints down and followed her mistress out of the room, taking care to bolt the door after her. They made their way along the covered walk way that flanked the courtyard on one side and the maze of rooms on the other until they reached the northern building, Madam Yeong's own dwelling. It was one of the four that made up this traditional Chinese housing quadrangle, a *si he yuan*.

Once in her own private reception room, Madam Yeong turned to Mui. "So how is she?" Yeong asked, her finely painted eyebrows raised in an exaggerated arc.

"She has calmed down. I promised that you would let her see her daughter if she cooperated and let me attend to her. I told her that Shao Peng will be well cared for and you would look after her like your own. She begged to be with her daughter. She became agitated every time she spoke of the little girl. So ... so I did as you instructed. I left the lamp of dreams burning in the room when I left her. She became calmer."

"Does she suspect anything?"

"No! She seems completely unaware. In any case she was exhausted and fell asleep soon after," said Mui. Cautiously she looked at her mistress. "Will you ... would you allow her to see her daughter? If I am to retain her trust, I have to be able to keep my promise. It will make it easier for us to persuade her to cooperate."

"So you have taken it upon yourself to promise something that does not lie within your authority to grant," cried Madam Yeong landing a sharp slap on Mui's face. "How dare you?"

"I am sorry. Please forgive me. I won't do it again." Mui trembled. "I only thought it would be best." She glanced at the rod hanging at the corner of the room. She sank to her knees, her head bowed, contrite.

Madam Yeong walked towards the rod and then, changing her mind, went to a round table at the far end of the room. She sat down on the ebony chair next to it. Perhaps the maid was right, she thought. Perhaps I should let Hua see her daughter. It would also make the little girl more pliable. She turned to the kneeling figure. "Get up! Go back to Hua and bring her to the western court. Give me some time to prepare the girl. I'll send you word when I am ready. Go!"

Mui got up from the floor, head bowed low, and shuffled backwards towards the door.

"Wait!" Madam Yeong commanded. "Make good use of the time you have with her. Win her over for me. Tell her my life history. It might make her feel able to trust me." Softening her stance, she said more gently, "And you, Mui. Remember! Next time ask my permission before making any promises."

MADAM YEONG RETRACED her steps to the western building. She was in no hurry and paused to look into the central courtyard. Four main buildings bordered the courtyard. They were not big as such houses go. The northern, housing her personal rooms, was the largest. The southern building, the living room that used to be shared by the entire family, was now a reception room for guests. Entry into the quadrangle was through it. The buildings to the west and east were for other members of the family and children. This was how Confucius said it should be, she thought. The entire complex built to reflect the five elements – wood, fire, earth, metal and water – and used in accordance with his philosophy. A murmur of exasperation escaped from her. What was the use of Confucianist principles at times like this?

When her husband died, everything had changed. She resumed her steps along the covered walkway, holding on to the carved wooden railings that separated it from the courtyard. As she approached the western block, she heard laughter and the muffled voices of children, girls! A feeling of guilt assailed her. The western building was for children but they were not hers. They were bought for the purpose of future sale, a contradiction of Confucian teaching. She muttered to herself, a prayer for forgiveness spoken half aloud. She unlocked the heavy door and slipped inside. As she closed the door, she looked across to the east. *Ah!* The eastern house! Here too she had contravened the rules. She no longer had any relatives. It was used principally to provide temporary accommodation for women who were to be consigned elsewhere. She pulled the door shut to obliterate the sight of it. She had broken every order and teaching of the great philosopher, teachings that governed the ethics and life of the Chinese. She preferred not to dwell on such matters.

Madam Yeong made her way to the inner rooms. She shrugged her shoulders. She did what she had to. How else could she survive and make a living? She had no husband, no family. They took everything away from her. She had only her wits. She opened the door to a large room. Inside were five girls of varying ages. Four of them were standing over a little girl in the centre, the new girl Shao Peng. They were teasing her, pulling her hair and tapping her shoulder, chanting all the while that she was a crybaby.

"Stop this!" Madam Yeong shouted. She clipped one of the girls. They immediately fell silent. Their brazen looks replaced immediately by ones of fear. "I will punish each one of you if I catch you teasing her again. Do you hear me?"

Gently she took Shao Peng's hand and led her to a chair. She sat down and, still holding on to the frightened little girl's hand, asked her to sit on a stool beside her.

"So!" she said. "Have you eaten?"

Shao Peng nodded.

"Did you like the food? Was it enough?" She reached over and gently stroked Shao Peng's face.

Shao Peng's eyes widened. She recalled the feast: chicken, rice, soup and green vegetables, food she had not tasted for a long while. And most wonderful of all, those sesame pancakes with a sweetness that she had almost forgotten. She nodded her head vigorously.

"And I see you have washed and changed. Do you like your new clothes?" she asked running her fingers lightly on the silky satin cloth of the girl's blouse.

Shao Peng again nodded her head vigorously.

"Would you like to stay here with me then?" Madam Yeong summoned up her sweetest smile.

"No!" said Shao Peng, suddenly finding her voice. "I want to be with Mama. Where is she? Where have they taken her? We need to go home. Father will be worried."

"*Shhh!* Calm down," Madam Yeong said planting a kiss on Shao Peng's head, "your mother is well and resting. You'll see her shortly. Don't upset her by whining. When you see her, tell her you have been well looked after. I will make sure that the girls do not bully you. They will look after you like their own sister. That is a promise."

She bent her head low and whispered, her voice cajoling and sickly sweet. "Like you they used to pine for their mothers. Now, they would not want to be anywhere else but here. And so will you."

Shao Peng looked up. She glanced at the other girls. Madam Yeong could see she had not won the child over. In the same sweet voice, she continued, "For now, if you promise to be good, I'll let you see your mother. You have to be brave though, brave for your mother. Something has happened to your father. Both of you have nowhere to go. So you will stay with me. Your mother will have to work for a living and cannot be here all the time. You must not upset her by complaining. You will try, won't you?" Her eyes held fast the little girl's; her expression implied that Shao Peng would only hurt her mother if she disobeyed.

Madam Yeong reached out for a tray of candied fruits and took a handful. "Have some of these. They are really good."

The little girl took the candied fruit. "What happened to father?" She wanted to cry. Seeing the warning look on Madam Yeong's face, she stifled her tears and swallowed hard, sniffling all the while to stop the tears but she could not stop her nose from running.

"Now, now," consoled Madam Yeong, hiding her irritation. "Take this handkerchief. Blow your nose and dry your tears. Your mother will be here soon. Your father..." She affected a huge sigh. "Your father has left the country. He won't be coming back. Don't tell your mother. It will only hurt her. Just say nice things, pleasant things. It will make her happy. Promise? Otherwise I can't possibly let you see her."

Although Shao Peng tried hard not to cry, tears oozed from her eyes. She wiped them away fiercely.

"And tell your mother, you like being here and that you are well looked after. You are, aren"t you?"

Shao Peng looked at the kind face before her and nodded.

❀ ❀ ❀

HUA WOKE UP. She felt as though her body did not belong to her, and that her limbs were disjointed and disengaged from the rest of her. She sat up and swung her feet to the floor. Her movements were languid. She felt lethargic and confused. Those dreams! They crept in and out of her sleep; they were so intense yet she could remember nothing.

Mui watched from the doorway. She had been waiting with a jug of hot water outside the room until she heard Hua's movements. She walked to the table by the bed and checked the oil lamp to make sure the opium fumes that had filled the room earlier were fully stemmed. She had only left it lit for a short time to calm Hua. The poor woman had obviously succumbed to the fumes easily even without smoking. She did not want her to become addicted, only calmed. A time might come when she would have to be truly introduced to the poppy; this, however, was not the moment. She took the jug and poured some water into a basin. Dipping a flannel into the warm water, she then wrung it out and brought it to Hua.

"Let me wipe your face. You will feel refreshed. You have slept for almost three hours. I'll bring you to see your daughter, once you have eaten." Mui smiled encouragingly, her eyes seemed tender with concern.

Hua tried to reciprocate the smile. She could not focus, neither her thoughts nor her movements. She stood up, swayed and fell back on the bed. "Can we go now? I feel so heavy, so tired even after sleeping. I want to see her now."

"Yes! Of course! You ought to eat first though. I have left two dumplings stuffed with pork and chives for you. You will frighten the poor child if you go to see her like this. We can't have you swaying and falling. Here, eat. They are delicious and a specialty of the cook." Mui held out a dish of steaming dumplings, wafting them in front of Hua's nose, hoping to tantalise her taste buds. Hua stared vacantly ahead, oblivious to her efforts. With determination Mui took a pair of chopsticks and, after deftly cutting the dumplings into smaller portions, fed Hua.

Hua sat and ate, her arms hanging limp by her side. Slowly with each mouthful, some semblance of normality began to return. Gradually her eyes focused while Mui continued her chatter.

"Shao Peng is enjoying herself. She is playing with her friends now. Earlier on she had a lovely lunch. She is quite contented, quite contented," Mui repeated. "Madam Yeong has taken to her. She is a kind woman, you know. She has had such a hard life. She lost everything, her whole family; her husband was accused of a crime against the imperial government and was executed together with her sons. They made her watch. She was left destitute until she found a benefactor who set her up and sponsored her business."

Hua pushed the chopsticks away. "Business? What business? She said she bought me. What business is that?" The cobwebs that had cloaked her mind were beginning to clear. She recalled the earlier words of Madam Yeong.

"*Aiyah!* It is just a loose use of the word. You were brought to her and she paid money to free you from those awful men who kidnapped you. That is why she said she paid good money for you."

"And that she would send me away? What does that mean?" Hua's agitation returned. She rose to her feet. Her eyes, glazed over just minutes earlier, became fiery. "I don't want your food. Take me to my daughter. I will repay her what she has spent on me. I will borrow from my husband's uncle."

"Stop! Stop! You will get me into trouble. And after all I have done for you. She only means that you will have to go away to work to repay the money she spent on freeing you from those animals. Everyone has to work for a living. Surely you cannot object to that?"

"I don't mind working," replied Hua, calming down. "I must see my husband first and for that I have to go home. He will be worried. I have to tell him what happened."

Mui looked at Hua earnestly. "I'm afraid, you can't. Madam Yeong had the same thoughts as you. She sent people to look for your husband, the minute she rescued you. She couldn't find him. He was gone. The army must have taken him. She has not given up and will continue to look for him; it is not safe for you to return home now. Don't fret! She always makes good her promises. Her benefactor knows many important people..."

"Mama! Mama!"

Hua swung round. Shao Peng ran to her followed by Madam Yeong. Hua swooped her daughter up in her arms. Madam Yeong and Mui stood aside. They dabbed their eyes as though overcome by their happiness in witnessing this reunion of mother and child.

"Are you alright? Did they hurt you?" asked Hua.

"No! I am fine. Madam Yeong has looked after me very well," replied Shao Peng. She could sense Madam Yeong's eyes fixed on her.

Hua turned around and looked gratefully at Madam Yeong. "I will work hard to repay you. I promise. Thank you! Thank you for rescuing us."

Chapter 4

"I DID NOTHING!" Wan Fook protested. "I know I should not have such a loud mouth. I should not have spoken about Ngao's wife in such a way. That said, I am sure those men had nothing to do with her disappearance. They are just wastrels, good for nothings; probably still sleeping off their drunkenness at this very moment."

Wan Fook tried to out stare his wife. "Look woman!" he jabbed a finger furiously in her face, "How can you possibly think that I have anything to do with Hua's disappearance?" His voice grew even louder in his bluster. "Couldn't she have just run off? Who would blame her? It is a miserable life up on the hill. It is all fine and noble for Ngao to say he wants a simple life for his family; to return to the happiness he had as a child when his parents were alive; that love is all that's needed."

He threw both hands up into the air in an exaggerated show of impatience. "Such trite and nonsense!"

Heong Yook held her temper. She wanted to shout, "Have you no shame to try to shift the blame on to Hua?" Instead, she said in a quiet voice, "The place was ransacked. There were signs of struggle. She could not have done all that on her own. At least try to speak to those men for my sake, for Ngao's sake. If they were not involved directly, they might have an inkling of who could have done it."

"Get Out! Leave me be," Wan Fook raged. Heong Yook stood her ground. Although she stayed with her head bent down and demure when speaking to her husband, he was in no doubt about her disapproval. He felt, even knew, though she had not said it in so many words, that she was accusing him of complicity with the men. He saw it in the stiff bend of her neck. If he could wring it he would. When she looked at him earlier, he felt her eyes boring into his very being. How dare she?

Moments passed. He raged and ranted. She continued to stand her ground, head bent. Unable to resist any longer, his bluster spent, he finally relented. "Alright, alright, I'll try to see what I can do. Tell Ngao he owes me."

He watched his wife's departing figure holding his back ramrod straight and his shoulders pulled back. His face was severe, forbidding and righteous. He could not keep up the stance for long. Once she had left the room, he slumped into his chair. He held his head in both hands. Bits of the men's talk came back to him. He got up and quickly left the house.

❀ ❀ ❀

IN THE WAITING room, Ngao sat drumming his fingers anxiously on the table. He could not wait any longer. Heong Yook had been gone for almost half an hour. Every minute lost could have implications for his wife and daughter. He hurried out of his uncle's house and made his way to the pottery in the adjoining building in search of the master potter. He found the old man sitting by the potter's wheel, with one hand resting on the idle machine and the other on his lap. The ground was littered with bits of unfinished jars, vases, bowls and plates. He had a faraway look in his eyes.

"Master Foo! It's me!" said Ngao. "They have taken my wife and daughter."

"What are you talking about? Who took them?"

Under his bushy eyebrows, bleached almost white, Foo's eyes were suddenly sharp and alert. He was very fond of the young man before him, his apprentice for many years. He had been sorry to let him go but he had no say in the matter. Business had been poor and, although Ngao never complained, he knew that his boss had been increasingly critical of the young man, taking it out on him whenever he could. In fact, he had been surprised to see Ngao come looking for work yesterday. Things must be very bad, he surmised.

"I don't know. Don't ask me why. I just have a gut feeling that..." He described to Foo the events of the previous day.

Sitting waiting for this aunt had brought back memories of his uncle's bad behaviour, the lurid remarks of the men around him and the looks exchanged between three of them in particular. The more he thought about it, the more convinced he became that somehow they had something to do with his family's disappearance. He had stayed back to have a meal in his aunt's house because she had asked him. To refuse would have hurt her. He remembered seeing them hurry away. He had thought nothing of it at the time. Now on reflection, he wondered why they were in such a rush to leave? Why had they cut short their drinking session with his uncle? Even his aunt had commented that it was unusually early for them to go.

"I believe my uncle called one of them Ah Kow," said Ngao.

"He is a trouble maker, living off the misfortune of others. If he is involved, you must act quickly. I can't help much except to tell you that sometimes your uncle visits them." Suddenly Foo became quiet. He was looking over Ngao's shoulders. "*Shhh!*" he cautioned pointing urgently to the street. Ngao turned around quickly. Through the open gate, he saw his uncle walking away in great haste, his face agitated.

"Follow him!" whispered Foo, "He might be heading there. Be careful!" He squeezed Ngao's hand.

Ngao hurried out of the gate in pursuit of his uncle. The street was busy. Day to day living had resumed until the next outbreak of violence. Tradesmen sat uneasily by the roadside hawking their meagre wares: a small basket of vegetables, a tray of eggs or a live chicken secured by a rope. All around them lay the debris of yesterday's insurgency. The traders had their ears tuned to sounds of gunfire, screams or soldiers marching. Their eyes, however, were fixed on their wares, ready to grab them and flee at the slightest sign of trouble.

Ngao mingled with the crowd keeping some distance behind his uncle. Wan Fook turned into a side road. It was quiet there. The crowd of the main street thinned out to just a few pedestrians, wheel carts and the odd sedan. No shop houses lined the road. Instead, walls bordered each side of it, interrupted here and there by vermilion painted moon gates that led into internal courtyards and buildings that were the residences of the rich. The rooftops of the buildings could be seen rising above the walls. Ngao hurried, quick-footed, eager not to lose his uncle but also wary of being seen. Here and there sections of wall had fallen into disrepair. Graffiti, imperial edicts and ragged posters of dissent adorned their once pristine surfaces. Someone had taken a pot of paint and hastily covered the protests, leaving the yellowed edges of the paper frayed and unsightly, the odd word peeping out in defiance. The imperial army had threatened retaliation against anyone found with such writing on their walls.

Suddenly his uncle stopped in front of a side entrance. Ngao saw him rap his fist on the wooden door: two slow knocks, three quick ones and then two slow ones. He heard the sound of a heavy wooden bolt being drawn. His uncle glanced furtively about him before slipping in. Ngao hurried towards the door. He stood there uncertain what to do next.

The sound of rattling jolted him. He swirled round to see a beggar sitting on his haunches and leaning against the opposite wall, arm extended, a begging bowl in his hand. Ngao ignored him. He ran until he reached the end of the wall and rounded its corner. There was no one there. A plum tree stood near the wall, its thick foliage hanging over it. Pulling a low branch towards him, he hoisted himself into the tree and clambered up until he could see over it. Three small outbuildings stood within this section. They were linked to larger grander buildings connected by a covered pathway. From where he was he could make out their ridged rooftops with their curved eaves sloping downwards. Reaching out from the tree he took hold of the protruding ledge on the top of the wall and hauled himself on to it. Once on the ledge, he searched for a way down. A small section of the wall was free from the adjoining buildings offering access to the ground some nine feet below. With a sigh of relief he saw the thick vines covering it. He grabbed hold of one and quickly climbed down to a dim narrow alleyway between the buildings.

It was quiet in the room. A soft breeze blew in through an open window. Heong Yook was seated with her hands resting on a table and clutched together as if in prayer. With an impatient shake of her head, she stood up; a second later, she sat down again. She did not know what to do. She had returned to tell Ngao of her conversation with her husband only to find the room empty. Ngao had gone.

Perhaps the maid would know where he was, she thought. She went to the kitchen, a domain she had visited no more than twice in all the years she had lived in the house. Complete silence greeted her. The stove was cold. Bowls and chopsticks lay unwashed by the basin. A half-feathered chicken lay on the wooden slab, a chopper carelessly set to one side. She looked at it with distaste. It would seem that the chaos in the city had also penetrated her household.

She bit her lip. She could not leave the house on her own to find out what was happening. Custom would not permit it nor would it be safe. Frustration welled up in her. She would not have been able go far even if she had wanted. She looked down at her feet, her incredibly small, three-inch feet shaped like a diminutive crescent moon enclosed in beautifully beaded slippers. Her parents had promised that binding her feet was for her own good, a prerequisite to finding a good husband and a mark of class. No one, they told her over and over again through all those years of suffering and pain, would marry her if she had unbound feet. Unbound feet symbolised lewdness. When they crushed the bones to bind the four toes and heel until her feet were the shape of a crescent, she had screamed in pain. She was just two, but she still remembered. They comforted her with tales of the beautiful consort Yao Niang. In 970 AD she had danced with feet bound by cloth on top of a pedestal of a golden lotus and won the heart of the Song dynasty prince, Li Yu. "Even three thousand buckets of tears are worth what it will achieve for you in the future," her parents had assured her.

She sat down. She thought of Hua with her unbound feet and her freedom to move. Envy filled her. Immediately she felt ashamed. This freedom might be no more if Ngao could not find her. She feared for them. She rose and walked slowly back to the main house, her long billowing skirt swayed with each step of her tiny feet, and entered the study. Her feet were already hurting. Pausing to rest, she surveyed the room. An idea flashed through her mind. Her heart quickened. She must enlist the help of Foo the master potter.

HUA SAT WITH Shao Peng on her knees. She placed her hand on her daughter's cheek and gently stroked it, tucking behind her ears the wisps of hair that had escaped from her pigtails. She could not believe how well her daughter looked. So Mui had told the truth. Madam Yeong had rescued them in a way. Otherwise they would still be in the hands of those men. She shuddered at the thought of what might have happened. With a muffled sob, she pulled her daughter towards her and hugged her tight, clasping her head close to her chest.

Madam Yeong and Mui exchanged a look between them.

"Have they really treated you well? Nod quietly, if so," whispered Hua in her daughter's ear. "I know you say they have, but tell me again. Don't worry they won't know what we are saying." She wanted to be sure her daughter had not been forced to lie.

Hua's heart lightened as she felt her daughter's nod. She looked up and saw Madam Yeong staring intently at her. She bowed her head once more to press her lips on Shao Peng's head.

"Listen quietly, your father has been taken. We can't go home immediately," she whispered. She held her daughter firmly to her. "Could you stay here with Madam Yeong for a while?"

Shao Peng buried her head closer into Hua's chest. Once again she nodded. She wondered how her mother knew about father. Madam Yeong had asked her not to ask for him and here was her mother telling her that he had been taken. Adults can be so confusing. She lifted her eyes to look at Madam Yeong and received a warning shake of the head. Shao Peng dropped her gaze immediately.

Madam Yeong drew closer to mother and daughter. She wanted to hear what Hua was saying to Shao Peng. She was not happy to leave them alone, nor did she want them to have a chance to talk.

"So have you thought any more about what I said earlier?" Madam Yeong asked Hua.

"Would you ... would you promise to find my husband? Would you help get his release?" Hua asked. "Mui said you know the district magistrate,"

"*Aiyah!* Money does not fall from the sky. I have to grease many palms before I can get to see the magistrate. Of course I want to help. Mui must have told you that my own economic situation is dire. So unless you do your bit I won't be able to do very much."

"I will work for you. I will scrub, clean, cook, anything. Can't I stay here with my daughter? Can she at least come with me?" Hua pleaded.

"I told you why Shao Peng should remain here. She will be well cared for. How do you expect to look after her while you are working? Think woman!" Madam Yeong pretended to be cross. She turned to Mui, indicating that she should take Shao Peng away. She wanted to keep Hua mellow until they had delivered her to the other end. Then it would be their worry, not hers. She did not want Hua taking her life or disfiguring herself as some did once they discovered their fate. It was far better to make them feel they were doing some good and to go willingly.

Hua held Shao Peng tight. "Please, please let her stay with me for a while. Don't take her away. I beg you."

With a great show of reluctance, Madam Yeong relented. "You have half an hour. Then I would like you to get ready. You leave this evening."

"This evening? So soon?" Hua broke down. Holding on to her daughter, she cried, "Please, please let me stay here a few days more."

"And risk the life of your husband?" Madam Yeong raised her eyebrows in shocked disbelief. Then she shook her head and shrugged her shoulders. "Well, it is up to you. You might as well not go. If we leave it too long to raise money to buy our way to the courts, I can guarantee your husband will be well on his way to the gallows." With an exasperated sigh, she left the room.

Chapter 5

Ngao stood in the shadow of garments hung out to dry in the backyard. He peered through a gap between them. His uncle could be anywhere. It was an innocent enough looking place. A well stood in the middle of a small plot of bare ground. To the left of him were the three small outbuildings he had seen earlier. Smoke rose from the blackened chimney of one of them. The smell of cooking drifted to him. He swallowed hard to quell his hunger pangs.

That must be the kitchen! Ngao thought. The other two must surely be the servants' quarters. They were too small to be part of the main residence.

He moved in the direction where he had seen his uncle enter. No one was about. Even so he trod carefully on the cobbled ground; it would be easy to trip and fall. Missing cobbled stones had left gaping holes making the ground uneven. The place had seen better days. The sound of people talking and arguing came from the kitchen. Suddenly someone came out carrying a big bamboo tray laden with food. Ngao drew back behind a large potted plant and stayed stock-still. He hardly dare breathe. He waited until the woman had moved away towards the main buildings in the quadrangle. She had not noticed him; she was too busy arguing with whoever was in the kitchen, her voice, loud and vehement.

He decided to take a chance and follow her. Crouching low he moved quickly searching for a bush or large flowerpot, anything that would provide some cover. He glanced anxiously over his shoulder, his heart lightened. There was no one. Relieved he straightened up. Crouching and moving furtively like he had been doing, he decided, would attract attention. Now that he was in the inner courtyard, he should walk normally. Perhaps he might be mistaken for a workman. Without warning the woman disappeared from view. He turned quickly and saw an entrance to the large building on his right. She must have gone in there and this must be the eastern building, he thought. He was familiar with the traditional layout of a *si he yuan*, four inward-facing houses, linked by a perimeter wall and sharing a central courtyard.

With great stealth he approached the doorway. A screen was set immediately behind it, hiding the interior. He peeped inside and saw the back of the woman disappearing into a hallway. There was no one about. He slipped in.

"Please let me see my daughter again. One more time! I beg of you. I don't want food! Just your help to see my daughter."

Ngao froze. The cry pierced his heart. He knew the voice. He ran towards the source.

Whack!

Ngao fell to the ground. He found himself manhandled and dragged on the floor back to the entrance, round the screen and out into the courtyard. He wheezed in pain as they kicked and rained blows on him, one after another. His face turned into a bloody pulp. He could hardly see the men beating him; just a blur of fists and feet. They flipped him over and tied his wrists and then his ankles. Unceremoniously they hauled him up, one held his ankles, the other his wrists. His head dangled face down. A sharp pain pierced through him as his back sagged with the weight of his body. He swung like a sack of coal as they carried him towards one of the outbuildings. He recognised it when he saw the well. Once there, they dropped him to the ground with a thud. His forehead hit the cobble stone paving and he could feel a stream of warm stickiness seep down his face. With difficulty he rolled over to look up at his assailants. Immediately a foot dug deep into his stomach. He drew his knees up and grunted. The foot dug even deeper.

"So! How did you find us?" asked the man who had his foot planted firmly on Ngao's stomach.

"Why are you holding my wife? asked Ngao grimacing with pain "Where is my daughter? What have you done with them?" He recognised the man. He was Ah Kow.

"We ask the questions. You answer. Understand?" Ah Kow kicked Ngao again shouting out a string of expletives. "That is for being impertinent."

The second man whispered urgently, "We don't have much time. We have to get rid of him. What shall we do?"

"Gag him. We'll take him to the gang master. He is recruiting. We might get some money for this lump. He'll ship him out and we'll be rid of him. Just knock him out to keep him quiet. I'll kill you if you let him escape! He knows too much. Do it! Now!"

Some distance away, in the doorway of the largest of the outbuildings, Wan Fook gasped. He stood frozen to the ground. Quickly he hid behind a thick doorpost. He did not want to be seen by his nephew. His knees were shaking. He had not expected to see his nephew here. He had come to find out for himself if Kow and his men were responsible for kidnapping Ngao's wife and daughter. He had come only at the insistence of his wife. He had been sure that he would be able to return home to brag that he had done his bit and report that his friends were innocent. He bit his lip hard. He blamed himself for the loose talk that had resulted in this situation. He rapped hard on the doorpost and waved Kow over.

"You promised me that you had nothing to with Hua's kidnap. You lied," he whispered. "You will get me into trouble. For goodness sake! Free the two women. And untie my nephew. Let him go. I vouch that you won't get into trouble if you do this."

"*Huh!* We get into trouble? *Huh!*" Kow snarled. With one sweep of his hand, he slapped Wan Fook. "You, you must be the one who brought him here. He would not have found us otherwise."

"No! No! I did not bring him here. I haven't even spoken to him since last night."

"And what do you think we should do now that he has found out?" Kow's voice was low and urgent. "The only alternative to shipping him out is to kill him. That is the only way we can keep his mouth shut. If we go down, you will go down with us."

"No! No! Don't kill him." Wan Fook panicked. He had almost yelped out his protest. He looked across at the unconscious Ngao.

Kow sneered and poked a finger into Wan Fook's chest. "Admit it. We are doing you a good deed. You were always jealous of your brother and his son, Ngao. This is an ideal opportunity to get rid of him forever."

Wan Fook looked guiltily away. In sporadic fits of jealousy over his wife's fondness for Ngao, he had said unforgivable things in the past. He had not meant it. Or did he, he wondered. He shook away his dark thoughts and turned once more to Kow. "What about Hua and Shao Peng?" he asked. He squeezed his eyes tight to block out the vision of the two in his mind's eye. Immediately his wife's face surfaced.

"That is out of my hands. I have nothing to do with them any more," Kow said with a grin. He threw a meaningful glance across the courtyard as a warning to Wan Fook. "And you had better not interfere."

IN THE BEDROOM, Mui heard the commotion. Turning brightly to Hua, she exclaimed. "*Aiyah!* How beautiful you look! If you will just cooperate and not sob, I will try to get Madam to let you see Shao Peng again before we leave. All I beg you to do is eat. The two dumplings you had will not sustain you."

"Did you hear the commotion outside?" asked Hua. She got up to go to the door.

Mui barred her way. "What commotion?" She pretended not to have heard anything. Hua was unconvinced.

"You must have heard it," insisted Hua. She looked at Mui incredulously. Again she made for the door. Mui placed a restraining hand on Hua's arm, smiling all the while.

"*Ahhh!* That noise! It is the workmen. They are repairing the door! Sit down. Eat and let me complete our preparations."

"I don't care how I look. I am going to work. I don't need to look beautiful." Hua grew increasingly agitated. She shook off Mui's grip on her arm and brushed off her attempts to come near her.

"Now, now. Don't make things bad for yourself. Think of your daughter."

Reminded of Shao Peng, Hua grew remorseful. "Please will you let me see Shao Peng? Will I be able to come back to see her every now and then?"

Mui nodded. "Only if you cooperate. I'll ask Madam Yeong. She has been so kind to you and you did promise that you would work for her to raise money for your husband's release. Just eat and drink a little."

I have to calm her down, Mui thought. It does not look as though she is going to go willingly. She sighed and went over to the table and poured out a cup of tea. Surreptitiously, with her back towards Hua, she drew out a little vial from her pocket and emptied a few drops into the tea.

Chapter 6

CANTON-BEILIU

THE LONG AWAITED rain pelted down. They fell with a ferocity that turned the road into a foaming grey river. It was like the heavens were being torn asunder to make up for the prolonged drought. The junks docked by the waterfront tossed and bucked, clashing against each other, hammered by the relentless beat of the rain. Lightning streaked the darkened sky lighting up the harbour.

A long queue of men stretched from one end of the dockyard to the other. They shuffled forward in the deluge with incredible slowness; men dressed in ragged cotton trousers and filthy tunic tops, their faces etched with despair and sadness. Water streaked down their cheeks like tears.

"You there! Get in line!" shouted a guard. He prodded the men, swinging his cane into their midst. Ngao, crammed among the shuffling bodies, tried to break free.

"I don't belong here. I am not here to sign up," he shouted. His voice would have been lost in the storm had it not attracted the attention of a guard standing close-by. Irate at the disturbance, the guard rushed over and brought his cane down with force. Ngao caught the cane and felt it cut deep into his palm. Uncaring he wrenched hard. The guard stumbled. Immediately Ngao was surrounded. The furore brought a motley group of men with pigtails to the scene. They pushed him down and kicked him.

"Now get up and get back in line," the guard commanded. Emboldened by his helpers, he prodded Ngao even harder. "He is a trouble maker. Watch him!" he said, bringing his cane down even harder on Ngao.

Ngao struggled to his feet. His knees buckled. Someone reached out from the queue and helped him regain his space in the line. "Don't resist," advised the man. "It won't do any good. You have signed up as far as they are concerned. Your family has taken their money. The men who delivered you said they were your brothers. They enrolled you."

"They are impostors. I don't have brothers. They have kidnapped my wife and daughter. Please help me escape."

"*Shhh!* Quiet! Don't get me into trouble. I couldn't help even if I wanted to. Look at me. I am in the same fix as you." The man glanced furtively in the direction of the guard. "You have made him lose face and you will pay. They," he said nodding in the direction of the guards, "don't like to be shown up. You nearly brought that one down to the ground."

"Who are you? Where are we going?" asked Ngao. He stared at the rugged sunburnt face of his helper.

"I'm Cheng. Don't you know anything?" He looked quickly at Ngao and saw his desperation.

Ngao shook his head. "Those men you spoke about. They knocked me out. When I came to, I was forced to join the queue. I know people are leaving the country all the time to seek work in foreign lands. So I guess that is what this must be. Other than that I know little. I do not know what work I am signed up for and where I am going." He clutched the man's hand. "I don't even know where I am. Help me," he pleaded once more, panic in his voice. "I need to find my wife and child. I cannot go. I have to get away from this place."

Cheng cast his eyes around him and shook his head almost imperceptibly. "We are in Canton in Guangdong province. That much I can tell you. I am so sorry I can't help you," he mouthed silently. "What can we do, hemmed in on all sides by guards?"

"Don't you have a wife or a child? Wouldn't you try to get away if you were me?"

"It is not a matter of wishing. It is a matter of what is possible," Cheng whispered softly, so softly that Ngao had to lean closer to him. "Don't say any more. The guard is looking in our direction. And you never know who might tell on you," he continued, glancing around them. Someone nudged them from behind. Cheng immediately took hold of Ngao's elbow, propelling him forward. "We have to keep moving with the rest."

Cheng dug his chin into his chest and hunching his shoulders he turned to look at Ngao. From afar, he was the picture of abject humility and despair. "I'll look out for you. That is all I can do," he said.

The ragged line of men continued to move towards a long wooden table presided over by five men. Above the sound of the splattering rain, howling wind and murmur of voices, was the rhythmic shuffling of feet. Suddenly the movement faltered. Instead of progressing from the table to the jetty where two vessels were docked, the men were ordered to take a number and adjourn to a large grey square building. "Departure has been delayed. It is too rough." The information was relayed down the line. Ngao looked at his companion. Their eyes met. Perhaps this would be my chance, he thought.

CRATES AND CHESTS of tea, silk and porcelain, all ready for export, lined the wall of the factory. It was one of the many on the strip of land between the waterfront and city walls where foreign traders were allowed to deal with government-approved wholesalers, the *Hong* merchants. Workmen were still busy off-loading containers carrying tea from the inland growing district of the region when they were ordered to stop and create a space in the centre of the factory to house the men. They came in droves. Wet, weary and hungry, they lay down to rest in any nook or space they could find. They had been on their feet for most of the whole day. Outside the rain continued relentlessly.

Ngao and Cheng squeezed into a space near the entrance. Despite the humid warmth emitted from hundreds of bodies crammed together, they shivered. Their clothes were wet. All round, men began to strip and Ngao followed suit. Clad in his loose black cotton trousers he wrung out his tunic. He looked around, marking out the doors, windows and the high walls. Guards were everywhere. In one corner a handful of Europeans stood apart from the mass of men huddled on the floor of the factory. Around them labourers were busy shifting crates.

Cheng tapped his arm. "Tea merchants," he said, "I use to work in this dockyard. I speak a bit of their language and acted as go-between for the *Hong* merchants. They come to buy tea and deal in porcelain on the side. They find it useful to ship them together. The porcelain," he said pointing to some of the crates, "cheap blue and white stuff mainly for domestic use provides additional ballast for their ships."

Ngao did not reply. He was not interested in the crates. He continued his surveillance of the place. He was searching for an escape route. His eyes strayed to a window. The latch seemed undone.

"It will be too difficult," Cheng whispered following his gaze, "difficult *and* risky." He squatted down on his haunches and bade Ngao to join him. Lowering his voice further, he asked him if he had a plan. "It is not just a matter of breaking free. You have to plan what to do after you have escaped as well. How are you going to return home? What are you going to do once you get there? I think it best to start your life anew in a fresh place, like I am doing. There is a fortune to be made out in *Nanyang*, Southeast Asia."

Ngao had no plan. His mind was swamped by thoughts of what might be happening to his wife and child. He did not know the port, the people or even the geography of the area. All he knew was that he had to get back to Beiliu to rescue his family. Cheng saw his desperation and his wild fiery eyes. "Think and plan. Don't act rashly!" he warned.

Ngao could hardly breathe. Every fibre in his body craved for action. He turned on his newfound friend. "Why are you so interested in me? Leave me alone." He brushed aside Cheng's hand. He did not want to hear that it was difficult, even less that it was impossible. He needed hope. Without it he would be left in utter despair. His frustration boiled over and he vented his anger. "I don't know you. We have only just met. Why should I believe in you?"

His raised voice attracted the attention of the men around him. In the tight confined space of the factory, tempers were easily frayed. His aggressive reply prompted others to edge closer.

"Watch your mouth!" one said, roughly pushing between Cheng and Ngao. "He helped you. Now you repay him with insults?" He leaned towards Ngao, his shoulders tensed, his fists ready.

"It is alright Kam. Thank you, Thank you," said Cheng. "We are only talking. He had a tragedy. He is just upset."

"Cheng is a good man. He too has had a tragedy. We all have had tragedies. That is why we are leaving China. That is why we have signed up to go to another land that offers us some hope. By signing up we are indebted and in the control of coolie masters. So don't think that you are special and have to be treated differently." Kam jabbed his finger into Ngao's chest and pushed. He continued, his face belligerent, "If you wish to survive, you should try to be on the better side of Cheng. He is the only one here who speaks some of the *gwei lo* language."

"*Mo kuan se. Suen le!* It is no matter. Leave it," said Cheng in Cantonese. "His family circumstance is worse than ours. We are leaving to earn for our family. He has lost his family."

Turning to Ngao, Cheng suggested, "Why don't you tell them what you told me?"

Ngao looked shamefaced at Cheng. "I am sorry. I have been unfair." He then turned to Kam. "I apologise. I am desperate. You see..."

❀ ❀ ❀

BACK IN BEILIU, Heong Yook sat in the study with her eyes transfixed on the wall painting behind the desk. She could not move for the beauty of it: the horses galloping at full speed, their manes flowing with the wind and muscles rippling with the effort. Her heart quickened: the calligraphy and the purity of the strokes in black on silk as white as snow had always set her heart racing. All manner of thoughts crossed her mind. Yes, Master Foo the potter must help her. Slowly she got up from the stool. Steadying herself she went around the desk and reached up. She unpinned the silken scroll and with great care rolled it up. My husband would be incensed, she thought. He would not forgive me. She went to the far end of the room where a tall rosewood cabinet stood. She unlatched the bronzed clasp that held the doors together. A smell of camphor wafted from its dark interior. She reached into a lower shelf. There was a painting here, she recalled. It was a present to them by an unknown artist in return for a favour from her husband years ago. She looked for the tag *'For Wan Fook'*. She took hold of the scroll, unrolled it and nodded. Her expression was grim. It would have to do. With all his worries, he might not notice until it was too late. Grasping the scroll under her arm, she closed the cabinet doors, making sure that the clasp was once more secure. Then she walked back to behind the desk and hung the scroll on the spot left vacant by the removal of the original painting. She prayed fervently that Wan Fook would not notice the switch. Picking up the painting of the horse, she left the room.

❀ ❀ ❀

THE ATMOSPHERE IN the warehouse was musty. A palpable damp odour rose from the cramped wet bodies. Several people groaned. A streak of light came through the window heralding dawn.

Suddenly the massive doors burst open. Several guards rushed in. "Get ready! Get in line! We are leaving!" they shouted.

Bodies unfolded and stretched. Cramped for hours and hungry, the sudden imminent departure took them by surprise. Mutterings of anger rippled through the crowd. "We were promised food," someone yelled. Others too threw in their protest. Soon an uproar of dissenting voices rose above the shouts and commands of the guards.

Ngao spun round in panic to face Cheng and Kam. He looked from one to the other. "I expected the wait to be longer. I need more time. You said there was another consignment of men waiting and that they would ship them out before us."

"Yes! That's right. A special depot is used to house people to be shipped out. I thought they would empty that first and then we would be sent to fill the vacated space and wait our turn. After all their boat was scheduled to leave before ours. It was done this way in the past when bad weather prevented vessels from leaving."

He looked around him and suddenly a flash of understanding crossed his face. "Perhaps ... That is it! They are moving us out first to stop any possible contamination of the tea! Our presence cannot be good for it; all that damp air!" exclaimed Cheng.

A guard moved towards them. Cheng made a show of getting ready to walk. He nudged Ngao.

"Get a move on!" shouted the guard, prodding them with his cane for good measure. "You'll get fed while we continue cataloguing you lot. Get in line!" He laughed at his own joke.

For him the consignment of people was just like a shipment of goods, a cargo, only more cumbersome as everyone had to be dealt with individually.

Outside the warehouse, the long table was in place with five men once again seated behind it. The queue shuffled forward. The guard prodded Ngao and Cheng again. "You two! Go to the front and form another queue. There!" he pointed to a spot in front of one of the men seated behind the table.

Ngao's face fell. His hope for escape was fast slipping away. The guard was quick to notice this. He pointed this time specifically at Ngao. "Go! Now!"

"Do as he says; there is nothing you can do," whispered Cheng from behind.

Reluctantly Ngao moved forward.

"Name?" asked the man seated at the table. He barely looked up when Ngao replied. He was too intent in finding the name in the columns of Chinese characters in the ledger. He grunted, wrote something in the book and only then did he look up. He gave Ngao no more than a perfunctory glance. His face wizened by the sun was openly contemptuous. He dabbed his pen brush into the black ink-stone and handed it to Ngao. "Sign here," he said turning the ledger round and pointing to a space next to some figures.

Ngao looked in horror at the sum. "What am I signing?" he asked.

"What are you signing?" the man echoed with a snarl, taken aback by the question. This was the first time anyone had been bold enough to question him. "You dare ask! You are signing to confirm the amount you owe us. That is what you are signing. You have already taken a sizeable advance. On top of that is the passage fare."

"But I didn't take any money from you?" protested Ngao. "I don't want to go so I don't need your passage fare."

"Too bad! You should have thought about it earlier. You have to go. You have already taken an advance and unless you can repay it with interest right now, you have to go to earn enough to repay us. Sign!" he barked. "Don't waste my time!" He beckoned to a guard.

The guard took Ngao's hand and roughly forced the brush into it before bringing it to the sheet of paper. "Sign!" he repeated after the man. Cheng whispered, "Just do as they say. You can't do anything else. You will just get beaten."

"Well said," drawled the man at the table. He looked on at the reluctant Ngao, a smirk played at his lips when Ngao eventually put his signature to the paper. "*Aaah!* An educated man I see. You have to learn the hard way. Guard! Take him and tie him to a post. Watch this one. You can never be too careful. We will be leaving soon."

❀ ❀ ❀

THE SUN SHONE fiercely and strong. Almost all signs of the previous day's violent storm had vanished from the dockyard. The jetty looked clean, washed by the torrential rain. Only a scattering of overturned crates and puddles gave testimony to its occurence. The throbbing activity of the dockyard had returned. Men hurried from jetty to ship, carrying crates on their bare shoulders, nimbly crossing planks to the anchored vessels. Further out to sea two fully laden steamships, the first of their kind, lay low in the water as they prepared to get under way. In the midst of this activity, Ngao sat with his knees drawn up. Both his ankles had been tied with a rough rope looped round a post. He alone was tied. The others had been cordoned off in an area that served as a rough temporary kitchen and canteen. He looked across to them. Cheng was hurrying towards him with a bowl in his hand.

"Eat! I managed to get an extra bowl. Quickly! Before they see us. The man doling out food was a mate of mine when I worked here." Cheng thrust the bowl of watery rice congee into Ngao's hands.

Ngao took the bowl with one hand and with the other caught hold of Cheng's forearm. He pulled until Cheng's face was level with his. "Thank you for the food. I am not ungrateful, but I need to escape."

"Listen, the more you complain, the less chance you will have to do anything, least of all escape," replied Cheng withdrawing his arm from the tight grasp. "Look here, if you had not drawn so much attention they would not have chained you." He squatted down. "Eat! That might be your last meal for some while." He cast a cautious glance around him. "There is no way you can escape. We are about to set sail. There is only one thing I can do to help. I can get word to your aunt of your whereabouts. We are going to be shipped first to Singapore. I learned that from the gang master."

Ngao opened his mouth to protest, his hand reaching out once more for Cheng's arm.

Cheng stopped him. "That is all," he said firmly. "I can't help you escape. I can't escape myself. In my case it is my own undoing. I gambled and to repay my debts I had to contract my labour. My wife and children have returned to her parents. Perhaps you could even say that I am running away. I know it is not the same for you."

"No! It is not the same." Ngao replied. He tried to keep his voice low; his face was contorted with pain and anguish. "What will happen to my wife and daughter? Who can help them?"

"You said you have an aunt. Perhaps she might be able to do something. Tell me her name. I will get word to her," said Cheng.

Ngao looked directly into Cheng's eyes. He could see nothing other than compassion. What could he do but trust him? He looked at his ankles tied tightly together and anchored to a post. Holding on to his bowl, tears began to well up in his eyes. They rolled down his cheeks; he wept unashamedly. "Her name is Heong Yook," he gulped, "she lives in the central quarter of Beiliu city, next to the Ong Pottery. Ask her to find my wife and daughter and contact me. I will be waiting for them." He knew he was clinging to a straw. Overwhelmed by fear for his family and frustrated that he could do nothing, he bowed his head in shame. Tears continued to flow unchecked down his cheeks, splashing on to his tunic top.

Cheng grasped Ngao's hand briefly. "I understand. But life continues. It would help no one by starving or by dying or by getting beaten. If it helped, I would be the first to tell you." He paused for no more than a second. "I have to get this message to a trusted friend. I'll come back."

Chapter 7

FOO WALKED QUICKLY down the street. He kept his arms carefully tucked by his side and his long wide sleeves covered his wrists and hid his hands. He held the pouch tightly in his palm. Few people were about. Some vendors continued to ply their trade by the sidewalk but sporadic outbreaks of violence during the morning had caused most people to remain in their homes. After almost three days of relative calm many did not believe the peace would hold. News from other parts of the city and the neighbouring province of Guangdong showed that the rebellion was continuing unabated and the death toll had risen to hundreds of thousands. Like his employer Ong Wan Fook and many middle and land-owning classes, Foo was not a supporter of the rebellion, much as he disliked the Manchu rulers and the corruption that had engulfed the country. He did not agree with the increasingly religious overtones of a rebellion that sought to replace traditional Chinese values and Confucianism with a form of Christianity he did not understand. The proclamation by its leader Hong Xiu Quan that he spoke as God was greeted with scepticism and disbelief. His claim to be the brother of Jesus Christ was ridiculed even more.

The potter kept his head down, careful to avoid eye contact with anyone in the street. The paving stones had been washed clean by the previous night's downpour. Each stone glistened. "Chaos!" he muttered as he stared at the clean paving and contrasted it with the filth and poverty that could be seen throughout the city. He quickened his steps as he approached his master's house only to slow down when he neared the entrance door. Reluctantly, he came to a stop in front of it. He fidgeted, shifting his weight from one foot to the other. He glanced anxiously up and down the street. He did not know whether it was safe to go in, but Mistress Heong Yook had made him promise to come to her once he had made the deal. With great trepidation, he lifted the copper door-knocker and rapped it gently four times, as agreed. He mumbled "*Choy! Choy! Choy!*" to ward off evil. They had agreed on that number to make sure that she would know he was at the door and come to answer it personally. No one would normally knock four times as the Chinese character *si* or four sounded the same as the word for death and was considered a bad omen. No one else in the house would answer such a knock. "The things she makes me do," he complained clutching the pouch even more tightly.

Within minutes, she opened the door and he stepped inside. A big crimson screen with paintings of the four seasons shielded the dark interior from the doorway.

"I can't invite you in," apologised Heong Yook. She was pale and anxiety caused her to wrinkle her brow. "It is fortunate that houses have screens at their entrance. We will have to talk here. Have you sold it?"

"Yes! Everything is in this pouch. It is the best price I could get. Times are bad. Is Master Ong back?" asked Foo. He looked anxiously over her shoulders. He did not wish to get more involved. "Please keep me out of this. I ... I ... do not wish to be embroiled any further."

"But Master Foo, I still need your help. Think of Ngao, and his wife and poor daughter. You know I am housebound. I cannot go out even in peacetime and certainly not now. I need your help to find out where they are. Even Ngao has vanished."

"No! No! Leave me out of it. I have already helped you to dispose of the painting. I would be imprisoned and sent away to have my hands chopped off if they thought I'd stolen it. So please, I don't want to be mixed up in this affair. All I can tell you is that Ngao followed your husband and therefore it is most likely your husband will know his whereabouts." Foo shivered as he thought of the enormity of what he had done. "I am an old man. I can't do much more. I have done what I can because I love Ngao like my son."

"You are right," conceded Heong Yook, "I should not place such a burden on you. You had better go. My husband is back. He looks out of sorts and is in his study. He did not notice that the wall painting has gone. He even looked at me as though I was not there!" She went to the door and eased it open carefully pausing every now and then to stop it squeaking. "Quick! The maids are back and might come at any time."

She bowed her head and whispered, "Thank you."

Taken aback, Foo returned with a bow that was even deeper locking his fingers together in a gesture of homage. He was older, but she was still his mistress.

Heong Yook stood still for a moment after Foo departed and then turned to return to the northern house. Once in her bedroom, she walked to her bed, an ornate structure with carved panels on three sides. She pushed aside the drapes and sat down on the thin mattress. She could feel the hardness of the wooden bed through it. Quickly she reached for the quilt rolled up at one corner and tucked the pouch into it. It would have to do for the moment as a hiding place, she thought. She will give the money to Ngao as soon as she sees him. It will help him. With this he won't need to leave China to find work. She got up ignoring the pain that shot through her feet. She was in agony; she had been up and about the whole day and was not accustomed to it. The pain coursed up her spine as she swayed unsteadily out of the room and made her way to her husband's study.

IN HIS STUDY, Wan Fook sat slumped in his chair, his legs stretched out in front of him, his eyes vacant. Every now and then, he would touch his cheeks. He could still feel the stinging slap that had been landed there. "What shall I do? What can I do?" he asked himself. His eyes swept unseeing around the room. He scratched his shaven forehead, his long nails leaving deep lines of red. "What have I done?" He panicked and pressed his fist into his chest to still the beating of his heart. "I have to pull myself together. I can't let Heong Yook see me like this," he muttered. He sat up and straightened his back, but he could not rid himself of the images of Ngao, head lolling, unconscious, kicked and beaten, his face a mass of purple bruises. He had not wished harm on his nephew or on Hua and the child.

"My big mouth!" he exclaimed, once more taking it out on his shaven forehead. In disgust, he took hold of his queue and pulled violently. "I am a coward. I always have been. If I were a man, I would cut off this pigtail and grow my hair. If I were a man I would brave the risk of beheading; I would keep to the teachings of Confucius and fulfil my filial piety."

He stood up and, raising his voice in remorse, recited, "For hasn't Confucius said: we are given our body, skin and hair from our parents; we ought not shave our foreheads. Shaving my head is a breach of my duty to my parents. Yet I do exactly that. I kowtow to the Qing command. I bring shame on my family. I fail my parents."

Visions of his nephew once more intruded into his mind's eye. His voice dropped to a whisper. "If I were a man I would have fought those scoundrels and rescued my nephew and his family. I deserve to pay penance." So saying he clawed again at his shaved skull.

When Heong Yook came into the room, she found her husband in a state of madness, alternating between remorse and anger. She watched as he switched from crying to inflicting violence on himself and then back to crying. He was totally unaware of her presence. She watched him walk up and down, muttering. Instinctively, she knew all her suspicions were confirmed and, worst of all, that Ngao and his family had come to serious harm.

She went to her husband and placed her hand on his forearm, stilling it even as it was reaching out to land another resounding slap on the owner's face for in the last minute, Wan Fook had taken to slapping himself.

"Stop this!" she commanded him. He spun round his mouth opened although no words emerged.

"Have you found Ngao and Hua?" asked Heong Yook more quietly this time. Her eyes were steely as she regarded her husband. She was disgusted with what she saw; the blubbering, stuttering man, full of self-pity and indecision. His quoting of Confucius teachings no longer held her in thrall. She had seen through them.

He shrunk from her; he couldn't meet her eyes.

"Tell me!" she demanded. She was no longer afraid of him. It was as though her reverence for him, the result of years of waiting on his very whim, had never been. She willed him to respond. She stood silent, just staring at him, waiting for an answer.

He sat down heavily and told her everything that he had witnessed. She listened without interrupting. When he finished, she said quietly, "You have to undo all the harm you have done. We have to rescue Ngao and his family. You owe them that much."

THIN SHAFTS OF light penetrated the tightly drawn window slats to touch the wooden floorboards of the room. They created shifting images of golden beams around which motes of dust danced and settled in turn. A strong sweet odour filled the warm air, its pungency cloying and intense. There was utter stillness except for the soft sounds of deep sleep punctuated by occasional moans coming from within the canopied bed in one corner. Someone opened the door, peered in and then closed the door again. Time slipped by. Slowly, the beams of light through the window slats shifted and then were no more. Darkness fell.

The door creaked open. Mui held the red lantern aloft and soft light flooded into the room. "Sir, I think she might have fallen asleep for she is tired," whispered Mui, miming her words with actions and placing a finger to her lips to demonstrate what she was saying. "She told me she is looking forward to being with you. Even then, she might push you away. If she resists, sir, it is only because she is new and very, very shy. They all do that. It is the shock, you see. She has not been with a man before."

"I would like to see her first," he said turning towards the bed. "Give me the light," he said pointing to the lantern, his voice hoarse. "Are you sure this is her first time?" he indicated with his thumb to make sure that she understood him. His Cantonese was basic.

Mui nodded vigorously. She recalled her instructions. "He would not know and we have prepared her body well, so tell him what he wants to hear. Virginity is not so important with them, even so, it is still prized," Madam Yeong had said.

Mui tiptoed to the bed beckoning him to follow, holding the lantern firmly in her hand. She did not wish to relinquish it. She did not wish him to wake Hua. She drew the drape aside gently and held the lantern behind the crimson cloth to reduce its glare. The pink glow lit up the bed. Hua lay in a deep sleep on her back, one arm across her chest and the other flung out beside her head. She was barely covered by the silk robe she wore; her chest rose and fell with the ebb and flow of her breathing. She moaned and turned on her side, curling into a tight ball. Her robe caught and uncovered her shoulder and neck. Mui looked at the man next to her, observing his tight breeches and his heavy breathing. She saw his excitement. She drew back slightly and let the drapes fall back in place. She indicated with her finger that she would leave the lantern on the table and with another finger on her lips, moved away.

Mui closed the door quietly behind her and sighed. She waited outside with her back leaning against the door, hands clenched. She would stay just long enough to be sure that the deed was done.

Cries of anguish echoed from within the room. "No! No! Get off me! Mui! Mui! Help me!"

Mui shut her ears to the cries from the room. She willed her thoughts to more practical things that she had to do, a drill she had practised many times or she herself would get into trouble. She would have to report to the Madam of this house. Her own mistress, Madam Yeong, had given her permission to stay on until Hua adjusted but Mui felt uncomfortable. She found Canton bewildering. It was huge and overwhelming.

Until this evening she had not encountered any westerners. They lived in segregation, outside the city walls, around the waterfront. Chinese law forbade their presence within the city walls. Yet, this man was here, bold and demanding. She was not familiar with such men and their strange language and even stranger sounding Chinese. She spoke no English and hoped that he understood her. She shrugged. He spoke sufficient Chinese to explain himself. She was told that Hua was fortunate that at least he was not as uncouth as others. At least, he spoke some Chinese and was most likely to take Hua on a more permanent basis if she pleased him. She heard Hua calling out for her, followed by scuffling and then an anguished moan. She hesitated and then moved quickly away.

❀ ❀ ❀

"YOU CAN'T GO. It is not a place for a respectable woman," protested Wan Fook. "You are my wife. What would people say?"

He wanted to shout, " I forbid it!" But all he could do was stutter and make feeble excuses. He knew from Heong Yook's withering stare that he had lost all credibility with her. "You will achieve nothing," he warned lamely. He fell back on his seat. Heong Yook sat down opposite him resting her forearms on the marble tabletop that separated them.

"We have to try," she said. "You told me that all Madam Yeong cares for is money. So we give her what she wants in return for Ngao and his family. You won't do it, so I will. I don't care what people say. I care more about my own conscience." Her voice was quiet. He could sense the steel and determination behind it. He dropped his gaze.

"We don't have the sort of money she would probably want. Business has been poor to say the least because of the rebellion and, and..." he stuttered.

"*Phhh!*" Heong Yook waved her hand dismissively. "I know all about that. I know our wealth is much reduced. But we still have some pieces of fine art. What are these set against their lives?

A look of sudden apprehension crossed Wan Fook's face. He spun round and stared at the wall behind him. He looked blankly at the picture. He did not recognise it. It barely covered the space left by the original. "Where is my painting? What have you done with it?" he asked even as he guessed what the answer would be. That was why she was so certain she would have the money to rescue Ngao and his family. Wan Fook's face turned purple with rage. He jumped up from his seat, toppling it over behind him.

Heong Yook remained unmoved. "I sold it," she answered calmly looking directly into his eyes, "because I knew you would not part with it. What is a painting for the lives of our own kin? Help me. Take me to that brothel, the place you've had no qualms visiting in the past, yet now, when you could do good there, have such reservations about stepping into it. Do it for me, for your brother, for your nephew."

THE SEDAN CHAIR bounced and swung as the two men broke into a trot bearing it along on the uneven paving stones. She could see the shoulders of the front bearer straining under the weight of the sedan. His tunic clung to his back soaked with sweat while his hair, tied into the obligatory queue, lay like a heavy greasy rope between his shoulder blades. Heong Yook looked out of the opening in the sedan. The street was deserted. Even traders desperate to earn a living had abandoned it following the previous day's clash between the rebels and government troops. She could see remnants of the conflict in the street. They passed an over-turned cart and a dog lying dead on its side, its wounds already festering with maggots. Heong Yook pressed her handkerchief to her nose and turned away.

Wan Fook had given her the address but had refused to accompany her, hoping this would deter her. It was only once again with the help of faithful Master Foo that she had succeeded in persuading the sedan bearers to brave the journey. Both men were related to Foo. They had protested and rolled their eyes in horror when they learned where she wished to go.

She heard them arguing heatedly with Foo. In the end they relented. She placed the kerchief this time to her brow to wipe away the perspiration that had broken out. Her hands were clammy and she could feel her heart beating faster and faster. She had said brave words to her husband. Now travelling by herself in the sedan she was frightened.

They turned a corner and entered into another street. The walls of the houses lining the street were splashed with paint. Black, red and yellow blotches hastily applied on writings, some of which were still visible like spidery webs gone awry. Big posters calling people to rise-up against corruption lay torn and crumpled by the roadside. She saw a beggar sitting with his back to the wall. The sedan drew closer, she looked out. She could not make out if he was dead; he was so still with his head drooped into his chest. The sedan passed the beggar and Heong Yook turned round to have a closer look. Flies congregated around an open wound on his leg and on his face He seemed oblivious. She drew back quickly. The men stopped. They lowered the sedan and shouted, "We have arrived."

"Wait here for me!" she instructed. "I hope I won't be long." She was determined to carry out what she had promised to do. She was not going to let them see her fear.

The two men exchanged a look. Under pressure, they had promised Foo that they would look after her. Nevertheless they did not want to hang around the street. They turned to stare at the beggar. He had not moved at all.

She saw their uneasy exchange. "I'll double your payment only if you stay. I'll pay when you take me home," she hastened to add. Without waiting for their reply she climbed out of the sedan, holding on to the carriage walls. Reluctantly, they stood and watched. They wanted to protest but they recalled their uncle's threat. Her movements were slow. She paused for a second to let her feet familiarise themselves, for the numbness to go, and with a brave face went to the door. She lifted the door-knocker and rapped loudly and urgently. Then she straightened her back and squared her shoulders in preparation for the confrontation.

"You had better go and get Uncle Foo," said one of the men to the other. "I'll stay here."

"PLEASE WAIT HERE." The maid indicated a chair by the side of a tall rosewood table. Her eyes were round with surprise when she opened the door to see a lady. She was not accustomed to lady visitors, especially one who showed such command and poise. Heong Yook had walked in without being invited and, brushing aside the maid's protestations, haughtily asked for her Madam. Short of pushing the lady out, she could do little else. If the lady did know Madam Yeong, she would be in deep trouble if she refused her entry. She stole a glance at Heong Yook, taking note of her clothes, her feet and her demeanour. "A proper lady," the maid concluded. "What could she want in a place like this?" she asked herself. So, hesitantly, she repeated her invitation to Heong Yook to sit and hurried to get Madam Yeong.

Left on her own, Heong Yook surveyed her surroundings. It was a largish room with black lacquered elm chairs and small tea tables arranged along one wall. To the left of her stood a tall red lacquered cabinet with a copper bolt in the centre. A console table with six small drawers and a vase of peonies stood by the moon-shaped window. There was little to suggest the place was anything other than an ordinary house and that this was the reception room in the southern building reserved for guests.

Throughout the journey she had fretted over what she would find in a brothel. She did not know what to expect, certainly not this ordinariness. Perhaps, she was at the wrong address. From a distance, she heard voices, young girls giggling. It broke into her thoughts and brought her back to the present. She went and looked out of the window opening onto the courtyard and saw young girls being shepherded from one building into another. Young girls, some as young as six! She started. "Shao Peng! Did she see Shao Peng?" She peered out again. They were gone. Her heart throbbed and her apprehension rose even more. She drew in a deep breath and exhaled slowly, repeating the process until she felt calmer. She would have to brace herself for the task ahead. "Be strong! Be strong!" she repeated over and over again. She went back to her seat and bowed in prayer to the Goddess of Mercy, mumbling her mantra as she placed both hands together on her lap. She was nervous, frightened, more frightened than she had let known. She did not notice the soft footsteps until Madam Yeong was in front of her.

"What can we do for you?" asked Madam Yeong. Her eyes narrowed as they swept over the tiny woman. She sat down on the chair on the other side of the tea table. Surely, she has come to see me about a recalcitrant errant husband, *Ahhh!* Men! She mused as she continued to size up her visitor.

Heong Yook looked up. She saw the exaggerated plucked brows, drawn like a pair of thin dark half-moons, the powdered face and dark red vermilion lips, painted into the shape of a bud. She was reminded of the paintings of courtesans in the

Imperial Qing courts. She had been forewarned of Madam Yeong's appearance, but even so she had difficulty concealing her distaste. "I come to appeal to you," she replied.

Madam Yeong raised her eyebrows. "Me? Appeal to me? How can a poor woman like me help the likes of you?" She brushed her skirt and returned Heong Yook's stare.

"I come to ask you, beg even, to release my nephew and his wife and daughter. He is called Ngao and his wife and daughter, Hua and Shao Peng. Please, they are very dear to me. I will do anything to set them free. Tell me how much you want."

Heong Yook had gone straight to the heart of the matter. She did not want to waste any time. Every minute lost would, she felt, have repercussions. Her husband had told her Madam Yeong's history and her lust for wealth. "Don't underestimate her," he had cautioned. "She has lost her whole family and channels her entire interest into acquiring wealth to protect herself. It is her way of avenging the wrong done to her. No one, she says, came to her aid in her hour of need and so, in her eyes, everyone was guilty and she wants to make them pay. Money is her God."

"Truly I do not know what you are talking about. Have you got the right person? What would I have to do with your nephew and his family? Who are you?" asked Madam Yeong, feigning surprise and indignation.

"My husband, Ong Wan Fook, has told me everything. I am not here to pick a quarrel. I am here only to appeal to you. I know that you once had a husband and sons and that you lost all of them. You must therefore realise how painful it must be to lose a loved one. So please release my nephew's family and return them to us. I ... I ... Here! I have brought all our savings." She placed the pouch of money on the table.

Madam Yeong rose from her seat. "I do not know what you are talking about. Leave! Leave now or I will have to ask the guards to evict you. How dare you come and make such wild accusations?" She pointed to the door, her face white with apparent rage.

Heong Yook did not move nor did she utter any further words. Her eyes held steadfastly those of Madam Yeong. She cannot fail, she must not fail Ngao and his family, she thought. When her husband told her of Madam Yeong's past, she was confident that she would be able to find a chink in the woman's armour. Surely she would have compassion for the suffering of others if she herself had undergone such pain? Heong Yook had been confident that no woman could be as cruel as her husband had made out Madam Yeong to be. Now she was not so sure.

"This is all we have," she said pushing the pouch across the table, spilling out some of the gold it held. If it was money, the woman craved for then she could have it.

Madam Yeong's eyes strayed to the pouch and lingered there. The gold gleamed invitingly. She made a mental count of the gold repeating again even while she was counting that she did not know what Heong Yook was talking about. "Ah Kow! Ah Kow! Help!" she shouted. Then swiftly leaning forward, she made to snatch the pouch off the table. Heong Yook anticipated the move. With one hand she snatched the pouch back and with the other swept the spilled coins into it. She held it to her bosom. She was unable to move. Her legs trembled. She could not believe her own actions.

"Hand that over. That is now mine. You cannot come to my house with your wild accusations and insults and not pay for it."

Heong Yook stood up and tried to move past her, but her legs were weak and she could not steady herself. She tripped, pushing into Madam Yeong and causing her to stumble. Heong Yook managed to catch hold of the table. She steadied herself, still clutching the pouch.

"Open the door! Open up!" came shouts from outside followed by vigorous pounding. The commotion was loud. It seemed like there was an army of men outside. "We know our Mistress is in there. Open up!"

Kow and his men had meantime rushed in. Caught off guard he waited for the instructions of his mistress. The banging and pounding from outside grew louder. Kow ran to the main door and peered out through a peephole. There were at least half a dozen men, burley men with long pigtails and shaven foreheads. He went to Madam Yeong and whispered. "I am not sure who they are. Could be Qing men or another triad. Not our faction. What do you want me to do?"

"Let her go," she said reluctantly.

HUA DRAGGED HERSELF off the bed. Her body ached. She grabbed the ends of her sleeves and pulled them down to wipe herself. She scrubbed and scrubbed, repulsed by her own body, adding soreness to the soreness that was already there. Her hair so carefully combed and pinned by Mui, was in wild disarray. It hung down her back and twined round her neck while strands clung wet across her face. Her thin robe was in tatters, torn by the struggle she had put up against the man. Her eyes darted around the room like a frightened trapped rabbit. He had left, but not without planting a kiss on her lips with the promise that he would return for her soon. She rubbed the back of her hand across her lips. She looked at the bed, the stains of blood and semen on the crumpled sheets and wept.

Holding what remained of her robe together, Hua went to the door. She tried to open it. It was locked from outside. She banged and shouted. Finally, exhausted she slid down to the floor. She sobbed, quietly, the sounds choked in her throat. She did not know where she was. She had no recollection beyond being dressed in Madam Yeong's house, bidding her daughter goodbye and then being abruptly woken up by a man on top of her. A shudder went through her. How could she face Ngao and Shao Peng? Her face burned red with shame. She felt dirty; her violation replayed in her mind. She got up and ran from one end of the room to the other. She found a basin with a pitcher of water. She grabbed the pitcher and poured water into the basin recklessly splashing it round her. She rinsed her mouth, letting the water run down her neck, on to her chest. Then, tearing an end off her robe she dipped into in the basin and washed. She cleaned and cleaned herself again, as though in doing so, she could return to what she had been; and in cleaning she could rid herself of the smell that clung to her.

Crrrk! She spun round. *Crrrk!* She saw the door squeak open, slowly, almost imperceptibly as though the person behind it was trying not to make a sound. Mui's head peered in. Hua rushed to the door. She pulled Mui into the room. Left! Right! Her palms connected with Mui's face. "Where were you? How could you?" Hua cried wildly.

Mui pushed her away and held her hands to her face to defend herself. "Stop! Stop! I am only doing what I am instructed. Don't blame me."

"I trusted you. I trusted you," wailed Hua.

Mui rushed out of the room and quickly drew the bolt. She did not know what to do. She listened to the cries from the room. She was not proud of what she did, what she *had* to do. But what could she do? She was just a pawn in Madam Yeong's hand, as Madam Yeong herself must be in someone else's. She comforted herself. This *fan qwei*, western devil, was not too bad, almost human. More important, he genuinely liked Hua and had already put in an advance for her. Mui shuddered. If Hua had not pleased the *fan qwei* she would probably be sent to the flower boats, floating brothels in the Pearl River that served foreigners outside the city walls and be passed from one client to another. Hua should count herself lucky.

The fact that this *fan qwei* had sufficient influence and resources to enter the city must be a testimony to his importance. Madam Yeong had told her that foreigners were forbidden to enter the city. At times, she said, the Madam in Canton would smuggle women into the foreigners' lodgings in their warehouses, or 'factories' as they call them, outside the city walls. She shuddered at the thought. She must find a way to calm Hua. She must not be seen in her present condition. She would be worse off than she was now if she did not maintain her looks. What is more, Mui would be blamed for her condition. The maid stood indecisive. The wailing continued in the room. "Perhaps I should come back later after she has calmed down," Mui told herself.

HUA SAT WITH her head hung low. There were no tears left in her; her eyes held nothing, just despair. How could she go back to Ngao? How could she meet the eyes of her innocent daughter?

Would these monsters ever set her free? She had been lied to, that was obvious. Shame and revulsion seized her again. She ran to the basin and retched, heaving uncontrollably. Slowly she slid down once more, ignoring the wet floor and slime. Her mind reeled. They would never let her go, she concluded. They would never let her see Shao Peng again. She had lost everything, her husband, her daughter. They were better off without her, a soiled and dirty woman. There was no point to her existence. Mui and Madam Yeong's promises were worth nothing.

She sat with her legs folded under her. Time slipped by. In the distance a cock crowed. A stream of weak light entered from the gap at the bottom of the door. It lit up the floorboards. She saw hairpins scattered on the wooden planks. Slowly she crawled on her knees to them. She gathered a handful in her palm and with great care selected the longest and sharpest. She held it aloft and looked at it as though mesmerised. Then she held out her wrist and slashed. The hairpin cut deep into the flesh. She sat looking at the blood flowing from her wrist. Gradually it formed a pool. For comfort she struggled to hold images and happy thoughts of Ngao and Shao Peng. The streaks of light into the room lengthened and the room grew warmer with the sunlight. She felt none of the warmth. "So cold," she murmured, licking her dry lips. Slowly she slipped out of consciousness; her eyelids fluttered and her breaths grew short.

The door creaked open. Bright sunshine flooded in. Mui took two steps into the room. Her eyes darted from the empty bed towards the window. She screamed. She ran to Hua. She tried to stem the flow of blood pressing her kerchief into the wound. Hua's eyes fluttered open; her lips moved. Mui bent her head to catch her words. "Please..."

Mui looked at Hua. The fear and sadness that had been in her face were gone. She looked serene. Gently Mui placed her hands on Hua's eyelids and closed them. Cradling Hua's head in her arms, she wept.

Chapter 8

"You should not have interfered! You have achieved nothing other than to embarrass me. What will people say when they hear that you went to a brothel? In fact you probably caused Hua and Shao Peng more harm than good. That woman might this very moment be plotting their demise to cover her tracks." Wan Fook ranted at his wife. He felt redeemed by her failure. He had lost face and needed to regain her respect.

Heong Yook sat silent, her head bowed. She ignored him even when he stopped in front of her to glare, his arms akimbo, tucked within wide black silk sleeves with white cuffs. Nor did she look his way when he wagged his finger at her. She was completely shaken by the incident. She admitted to herself that she had been naïve; she had not expected events to unfold the way they had. She had been sure there would be a sense of mercy, of goodness within Madam Yeong that she could reach out to, particularly when she was willing to give the woman gold.

"If I had not called on Foo to send more men along, you would be in trouble now. It was lucky that they set out immediately and met one of the sedan bearers on his way to Foo. He showed them the way to Madam Yeong's place; otherwise they might not have arrived in time."

He did not tell Heong Yook that Foo had chastised him for not accompanying his wife. It was this chastisement from an old master potter who had been with his family for more than three decades that shamed him to action. After all, Foo was like an uncle to him.

Heong Yook raised her head and looked him in the eye. He could see that she was not moved by his words. She still blamed him.

"So what do we do now?" she asked. "Leave aside what I did wrong. After all I went on my own because you did not go with me. We can't leave Hua and Shao Peng in that house. I am sure they are there. And we still need to find Ngao."

"Did you not hear what I said? It is no use," he shouted. He slammed his fist down in exasperation. "She has all the officials in her pocket. She has oiled their palms. If she has not retained their services they are probably using her brothel. She learnt her lessons well. Since her husband's execution, she knows that her survival depends on conniving with and corrupting officials, not opposing them like her husband."

"We have to do something!" retorted Heong Yook. "You know her men, the very men who took Hua. You were the cause of their kidnapping with your loose talk. Surely you can talk to them?"

"I have tried. It is no use," replied Wan Fook, angry to be reminded of his role again. He gingerly touched his face remembering once more the slaps and punches he had received. He sat down heavily on a chair next to her. "I am sorry. I truly am. I have not been a good husband. I should have known better than to talk about Hua to those men. I was drunk. I should have known that it might arouse their interest in her. This is hindsight that I did not have then."

He looked at his wife and then dropped his eyes. "When men go to Madam Yeong's place," he explained softly, "they do not think of how the women get there. I, for one believe, at least like to believe, they are there out of their own choice. Perhaps we blind ourselves to ease our conscience. In truth, I did not think of it at all. It never occurred to me my loose talk that drunken evening would spiral into their kidnap."

They sat in silence, each lost in their own thoughts.

MUI WENT TO the western quarters in search of Shao Peng. It was almost two days after Hua's death. She had just returned to Beiliu and spoken to Madam Yeong, who while shocked seemed to have taken the matter philosophically. "Well, these things happen, though luckily not often." If she regretted Hua's death, Mui saw no trace of it in her face.

"Don't tell Shao Peng," Madam Yeong added. "You will have to find ways of fending off her questions. We had some trouble here while you were away. Her aunt came looking for her. So I am making arrangements to ship her out. It is a shame. I had intended to bring her up in this house myself to groom her for greater things. It will not be prudent to do that now. Her mother's death and the aunt's suspicions will make it awkward if not impossible."

Mui moved quickly along the covered walkway that linked the different buildings. There was no one in the courtyard. She looked towards the entrance of the western quarters. One of Kow's men was stationed nearby. He looked bored. She smiled at him and went into the building. It was dark inside. The rooms in this part of the quadrangle were always dark. Like all the buildings in the quadrangle, there were no windows facing outwards to the streets. Light came in mainly from the courtyard, filtered through the covered walkway. As a result the western buildings, which faced east, received relatively little light in the afternoons. She found Shao Peng sitting on her own. Mui smiled at the other three girls who shared the room. Then she went over to Shao Peng.

"You are back!" exclaimed Shao Peng. Her face brightened and she smiled. "Where is my mother? Is she back? Can I see her now?"

"*Shhh!* I came back alone. You know that she has to work," replied Mui. She saw how the light went out of the little girl's eyes. She looked towards the other girls who were busy playing. She bent her head close to Shao Peng and whispered, "I am going to try to take you away from here. You remember your mother speaking about your father's uncle. Would you like to go there?"

"Why?" asked Shao Peng. "I want to stay here to wait for my mother. I don't mind it here. I don't know my uncle."

"*Shhh!* Lower your voice." Mua looked towards the three girls. They did not seem to have heard Shao Peng's outburst. "You can see your mother there. Your father might also be waiting for you with his uncle." Mui felt she had to throw in an additional incentive to persuade Shao Peng to leave.

Shao Peng looked perplexed. "Is mother not coming back here?"

"No! Not here. It is safer for you if you go to your uncle. Trust me."

The little girl hesitated. Mui took hold of her hands. "This is what your mother wished me to do. I am repeating her words. You will listen to her, won't you?"

Shao Peng nodded, her eyes intent on Mui. Her mother had said, before she left, that she could trust Mui. So she listened closely.

"Then do as I say. We will have to leave this house quietly. You must not tell anyone what I have said if we are stopped from leaving. Promise?"

Shao Peng nodded, her eyes round with excitement.

"Then come along. You have to be brave. Whatever people say or ask, just reply that you are following Mui."

Mui took Shao Peng's hand and stood up. She went to the three little girls, still engrossed in their play. "I am taking Shao Peng to Madam Yeong. If anyone asks just tell them that." She smiled encouragingly. "We will be away for a while, so continue your play." She patted their heads. "Someone will bring your lunch soon, don't wait for Shao Peng."

They left the room and then made their way out of the western building. Mui smiled gaily at the guard stationed outside. "Have you eaten?" she asked.

He gave her a rueful grin. "I hope soon," he replied, his stomach was rumbling with hunger. "Where are you taking her?" he asked, narrowing his eyes and nodding in the direction of Shao Peng. "I have strict orders to guard this house and not let the girls leave."

"Don't worry," laughed Mui, "she is with me. She is going nowhere. Madam wants to see her and asked me to fetch something from the kitchen along the way. I'll tell Madam what a good guard you are. You are truly attentive. No wonder she speaks so highly of you." She tapped him on his arm teasingly. "I'll make sure that the maid brings you something good to eat when I see her in the kitchen."

He relaxed, pleased with the flattery. "Do that," he said cheekily. "I will reward you myself." He laughed out aloud.

"*Aiyah!* Don't say such things. I may take you up on it," replied Mui with a coy smile.

Holding tightly on to Shao Peng's hand, she walked quickly towards the kitchen in the southern outbuilding. The guard looked on amused. He was certain that the maid had a crush on him.

Mui went into the kitchen. She stopped, turned and peeped out the doorway. The guard was looking away. She greeted the cook merrily. "I am looking for a pair of scissors for Madam Yeong." She rummaged through the drawers. "Ah! Got it. I am going to the back garden to cut some flowers for her. Come, Shao Peng." she said. She gave a final nod to the cook, who barely gave her a glance, and went out. She did a quick reconnaissance. Holding Shao Peng's hand, she hurried to the back of the building. She walked past the clothes-line and went to the wall. Sheet upon sheet was hung out to dry. They fluttered gently in the wind hiding Mui and Shao Peng from view. Mui motioned the little girl to come closer to her. "I am going to help you up. Climb up those vines until you reach the top and then lie flat on the wall's ledge. If you see anyone, warn me softly. Make a hissing sound like this," she demonstrated expelling air through her teeth. "Wait there for me. I will follow. When I reach the ledge, I will help you down the other side. There is a tree that we could use to climb down."

She lifted the little girl up and placed her feet on the vine. "Here, grab hold of the stems. They are strong. Don't be afraid. I'll catch you if you fall. You won't. Just don't make any noise. We do not want to attract any attention."

Shao Peng clambered up. Mui reached up to support her bottom. Shao Peng hauled herself up step by step on the vine. She showed little fear. Her sturdy little legs were used to climbing the hillside with her goat. Soon she was on the ledge. Mui followed, moving quickly. Once on the ledge, she reached up and caught hold of a branch of the tree. Holding it firmly with both hands, she coaxed Shao Peng to her. "Hold on to my back. I am going to try to move along the branch. If we reach the tree trunk we can climb down. If we can't make it to the trunk, our weight should be enough to bend the branch down low enough for us to let go and land on the ground. We are not very high. Don't make a sound if we fall, even if it hurts. Understand?"

Shao Peng looked uncertainly at Mui. Mui returned an encouraging smile. Her heart was pumping. The ground seemed incredibly far below. "We'll be alright. Come! Hurry!" she said looking anxiously around to see if anyone was in view.

Shao Peng clambered up Mui's back wrapping her arms tightly around her neck.

"No! Not around my neck. Thread your arms under my armpits and then hold on to my shoulders. Tightly!" Mui took one final look in the direction of the quadrangle of buildings then swung forward leaving the wall. Her legs dangled. Shao Peng twined her legs round Mui's waist. The branch dipped with their weight. Holding the branch with one hand, she swung the other forward to move along the branch. She felt her shoulders wrenched and pain shot through her arms. The branch creaked. With alarm she saw the branch tearing from the tree. "Hold on to me," she said. "We are going to..." With a resounding creak, the branch dipped further down, swaying perilously. "I am going to let go. Hold on," warned Mui.

They fell. Mui landed on her back, Shao Peng under her. She rolled over. "Are you alright?" asked Mui. Shao Peng lay winded for a moment and then grinned. They had landed on a heap of compost; decayed leaves from the plum tree that had accumulated over the years. "Good, we have to hurry before they discover we have gone."

HEONG YOOK DID not know how long they had sat there not looking nor speaking to each other. It was late afternoon. Her silence irritated him. Wan Fook did not know what more he could say to assuage his wife. He switched from contrition and regret to indignation. How dare she takes a position so opposed to his? He told himself that any other man would not have put up with such nonsense from a wife. She should obey him without question. She was lucky he had not taken any secondary wives and concubines, he thought. And to think that she sold his precious painting and her jewellery as well without consulting him! He stole a glance at her. Her face remained stony. Throughout she had not even glanced at him as she sat tight-lipped. He tried to muster anger but he could not. He knew he was at fault. Not perhaps intentionally. He also knew that he had not been kind to Ngao in the past and he had buried that guilt deep inside him by his bluff behaviour.

The atmosphere was unbearable. He stood up to leave the room. Just then a maid hurried in. "There is someone to see you," she said. "I asked him to wait. He said he has news of your nephew, Ngao."

Heong Yook stood up at once, holding on to the table to steady herself. "Send him in," she said. Turning to Wan Fook she told him to stay. Within seconds, the maid returned with a man. Dust combined with sweat streaked his face. Heong Yook regarded the man with great apprehension, not so much because of his appearance, but because of the news he might bring. She did not wait for Wan Fook to speak. "*Xiansheng!* Sir! What news have you of Ngao our nephew," she asked immediately.

"I come from Canton. By this time, the vessel with Ngao on it will have left the port for Singapore and Malaya."

Heong Yook gasped. She swayed and sat down on the chair again. Her face was bloodless. "*Sing ah poh! Ma lai ya!*" she repeated, mouthing the syllables uncomfortably. She turned desperately to Wan Fook. "What are they? Where are they? Why did he go?"

"Your nephew Ngao didn't go by choice. Cheng my kinsman sent me here to tell you. Cheng is with your nephew now. They are both on the same vessel. Ngao was badly beaten and apparently men claiming to be his brothers sold his service to the gang masters recruiting for the pepper plantations and tin mines in Malaya. Now he will have to work to repay the advance taken by them. He is worried about his wife and daughter and asked if you will find them and let him know."

The enormity of the information was too much for Heong Yook. She trembled. She was at loss. She didn't even know where Malaya was. All the classical learning that she had been so proud of, including her skill in poetry and calligraphy, was of no use in a situation like this. For once that late afternoon, she looked to her husband for guidance.

Wan Fook ignored her. Instead he asked, "Which is his first port of call?

"Singapore," came the reply.

"How can we get in touch with him there? Do you have an address?" asked Wan Fook.

"I'll help you with that if you wish. I have a brother-in-law Lim Eng Kim in Singapore. We have an arrangement with the shipping vessels to deliver our letters. Although the system is complicated, it has worked for us. I can explain. Have you found them ... I mean Ngao's family?"

"*Dui mm qi!* I am sorry! I forgot to ask your name," replied Wan Fook ignoring the question. His manner was solicitous as he invited the man to be seated.

"It is Loh Ah Fatt. People call me..." A commotion broke out. Raised voices arguing rang through the house and then the sound of pattering feet running towards the room interrupted his reply. All eyes turned towards the entrance. The maid was back again; this time she had a woman with a young girl.

"Master! Master! She forced herself in, insisting that she has to see you," cried the maid, pointing to the woman with a pock-marked face and a girl who had meantime run ahead of her.

Heong Yook's hand fluttered to her mouth. The girl! Could she be Shao Peng? Where is Hua then? And who is this woman? Heong Yook was finding it difficult to take in everything.

Slowly she rose from her seat and beckoned the little girl to come to her. Shao Peng hid behind Mui's *samfoo* trousers. Heong Yook turned to Mui. "Who are you?" she asked. "And this is...?" She pointed to the little girl who stood wide-eyed and frightened. But in her heart, Heong Yook already knew. The little girl was a spitting image of her mother.

"I'm Mui. I work for Madam Yeong. I am her bondmaid. This is Shao Peng, your nephew's child. I bring news about her mother, your nephew's wife, Hua." Mui fell on to her knees, head bowed low in abject humility.

Heong Yook gasped. A premonition of the vile things that could have happened to Hua flashed through her mind. She turned to her husband and, leaning close to his ears, whispered, "Please would you take Mr Loh to the next room. I want to speak with this woman on my own." She did not want others to hear her news without knowing what it was. "Could you deal with him and ask him for his address? We might need his service."

"Perhaps Mistress, you should take Miss Shao Peng aside as well. What I have to say is not for her ears," said Mui.

Chapter 9

SINGAPORE

THE JUNK MADE its way towards the harbour. The men were brought on deck. There were hundreds of them. They trooped out in droves from the hold where they had lived packed like sardines. They were hungry and tired. They had been confined in the dark for well over a month. Sickness had run rife during the journey. About a third of them had perished, their bodies unceremoniously thrown into the sea. Of the survivors who stood jostling against each other on deck, their sufferings were plain for all to see. Their eyes were sunk in their cheeks and ribs protruded through their exposed torsos.

The journey from Canton had been rough. The South China Sea under the sway of the northeast monsoon had bucked and tossed the boat for days on end. Packed deep in the belly of the vessel, the men had suffered unspeakable conditions. Now dazzled by the sun, many could hardly open their eyes. The stench of sickness and unwashed bodies was only partially obliterated by the tangy salt air. Yet on that day the sun shone down turning the sea into a clear crystal blue broken only by the white caps of transient waves. The brightness made a mockery of the inhumane treatment that the men had endured.

Ngao tried to steady himself as the junk rolled. He planted his feet wide apart, pushing into others standing alongside him. A sudden jolt from a wave sent him stumbling but not far. Bodies packed against bodies buffered him, keeping him upright. He looked towards the approaching land and saw a large outcrop of rock to the west of the harbour. Vessels of all shapes and sizes swarmed the waters. Slowly, the junk came to a stop. He looked across and caught Cheng's eyes.

"*Sin Kong!* New Harbour! Get ready to disembark. Move! Move! Make way for me," shouted a sailor. He barged straight through the throng setting loose a bout of pushing and a string of curses.

Whack! A cane came crashing down into their midst, followed by more blows. The jostling stopped although the murmurs of discontent continued *sotto voce*. Slowly the men moved forward and down the gangplank to the dock. Ngao felt his legs turn to rubber. He found it hard to balance; the ground seemed to rise and fall like the swell of the ocean.

"*Heh! Nei! Nei! Nei! Hang lei*. You! And you and you! Move over! Form a line!" someone shouted in Cantonese. Groups of men in loose tunics with Mandarin collars and black trousers stood with books in hand, shouting at the disembarking coolies. Dialects of the southern provinces of China bounced from one end to the other: Hokkien, Teochew, Cantonese, Hainanese and Hakka. While some of the men had long pigtails, many did not. There was no compulsion to keep them; the *Qing* command weakened by distance. Amidst the groups of Chinese were men with darker complexions wearing different clothes and headgear. Ngao stared at the unfamiliar sight. He had never seen anyone wear a cloth wrapped round the waist. Standing separate from the crowd stood a small group of Europeans. In pressed dark trousers and long sombre coloured jackets with high collars and silk cravats round their necks they stood out from the colourfully dressed assembly of men.

"Keep close so we will not become separated," prompted Cheng, positioning himself behind Ngao. They moved forward.

Ngao saw a group of Chinese examining him. An earnest consultation broke out between two men.

"Who are they?" asked Ngao. He was apprehensive yet excited at the same time. A surge of adrenaline replaced his earlier fatigue.

The two men came over and pointed with canes at the line of coolies. They counted out about thirty of them; Ngao and Cheng found themselves included in the group. They were directed to a compound to the side of the river mouth. Two- and three-storey terrace houses, painted in pastel shades of pink, blue and green and reminiscent of the buildings in China, bordered most parts of the river as it wound inland. It was almost a replica of a Chinese street back home with the exception of one building, Ngao thought. It caught his eye: an imposing warehouse with numerous pillars. Across from the row of houses were more buildings, all two- or three-storied terraces with narrow fronts that backed on to each other. The river was crowded with barges and *sampans* laden with goods. The whole place was bustling with activity: men pushing carts; men loading and unloading; men pulling rickshaws; men bargaining, talking, shouting, arguing: an explosion of sounds and smells.

"What's happening?" asked Ngao. Cheng placed a finger on his closed lips gesturing to his friend to keep quiet. He was listening intently to the exchanges taking place. Ngao recognised the captain of the junk walking towards them, a ledger and an abacus tucked under his arms.

"So you have chosen," he hollered as he approached the men in tunics. He gave a perfunctory sweep of his arms in the direction of Ngao and Cheng. "Good men, all farmers and strong. Make good coolies," he said. "They are from Guangdong and Guangxi and are mainly Hakkas; so they speak your dialect. But it will cost you," he continued with alacrity. A smile creased his face, softening his stern features. Someone hurried to get him a stool. He sat down, set the ledger on his lap and flicked it open. Looking at Ngao and the men with him, he began ticking it, calculating all the while with his abacus. The clicking sound of the black wooden beads echoed, *click! clack!* Finally he wrote a figure on a piece of paper and pushed it towards the waiting men in tunics. They shook their heads in response. With a flourish, they deftly countered with another figure on their abacus. The clicking went on, punctuated with sharp inhalations of breath and curses.

Ngao looked on. Once the excitement settled, he began to understand the exchange between the men. The Hakka and Cantonese spoken began to take a familiar form. Without warning the haggling stopped.

One of the men in tunics came over to them. Short, tanned brown as nutmeg, his manner was brusque. "All of you will be working for me," he announced, "I am Chow See Kok, your boss. You may call me Mr Chow. I have settled the debts you owed the captain whether they were advances paid to your kinsmen, passage fares, food, or anything at all. You now owe me and in return you will work for me. Your debts will be deducted from your wages."

"What will we be paid?" asked Ngao in a whisper.

"Speak up!"

Ngao repeated his question. Chow See Kok's eyes narrowed. "You will be told in due course."

"But how will we live?"

"All taken care of. Don't worry. We'll cover all your expenditures and deduct them from your wages at the end of the month. Here," he waved a piece of paper, "are the rules of the *Hai San hui*, a society for men of Hakka extraction such as yourselves. I will arrange for someone to read them to you. You will all belong to it."

He paused and eyed each of the men intently. It was obvious that not belonging was not an option. Ngao looked uneasily at his friend, Cheng.

"Make sure you understand and abide by them," continued Chow, waving once more the piece of paper in his hand. It will make your life much easier."

He mustered a smile, his eye on Ngao. "Go to your quarters now. You will meet other members of the society. Tomorrow, you will begin the journey to the mainland of Malaya. Your first stop will be Johor."

"It's alright," whispered Cheng not wishing Ngao to ask further questions. It would draw too much attention. "I have a kinsman here in Singapore. I have heard him mention the *Hai San*. He will explain everything to us."

❀ ❀ ❀

NGAO AND CHENG huddled together, heads close. They spoke in whispers. Most of the others in the room were asleep. It was dark and humid. The sounds of sleep echoed in the confined space and the night air was suffused with the hot breath of sleeping men.

"Two dollars a month! How many years will I need to save enough to be free?" asked Ngao. "By that time, even if I can raise enough to pay my passage to China, I will probably have lost any chance of seeing my wife and daughter again."

"*Maan maan lai.* You have to take things slowly. We've only just arrived. Don't think so far ahead. Above all don't give up hope. Not yet. I have asked Eng Kim, my relative here in Singapore, to inform your aunt of our whereabouts. He will get in touch with Ah Fatt, the one I entrusted in Canton with your message to your aunt. He will get word back to us. I have great faith in him."

"Whereabouts? I don't even know where I am or will be. Didn't you hear? We are not going to be here for long. We are to be shipped out to ... to ... Johor! And where is that?" Ngao grew more and more distressed as he spoke. "We were at sea for a month. A month! My family might be dead even as we speak!" His voice cracked.

Cheng placed a hand on his friend's shoulder to reassure him. "They have a system of communicating here. My cousin says he sends money home and receives letters from his family. They even have letter writers, just like in our villages back home. At least you don't have to pay for their services; you can write. Look at the positive side," said Cheng jokingly in an attempt to lighten Ngao's mood. Cheng slid onto his narrow camp bed drawing up his legs within its narrow confines. The thick piece of patched sailcloth strung between a wooden frame sagged with his weight. "Get some sleep. We start early tomorrow."

Ngao got on to his camp bed. It creaked and wobbled. Abandoning it, he lay on the floor. The cold cement was hard and unyielding. He had nothing with him. Even his clothes were borrowed. A sense of despondency rose in him. Hua's face intruded into his mind eye. She had looked so troubled when he told her that he was going to Beiliu. He should have listened to her and stayed at home. If he had not left, none of this would have happened.

He turned on to his other side, deliberately willing himself to think of other things. He breathed deeply. Images of the harbour returned; he recalled the vibrancy of the people in the dockyard and the prosperity! Yes! Prosperity! He did not expect that. Cheng's cousin Eng Kim came in to his thoughts. He must have done well. He owned a shop and was involved in a string of other activities! Cheng said he had started out just like them. Hope welled up in him. Cheng was right. There was nothing he could do about Hua and Shao Peng beyond getting in touch with his aunt. He would just have to work as hard as he could and save fast to return to China. Perhaps a miracle had happened and his aunt had already found his family. Perhaps he would do well like Cheng's relative. Fatigue overtook him. He fell into a deep sleep, the first since leaving the port of Canton.

NGAO WOKE WITH a start. It was still dark outside although the first sunrays had appeared behind the heavily clouded skies. He sat for a moment, mastering his thoughts, his feet still unfamiliar with the firmness of the floor beneath them.

All around him people were waking up; bodies unfolded; whispers soon turned to loud chatter. A sense of excitement filled the air. Almost without warning, the sliver of light that penetrated the room became bright sunshine.

"Zao fan! Breakfast!" someone shouted, hitting a gong. The men shuffled out. Immediately outside the building was a big table with a cauldron sat on a charcoal brazier. Steam rose from the pot. Ngao and Cheng took their place in the queue. Taking a bowl and chopsticks in hand, they waited their turn for food to be doled out. Ngao felt his stomach churn with hunger. He thrust his bowl forward and received two ladles of rice porridge, a small piece of salted fish and a sprinkling of pickled vegetable. His eyes lit up. He was ravenous. Cheng grinned. "At least we are fed," he said. Ngao inhaled the steam from his bowl. It was sharp and pungent. It reminded him of home and the huge brown pickling urn behind his house. He tried not to extend that memory to include his wife. He shut his eyes but try as he did, she was there. She was always preserving one thing or another: leafy vegetables, turnips or even eggs. He frequently teased her about it. She in turn would wave him away with a smile and a retort that he did not complain when she placed it on the table. He turned abruptly away. Cheng sensed his change of mood and followed him.

They took their bowls and squatted companionably outside the doorway. Others followed. Hardly a word was exchanged between them. Hungry they tucked in, slurping the piping hot gruel between sips of pale golden tea. No sooner had they finished, Ngao saw a man walking purposefully towards them. He saw the others rise to their feet. Cheng followed suit and prompted Ngao to do the same.

"I am Lee Sik," announced the man. "I am your foreman. You report to me." He looked at the medley of men, examining them one by one, allowing time to let his introduction sink in. "If you have any problems, complaints, questions, anything at all, speak to me. As you might already know, our boss Mr Chow has decided to move into new grounds in Johor. You will be planting pepper. Johor is just across the narrow channel that separates Singapore from the mainland. We will be leaving today."

"So soon!" exclaimed Ngao.

Thinking that Ngao wished to remain in Singapore, Lee Sik replied, "You will see that within months, our new estate in Johor will be similarly transformed. So do not despair when you are confronted with jungle. A little town will soon be in place; just like here. All this was agricultural land before. We grew nutmeg, pepper and gambier. Look at it now!"

No one replied. Lee Sik looked from one man to the other taking measure of them.

"Can I send a letter to my family before we leave?" Ngao asked.

"No time for that now. You can write when we arrive in Johor. Someone from *Hai San* will help to send it to your family. Quick! Move!" His early easy manner changed; his voice became commanding, assertive.

Ngao stood for a moment, his feet planted on the ground. He felt his toes squash the thin soles of his cotton footwear. He was so tense that he could not uncurl them. He wanted to plead again, but Cheng dug a fist into his ribs and urged him to move. "No point arguing with him on your first day. My cousin will help us. We'll find a way."

Ngao brushed away Cheng's hand. He turned to speak again but the foreman was already striding away.

"We'll work something out," said Cheng "I promise."

Chapter 10

JOHOR

NGAO STEPPED ASHORE with the other men and made his way along the beach. Even the breeze was hot. He touched his neck; it burned. He like many others had cut off his queue on the boat, a symbolic gesture of change and a new life.

They made their way inland. The white sand gave way to patchy undergrowth. Coconut palms and wooden houses on stilts dotted the landscape. It was green everywhere, and the rich smell of vegetation scented the air. A sense of calm descended on Ngao. He looked towards the others. They too stood transfixed by the newness of it all.

Men and women came out of the huts to stare. Their brown faces broke into wide grins. They wore sarongs with hues ranging from the deepest reds and blues to colours of mushrooms and forest greens. Colourful and barefooted they formed a startling contrast to the Chinese men with their severe grey tops, loose black cotton trousers and cotton shoes.

For a moment, silence prevailed interrupted only by the buzzing insects. Then the stillness broke: children ran and crowded round them. They shoved and pulled reaching out with brown hands to touch the men's clothes. "*Orang Cina! Orang Cina!* Chinese men! Chinese men! Distracted by the children, Ngao did not notice until later a single file of men had emerged as if from nowhere. The leader, resplendently dressed, had a cloth headgear the like of which Ngao had never seen before. Turban-like with a stiff border it gave the wearer height for most of these people were slim and had small frames.

"*Selamat datang!* Welcome!" he greeted. His voice boomed above the cries of the children.

Ngao glanced quickly at Cheng. He did not understand what this newcomer said. His ears, only recently accustomed to a medley of Chinese dialects in Singapore, did not recognise these melodic modulated round sounds.

The foreman Lik See, however, appeared not to have any problems. He strode quickly to the front and bowed low with his arms raised and his hands clasped together. "*Temenggong!* My Lord! *Selamat petang!* Good afternoon! I come as Mr Chow's representative," he said in the same tongue.

Temenggong Ibrahim smiled. "So these are the men you will use to farm pepper and gambier?" He stood appraising them, his eyes resting on each man, briefly noting their leanness and wiriness. Not an ounce of spare flesh showed, quite the contrary, many of them were thin to the point of emaciation. He wondered about their strength. Previous consignments of Chinamen had been similarly bedraggled yet they proved to be good workers so perhaps he should not prejudge.

"Yes. We are expecting another consignment of coolies from China soon. We will start with them for now." Seeing the scepticism in the Temenggong's face, Lee Sik continued, "They are strong; they suffer from nothing that a good meal will not sort out." Quickly he took a pouch from the bag slung round his neck. "My boss, Mr Chow, sends you his warmest regards," he said. Still bowing low, he presented the pouch reverently with both hands to the Malay chief.

"*Ahhh!* The good Mr Chow," the Temenggong exclaimed feeling the weight of the pouch in his hands. He seemed pleased. "We have done good business before and I hope we will continue to work well together. I have news that will make him happy. Come! Let us go in and have some refreshments. Your men can stay here to rest. I will arrange for someone to bring them food."

THEY WERE HOUSED that evening in a long wooden shack. Ngao squatted, hunched over an old wooden casket. In the dim kerosene light, he wrote with the pen brush he had borrowed from the foreman. He had much to say and ask of his aunt Heong Yook and doubted whether he could cram all of it on the piece of paper he had been given. It had been years since he had written anything and the strokes did not come easily. Neither did his words and thoughts. He could not condense his emotions in a logical way. There was so much he wished to say. Should he tell his aunt of his suspicion of her husband? He might antagonise her instead of winning her help. If she did not help him, he had no one else to turn to. Writing the letter reinforced his worries and fears. He looked at the curious faces of the men around him, each with their own tale of sorrow, suffering and aspiration. The excitement he had felt on arrival evaporated. A splodge of ink fell on the paper; he placed his brush down.

Cheng sensed his friend's distress. "There is no point worrying about things you cannot do anything about," he advised. "Our foreman Lee Sik will be here soon. Finish the letter! Write from your heart! Your aunt will understand, if what you told me of her is true."

Ngao resumed his writing. Cheng saw his friend's initial hesitation, and then all of a sudden Ngao began to write confidently; his strokes flew off his pen brush. Soon the page was filled.

"Our foreman has long life!" commented one of the men crowded in the room. He had been trying to look over Ngao's shoulders. "You mention his name just minutes ago, and he is here. Look!"

Lee Sik had come straight from his long talk with Temenggong Ibrahim. If he heard the light-hearted comment, he showed no sign of it. Instead he drew a stool into the men's midst and sat down. "It is finalised," he said gravely. "We have been granted the land. Tomorrow we will make our way up the river on foot. Our task is to clear the jungle and prepare the land for planting. So have an early night. We move at dawn."

He got up and made for the door, giving little opportunity for the men to ask questions. A disgruntled muttering broke out amongst them. Ngao followed him with Cheng close by his side. "Sir, you said you would help me send a letter to my family. I have written it."

Lee Sik turned impatiently. He stared at the letter in Ngao's hand. For a moment he looked as though he could not recollect what he had promised and then he took the piece of paper. He glanced cursorily over it and then placed it in his pocket. "So you can write!" he said, a flicker of respect crept into his voice. "Come, let's go outside where there is more air. You too, Cheng; I would like to talk to both of you."

They wandered out of the hut. An oil lamp hung outside cast a yellow glow on the dirt ground. Tiny insects buzzed around the light, drawn to its bright glow. There were hundreds of them, their wings stretched out to reveal tiny transparent membranes with veins like those in a leaf. They hovered round the light buzzing with intense activity and then, without warning, they fell, shedding their wings. Soon the ground was heaving with the wingless insects. The night air grew heavy and humid and, without warning, lightning flashed cutting the night sky with bolts of white silver.

"Termites! It will rain soon. And it will be a muddy journey up river," explained Lee Sik. He turned to the two men. The light lit up their faces, one young, the other older; open honest faces. He had been observing them and had liked what he learned. The man Ngao in particular caught his attention because he was among the very few who asked questions. There was intelligence and thought behind them. That together with his diligence and ability to read and write would come in handy.

Lee Sik was uneasy after the long discussion with the Malay chief. All the men under his care were newly arrived. He did not know them. He needed to cultivate a few he could trust. He threw another appraising glance at his companions.

"I'll make sure the letter leaves on the first boat to Canton," he promised Ngao. He saw how Ngao visibly relaxed after this assurance and resolved to find out more about him. First, however, he had to prime the two men about the present situation and set them a task as a test.

"When we go up river and start work on the land, I want both of you to be my eyes and ears. Be vigilant. Things are a bit sensitive here." Lee Sik saw the immediate wariness in their face. He could see that they are wondering why he was saying this; why he had chosen them to look out for him.

"Most of the land in Johor is leased out to the Teochew people for planting pepper," Lee Sik continued in a hushed voice. "They are long established in this area, some were even born in this country. The Temenggong has now granted our boss Mr Chow, a Hakka, the right to farm pepper. There has been bad blood between the different dialect groups. They, backed by their societies, have had numerous battles. The Teochew clan will probably see our coming into Johor as an incursion into their territory. I do not wish to step on their toes. That said, I don't want to lose out to them either and will certainly not *kowtow*. Once we show fear, they will push us even more."

"If there is bad blood between the different dialect groups, why did the Malay chief grant Mr Chow the right?" asked Ngao.

"Wouldn't that guarantee to turn the whole place into a warring state?" asked Cheng.

"And do we have enough people to fight them off? There are only thirty of us," added Ngao.

"That is precisely why I ask you to be my eyes. Without reinforcements, we do not have enough men to engage in any fight. So I would like to avoid it if we can. As to why Chow was given the lease, I really do not know. They both met in Singapore and apparently hit it off. Mr Chow can be a very charming man when he wishes to be."

"Perhaps Mr Chow made a better offer," suggested Cheng.

"Yes, and perhaps the Malay chief did not want to depend on one party and this is a ploy to play one against the other and help bid up the price of the land," volunteered Ngao fascinated by the intrigues that were emerging.

"We can but speculate," replied Lee Sik. "Whatever it might be, we are likely to have trouble. I need both of you to look out for me. "

Lee Sik was impressed. He had not expected any business acumen. He was told that the younger man was a farmer and the other had worked in the Port of Canton. But then, Mr Chow and he himself had not been businessmen in their previous lives. They had come to Singapore as coolies, a name derived from the Chinese characters *ku li* or bitter strength! Men who were driven by hardship in China to sell their strength for money! Such men like his boss were not to be despised, he thought, and neither were the two individuals in front of him.

❀ ❀ ❀

THEY MOVED AT the break of dawn. Each man carried a little packet of rice wrapped in banana leaves. They ate even as they made their way up the river. They looked at their rice provision with suspicion, sniffing it and looking at each other, puzzled. It smelt different, a rich unfamiliar smell. But hunger gnawed and soon they were shovelling the rice into their mouths, marvelling at the sleek oil left on their fingers. "What did they put into the rice?" asked some suspiciously.

Lee Sik's gestured at the surrounding trees. "What do you see?" he asked pointing at the tall coconut palms that seemed to grow at every corner. "The oil comes from the milk of those nuts. Be careful not to stand for too long under a palm tree. A coconut could fall on your head! I have seen skulls cracked by them," he warned, amused to see many immediately scurrying from under the shade of the trees.

Further up river, the rain had created eddies of brown mud that sucked at the men's feet. Each step was a battle. Ngao's feet sank ankle deep into the brown slurry. The mud clung to his feet like a jealous lover resentful at parting. He looked round him and saw the others struggling. A man fell, his arms flailing in the air in vain to stop the fall; there was nothing to hold on to. He glanced at his friend Cheng. *Plop!* Something had fallen off Cheng's exposed leg. They had all rolled up their trousers. A small patch of red appeared. Blood! *Plop!* Another patch of red oozed out. He shouted to Cheng, and looked down on his own legs. Leeches! Big fat leeches, feasted to their fill, fell from him only to be replaced by others. He yanked them off squashing them. Soon all the men were wildly ridding themselves of the leeches.

Ngao pointed to the higher ground. "Its drier there and we can walk faster and better," he cried. Before Lee Sik could reply the men were already clambering up. They hauled themselves up, grasping the long grass, their muscles straining with fatigue. Lee Sik ran after them.

"Wait!" he bellowed. "I said to walk along the riverbank. Don't encroach on the pepper plantations. We were given permission only to follow the riverbank. So if you find that you are walking into a plantation, come back down to the bank. I do not wish to have a gang war before we even start work."

He nodded curtly to Ngao. His face was tinged red with annoyance. "You check with me next time before coming up with suggestions. Remember what I said last night!" He pushed his index finger into Ngao's chest, held it for a moment and then released it. "You make sure that they follow my instructions. First sign they are on plantation land, they are to run back to the riverbank, understand?"

Ngao nodded and mumbled an apology. He ran to catch up with the others. They walked keeping an eye on the river and inland terrain. The sun was overhead. Bright sunlight seeped through the canopy of trees turning the early wetness into a bath of humid air. Mosquitoes came out in droves, latching on to any exposed flesh, their proboscises digging deep into arms, legs, faces and necks. Little fiery red wheals soon covered arms, legs, necks and faces. The men scratched and slapped in vain attempts to drive the insects away. There was little let up from the insects as the men pushed through the dense jungle. Hours passed. Their footsteps grew slower. Weariness began to take over.

Lee Sik nodded to Ngao and Cheng. "Let's stop to rest and eat. You two go ahead and make a quick recce. See if we are near any village, plantation or settlement? Come back quickly."

The men threw themselves on the ground swiping wildly at the mosquitoes. Many were past caring. Scratched, bitten, infested with wounds still raw from leeches, they sat on the ground, now dried by the sun, gazing at the ants on the ground and the flies. They sat waiting, too tired to move.

From a distance, Cheng and Ngao shouted. "No plantations immediately ahead; just a small settlement. Beyond the settlement, we caught a glimpse of pepper plants."

"You have half an hour to rest. Then we leave. We have to reach our site by nightfall. You heard them. Remember, after the village take the path along the riverbank. Do not step foot on the pepper estate."

❀ ❀ ❀

IT WAS ALMOST pitch dark when they arrived at their site. The sun that had shone so harshly throughout the day disappeared below the horizon without warning. Plunged into a steamy darkness they held on to each other on the last leg of the journey along the riverbank. A slip could mean the end. The rustle of the long grass could herald a slithering snake; on the riverbank it could also mean crocodiles.

"We will eat. A hot meal!" said Lee Sik encouragingly. He sensed the men's weariness. He did not have to look at them to know it. He could hear their fatigue for in the last hour, their walk had turned into a shuffle. More and more men began to stumble. "A hot meal and you will feel different."

"What would I give to have a wash!" one exclaimed.

"Not tonight, unless you wish to brave snakes and the like. The natives do wash in the river. We will have a better idea of where best to do it tomorrow in daylight. Now we must make a fire and prepare our meal. Food! Food is what we need," he said brightly to inject some enthusiasm amongst his men.

Lee Sik divided them into groups, some to fetch water from the river, some to clear a rough patch of ground where they would camp and some to collect kindling and wood for a fire. He drew out a small sack of rice and emptied half the contents reverently and carefully into the pot before tying the sack tightly. He then made his way to the river. He found some of the men standing hesitantly by the bank; one of them was Ngao.

"Is the water good to drink?" asked Ngao, turning around when he heard footsteps. One of the men had complained that the water tasted foul because of the mud that had been churned up. "We can't see much in this light."

"Tomorrow we should be able to find a source of clean water," Lik Sik replied. "Most of the rivers come from the mountains and, unless there is a village upstream, the water should be fine. Let's go beyond that bend over there. The trees are less dense and there is a bit more moonlight. Come with me. Don't disturb the riverbed or it will stir up the mud."

Both men walked on, leaving the others. The air grew cooler. Moonlight threw a silvery cast on the water. Against the deep darkness of the night the ripples of water turned into liquid pearls and rocks and pebbles showed up like glittering clusters of mysterious jewels.

"There! The water there looks good. Even in this light, it is clear. It is shallow water. Go!"

Standing ankle deep in the river, surrounded by the stillness of the night, Ngao felt a sense of peace. He lowered the bucket and filled it with the clean cold water. Perhaps, he thought, Hua and Shao Peng are with his aunt this very moment. A tear rolled down his cheeks; he brushed it away quickly. A few feet away on the riverbank, Lee Sik stood looking on, wondering at what was passing through Ngao's mind. The moonlight shone on the lone figure standing in the river. He saw how Ngao closed his eyes and moved his lips as if in prayer. He made no attempt to join him; he realised he needed to give him space.

By the time they made their way back to the site, the men had cleared a rough patch of land with their machetes. In the middle stood a pile of dry wood. "So how do we light this?" they asked.

"With a fire piston." Lee Sik went quickly to his bag, rummaged and then brought out a wooden tube with a plunger. He took some tinder and packed it into the bottom of the tube and then he pushed the plunger down hard. Releasing the plunger, he emptied the smouldering tinder into a pile of kindling. Immediately the fire took. "This," he said proudly, "is a device adapted from the blowpipe used by natives to hunt."

With the fire lit, the mood in the camp changed. A stove was improvised and the pot of rice placed on it. Smiling broadly, Lee Sik fished out from his bag two small salted fish, a little squashed and rough at the edges, but still fish! He had bought them on an impulse at the last village they passed. The men had looked so weary and forlorn. "A treat," he said, pleased with his forethought. He waited until the bubbling had simmered down and the rice grains had absorbed the water; then he plopped the fish in and closed the lid. "A few minutes and it will be ready." He sniffed the air and saw the men doing the same. A pungent salty aroma, a reminder of the sea filled the air. It was something that he knew the men would delight in and sure enough he saw some of them swallowing hard.

"Tomorrow," he continued, not wishing to show too much softness, "tomorrow, we will begin our real work. Mr Chow has engaged someone to tell us about pepper planting. He will arrive with a small boat and provisions."

Chapter 11

BEILIU CITY

HEONG YOOK SAT next to Shao Peng. Scrolls of paper littered the table. An ink tablet stood at one end. Holding her wide sleeves, she dipped her pen brush into a little water and then applied it to the ink tablet. She worked the brush until the ink was velvety smooth and even. With great care she held the brush with her thumb and index finger, supporting it with the middle finger and then lightly resting her wrist on the table began to write.

"See Shao Peng, when you write you have to follow a certain order in your strokes so as to achieve a balance in your calligraphy. You write from top to bottom. Take the number three; it contains three horizontal strokes, you write the top stroke first and make your way down. Here, I will show you." She placed the pen brush in the little girl's hand and holding it in her own, demonstrated the writing. "Don't press down too hard, it will smudge. The pressure should be such that the strokes flow with grace and allow the ink to spread in a way that reveals the tenderness and reverence you give to the brush: slightly harder when you first touch the paper and then tapering it gently. See how a stroke is not a hard uniform line but is of different widths and shades."

She held on to Shao Peng's hand and wrote the letter three over and over again, praising her ward each time.

"In characters where there is a left part consisting of several strokes and a right one, also made of several different strokes, you have to finish the left before proceeding to the right," continued Heong Yook. "The horizontal stroke always precedes the vertical and when you have diagonal strokes like in the word *ren,* people, you stroke down from right to left and then stroke from left to right; never the reverse. We'll just start with these simple characters before going to the other ones. Then we'll take a break." She smiled and gently pushed Shao Peng's fringe from her eyes. "What would you like to do after?"

"Play, I would like to play," replied Shao Peng, without looking up. Her lips pursed with concentration, she wielded the brush as she had been told. Heong Yook's eyes were tender as she looked on. Moisture gathered in their corners; she blinked it away. Her mind went back to that fateful day when Mui arrived with Shao Peng. Mui had insisted that Shao Peng should not be present when she spoke and she soon understood the maid's reticence. It was futile, probably harmful for the child to learn all that had befallen her mother. Heong Yook's first reaction was to send Mui away, even report her to the local magistrate. She was glad now that she had resisted the urge to punish her. Mui was devoted to Shao Peng and she, after all, was the one who had saved her.

"What would you like to play?"

Shao Peng stopped and pressed the top of the pen brush on her lip. "Where is mother? When will she come back? We used to play house. She taught me cooking and I helped her in our kitchen. I loved scrubbing eggs; she preserved them with a gooey mixture. It was fun working with the goo."

"Since your mother is not here, would I do instead? I am not good with cooking. I will learn with you. Let's go to the kitchen and get the cook to teach us. Would you like that?"

"When will mother come back?" Shao Peng asked again. "You said you would tell me. When can I go home?"

Heong Yook's lips trembled. Shao Peng had increasingly asked for her mother. She did not know how long she could keep the truth from her. She bit down hard on her lower lip and smiled. With forced joviality, she said, "*Ahhh!* I don't know. We have not heard from her because she is working very hard. I would have to ask Mui. Don't you like it here?"

"I do, but I miss mother and father."

"I might have some news of your father soon. You remember that gentleman who was with us when you first arrived. He said he'd let us know by and by. I will tell you as soon as we have news. I promise." She placed an arm around the little girl, lowered her head and nuzzled her neck, feeling the softness of it. "I promise," she repeated. "Finish your writing and then we'll go to the kitchen together."

❀ ❀ ❀

SINCE THE SHOCK of finding out her own fallibility, Heong Yook had taken great pains to learn things that she never bothered about previously. She was completely taken aback by her own ignorance of what was happening outside the confines of her home. The existence of women like Madam Yeong and their philosophy in life, if that was what it could be called, was a revelation, even more so her husband's confessions. Yet what really took her by surprise was her ignorance of geography. To be shamed in front of a stranger for not knowing Singapore was bad enough; to have to ask help from her husband was even more of a let down. She had always harboured secret thoughts that she could be a scholar. Custom did not permit her to declare so; nevertheless, she flirted with the idea and relished it. She now realised her knowledge of classical learning, calligraphy and sewing was no preparation for real life.

She had never visited any city other than Beiliu, let alone another country. She did not even know Beiliu city beyond the few times she had ventured out in the sedan. Even then her glimpse of the outside world was through a heavily curtained tiny window. Like all Chinese scholars, she believed that China was the centre of the world. There was nothing a Chinese could learn from outside. Apparently times had changed. Perhaps that was why foreign powers were gaining an upper hand. What Mui told her about the foreigner and Hua shocked her to the core. How could such things be allowed to happen on China's own soil? Her whole being cried out for those involved to be punished, but how?

She was determined that Shao Peng would not be similarly disadvantaged. She must acquire all the practical skills that Heong Yook never had. She must learn reading and writing, of course, but that should not be all. She looked at her feet, the scourge of her life and once again wished she were young and could start all over again. In Mui she found a source of information of the outside world she did not know. She was willing to learn even while it repulsed her.

She sat, her mind full, looking on while Mui and the cook vied to teach the little girl the rudiments of cooking a simple dish of steamed chicken rice.

"Why don't you joint the chicken instead of steaming it whole?" asked Mui. "Here, let me show you."

The cook ignored her and directed her answer at her mistress. "I am in charge of the kitchen so I do as I feel best. That is how I cook it. Mistress, do you like the dish that I prepared?"

She threw a cutting glance at Mui, her knife held mid air from the chicken on the chopping board, before raising an eyebrow in question at her Mistress. She had initially been very pleased that at last the Mistress was aware of her value and even deemed to enter this part of the house. Now all that had been spoilt because of the new intruder. What does this woman know about cooking she asked herself? There was something fishy about her presence. She never replied directly to any questions about her past. She flashed another venomous glance at Mui, and with a quick slash of the chopper, dismembered the chicken neck letting it roll off the board.

Heong Yook saw Mui was about to retort. She was all worked up, her cheeks red and her hands clenched. At times like this, she questioned her decision to keep Mui and not to throw her over to the authorities. The animosity and rivalry between the two women were getting on her nerves. Why couldn't Mui understand that she could not just walk into a household and take over from the other servants, particularly from the cook?

"We will have it cooked whole just like we like it and then perhaps we could also try it jointed another day. What do you say?" Heong Yook asked the little girl, her eyes all the while on the Cook, willing her to put away the knife she was holding so precariously.

Shao Peng had obviously sensed the tense atmosphere in the kitchen and was looking from one woman to the other. "Are they quarrelling?" she asked.

"Of course not!" replied her great aunt putting on an amused expression. "Adults always have these sort of discussions. Don't they?" she asked flashing her eyes with displeasure at the two women. "Just watch cook carefully and perhaps we could let you try to repeat the same dish some day. Go, go and help her out."

She turned to Mui. "Why don't you help me sort out some of my clothes. I have put a pile of them aside. I think they might be suitable for a quilt. Go! Sort them out by colours." She pretended not to see Mui's reluctance to leave the kitchen. "Master will be pleased if we quilt for it will put the old clothes to good use. It will also be a saving as we would not need to buy new beddings to replace the worn out ones this winter."

Wan Fook had complained that times were hard and they were taking in two more people to feed when their resources were already strained. He had wanted to get rid of some of the staff but Heong Yook could not bring herself to do it. After all they were either people who had worked for them all their lives or bondmen. She chided herself. Perhaps she should have persuaded the cook to teach Shao Peng to use cheaper cuts of meat, instead of chicken. She looked across. The cook was immersing the chicken into a pot of fast boiling water. Then after about some minutes, she quickly lifted the pot onto a cold stove and clamped a lid on the pot.

"It will cook in the heat, without further boiling," she told Shao Peng. "This way the meat will be moist and tender. We now prepare the sauce. We need scallion, ginger and a dash of sesame oil. Come, I'll show you how to grate ginger..."

"Mistress! Mistress! He is here," cried Mui running back into the kitchen.

"Who?"

"The man who was with you when I first arrived. He calls himself Ah Fatt."

Heong Yook stood up. Her heart thumped. "Show him to the sitting room and tell my husband." She glanced over at her ward. Shao Peng was engrossed and did not look up. Perhaps it was best to leave her here while she saw the man. He might have news that Shao Peng should not hear, at least for the moment. She walked slowly and with difficulty out of the kitchen into the courtyard cutting across it to the living room in the southern building. She was determined to do everything on her own without the assistance of a maid.

THE BEDROOM WAS dim with the exception of a lantern hung above the little round table of pale marble. Shao Peng sat on a marble stool next to it. Her feet dangled just above the floor. It had been an exciting day for her. Her eyes twinkled. The cook had given her so many titbits she was full to the brim. She had been told to wait in the bedroom. What she really wanted to do was rush off to Mui and play with the clothes that were in the basket. Perhaps, they would let me wear them and pretend to be a grown-up, she thought to herself. She slipped off the stool and spread her arms wide. She twirled round and round, and then tiring of the game, clambered back up onto the stool, just in time to see Heong Yook come into the room.

"So," said her great aunt approaching the table, "you have cooked your first meal. Cook said you did very well. Did you enjoy yourself?"

"Yes! She said she'll teach me another dish tomorrow. This time we'll be doing something sweet."

Lowering herself onto an adjoining stool Heong Yook brought out a piece of paper from her sleeve pocket, "Shao Peng," she said softly, "we have news of your father."

Shao Peng slid off her stool and immediately went up to her great aunt.

"Look, a letter from him. It is from Malaya. He is safe." Heong Yook put an arm round the little girl and held her close. Ever since she heard about Ngao's abduction from Ah Fatt she had worried for his safety. She smiled, a wide beam that lit up her face. Her prayers to *Kwan Yin* the Goddess of Mercy had been answered. She made a mental note to give a donation to the temple of the Goddess. The letter had not come soon enough. It was becoming increasingly difficult to fend off Shao Peng's questions.

"Malaya? Where is Malaya?"

Heong Yook blushed. She had not known until her husband told her. That whole wide world with all those different places that even the messenger Ah Fatt seemed to know but not she, an educated woman.

"Can I go to see him? Why is he in Malaya and not here?"

"I'll explain why he is in Malaya later. Shall we read what he says?"

"Please, please," cried Shao Peng running behind her great aunt to peer at the writing. She did not understand the page of intricate dashes and strokes, like little framed pictures. She had never seen her father's writing before. She did not even know he could write. "Father wrote this?" she asked wide-eyed. "He never taught me to write."

"Your father went through a disenchanted ... a bad period; he was disappointed with people and with society. I will tell you more about it when you are older. He left everything and went off with your mother to live in the hills. Back to nature, he said, to lead a simple life away from the corruption of the city." She stared at the wall unseeing, pensive. Shades of grey reflected in her eyes as though she was looking inward, her memories pressing on her. "I believe my son might have contributed to his flight," she said. Images of her son bullying Ngao came to her mind. "Your father never complained. He left us and became a farmer. However I always insisted that he learn. Even, when as a child working in the pottery, I made him study. So yes! He writes and writes well."

Shao Peng was looking at her in expectation. Something in her look stirred Heong Yook and brought her back to the present.

"Forgive the ramblings of an old woman. Shall I tell you what the letter says?"

She held the letter some distance away from her and took a deep breath. Her hands shook and she held the letter so tightly that the knuckles of her hands turned white. Her eyes glanced quickly over the letter. She swallowed but all moisture in her mouth had been sapped dry.

My great esteemed Aunt,

I am in a place called Johor in Malaya. It is only a short distance from the island of Singapore where I first landed. By now, Ah Fatt must have told you of the circumstances of my being here.

Heong Yook saw that the characters were smudged and rewritten several times.

> *I was taken by force, then sold and shipped out here. I do not wish to dwell on these matters although you should know of the place where it happened. It could give clues as to my wife and child's whereabouts. It is in a siheyuan in Jiu lu, a side street in the western quarter of the city. Ask Uncle Wan Fook; he knows it. I hope, however, that you have already found Hua and Shao Peng. I worry about them and think of them every day. Their faces appear in my dreams and in my waking hours. I cannot tell you how I feel when I think of them. I regret and blame myself.*
>
> *If Hua and Shao Peng are still not found, please help me find them. Don't give up on them and let me know. Whatever happened tell Hua I love her. I don't care about the past. Please help me; help them.*
>
> *Give your reply to Ah Fatt who delivered this letter and he will see that it reaches Hai San and the Society will ensure that it reaches me. It will be many years before I can return. I have no money to pay for a return passage and I am bound to my master until I repay my debt. I will work hard. Perhaps if things settle down and Hua and Shao Peng are found they can come here. It is a place where many have done well. We can start our lives afresh.*

Your obedient nephew, Ngao

"Tell me. You said you were going to tell me what papa has written," cried Shao Peng wondering why her aunt should be so silent and pale.

"Yes! Yes of course! Your father says he is well, thinks of you and your mother all the time, that he is working very hard and that ... that he will be back when he is rich ... and perhaps you can go visit him."

"Does he say why he didn't take me with him? Why did he go to Malaya? You said you would tell me?"

"He went to earn a better living for you and your mother. He could not take you with him. They don't take little girls."

Shao Peng began to cry, big drops of tears trickled down her cheeks. "And mama? Where is she?" she howled. If I can't go with papa, then why can't I be with my mama?" She was inconsolable. "Why isn't she here?"

Heong Yook gathered the sobbing girl into her arms. She had no reply. She still had not worked out how to tell Shao Peng that her mother had died. The child's tears seared hot on her chest. "Your mother is ... working." She placed her face close to Shao Peng and held her tight rocking gently. "Everything will be alright. Your father is alive and fine. We should be joyous that he is safe."

LONG AFTER SHAO PENG had gone to sleep, Heong Yook remained awake in her bedroom, alone. The candles had burned low leaving a waxy uneven stump and a fast dying flickering flame. So Ngao must know that Wan Fook had been instrumental in Hua's disappearance. Why else would he have said that Wan Fook knew of the place? She blushed with shame and anger stirred afresh against her husband. Yet Ngao asked her to help. That was trust indeed and she must do everything in her power to undo the harm her family had done to him.

Chapter 12

CANTON

EDWARD GRIME STOOD with his hands clasped behind his back, legs astride, looking out of the window. He was in his room in one of the thirteen 'factories' in this small area of the Canton waterfront designated for foreigners. His room in the upper floor, the largest in the factory, was spartanly furnished to suit his bachelor existence. The windows had solid teak frames and glass panes; the few pieces of furniture in the room were all Victorian and left by his predecessor, who wanted nothing foreign ... Chinese ... in his living quarters.

He stared unseeingly through the window towards the ships and junks afloat on the Pearl River. They were of all sizes, colours and styles from lowly sampans hawking fruits, vegetables, meat and poultry to the colourful flower boats – the Chinese euphemism for floating brothels – and the impressive ship commanded by the *hoppo*, the Chinese official responsible for collecting maritime custom duties. Chinese vessels dominated the river. Western ships like the newly introduced steam vessels were too large and their draughts too deep to navigate the Pearl River. They had to anchor out at sea.

He frowned as his thoughts went back to his secretive visits within the city walls of Canton. He had been stationed in Canton for almost a year. It was a solitary existence; westerners were not allowed to bring their wives with them. Nor were they able to consort with any Chinese, let alone Chinese women within the city wall. Their contact with the local populace was limited to the officials appointed by the Chinese government, the boat people who supplied them with provisions and workers in the dockyard and factories. They could move only within a designated strip of land bordering the Pearl River and outside the city walls, an area no larger than a few acres. Grime felt his existence almost claustrophobic. He recalled the one occasion when, driven by loneliness, he had visited a floating brothel. He had felt ashamed after that. For the most part, he had kept aloof from the activities of the others. He had considered himself a passing visitor not inclined to mingle with the Chinese socially. That was until he saw the paintings of the famous Guan Lian Chang. It opened his eyes. It gave him a view of what Canton, the city within the walls and forbidden to foreigners, was really like. He had been so intrigued that he decided to study Chinese and to visit the city, both of which were prohibited by the Chinese imperial government.

Edward Grime's fascination for Canton developed into an obsession following his introduction to the Flower House. At first his visits were just for the entertainment: he was captivated by the music, wine and beautiful dancing women. The secrecy and the forbidden element added to the excitement.

With time his attitude changed. He had never experienced such solicitous care and attention to his every need. Tired of fleeting companions, he had asked for someone to whom he could have sole access and he was richly rewarded. Hua was beautiful and unlike any of the women he had been with. He had been assured that she was willing although he had also been forewarned that there might be resistance. This he had been told should not be taken as a rejection of him. He had been primed to interpret it as shyness. "Was I too rough with her," he asked himself. He closed his eyes. He recalled that she did push him away and had cried. No he surmised. Her pushes were without force, half-hearted, he thought. It was not by someone that was not willing. Perhaps he could have been gentler. She was so tiny, so delicate. Was that why Hua was no longer available? Had they found another wealthier benefactor for her?

He sighed. He had been looking forward to a long-term relationship, someone he could be with, until his return to England. "Confound this country! Confound this post! Confound women!"

He strode to his desk. He sat down and pulled a sheet of paper out from its drawer. He paused with his pen held midway, staring at the blank wall in front of him. Minutes passed. Pushing aside his guilt, he wrote:

My Dearest Wife,

There is not a day that I do not think of you and...

Chapter 13

JOHOR

THE MID-DAY SUN shone on the vast expanse of burnt ground. Charred stumps protruded from the soil and severed branches lay limp and grey. Here and there the fire continued to smoulder sending waves of heat and clouds of ash into the air. The men tied strips of cloth round their nose and mouth to protect them from the choking fumes. They stood with their faces smudged black, their skin scorched red and their arms scratched and burnt, waiting for the fire to go out completely. All they could hear in the apocalyptic landscape was the sound of the wind and the crackling of the still smouldering embers. There were no birds, insects or other animals. They had either fled the fire or been consumed in the flames.

Ngao felt the heat through the thin soles of his shoes or what was left of them. Every muscle in his body ached. They had been felling trees and slashing the dense forest undergrowth for weeks before this final act of burning. He stood drained of energy at the edge of the cleared forest mesmerised by the flickering flames. Hua's face came into his mind's eye. He felt guilty. He had not thought of her during the mad rush to clear and burn the forest, except at night. The nights were the worst. Images of her and Shao Peng intruded his sleep. He had tossed and turned; feelings of panic had alternated with helplessness and anger, feelings that had left him soaked in sweat. Try as he did to shut them out, he failed. What happened? What terrible acts had they been subjected to?

A loud cry jolted him out of his reverie. Someone had burned himself.

"Over here," shouted Lee Sik breaking further into his thoughts. He gesticulated to his men. "Come, we'll douse the fire. It is not safe to stay too close. If the wind increases or changes direction, you could get badly burnt." He had seen men in flames because their clothes had caught fire from the cinders and ash. The cry from one of the workers was a sharp reminder.

"It will take forever," grumbled one of the men. They moved in the direction of the foreman, skirting the scorching ground; a file of tired men. A few disgruntled remarks were soon followed by others.

Lee Sik saw how the men moved, feet dragging over the ground and their shoulders weighed down. He heard the low rumblings of dissent and looked for Ngao and Cheng. He met their eyes. He gave an imperceptible nod and a look of understanding crossed his face.

"Seeing how hard you have worked you might want to take a rest first. Go down to the river where it is safer and take a bucket with you anyway. Bathe if you need to. I will get the cook to make tea. We three will finish the job," he said, pointing to Ngao, Cheng and himself.

The men rushed down to the river, collecting buckets on the way. Once there, they stripped off casting their dirty, soot and sweat-sodden clothes onto the riverbank. The river, a small tributary that flowed direct from the mountain, gushed sweet and cold. It was quite shallow near the bank. In parts, the water flowed like liquid mercury bouncing off pebbles and stones. Droplets sprayed high into the air. They caught the sunlight and shimmered like a thousand gems. No boats could navigate this part of the river. It was too shallow. The boat that brought their provisions had stayed on Sungai Johor the main river. Here the water was fast moving and free from leeches, making it an ideal place to bathe. Once revived and cleaned the men clambered back on to the bank and retrieved their clothes. They washed and wrung them out then put them on still wet, the cotton sticking to their skin. A sparkle had returned to their eyes. They stood in the sun to dry, faces turned skywards.

It was some time before the three finished dousing the ground and were able to join the rest of the men. They ambled to the river and sat down by its bank to watch the revelry, too tired to even wash. By that time, many were already laid on the ground with their eyes closed and a smile on their lips. Others turned to nod at the three, a friendly overture of thanks not quite spoken but nevertheless there in the tilt of their heads, the affable shine in their eyes. It had been weeks since they were given a real break from their labours.

"I caught both your expressions. It made me realise that I have been driving the men too hard," confided Lee Sik. "I was so wrapped up in getting the job done and secure, I would have gone on and on. If I had not allowed them a break I could well have had a rebellion on my hands."

Lee Sik realised that Ngao and Cheng were his bellwether for managing the men. He had been right in their assessment. If they said that they were tired, it meant they really were tired. He was learning fast that he could not extract work from unhappy men. Up until recently, the *Hai San* Society to which they all belonged had been a powerful binding force. He had relied on it to get the men to obey. It gave material support and help to members and in return demanded complete loyalty. Members were even expected to lay down their lives in battle for it. Oaths were sworn and complex rituals undertaken as part of their initiation. From Ngao and Cheng he learnt that compassion can harness more loyalty than any oaths. He recalled Ngao's reaction when he had promised to send his letter on to Canton and Beiliu. He knew he had earned a lot of credit from that one compassionate gesture.

"So! What do you think of the clearing?" he asked the young man, wishing to strike a conversation. "You were a farmer, I hear."

Ngao shrugged non-committedly. He did not think much of the slash and burn although he could understand why it was used. It was fast and perhaps the only way to make any headway in the impenetrable jungle. They had only basic tools. He looked at his hands. Burn and scorch marks marked them. Blisters grew like raw welts on his palms, some already bursting as a result of the incessant chafing of the *parang* he used to clear the undergrowth. Rather than reply to Lee Sik's enquiry he asked a question that had been on his mind.

"The man who came to talk to us about pepper planting said it will be three years before the plants begin to bear fruit. He also told us that full production begins only in the seventh or eighth year and then continues for a further thirty years." Ngao paused and looked at his foreman. "So what will we do after we have planted? Do we just stay here until the first crop is harvested? Will we be stationed here for the entire life of the crop?"

"No!" replied Lee Sik. "A few of you will have to stay on to tend to the plants, others will go on to new things."

"What things?"

"You will be told when I am ready." Lee Sik was amused that Ngao had tried to side track his original question. "I asked you about the land clearing. You have not answered."

"This is the first time I have cleared land this way. In Yuzhou I did not burn to clear the land. I know of an old man who did. He lived in the village at the foot of our hill. He said the soil was very fertile in the years immediately after but later nothing grew."

"That happens only if you put nothing back into the soil," replied Lee Sik, mildly irritated. "This was the problem the natives in this country faced and why they moved from one piece of land to another causing a lot of damage. It explains why they cannot grow pepper and we can. They only cultivate tapioca, sweet potatoes and the like, plants that have short life span. Moreover we will be introducing irrigation, which should help further. Well, we should not waste time talking." He got up. "It is time to resume work."

"Wait!" cried Ngao. "Please, I have one more question. If we are to be here for possibly a long time, can we bring our families over?"

Lee Sik stared at Ngao for a time. An amused glint appeared in his eye, followed rapidly by one of sympathy. "Don't you know? The Chinese government does not allow women out of China. Didn't you notice in Singapore that there were hardly any Chinese women? Come, we have to get back to work."

❀ ❀ ❀

AT THE BREAK of dawn, Ngao stole out of his bunk bed and reached over to tap Cheng on his shoulder. He was impatient. They had talked till late the previous evening. He was shocked to discover that women were not allowed to leave China. How was he going to get his wife and daughter over to Malaya? Since his letter to his aunt, he had made himself believe that Hua and Shao Peng would be found and that they would be reunited in the future. It was a hope that held him together and kept him sane. He was near panic with Lee Sik's disclosure.

"But I have seen Chinese women here," he insisted. "Remember when we passed that little one street town with two-storey shop houses some four miles from here? Didn't we see a Chinese woman? She was carrying a child on her hip and stood outside a grocery shop."

"Yes, we did indeed," replied Cheng. He too had been taken aback by the foreman's revelation. "It is true, though," he rejoined, "I didn't see any Chinese women in Singapore."

"I must sort this out," replied Ngao. "I told my aunt that I would send for my family. Lee Sik might not know everything. Who do the men marry if there are no Chinese women? If there are Chinese women, then there must be provisions for them to leave China. We should have asked your cousin in

Singapore. Even if it is not allowed, there must be ways around it. How else would that woman be here?"

They decided to make enquiries in the town. Today would be their first real break in more than a month. Ngao shook Cheng's shoulder again eliciting a groan from his friend.

"Wake up! If we leave now, we will avoid at least some of the heat and return in good time. It is a long walk and Lee Sik said he wishes to see us in the afternoon," whispered Ngao. "Quick!"

BY THE TIME they reach the little township it was mid morning. The town consisted of a single street with about five or six double-storey shop houses on each side. Leading up to it, however, was a scattering of wooden houses built on stilts. Beneath the houses, hens roamed freely. Behind them loomed the jungle, dense, dark and forbidding. Men and women with complexions the colour of mahogany mingled freely in the compound surrounding the houses. Since arriving in Johor they had not had anything to do with the local villagers. The people stared with open curiosity at the two men, stares that they equally reciprocated. The idea of wearing a cloth wound round the waist was foreign to Ngao and Cheng. They marvelled at how men and women interacted without restrictions, a custom that would have been taboo in China.

Ngao and Cheng walked up the street past the shops to the outlying areas and back again. Where possible they took advantage of the shadows cast by the double-storey buildings to keep out of the sun. They could feel it burning their skin. People came out to stare. They felt conspicuous; everyone must know everyone else and they stood out as strangers. In this part of the town, only Chinese men were about. Ngao and Cheng looked furtively into the open doorways of the shop houses in the hope of seeing a woman, a Chinese woman. The shops were mainly provision stores; one seemed to be an outlet for pepper. Baskets and baskets of the dried berries stood in front of the doorway.

Do you remember where you saw her?" asked Ngao. His stomach churned, because he had not eaten anything. They had left before breakfast. The smell of cooking hung heavy in the air: garlic, soya and something spicy and citrusy that titillated his palette, the familiar and the unfamiliar odours mingled to taunt him.

"Not really. It must be on this main street. These shop houses are like the ones we have in China while the other houses on stilts belong to locals. We could not have seen her there. Lee Sik calls the locals *Malai*. Did you hear them? I could not understand what they were saying."

"I didn't either. We have to learn their language, the sooner the better," said Ngao.

A boy appeared on the street. He was about ten or eleven years old. Ngao clasped the forearm of his friend. "Follow the little Chinese boy. Where there is a child, there must be a mother. A Chinese mother in this case."

They walked quickly to keep up with the boy. The lad skipped and hopped some of the way and ran the rest. Suddenly he turned onto a little path that skirted around the back of the shop houses. They followed. Within minutes they found themselves in the backyard of one of them. A woman was sitting on a stool underneath a fruit tree with a fan in her hand. The little boy ran to her.

"*Adoi! Kenapa bagitu kotor*! Oh dear! Why are you so dirty!" she asked with an indulgent smile. She looked Chinese yet she wore clothes that Ngao and Cheng did not recognise. It was a muslin top of some sort with again a cloth wrapped round the waist, much like what they had seen the natives wearing! And what was more astonishing, they could not comprehend what she was saying. Whatever it was, it was not Cantonese, Hokkien, Hainanese or Hakka nor any of the Chinese dialects they knew. They looked at each other in bewilderment. For one moment, Ngao's heart had leapt. She had pale skin, long eyes with epicanthic folds and a rather round face. She would have been the evidence he was looking for: that Chinese women were allowed out of China.

"What are you doing here?"

They turned and came face-to-face with a man. He had crept up on them and stood glowering, his forehead puckered up into two deep ruts between his bushy eyebrows. His face was dark with rage.

"I saw you following my son. What do you want?' demanded the irate man first in Teochew and then in Hakka when he saw their blank faces. "You are on my land!" With his other hand, he waved to the woman indicating that she and the boy should go indoors.

"Please excuse us! We didn't mean any harm. We are new here. We are working for someone called Chow See Kok and our foreman is Lee Sik. We are clearing land to plant pepper."

"Why are you here and not back where you belong? Why are you following my son?" growled the man.

Ngao and Cheng looked at each other. They realised that their actions had been too precipitous and open to misinterpretation as to their intent.

"We are sorry," repeated Ngao. "We were wondering if there were Chinese women in this country because we have been told that they are prohibited from leaving China. We saw..."

"What?" the man growled. "Looking for women already when you have only just arrived? I will speak to your boss. Make no mistake we already have great reservations about you lot. The Temenggong in the past has always given the rights to pepper planting to the Teochew people. We do not want you Hakkas here. Forget any thought of interfering with our women."

"I am sorry. I don't mean it that way at all," blustered Ngao.

"Out! Out! Right now! One minute more on my land and I'll..." yelled the man.

Cheng came forward. "Please sir, my friend meant no harm. He is trying to find out if he could bring his wife over from China. He has been told that Chinese women are forbidden from travelling outside China. So we are trying to establish if this is true. If there are Chinese women here we would like to know how they succeeded in coming to this country."

The furrows that had marked the man's forehead relaxed visibly. His jaws unclenched and his thunderous expression was gradually replaced by one of understanding and amusement.

"*Ahhh!* That was why you were following my son. You think that a child will obviously lead you to the mother."

"Exactly! Please would you tell us how your wife was able to get permission to come here?" pleaded Ngao. "I am hoping to send for my wife."

"She was born here," replied the man. "Her family has been in this country since ... I do not know ... perhaps, hundreds of years," he continued. "But it is true. Chinese women are not allowed to leave China. Look it is a long story. I suppose

I cannot expect a newcomer to know the background and history of this place. I can't stay and talk to you right now. I only popped back to fetch something from my house. I have business to attend to. Can you wait a couple of hours? Do you have the time?"

"We don't. We have to get back to the camp," explained Ngao. "We can return another time."

"I am Kam. Just call me by my surname. Everyone calls me *Towkay* Kam, boss-man Kam. Why don't you come and look me up next time you are in town? I'll explain then." He looked kindly at the young man and his companion, slightly abashed at his earlier rudeness.

In the upper floor of one of the houses two women looked out through the curtains at the scene below. "The young man is good looking," said the younger woman. The older one quickly drew the curtains tight. "Don't you let your father hear you saying things like that!"

Chapter 14

IT WAS TO be several weeks before Ngao could go into the town again. The pepper planting was in full swing. The ground was dug, stakes driven into it to support the pepper vines and the cuttings planted and watered. Under the hot blistering sun, Ngao worked with unrelenting energy, spurred on by the foreman's tales of success achieved by men like him. They fired Ngao's own ambition to earn enough to send for his family. Now that he had spoken to Kam he was sure there must be a way. He had dreamt of Hua and Shao Peng twice. Once he saw them with his aunt. In his dreams, Hua had told him she was waiting for him and even now he could feel the kiss she gave him. Another time, he saw her in a kitchen with Shao Peng. He did not know the place. Hua had turned round and said she was preparing his favourite dish. He treasured these images.

They reinforced his ambition to bring his family to Malaya. He blotted out all other thoughts. He refused to believe that they might not be found. He was convinced that his aunt would not let him down.

Over the long evenings, he learnt from Lee Sik that Kam was a pepper and gambier dealer. Besides this, he also owned a provision shop and herbal store, dispensing cures and traditional herbal remedies to all and sundry. Chinese medicine shops were quite an industry. Eng Kim, Cheng's kinsman in Singapore also had such a store. Sickness could spread rapidly amongst those who work in the plantations. Except for the local doctor, a *bomoh*, whom Lee Sik had described as more a sorcerer than a medical man, Kam's herbal storekeeper was the closest thing to a physician in the area. As to the question of Chinese women, Lee Sik merely shrugged. "Let Kam tell you. He is privy to such information more than me because he has local family connections."

"What do you mean?" asked Ngao.

Lee Sik smiled. "He has been here for a long time. Ask him. I know little about the history and social structure of this country. My main aim is to make as much money as I can and return to my family in China. I have no ambitions to bring them here. I am a transient. My wife and children are with my mother. I look forward to the day when I can go back a wealthy man."

It was late afternoon when Ngao reached the town. He had left Cheng behind in the camp; he had looked pale and sickly. He was worried about his friend's health and did not want to leave him but Cheng had insisted that he went. The humidity enveloped Ngao like a cocoon. He passed the cluster of wooden houses on the outskirts of the town. People sat with their eyes closed in a state of heat-induced somnolence, under trees, beneath the platforms of their houses, anywhere that provided shade and a reprieve from the sun. Bunches of ripe bananas and coconuts lay on makeshift stalls suffusing the air with a heavy sweet aroma. The more he saw of the country, the more he liked it. This was a land of abundance and opportunity. The only missing element was his family. He did not mind the hard work and the harsh conditions if he could see prospects at the end.

He smiled at one of the locals and was rewarded by a cheery flash of white teeth against brown skin. "*Selamat tengah hari!*" Good afternoon!" Already he was grasping a smattering of the language. And of course, he was beginning to learn the other Chinese dialects.

Ngao walked into the main street. It was buzzing with activity. A consignment of pepper berries had arrived in baskets balanced on poles borne by Chinese coolies on their shoulders. The loads almost weighed them down. He could see the strain on their body, the sweat on their faces. The berries had been soaked and then dried in the sun. In three years time, he might be one of these men carrying pepper berries into the town. He walked into their midst. A hush fell where previously there had been excited chatter. The workers eyed him with a mixture of curiosity and suspicion. They made way for him unwillingly. Ngao knew they were from the adjoining rival Teochew-owned plantation. He nodded to them and continued to look for Kam. He found him squatting down on his haunches examining the berries for their quality.

When he spotted Ngao he called out, "Go to the backyard. Wait there for me. I'll come when I am finished here."

❀ ❀ ❀

"SO! WHERE IS your friend?" asked Kam as he showed Ngao into the house through the backdoor.

"In the camp. He is not feeling well. He has some kind of fever," replied Ngao. He frowned recalling the perspiration on Cheng's face. "He is shivering and complains of intense headache. Perhaps you can suggest a remedy."

"Oh dear!" Kam's voice trailed off. "I'll send my man over immediately. He dispenses herbs in my store and will be better placed to diagnose how to treat him. You and I can have our chat here while he does that." He indicated a seat by a table. "I'll tell him now. He is just next door."

The house was cool in contrast to the heat outside. This must be the kitchen, thought Ngao as he sat down. Three charcoal braziers stood in a row on a raised cement platform. Next to the stove, various pots and cooking utensils could be seen through the netted doors of a cupboard. Further within the long narrow house was an open courtyard. The sun shone directly into it illuminating the otherwise dark interior of the house. Pots of plants stood at random on the cemented floor of the courtyard. A well stood in the middle. Beyond the courtyard, a tiled wall spanned the entire breadth of the house broken only by a narrow doorway. It must lead to the front of the house, Ngao thought. He could not see beyond the wall. The house, 70 feet or so deep, had a very narrow frontage. Lee Sik had explained that the narrowness of the buildings was because shop owners were taxed according to the width of the shops. By the wall, a covered stairway led to the upper floor. He could see movements behind the windows overlooking the courtyard.

Kam returned just in time to catch Ngao looking up in the direction of the windows. He explained. "My wife and daughter. They watch the world from the upper floor; they are always looking out to the front of the house and into the courtyard. There is even a peephole in the floorboards for them to peer through to the sitting room in the front of the house. They spy on me when I bring important guests home." He laughed. "A woman's world! I rarely allow them to venture out, except on auspicious days when I give my wife permission to visit her parents. And of course, my parents who have precedence over hers stay in this house. My wife must pay my mother first allegiance; the rules of Confucius prescribe it, even though she may not like it."

"Was that your wife we saw the other day?" Ngao asked hesitantly, ignoring the reference to important guests and the hint of contention within the family. He knew full well that he did not rank as one of Kam's important guests; he had brought him through the back door! "She spoke a language with intonations very similar to the ones I hear the Malay people speak," Ngao said.

"*Ahhh!* You are curious! I like a man who comes straight to the point. My wife is a *nyonya*, a *peranakan*. Her great grandfather was Chinese but her great grandmother was a Malay woman," he said. "My wife speaks Malay, her preferred choice of language although she also speaks Chinese, principally Hokkien. Her family came from Penang."

Kam leaned closer towards Ngao and winked. "There was little choice for Chinese men in those days. The Chinese have been coming to this land since the 1400s, perhaps even earlier. They came mainly as traders. Some were also Muslims. If they opted to live in Malaya, they had to marry the Malay women here. It was not a bad arrangement. Over the years the

Malay bloodline in such marriages declined. My wife's mother married a Chinese man, as did her mother, and by the time my wife married me, there was little trace of her Malay ancestry except in terms of language and the style of clothes she wears."

"So it was true; Chinese women were not allowed to leave China," said Ngao, his anguish causing his voice to waver. "What about now?" he asked holding to a faint hope that the legal system had changed.

Kam shook his head. "The same restrictions on women's emigration apply, but now Chinese men in this country can marry *nyonya* ladies. Like I have done," he beamed. "My daughter is much sought after."

From the windows overlooking the courtyard, the two women looked on, their ears pressed close against the window to catch what was being discussed. They saw the distress in the younger man's face and his hurried departure. The younger woman looked at the older with dismay.

"I told you not even to contemplate it. He is married and hopes to bring his wife here. He told your father," her mother said.

NGAO HURRIED UP the slope with a bucket of cold water, sloshing it over his bare feet as the bucket banged against his leg. He had gone upstream to collect the water to make sure it was clean. He arrived back at the camp and made his way to the open-air makeshift kitchen. The cook had just finished preparing food for the evening meal and there was still a small fire left over from the cooking. Ngao snatched a pot from the side and measured five cups of water into it. Next he took the pouch of herbs and emptied the contents into the pot before setting it on the fire. The potion had to be simmered over a low heat for at least three hours until the infusion was reduced to one cup. He had not expected Cheng's condition to deteriorate so rapidly. He hurried to him with the bucket of remaining water. Setting it down by the camp bed, he tore a piece of cloth from his sleeve. He wrung it in the water.

"This will help cool you and bring down your temperature," he explained.

Reaching out he made to place the cloth on Cheng's forehead but Cheng forestalled him grasping his arm with an unexpectedly tight vice-like grip. His hand was feverish and damp. "I don't think I'll make it," Cheng spluttered and coughed, heaving and fighting for breath. His skin, marked with a deathly pallor, shone with perspiration and his lips were dried and blistered. "I heard the herbalist say to Lee Sik that few people survive the shivering disease." He beckoned Ngao to come closer to him; his voice grew weaker. "Already three have died from this very camp." His breath burnt hot on Ngao's cheeks. "Search in my bag ... under the bed. I have a little cloth bag in there. I brought some savings with me ... my cousin Eng Kim in Singapore has also given me some money to help me repay what I owe for my passage from China." Cheng's chest heaved uncontrollably. His breathing became ever more raspy. "Take it," he continued, his voice hoarse, " and send it, together with the wages owed me, to my wife." Another bout of shivering overtook him and he began to wheeze. "I ... I have spoken to Lee Sik. He ... he'll let you have them." He fell back on the bed. "You are a good man. You have looked after me well..." The effort of speaking had totally exhausted him. He closed his eyes.

"Don't speak like this. You will get better. You have to make yourself believe you will be all right," coaxed Ngao applying the cloth to Cheng's temple. "Fight it. You have taught me so much. You taught me to believe in myself. You have to do the same to set me an example." His voice broke. He held his friend's body as it went into another convulsion of shivers. "Whom do I talk to if you are not around? Stay with me! Hold on! Everything will be fine."

Even as he spoke Cheng's body went limp, his eyes glazed over. Hot tears gushed down Ngao's face. He sobbed uncontrollably. All the pent-up emotions he had hidden from his friend during his illness came to the fore. It was as though his last connection with the past was gone. He was more alone than ever.

❀ ❀ ❀

NGAO HELPED BURY Cheng. The heat did not allow them to wait for the arrival of his kinsmen from Singapore. Only Lee Sik and his fellow workers attended. The burial spot was a little patch of ground under a tree, some distance from the pepper field. Instead of three plots there were now four.

After the men disbanded Ngao walked alone to the river and sat down on a protruding rock beside it. Lee Sik had given him some time to himself after the burial. He searched in his pocket and fished out a letter. It had arrived the day he went to see Kam. It was waiting for him when he came back from the visit. Ngao opened it and ran his eyes over the contents one more time.

My beloved Nephew,

I am so happy that you are well and working. We have found Shao Peng and she is with me. She has not come to any harm and is growing up fast. She learns well and I teach her reading and writing. She is learning to cook and sew and seems content but I know she misses you. We talk about you everyday.

Sadly, however, Hua has passed away. The circumstances of her death are not clear. Perhaps she died of a broken heart. She asked for you to the very end. I have not broken the news to Shao Peng. I want to give her time to recover from her traumatic experience before telling her.

You can leave Shao Peng with me as long as you wish. She will be like a daughter to me. Tell me when you wish me to send her over to you and I will do so. She is young and will need someone to accompany her on such a long journey. I worry about the journey. I shall wait for your answer. You might decide differently now that Hua is no longer with us.

I pray for you my nephew and I am so sorry your uncle has inadvertently caused this tragedy. I am working towards bringing the criminals to justice. Times are bad here and corruption is widespread. It will be a difficult task but I have not given up.

Take care, your loving aunt Heong Yook

Ngao traced his fingers over his wife's name. He felt his world collapsing about him. The hurt in his chest was like a wound that left him utterly drained. He would never see Hua or hold her again. What did his aunt mean when she said the circumstances of Hua's death were not clear? Why did she not say anything about how Shao Peng and Hua were rescued? Or did they only manage to rescue Shao Peng while Hua died alone? Was that why they did not know how she died? That could not be. Surely if it was so, his aunt would have told him. The letter was mysterious. It raised more questions than it answered. He had been tortured by thoughts of what Hua and Shao Peng might have been subjected to ever since their disappearance. He had kept those thoughts hidden. He had not even discussed them with Cheng. Did those men ... did they...? He could not bring himself to voice out loud even to himself the words rape or molest. He had forced himself to wipe them out of his mind and to believe that his wife and daughter would be rescued. He would not, must not, dwell on such ugly speculation. Especially now! Not when his wife was no longer. He had to preserve her as he remembered her, beautiful and pure. He winced with pain as he choked back tears.

He gazed at the letter again willing it to reveal more. It sounded odd. Cold even in its absence of details! So ordinary when the most abysmal and outrageous had happened! There was no mention of the kidnappers. He had so many questions. Did his aunt go to the address he had given her? Was that how they managed to find Shao Peng? He got up. He must find a way to get her over to Malaya. He had nothing to return to in China.

Chapter 15

BEILIU CITY

AFTER A TEMPORARY lull, the city of Beiliu was again embroiled in fighting. The Taiping Rebellion had entered a new phase. Government troops were out in full force against the rebels. News that the rebel leader Hong Xiu Quan had gone into hiding confused people. Chaos reigned in the streets as the rebels led by Hong clashed with the splinter group under Hong's former associate, Yang Xiu Qing. At times, it was impossible to distinguish between the different factions engaged in battle; hand-to-hand and street-by-street. Dead bodies littered the streets.

Mui, sent to the markets to forage for food, came back with stories that thousands had died during the course of a week's battle. Some claimed millions of people had died in the two provinces of Guangxi and Zhijiang since the start of the rebellion. Mui panted with excitement as she relayed her tales. She relished the telling of them and the shock looks on the faces of her mistress and fellow maids. The latest news was that the Imperial Qing Government had persuaded the Europeans to enter into the foray and that the middle class and traditionalists, long sceptics of the rebellion, were beginning to turn against the rebels.

In the household of Heong Yook, life continued. Food had become scarcer and more difficult to obtain. The food markets were continuously being disrupted by the fighting. She was secretly glad that they had Mui to rely on for she was the only one brave enough to venture out. The family lived in constant terror. Doors were bolted and chained. They took turns to remain vigilant even through the night. Her husband had locked himself in his study. The pottery was closed.

"Mistress, it is bedlam in the streets, though I understand that out in the territories granted to foreigners, business goes on as normal," said Mui when questioned by Heong Yook. "Ships are still leaving with full loads of tea, porcelain and labourers for *Nanyang* and *Kam San*. They say that the demand for our labourers in Southeast Asia and the Gold Hills of California's is insatiable."

"Did you find out if is possible for women to board these vessels and buy a passage to this place they call Singapore?"

Mui giggled. She and she alone found the chaos exciting and could laugh. At times Heong Yook suspected her of enjoying the role she had carved for herself as a bringer of sensational news. "Yes!" Mui said and turned her face away to put a kerchief to her mouth to hide her laughter.

"And! What did they say?" asked Heong Yook glaring at Mui, her voice sharp.

"The Government does not permit it. This does not mean much in practice. Women are in some of these boats anyway. You won't want to know, Mistress. Your delicate condition would not like to hear this," Mui continued slyly. She enjoyed teasing her Mistress whom she considered naïve and totally inept in the more practical world that she, Mui, inhabited. She also did not know why her Mistress should be interested in the matter and was hoping to tease out some information.

"Tell me!" insisted Heong Yook.

Mui lowered her voice into a conspiratorial whisper. She was enjoying the drama. Her new mistress's household was very staid in comparison to what she had been used to. "Only women of poor morals, flower girls and the like, go on these ships. It is still illegal, but gang masters smuggle them, sometimes by force, to sell their services abroad. Apparently there are hundreds of men to one Chinese woman in these places. Imagine! Madam Yeong had considered sending Shao Peng's mother to Nanyang, if she were to fail to please in China." Mui stopped abruptly aware that she had said the wrong thing. Heong Yook's face was white as sheet.

"I'm sorry. It just blurted out. I'm so sorry," Mui cried in fear.

Heong Yook turned abruptly away. "Leave me! I have to think," she ordered. Her voice was sharp, sharper than at any time Mui could remember.

Mui did not want to leave. She needed to re-establish a connection with her mistress, ingratiate herself again. She could see her anger and disgust. Mui had wanted to keep a piece of information to herself until a more opportune time. She felt she had to use it immediately if she were to regain favour. "I have one piece of news that might interest you. I found out the address and name of the man that ... *ah* ...

ah ... Shao Peng's mother ... you know... I mean..." She looked from under her eyelashes to see the effect on her mistress. "He is an important foreigner, an Englishman and the Second Superintendent of Trade."

Chapter 16

SINGAPORE

THE MARKET RESOUNDED with people talking at the top of their voices. All the dialects of southern China seemed to be represented; their sing-song intonations rose and fell according to the fervour of the argument and haggling. Interspersed with the buzz of human voices the abacus clicked and clacked. Ngao stopped to listen more carefully. He had started distinguishing the different dialects. Communicating with other Chinese was not an insurmountable problem because he could always write his questions down. The written word remained the same no matter how it was spoken. It was not as convenient, however, and many people could not read or write.

It was good that his ears were becoming attuned to the cadences of the different dialects. He was a Hakka and many Hakka people had settled in parts of the Guangxi province where Cantonese was mainly spoken. But Teochew! He closed his eyes to focus on the sounds. Yes, there was a predominance of Teochew being spoken in the market. This must be the market Lee Sik had spoken about. His foreman had warned him that the British had divided the island, by ethnicity, into separate districts. The Chinese were allocated land to the southwest of the Singapore River. Within this, there was the Teochew area, the Hokkien area, the Cantonese area and so on. The Malays were on the other side of the river in villages they referred to as kampongs. The Indians were segregated mainly in an area called Serangoon while the Europeans congregated further to the north and east of the river.

Ngao left the market and headed in search of the road that would lead him to Mr Chow, the man he had met when he first landed on the island, the man who was the ultimate boss of the company to which he now owed his passage from China, and the man Lee Sik said he was to owe his entire loyalty.

"You'll find him in his opium outlet. He'll be waiting for you. He knows you are coming in my place. Only after you have seen him are you to seek out Cheng's kinsman."

Ngao had looked in horror at Lee Sik. "Isn't it illegal? In China, the imperial government has long sought to wipe out the opium trade. I don't..."

Lee Sik had silenced him with a ferocious stare. "You are not in China and even there, despite what the imperial forces decree, opium is rampant, thanks to the British. Here, you will find it is legal. The British allow the opium trade because it is a major source of revenue for them. Two thirds of their total revenue comes from opium. It is a common fact. As the government in this island, it has the monopoly of the trade and farms it out to the merchants. Mr Chow is only a small cog in the wheel in this sense. He, like the other Chinese in the rest of British Malaya, pays his due to trade in it. Go! And keep your opinion to yourself if you value your life."

The foreman had then grasped Ngao's shoulder, his fingers digging deep into his flesh. "Don't think of escaping," he had said softly to the shocked young man. "We have looked after you well and treated you well. Think of it this way. The coolies have no entertainment, life is hard, and there are few women to comfort them. Opium and gambling are two entertainments they do have. Life is complicated. You will appreciate this with time."

Ngao collected himself and walked quickly on. Lee Sik's tone and implicit threats haunted him. This was a side of the foreman that he had not encountered before. His head spun with conflicting thoughts. Hitherto the foreman had been good to him. Indeed he owed Lee Sik for the favours granted to him, such as this trip to Singapore. He had wanted to come to Singapore to find Cheng's kinsman Eng Kim and give him the money that Cheng had left. He had promised Cheng he would arrange for it to be sent on to Cheng's wife. He had also wanted to make enquiries about the possibility of sending for his daughter. He had not lost hope. It was Lee Sik who had given him the opportunity to do these things. In return the foreman had entrusted him with the task of seeing Mr Chow to do a little job. Ngao could not fail him.

He turned into a street. Rising above the skyline of the double storey Chinese shop houses was a building the like of which he had never seen before. It had figurines of dark men and women clustered together in various poses, layer upon layer of idols, colourful and unfamiliar to his eyes. He walked on, his eyes returning to the building again and again. He saw men, dark as coal and dressed in what looked like loincloths entering it, shedding their footwear at the entrance. He surmised it was a temple. Why, he wondered, was there an Indian temple in the middle of a Chinese street? Weren't the districts supposed to be divided by ethnicity?

He arrived at the address given to him. He stood in front of the door uncertain what to do next. The frontage of the building was narrow like those in Johor. The door was closed. He rapped twice, as he had been told. The door opened a mere crack. Ngao uttered the word '*mang*' or grasshopper, the code word for opium. The door opened wider and he stepped in. Standing immediately behind the door was a rough wooden panel. He stepped round it and into the dark interior and was immediately engulfed by a heavy, sweet, sickly odour.

❀ ❀ ❀

NGAO RECOGNISED MR CHOW instantly. He was seated behind a table. With him were five men, wiry, strong individuals. Their trousers were rolled up revealing sturdy sinewy calves. Several big chests stood beside the table and they were foraging inside, lifting huge balls from within and counting them. Hesitantly Ngao approached the table. He stood in front of it, his hands, damp and clammy, clasped together. He did not know what to do with them. He bowed his head slightly. "Mr Chow?" he enquired solicitously.

Mr Chow cut an ordinary figure dressed in loose black silk trousers and white cotton tunic with the traditional frog buttons, that was until you looked him in the eye. His eyes were shrewd and sharp. They measured Ngao and gave no signs that he knew him. "Yes!" he barked. "And you are?"

"Ngao! Lee Sik sent me. He said you wished to see me." Ngao made no attempt to remind him that they had met; that it was Chow who had recruited him. How could he remember when it was just a fleeting moment? Chow must see hundreds if not thousands of similar coolies.

"*Ahhh!*" said Chow, his demeanour relaxing, "I have heard about you from Lee Sik. How is the pepper planting?"

"Foreman Lee Sik sent me to report to you. He is sorry he can't come himself. He could not leave the plantation because of matters that need his personal intervention. The land has been cleared and the pepper planted. Still the plants have to be watered regularly and, of course, there is the weeding. He is supervising the construction of an irrigation system. The men are inexperienced and only Lee Sik knows how to do it. He has also started building more permanent lodgings. Until now, we have been living in makeshift quarters. Our attention has been devoted to clearing the land and planting."

"Good! Lee Sik is a good man." Chow looked at his hands. The nail in his small finger was long, so long that it curled like a talon, an affectation of old Mandarin scholars. "And there is no trouble with our neighbours?" he asked softly, his eyes peering up from lashes that would have made him look effeminate, but for his build. His body was heavy and solid.

"Not so far," replied Ngao. He was not sure if he should mention the skirmish they had with the adjacent farm. He decided against it. Lee Sik had not said he was to mention it.

"Well, there will be soon. Tell Lee Sik to be prepared. We cannot afford complacency!" Chow's eyes glinted with sudden ferocity. It took Ngao by surprise.

"As you might have already been told, the neighbouring plantations are not happy that Temenggong Ibrahim has granted us the lease to plant pepper," explained Chow. "He is the Malay chief in Johor. You must have seen him. In the past he has mainly given leases to the Teochews, giving them the right to call themselves Kangchu, or Lords of the River. They no longer have that entitlement." He broke off when he saw Ngao's puzzled face. "After the name of the lease, you see. The lease is called *Surat Sungai* or River Letter."

"Lee Sik has told us about the bad blood between the Teochew clan and yours," said Ngao.

"Not between the Teochew clan and mine but also yours." Chow glared fiercely at Ngao. "You have to get this into your head. You are part of this *kongsi* and the *Hai San* society. Remember that!" He glanced sharply over his shoulders at the five men with him and they edged closer around their boss. "The reason I ask for you is this," continued Chow pointing to the chests. "You know what they are?"

"Opium?" he replied hesitantly, keenly aware of the six pairs of glowering eyes on him

"Yes! Opium or *chandu* as they call it here. Some of the other clans are trying to muscle in on our territory. I have the sole franchise to trade and distribute it for two more years in Singapore." Chow's voice became querulous. "Quantities are now being smuggled into this island and I won't have it. I want to pay back these infringers. I want you," he said pointing his finger at Ngao, "to move a small amount of opium into Johor, their territory. Call it a test run! In any case, Lee Sik's men, your colleagues, will need them. I will not have my men cavort with another supplier!"

The unease felt by Ngao multiplied. Was this what he was expected to do to pay back the favour he owed the Society? Whatever it might be this was something he could not and did not wish to do. Yet he also knew he could not protest outright. He saw the sneer on the men's faces, daring him to protest. He had to think it through.

It never occurred to Chow that one of his men might have reservations on moral grounds about dealing with opium. To him the use of opium was as normal as eating and drinking. After all, what could the men do after their hard toil? There were no women, no wives to return to, nor families to offer comfort. They had only two things: opium and gambling. And it was all legal and sanctioned by the Government. He saw the apprehension in Ngao's eyes. He mistook it for fear. "Don't worry. I am not asking you to move large amounts. This chest here holds forty balls of opium. That should be sufficient. I sell between forty-five and fifty chests per month to the whole of Singapore! Your camp is quite small and they will be mainly beginners to the smoke. One chest will be enough."

Ngao looked furtively at the burly men surrounding Chow. He could not say no. That would be the end of him and he needed to survive for his daughter's sake. He would ask Cheng's kinsman for advice. He would have to think on his feet.

"When do you wish me to move the opium?" he asked with more confidence than he felt.

"We will wait for the next consignment of water to the island. Water is transported in the island by bullock carts. We'll smuggle the opium to the mainland using them. Water carts are a common sight. No one would think anything amiss if you brought a water cart to your camp," said Chow with a wink. He was pleased with Ngao's quick positive response.

Weighed down by the magnitude of the task, Ngao became so anxious he could hardly bear to remain a moment longer. He was sure that his distress would show through his bravado.

"I have some business to attend to," he explained. "One of the men died. He was my close friend. I would like to return his belongings to his kinsman in Singapore and Lee Sik has granted me permission. May I leave now?"

"Of course!" exclaimed Chow, "and if there is anything that we can do, let us know. We always look after our own. Was he appropriately buried?" The compassion in his face was a stark contrast to his earlier fierce bullying stance. It bewildered Ngao.

"We could not bring his body back to his kinsman. The body was decomposing rapidly with the heat. Lee Sik was worried it might lead to fear within the camp because the men are superstitious. He was the fourth person to die of the fever. We buried him as best as we could."

"Well then. Let us know what his family needs. We'll help to the extent we can."

Ngao thanked him and was about to leave when Chow, waving to the interior of the shop building, asked, "Would you like to take a rest in the parlour behind? It will be on me," he added generously.

Ngao could make out the faint spirals of smoke seeping out from within the dim interior. The sweet sickly heavy odour struck him anew. He saw a man emerging from within, his eyes glazed and his movements languid and detached. "Another time," he forced a smile. "Thank you. I have to find Cheng's kinsman."

"Take a look. There is no harm," coaxed Chow. "*Ah pian*, the opiate has wonderful attributes and is known to kill pain and cure all manner of sickness, even those of loneliness."

Ngao had no choice but to oblige. He went into the hallway and then through a door. The air was thick and pungent. Here and there were rough wooden cots, double decked or single. Men lay on them, their heads resting on porcelain and ceramic 'pillows'. They were oblivious to the discomfort of these hard two inch thick hollow boxes, their lips moulded around their pipes of dreams, sucking and breathing, their eyes in a dreamy haze. He stood as long as he could bear and went quickly out. Once on the street he breathed deeply to clear his lungs.

IT WAS LATE afternoon before Ngao found Eng Kim, Cheng's cousin. The sun had slipped below the skyline of the shop houses, throwing one side of the street into dark shadow while the sky remained bright above the rooftops. He looked up to the curving eaves of the Soo Temple of the Goddess of Mercy, each eave emblazoned with a magnificent dragon with its thrashing tail caught by the setting sun against the bright blue sky. The walls were painted pink and pale green while the roof tiling was dark green burnished with crimson edges. He stepped over the wooden threshold of the doorway into a courtyard. To his right, he could see the hall for ancestral worship and a place for the plaques of important clansmen. The intricately carved plaques applied with gold leaf stood resplendent next to paintings of prominent patrons. In the central hall, straight in front of him, stood a vast brass cauldron for joss sticks. Behind it was the statue of *Kuan Yin*, the Goddess of Mercy. To his left was the Hall of the Warrior God. He walked across the courtyard and made for the interior. Incense filled the air and a bell chimed breaking the silence.

He was shown into a small dusty cubicle with roll upon roll of tightly bound scrolls. Calligraphy against painted backgrounds of waterfalls and limestone rocks lined the walls. Eng Kim was bowed over his desk, his pigtail hung long and thick behind his back. He was engrossed in writing but rose on Ngao's entry. His eyes strayed immediately over Ngao's shoulders.

"Where is Cheng?" Eng Kim asked. When he saw Ngao's expression, his smooth round face broke into a frown. He fell back on his seat. "Is he ill?"

"He passed away. He caught the shivering illness. I have brought his belongings here and would like to send them back to his family. May I borrow some writing material so that I could write a letter to bring them some comfort?"

A shadow passed fleetingly across Eng Kim's face. He moved his lips in silent prayer and looked away as if to collect himself. When he returned his gaze, Ngao could see the sorrow and stoicism in his eyes.

"We'll arrange for prayers to be said. It is a terrible tragedy that happens far too often. I shall miss him. His family will be devastated, especially his wife. I had thought that within months, with my help, he would have saved enough to repay his debts and passage fare. I had planned to give him more money. It was not meant to be. Life is fated."

The two men fell into silence. Then Eng Kim said, "Cheng spoke highly of you. He said you read and write. I was the one who forwarded to you the letter from your aunt. I sent it on to Johor. I hope it arrived safely."

"It did and thank you."

"*Mei wen ti!* It's no matter! It was my annual trip to China anyway. Ah Fatt, who was to have collected your aunt's letter to you, could not leave China because he had to attend to some personal matters. So I just stepped in." He pointed to his pigtail. "That is why I keep this, to avoid any trouble when I step into China."

"You saw my aunt?"

"Yes! I made it a point to visit her when Ah Fatt told me to help out. She is well."

"Did you see my daughter?"

"No! I spoke only with your aunt."

"I am trying to find a way to bring her over. She is barely seven. Would you know how Chinese women are smuggled out of China?"

"I would not advise it. You will put her in the hands of thugs. She will be immediately in the company of undesirable women. Have you passed the brothels in the street? Did you see how they were? You just have to be patient. A movement is underway to get the Imperial Government to lift the ban. Some English merchants are even considering paying a bonus to men who bring their wives with them when they come to Singapore though with the Chinese government so set against it at the moment, it is unlikely to work. The imbalance between men and women is causing great social problems and is a headache for the British administration. There are twenty Chinese men for every Chinese woman in Singapore! But who knows?" exclaimed Eng Kim taking pity of the young man and not wishing to destroy his hope. "Perhaps with persistent petitioning, there might be a chance that the ban will be lifted."

He reached out and touched Ngao's arm gently, "The main thing is to succeed here. Make a fortune and eventually your child will be able to come." The sadness and despair etched in Ngao's face touched him.

"My debts are high. Prosperity is a distant dream. I owe Mr Chow, not only the passage fare but what has been advanced for my daily living and given to the thugs who sold my labour. My earnings are too small for any chance of freeing myself any time soon."

"You will be surprised how quickly one can save if you are willing to work hard. Unless of course, you fall into bad habits like gambling and opium!"

"Opium! I need your advice," Ngao said reminded of his quandary. He liked Eng Kim's plain talking and instinctively trusted him. Cheng had said that he was reliable and honest. He related Mr Chow's orders.

"You have to do what he asks," Eng Kim; face was grave. "There is no way out of it unless you wish for death." There was no hesitation in his answer. "Morality is a luxury that you do not have. Do it and then find a way out of his employ. Chow is not a bad man; some even describe him as kind. He goes out of his way to protect and support those who are loyal to him. Nonetheless he is a tough businessman. He sees opium as pure business. He sees himself as a king protecting his domain."

"How can I leave his employment? Moreover I feel I owe Lee Sik, my foreman. He has been good to me."

"Everyone here is out to do the best for himself. They will sympathise if you leave for better opportunities. What they will not condone is disloyalty or failure to carry out orders. You understand the difference?"

Eng Kim examined the troubled young man before him. "I'll lend you the money to repay your debt," he said after some time. "I need someone with the ability to read and write. I would have taken Cheng on if he could read and write; well that is all in the past." A momentary tinge of remorse crept into his voice and then it disappeared. He straightened his back and continued, "I am expanding my business. Many places are now opening up on the west coast of Malaya following the discovery of tin. Chinese people are going in droves to prospect for the metal. The Malay chieftains are leasing out land to these prospectors. I aim to supply them with food. What do you say?"

Ngao looked dumbstruck.

"I know Chow," said Eng Kim. "He is a valuable patron of this temple. I'll talk to him and sort something out, but only after you have delivered his opium. This way you will not offend him. Come, I'll show you to your lodgings for the night."

THE ROOM WAS stifling and hot. Seven of them were packed into a confined windowless space. They shared bunk beds, body pressed against body. Ngao could not sleep. He swung his leg over the bed and connected immediately with a bowl and spoon on the floor. He remembered it belonged to the man who lay next to him. He looked anxiously around, concerned that the noise would awaken the other occupants. No one moved. The men lay in deep sleep, uncaring; their breathing, a cacophony of muffled noises, punctuated by the occasional snore. They were tired and dead to the world. Slowly he got into a sitting position, cringing with each creak of the bed, before slowly standing up. He tiptoed towards the door, mindful of the belongings scattered hither thither on the floor. There were no cupboards for their possessions. The odd bundle of clothes, bowl, teacup and kettle just sat on the floor where their owners had put them. Ngao grimaced. He knew such lodgings were not uncommon and he should not complain. A single room can house a whole family with the father, mother and four to five siblings sharing the same space, he was told. And there were many similar rooms in the house with people all packed together like pickled vegetables in a jar!

He went out to the dark hallway. It was quiet except for the sounds of sleep. He leaned against the wall and breathed deeply. "What should I do?" he asked himself. "How can I smuggle such a vile thing as opium to feed my fellow workmates? How can I not do it?" His mind whirled, fogging all his thoughts. One pushed and countered the other. He stood in the hallway numb with worry. He stayed there until the early sounds of morning broke. Men came out of the rooms and made their way to the back of the house to the lone latrine shared by everyone. A long queue formed. Impatiently, Ngao walked out of the hallway and out of the house. His thoughts were no clearer than they had been. Only the image of his daughter Shao Peng remained fixed in his mind. She was all·he had. He choked back his tears for Hua. He had to be practical. He had to focus on Shao Peng.

Chapter 17

Canton to Beiliu City

Wave upon wave of Chinese pressed into Respondentia
Square outside the city walls of Canton. They turned what
was normally a peaceful market place into a heaving mass of
bodies. The arrival of Chinese troops failed to dispel the mob.
It attacked the foreign factories with stones. Feelings were
running high. Two English sailors had killed a Chinese woman
and the Chinese authorities decreed that they be executed in
the square. The English Captain had protested and moved in
with his sailors to prevent the execution. Fighting had broken
out. The uproar stemmed from an earlier incident in which a
group of Englishmen had killed a Chinese man. The Chinese
court, under pressure from the foreign forces, had imposed a
paltry penalty of £4 on one of them and freed the rest. The
people of Canton were outraged and their anger had continued

to simmer until this latest incident. People rushed in from all directions. Streets feeding into the Square were soon packed to the brim. Sporadic fighting broke out. A batch of armed foreigners wounded several Chinese men, adding further fuel to the uproar.

Edward Grime ran from his factory towards the Square. He made his way to the soldiers congregated there. "Ask the captain to do something. Fire shots into the air to disband the crowd," he commanded his interpreter. He could not speak directly to the captain. He was not supposed to know Chinese. "The mob will try to burn the factories like they did two years ago and then there will be consequences. We will not allow our property to be endangered!" He shouted at the top of his voice to be heard. The captain looked at him, eyes narrowed, his face inscrutable like a mask of stone. He was unmoved by the impassioned plea.

"Ask him to return to the factory for his own safety," retorted the captain addressing the interpreter, with barely a further glance at Grime. "Tell him that the factories are on Chinese land!" With a curt nod he turned his back and continued with his soldiers towards the centre of the square.

The crowd parted, like corn yielding to the force of a tornado, to make space for the soldiers. A hush fell. They watched the two sailors being strung up. The air was palpable with tension and anticipation. The only sound was rasped breathing. All eyes were on the two sailors. The two men stood with their feet barely touching the stools. There was a quick jerk. The two bodies swung like puppets in the air, their heads slumped forward and their bodies convulsed. The crowd cheered.

Grime looked on in horror. There was nothing he could do. From the corner of his eye he caught sight of a fire in one of the factories. He turned and ran towards it, ordering his men to follow. "Attend to the factory," he hollered. "And you," he commanded the man next to him, "gather others and make for the Church. Guard it!" he bellowed pointing to the Anglican Church, the pride and joy of the foreign community. The church spire dominated the skyline, obliterating the pagoda in the background to the chagrin of the local people. They viewed it as an eyesore and a constant reminder of their own failure against the might of the foreign powers. It was almost inevitable that someone would attempt to torch it.

Mui followed Grime, fast footed, hiding from his view. Her mistress Heong Yook had asked her to look for the Englishman. She had been loitering the whole day on the waterfront to catch a glimpse of him. Her contacts said he had not been to the Flower House for some time. Her mistress had given her no other instructions than to watch him and find out where he lived.

She walked quickly pushing her way through the crowd, stopping at intervals to stand on tiptoe to peer over the shoulders of people in front of her. The fire had spread to *Zhu lu,* Hog Street; the corner candy shop was ablaze. She took her eyes momentarily off her quarry ... and lost him. Mui stood confused. She looked to the left and right of her and then she caught sight of him again. A line of men was passing buckets of water from one to the other. Grime was directing them. She edged closer. She made up her mind. She would stay on his tail until she found out which of the thirteen factories he lived in and then she would make more enquiries.

BACK IN THE city of Beiliu, Heong Yook fretted. There had been no news from Mui. With some reluctance she went to the study to seek out her husband. His door was bolted from within. It had been so for months. Food was delivered to him and left at the door. He rarely came out, preferring his own company. He had lost face and could not bear the scorn of his wife. He felt everyone knew what he had done and looked at him with accusing eyes. In particular, he avoided Shao Peng; she reminded him too much of Hua.

Heong Yook knocked on the door. There was no answer. She tried again, this time calling his name. Things could not go on like this she decided. Punishing him would not solve anything. She feared he might do something drastic. Hua's suicide had affected him greatly. Might her husband be contemplating the same fate, she wondered. She banged even harder. She pressed her ears against the door. She heard breathing and for a moment she was not sure if it was her own. She pressed her ears even more closely to the door feeling the hard grains of the wood on her cheeks. Suddenly she stumbled! The door was yanked open from within and Wan Fook stood before her, dishevelled and his eyes half crazed.

"What do you want? Can't you leave me alone?" he growled.

"We need to talk. The whole city has been thrown into even greater madness. The fighting has worsened. I don't feel safe. Moreover, we have to decide what to do with Shao Peng."

Wan Fook stepped back into the room. With an air of resignation he motioned her in. She followed and found herself immediately assailed by the sourness of the air. All the windows were closed and the room was almost in complete darkness. She made her way to the windows, swaying on her tiny deformed feet as she did so. Quickly she flung them open and a rush of fresh air rushed in. She inhaled deeply.

"So! I even smell bad!" He stalked to the window and stopped within a foot of her. "Why do you need to talk to me? I am no longer the man of the house. You have reduced me to this," he said, indicating with his thumb and index finger a miniscule measure.

Heong Yook turned to face him. She did not intend to restart their quarrel. Over the weeks and months, she had reflected on what happened. Perhaps she had been too harsh. She had to forgive and forget because the alternative would be even harder to bear. Divorce was unheard of and was not an option. A man might easily cast off his wife; she as a woman did not have the same right, no matter that her husband commits adultery, has many concubines or mistreats and abuses her. She told herself over and over again that beneath it all, her husband was a good man. He had been led astray. She must draw a line under all that had happened because nothing would bring Hua back. She needed her husband's knowledge of the world and his contacts to find a way of getting Shao Peng to Ngao. She could not rely totally on Mui. She took in his reduced state and her heart softened.

"No you don't smell bad. I opened the windows to let in fresh air. Sit down. I need your help. Despite what has happened, you are still the head of the family. You are needed more than ever at this time of crisis."

He looked up astonished at her sudden change. "Are you sure?" he asked. His voice quivered.

She nodded, sat down and took his hands in hers. She was determined not to fight him. "There are a number of things we have to discuss. One thing you should know is that Ngao has written. He is safe. He wrote from a place called Johor. Here," she said fishing a letter from within her tunic top, "read this."

Wan Fook took the letter from her. His hands shook. He was wary about what he would read. He read it twice and looked up. "He...he seems well. He sounds positive." He was relieved that the letter had not been accusatory. He looked at the date of the letter. "But this arrived some time ago. You said nothing! I was ridden with guilt. I thought ... I thought he was dead as well and that I was the cause!"

"I couldn't tell you because you were unapproachable. And I had to think," Heong Yook said lamely. "Can we get Shao Peng to him?"

"Women are not allowed to travel out of China. This is to ensure the men return. Don't you know?" He looked at her with eyes mirrored with concern.

"I know, that is, I do now. Mui told me. I have sent her to Canton. She is trying to find the Englishman who raped Hua."

"Why? Why are you trying to rake up the whole thing again? What good will it do? What can you do? Bring him to trial? Does this country look like one where any form of justice can be found?" His voice grew in volume; the frustration he felt against his wife rebounded. He flung out his arm and nearly caught her cheek, as he pointed in the direction of the outer walls of his house. "We have a civil war! We are also at war with the foreigners. Who would take the word of a brothel maid?"

"I agree with you. I had this idea that if we find the Englishman, we can use our knowledge of his deed to make him help us."

"Blackmail him?" asked Wan Fook, his eyes round with horror.

"I didn't use the word blackmail," retorted Heong Yook but she kept her voice soft and placating. "Perhaps that is what it would be called. I prefer to call it pragmatic justice." She sat still allowing him to shout and rail at her. She was not going to respond. She looked down at her feet until he quietened.

"Who is he?" Wan Fook asked quietly once his temper was spent.

"Someone important. Mui has gone to confirm this and will let us know when she comes back. Can you help? You have contacts in the foreign territory of Canton, don't you? You export porcelain through them. Can't you see one of your friends in the *Co-Hong*, the guild of merchants? It has the monopoly of trade with the foreigners and will surely know him." Her eyes held his. She took his hands once more in hers. "We have to help Ngao, to redeem ourselves for the bad that has happened to his family."

Chapter 18

FROM THE SHELTER of the covered way that fronted the shop houses, Ngao looked across to the opposite buildings. The street was congested: men hurrying, men selling their wares, men with horse carts, and men drawing carts and rickshaws, no different from the beasts of burden trotting alongside them. This was the part of Chinatown in Singapore called *But Yeh Teen,* or where night never falls because there was always activity. The water cart stood at the side of the road. It was an innocuous two-wheel vehicle hauled by two bullocks, one of many seen on the island. Between its two wheels was a platform on which sat a huge wooden water barrel. The bullocks stared limpidly at the scene around them, swishing their tails languidly.

Ngao hurried across to Chow's men standing guard by the water cart, their arms akimbo, sleeves rolled up and frowns on their faces.

"You are late," snarled one of the men.

"I am sorry. Shall I load the cart now? Would you please explain how best to transfer the ... *mang*... grasshoppers to the barrel?" asked Ngao. He was flustered, having spent the last forty minutes or so walking to and fro to clear his mind. He knew he was late.

"Huh! If we had to wait for you to do that, we might as well carry it over to Johor ourselves!" exclaimed one of the men. "It's all done. It is in the barrel and there is a false lid you remove to get access to it. Make sure the lid is tightly shut and drive carefully. You do not want to risk overturning the cart. It is now much lighter than normal with the barrel empty except for its new contents."

"What if someone asks me for water?"

"Tell them you have none; that the barrel has sprung a leak and you are on your way to get it repaired. Make up a story. Use your brains. *Fan su tow!* You have a sweet potato for a head!"

"And," added another of the men, "see that you deliver it safely to Lee Sik. We have counted and weighed the consignment. Every single ball!" With a swift motion of his index finger he indicated a slashing motion across his throat from left to right, "Be warned."

Ngao clambered up on to the cart. He donned a wide straw coolie hat, shielding his face from the fast rising sun. Sweat streamed down his back. He was tense with nerves. "I'll make my way now. Thank you. I am sorry I was late." He bowed and then gently prodded the two animals forward.

The cart lurched forward and then settled into a gentle rhythmic pace. The bullocks swished their tails and flies rose and then fell again to congregate on their haunches. A reflection of life's tapestry, repetitive and persistent. The water carrier vied for space in the narrow streets: carts, people and animals moving in tandem. Slowly as they left the main thoroughfare and headed towards the harbour, the noise and bustle settled. Arrangements had been made for them to board a boat that would take them across the Straits of Johor, the narrow strip of sea between Singapore and the Peninsula of Malaya. Ngao sat holding onto the rein, his body moving gently with the motion of the cart, his eyes looking at the scenery unfolding before him, yet unseeing. The tension in his body grew until the muscles across his shoulders and between his shoulder blades were a hard unremitting source of pain. He pressed on, not stopping once. Gradually, the turmoil in his mind eased and in its place, the image of Shao Peng rose once more, followed rapidly by Hua's.

"I have to do this for Shao Peng. Hua would expect this. I have to stay alive. I will make up for this deed," he vowed. He pushed aside the heavy guilt that lay in his heart and thought of what Eng Kim had said. "Was there another alternative to what he was doing now, except to be killed? Would his death stop the opium from being brought into Johor?"

"You did well," said Lee Sik as the last ball of opium was unloaded. "Did you have any trouble?"

"No! When I passed the township, there were some curious looks but bullocks and cows are not an uncommon sight and I had my story ready."

"Good! We don't want to have a gang war on our hands. Mr Chow's franchise to trade and distribute opium does not extend to this area because Johor does not fall under British rule." Lee Sik closed the chest, locking it securely before putting the key away. He straightened up and turned around to fix his penetrating gaze on Ngao. "I was told that you will be leaving us soon."

Ngao started guiltily. He was astonished that Lee Sik knew and wondered if he minded. He thought that Eng Kim would need to approach Mr Chow and some time would lapse before news would reach this outpost. How did he know so quickly?

"Don't worry. I won't put anything in your way though you should have told me of your plans beforehand," he said with a hint of reproach in his voice. "The first phase of the hard work is already completed. In any case, you will be with us for at least another month. Mr Chow, our boss wants you around for another job before releasing you."

"What does he want me to do?" asked Ngao. He feared that it would be something to do with the distribution of the opium. He did not know how he could cope with it. He must find some way to undo what he had done. No matter what he said to excuse himself he had now connived in the evil deed of opium distribution. Guilt lay on his heart like a rock. He saw the foreman watching him.

"Are you worried? What about?" asked Lee Sik.

"Nothing," replied Ngao mustering a smile.

"The opium?" asked Lee Sik seeing the dread in Ngao's face. "We are not going to distribute it here. It is not our turf. It is for our own use."

"Won't it destroy our men? Please, I feel really bad... I don't want to be..."

"Stop! I didn't hear that. I shall also ask you not to say more. The matter stops here. Understand! I say it one more time. Don't test my patience. The British government holds the monopoly on the opium trade and licenses Mr Chow, for which he pays an enormous sum of money, to distribute it in Singapore. It is all above board. Money talks."

Ngao looked away. He wanted to say that it was not above board in Johor. Mr Chow did not have the franchise to distribute it in Johor and he should also not supply his own coolies there. He refrained. Eng Kim had told him of the punishment meted out for disloyalty and disobedience was counted as disloyalty. But he could not stop himself completely. "Do you agree with me it is not good for the men?" He said it so quietly Lee Sik had to lean closer to catch what he said.

"What I think is of no account," said the foreman. "We are here to carry out orders. And my order to you is that you will lead a party of men further north into the jungle. Mr Chow wants a report on the activity there. Don't ask me why. He is keeping it close to his chest. I will let you know more when the time is right."

He brushed pass Ngao and as he did so, he said, "Mr Chow has no intention of feeding it to his own men. He was just testing you."

Ngao stared at the departing back of the foreman. He was puzzled. What would the opium be used for then? Which version of Lee Sik's reply was the truth? And how did Lee Sik read his mind?

Chapter 19

CANTON

WAN FOOK SAT in the hallway of the Guild of Merchants. He had been waiting for hours. There was still no sign of any of the *Co-Hong* members. They were huddled in the main hall holding secret discussions; the meeting had been going on for days. This was Wan Fook's third visit; each of his previous trips had been in vain. He was turned away; they had no time for him. There were urgent matters at hand. From snippets of conversations between sessions, he learnt that all was not well. The foreign enclave outside the city walls had been burnt down. Fires had broken out often in the past, but this time the entire area had been devastated by the flames. Almost all thirteen of its factories had suffered. Trade was disrupted and the *Co-Hong* stood to lose almost everything. There would be no exports of tea, porcelain, and labour. Already there was speculation that the foreign enclave would eventually move to Shamian Island or even Hong Kong! Everything would be disrupted. Then, just when it seemed things could not get any worse, a messenger had hurried into the Guild, panting and shouting, "We are under attack."

The commotion brought the merchants out of the room. "Calm down! Explain yourself!" they commanded him.

"The forts are taken, all four of them, and twenty three Chinese junks have been destroyed. At this very moment foreign ships are firing into the city and parts of Canton City wall have been battered," cried the messenger. He ignored the reprimands levelled at him to speak more slowly. His breath came in rapid gasps and his eyes were wild with excitement.

The news created even greater furore. Everyone spoke at once. The noise level rose to fever pitch. All attempts to keep the discussion calm and collected vanished.

Wan Fook went over to one of the guild merchants he knew called Tan and pulled gently on his friend's sleeve. "I need to see someone called Edward Grime, the Second Superintendent of Trade. Will you help me?" he asked urgently

"Bad time to see any of them," Tan replied. "He is very approachable normally and, of all the foreigners, he is probably the one most sympathetic to us. But as you can see now is not a good time."

"Why has the dispute escalated so fast?" asked Wan Fook.

"It's the same old story. The British are demanding that China legalise the opium trade to enable them to bring even more of it into China. They want the entire country to be opened up to their merchants. China has always rejected these demands. We all know that they get around the restrictions on the opium trade by using local Chinese vessels to bring it in; they allow them to fly British flags to protect them. Well, this time Chinese officials have ignored this by boarding a Chinese-owned ship called the Arrow, suspected of smuggling opium. The newly appointed British consul, Parkes, insists that the vessel was flying a British flag and hence boarding her was an insult to the British Government. Ye, the Chinese officer responsible for the search, argues the vessel had not renewed its registration under the British flag. When they inspected the vessel's license, they found its British license had expired. This, the Chinese authorities maintain, gave them the right to check the boat because its status had reverted to being Chinese. Apparently the explanation has not satisfied the Consul. He deemed it a great insult and has instigated the attack of our city. I think they were just waiting for an excuse."

"They must know that with the Taiping rebellion and our lack of troops, we are in no position to protect ourselves," cried Wan Fook. "If they win this war even more opium will be forced on us." He recalled his son's addiction. He had not seen him for years. He dreaded to think what would happen if the drug were to be allowed freely into the country.

"You have to excuse me Wan Fook," said Tan. "I have to get on with what I was doing before the interruption. Go back to your wife; there is nothing you can do here."

Mention of his wife brought Wan Fook back to his mission. He could not leave without finding the whereabouts of Grime. "Please can you help me? I cannot return home without seeing this officer," said Wan Fook.

"I can only direct you to where Grime *might* be," Tan replied. "He is moving his factory to Shamian. So he might be in either the foreign enclave in Canton supervising the move, or on Shamian itself."

❀ ❀ ❀

"Sir! This is the building. I saw him enter through that door. I asked around and was told that he lived on the first floor," said Mui. "He is not there any more." She was excited and pointed with jabbing motions at the building in front of them.

Wan Fook looked up and around him. He had never been to the foreign enclave in Canton. Although he sold porcelain for export all the sales were handled by the *Co-Hong* and Tan was one of his principal business contacts in the Guild. Despite the fire damage, what remained of the buildings showed that they were once very grand. The one in front of him had long windows with wooden shutters that were totally different in design to those in the Chinese dwellings familiar to him. Many of the shutters hung perilously askew while others were scorched and blackened by fire. Parts of the wall, once white, were torn down. Inside, the wooden ceilings had collapsed. The place had been ransacked.

"You are probably right. He is obviously not here. The place is empty. Where is Shamian? I was told they are moving their quarters there," said Wan Fook.

"No! Not Shahmian. If he is not here, then he must be on Honam Island. They will move further up the river to Shamian Island eventually. They are in Honam now," Mui insisted with great pride. "I followed them. The *Co-Hong* merchants are too frightened to see for themselves. So you cannot rely on what they say."

"Will you recognise him?" asked Wan Fook. "You say he spoke Chinese."

"Yes! He did and I will make sure he remembers me," said Mui.

"Do you know the way to Honam?"

"Not far!" said Mui excitedly. "Near! Very near! It is just across the Pearl River," she explained.

EDWARD GRIME WAS troubled. He was not persuaded that an outright second war against China was justified. In fact, it was unjust. He knew that many British vessels and Chinese vessels flying the British flag carried opium; opium that was grown in India by the British East India Company and destined for China despite it being banned by the Chinese Imperial Government. He knew he was not the only one against the opium trade. His friend and confidante, Sir Charles Elliot, was of a similar mind and had written of his inability to countenance the "disgrace and sin" of such a commerce to Lord Palmerston. Back in England, many parliamentarians denounced the war, particularly Gladstone who openly criticised Lord Palmerston's support for the contraband trade. Grime's own family had voiced their concern. Despite the outcry, the forced imports of opium into China continued. Palmerston had turned the table on those who criticised the trade by calling them unpatriotic.

Grime surveyed the street before him. The transfer to Honam Island had been hurried because of the fire. It had spurred anger amongst the foreign traders and his fellow Englishmen in particular. He did not know if the fire was deliberate. Over the years there had been many such incidents, some deliberate and some accidental. He recalled a fire that started in a pastry shop and destroyed four buildings. It would have spread even further but for the joint efforts of the

Chinese and the foreign residents in dousing the fires. After all, the Chinese merchant guild, the *Co-Hong* stood to lose just as much if not more then the foreign merchants. This time, however, help had not been forthcoming from the Chinese. He saw for himself the rising tide of feeling against the British after the hangings in Respondentia Square. A fire also occurred that day. Luckily it did not spread. This time, they had not been as lucky.

He turned abruptly away from the street scene. He wondered if he would have helped douse the fire had he been a Chinese. "We have bombarded them with too many demands" he muttered to himself. The last had been that the trial of any Englishmen caught breaking the law on Chinese soil should be conducted in an English court. This had aroused a great deal of antagonism because those arrested were immediately released on their return to England. So when a fruit stall was kicked over by foreigners and the owner beaten up, all hell broke out. No wonder, the Chinese had taken on the role of executioners in Respondentia Square. Perhaps, this time the fire was not accidental.

He crossed the street to his temporary quarters; his steps echoed on the granite cobbles. His mind strayed to his own deceit. He was immediately filled with an intense regret. He too had not behaved well to the locals. That woman Hua, he wondered. What had happened to her? How could she have vanished into thin air? He had been looking for her ever since that night. In his loneliness, he had pined to have a stable relationship, encouraged by stories of those who had successfully formed such extra-marital liaisons in foreign lands. A warm body and welcoming arms to comfort him were all that he wanted. He sighed; he had allowed himself to be carried away by his own fantasies.

A hand caught his sleeve as he stepped over the doorway's threshold. He turned.

"*Gei de ngo ma?* Remember me, Sir?" asked Mui in Cantonese.

Edward Grime stood rooted, one foot across the doorway's threshhold, the other outside. He stepped back out of the doorway and into the sunlight. He could not take his eyes off the woman and the man next to her.

"I brought you to Hua's room," she persisted looking him straight in the eye, stare for stare.

He remembered her, down to the pockmarks on her face. He could not speak. His mind reeled. What does she want? Is this a trick of some sort? Or has Hua a message for me? His heart leapt at this possibility. Perhaps she has changed her mind and will see me now, he thought.

"She is dead, sir. *Sei le!* She killed herself after you left her. She was ashamed. You defiled her and she killed herself because she was ashamed. She couldn't face her family, her husband and her child. You did that to her, sir!"

He turned a deathly pale. "She is dead?" He felt as though his knees would buckle. Then his face regained its colour. Husband? Child? He narrowed his eyes fixing them on her. "You are lying!" he exclaimed. "Why should I believe you?"

"She is dead sir because you defiled her," insisted Mui loudly this time. "You came into the city against the law."

Her voice attracted a few passers-by. The street was busy. All heads turned to the shrill voice of a woman. It was rare to see a white man being so accosted. A clerk came out of the doorway and peered at him with a questioning look, "Alright sir?" he asked, before retreating back into the building when Grime waved him away.

"Come in! We'll speak in my room," said Grime quickly. He needed to silence this woman. "And you too," he said turning to Wan Fook who so far had not uttered a word.

He led them into the building and up a stairway. They walked along a narrow passageway to a room at the end. He ushered them in and closed the door.

"Are you telling me the truth? And who is this?" he asked pointing to Wan Fook.

Wan Fook drew himself to his full height. "She is telling the truth. Hua, the woman you consorted with, was my nephew's wife."

"Sir, I had no idea that she was married or unwilling." He turned on Mui. "You told me that she was willing," he cried. "You said to expect a show of reluctance because she was shy and very new to the establishment. I ... I thought she was a virgin. How could she be married? There was evidence of blood," he added lamely, his eyes went from Mui to the man before him.

Mui gave an inane giggle. Wan Fook glared at her so hard she stopped immediately.

"You thought wrongly," said Wan Fook, his face grim. "She was not there of her own will. You raped her! I come to warn you that we are going to report this, both to the Chinese authorities and to your government. We will write a letter to *The Times*, your national newspaper. We'll publish the story in Canton itself. We have many witnesses."

Grime sat down. He buried his head in his hands. He was shocked. How could he have been so stupid? So gullible! He had been manipulated. His base desire had obliterated all rational thinking. He had behaved no better in his dealings with the Chinese than those he criticised. He thought he could buy love. He had made excuses for himself and clouded his vision. Yes he was lonely. He had wanted a long-term relationship and had thought it was reciprocated. He was told Hua was looking for a man, a husband even. Was that sufficient excuse for what he did? He thought of his own family and his standing in the foreign community. There were already many in the British India Company who thought him too pro-Chinese. This would play into their hands. At best he would be laughed at as a Chink lover! At worst, a rapist and murderer.

He shook himself in disgust. Even now he was thinking of himself when he should have been thinking of the poor woman who had been trapped between him and her procurers. She had paid a heavy price. He was ashamed. He felt their eyes on him. He raised his head and forced himself to look at Wan Fook. He saw the glimmer of uncertainty in Wan Fook's eyes. With a flash, Grime understood what was happening. He realised that they wanted something from him. They could have done all that they threatened without coming to him. They came for a reason.

"What do you want?" he asked.

"Help Hua's daughter! Help Hua's husband! Redeem yourself," said Wan Fook.

He recalled that his friend had told him that Grime was a good man and sympathetic to the Chinese. He suspected Grime had been fooled, a suspicion confirmed by Mui's giggles. He had never liked the woman, never trusted her. He could empathise with Grime because he too had allowed himself to believe what was convenient for his conscience.

"How?" asked Grime.

Wan Fook took a seat opposite Grime and explained. He saw the emotions that passed over the man's face when he told him of Hua's kidnap, the forced deportation of Ngao to Singapore and the plight of Shao Peng left motherless and separated from her father. "Help her go to her father. We can't get a safe passage for her."

"Chinese women are not allowed to leave China. Nor would it be safe do so at the moment. Still I will try to find a way, though it will take time for me to arrange it."

"It does not have to be done immediately. We just need to know it can be done so that I can reply and make a promise to my nephew. I do not want to promise to send his daughter over and then find we cannot do it. I have failed him too many times." Wan Fook lowered his voice and leaned forward. "We hear this rumour that you might move to Hong Kong. Is this true? How then could we get Shao Peng over to you?"

"I shall find a way. I will not forget," promised Edward Grime.

"How can we trust you?"

They locked gaze. A flicker of uncertainty crossed Grime's face. Wan Fook saw it and became apprehensive. He sat back and repeated his question.

"You have my career and reputation in your hands. I will carry out my promise. I give you my solemn word. I am truly sorry. I wish none of this had happened. It was not my intent to cause her harm. I know 'sorry' sounds futile and trite for what has happened and nothing I do can bring her back." Grime struggled to contain his shame and regret. Mixed with it was fear. His words came out in spurts and starts.

In that instant Wan Fook saw before him not the high ranking officer, no less than a Second Superintendent of Trade in the British Government, but a lonely vulnerable young man separated from his family. He found himself drawn to Grime. He could not explain why, perhaps, he reminded him of his own mistakes and weakness.

Chapter 20

SELANGOR

NGAO LAY ON the straw matting, staring at the starlit sky. The night sounds of geckoes mingled with the steady humming of mosquitoes. It was too hot in the narrow confines of the wooden hut. Out in the open, there was at least some breeze. He had left the men in the hut. There were five of them. He closed his eyes but sleep escaped him. He could not stop thinking of Hua and Shao Peng. He felt a deep sadness like a lump that would not disperse and remained lodged in his heart. A tear seeped from the corner of his eye. He brushed it away. During the day, he was fine. Relentless work pushed everything aside. It was at night that thoughts of his family encroached and occupied his entire being. In moments like this when he was alone with his thoughts, he could not believe what had happened. He whispered Hua's name and a sharp pain went through him. He willed the thought away. "For her sake and our daughter, I have to make good," he vowed aloud. "I have to earn sufficient money to bring Shao Peng over. There must be a way to get her a passage." He forced himself to focus on this.

They had arrived in Selangor the previous day. The journey had been long and arduous. They had travelled in a bullock cart carrying their mining tools: spades, trowels, forks and wooden pans. He was told to lead five men north of Johor to Ulu Klang in Selangor to look for the best mining area.

"Start with the river," Lee Sik had instructed. "The tin ore, I am told, is generally located in the gravel along streambeds. Panning the riverbeds should be easy enough once you have been shown how to do it. You have two men – Hong and Lok – in your team who have experience and will be able to assess what you find. This should give you some idea of the potential richness of the area. Mr Chow wants to know before committing himself; he is in negotiations with Raja Abdullah of Selangor to lease the land for mining. Look around at the competition and report back."

Lee Sik had paused then to look appraisingly at Ngao. By now Ngao was familiar with the hard measuring stare directed at him. "You showed great foresight in learning the native language," the foreman had conceded with grudging respect. "The boss must think highly of you to give you such responsibility. So take care that you do well by him. One other piece of advice: what the two new men do is not your concern. They are the boss's men. They do not report to you."

Ngao opened his eyes and studied his surroundings. A sliver of moonlight penetrated the tree canopy. A light breeze had picked up. Branches swayed and leaves rustled. In the distance, a tiger roared. Two men had been mauled to death in the past month by tigers in one of the pepper estates in Johor. Perhaps he should return to the hut; the thought, however, made him feel claustrophobic. So he remained where he was under the night sky and closed his eyes again.

He could not sleep. The two new men Hong and Lok intrigued him. They were not part of the team that had been involved in the pepper planting in Johor. He had not met them until the very day that he received instructions for his mission. They kept to themselves and had a box that they carried wherever they went. It was not his concern, he thought. His mind wandered. A picture of a house with his daughter rose in his mind. Once I am settled, I must save enough to have a place of my own; a place for my daughter, he thought. I will make it come true. I will write to Aunt Heong Yook to tell her. In this way, Ngao directed his mind to the future, filling it with positive plans. It was his lifeline, the only way he could survive after the tumultuous events of the past year.

AT THE BREAK of dawn, Ngao left with his men for the village. Hong and Lok still carried the box between them. Ngao ignored them. Well, he thought, casting a glance over his shoulders at the men, they are not my concern. If they wish to carry a heavy load, then let it be. Perhaps it contained the remains of some ancestors that needed to be buried at some specific place.

The morning air was infused with moisture. Ngao could feel it on his face and arms. He inhaled deeply the rich scent of the earth and vegetation. He liked it. He liked what he had seen of Johor and he liked it even more here in Selangor. There was space. Shao Peng would like this place, he told himself. He reflected on the living quarters in Singapore and shuddered at his recollection of sharing sleeping quarters and a single latrine with thirty others.

They made their way along the rough-hewn path, their feet pressing deep into the rain soaked soil. It took some minutes to reach the top of the slight incline. Looking down into the valley below they could see buildings and houses.

He led the men down the hill and, as they got closer, Ngao could see to the west, the Malay village he had been instructed to reach. Lee Sik had called it a kampong. It consisted of a core group of wooden houses on stilts. Juxtaposed to the village was a single road with about a dozen shop houses, not unlike those in Singapore, on either side; then, still further to the east, lay a cluster of huts some little more than lean-tos. Some square and others of indeterminate shape, they were scattered around with no apparent order. From where he stood, it would seem a whole new settlement of huts and lean-tos had grown hodgepodge with little relevance or connection to the original village. Despite the early hours, people were up and about in this new settlement. Men with wide brimmed hats were selling fruits and leafy vegetables. Some were busy arranging stalls. He saw a man set up his charcoal brazier ready to dish out rice congee. People sat on their haunches or on stools around portable tables eating breakfast. He looked with astonishment at the unfolding scene, almost like Singapore's China town in miniature.

He hurried towards the kampong. He had been told to present himself to Raja Abdullah. "You will know his residence when you are there," Lee Sik had said.

Amongst the group of wooden houses on stilts, set well back, was a building bigger and grander than the rest. Raised above the ground by some two metres and resting on about twelve pillars, it retained much of the traditional architecture. The dark wooden carved railings of the veranda gleamed richly against the whiteness of the walls in the front of the house where plaster and brick were used. The rest of the house was constructed of wooden panels, each one with its own intricate carvings. Even the windows and doors were similarly carved.

Ngao made his way towards the building with his men. "This would be a true test of how much Malay I can speak. I hope the hours spent learning it in the evenings have been worthwhile," he mumbled.

By the time he reached the stairway leading up to the house, Raja Abdullah was already out on the veranda surrounded by his men. Ngao know him from the description he had been given and his distinctive headgear. The Raja gave a cursory nod towards Ngao; his eyes were watchful and wary.

Ngao raised both hands clasped together in greeting, a gesture he had observed in Johor. "*Selamat pagi!* Good morning!" he said.

"So you speak Malay?" asked Raja Abdullah. He was pleasantly surprised. "My father-in-law, the Sultan, will be pleased."

"*Sikit!* A little," Ngao replied. "I learnt it in Johor from the villagers; it is very basic and I hope you will forgive me if I mispronounce and make mistakes." He was surprised at the informality of the Raja. He expected more pomp and circumstance. He had thought he would be ignored because of his lowly status, a concern he had expressed to Lee Sik when he told him that he was to represent Chow.

Lee Sik had scoffed and told him not to be concerned about such matters. "If the Raja wished only to speak to people of noble birth or rank, then he would not have many to converse with. Moreover, you speak Malay. He will like that."

"You have something for me?" asked Raja Abdullah, waving them up the stairs to the veranda. He looked expectantly at Ngao, a half smile hovering around his lips and a twinkle in his eye.

Ngao looked puzzled. Before he could reply, Hong and Lok had hurried forward and presented their box to the Raja. Ngao looked on with trepidation. Although he did not know what was going on, he did not wish to reveal his ignorance. He tried to catch the eyes of Hong and Lok. They steadfastly avoided eye contact.

The Raja opened the box. "*Chandu!*" he exclaimed, the hitherto half expectant smile broke into a wide grin. "Good!"

Ngao started; his eyes darted to the ball of opium in the Raja's hand. Suddenly everything fell in place. The opium he helped carry from Singapore was not for distribution in Johor, not even for the pepper plantation workers. In that respect Lee Sik did not lie. His employers were playing with him. It was for Raja Abdullah in Selangor. So Mr Chow had not trusted him as much as he was led to believe. Perhaps Ngao's misgivings about the drug had got back to him. To stop him from suspecting, they had transferred the opium from the original chest to a box.

Ngao fretted. Once more, he found himself involved with opium and like before he could do little about it. He looked on while the Raja examined the contents of the box. Satisfied, Raja Abdullah looked up and flashed another smile at Ngao. "So, let us settle the matter. Come into the house. I will show you the map and boundaries of the land I propose to lease to Mr Chow. You may take your men there and do a little prospecting to satisfy him. But I expect an answer soon. I have many people wanting to lease the land. And," he pointed at Ngao, "after all this is finished, you and I have other business to conduct. Your future boss, Lim Eng Kim has already been in touch."

NGAO WAS PREOCCUPIED during the entire journey to the river. He felt manipulated, a cog in the wheel with no control over anything. The morning's handing over of the opium to the Raja still troubled him. He wanted no part in it yet he was involved anyway. He was unhappy that both Chow and Eng Kim, his present and future boss, had withheld information from him. They placed him in impossible positions and then expected him to comply. Ngao was uneasy. He was suspicious of what further plans they might have for him. Eng Kim had not told him that he had been in touch with Raja Abdullah.

The bullock cart carrying the six men moved slowly along the rough path of the riverbank. There was little chatter. Ngao was engrossed with his thoughts, while Hong and Lok maintained their customary silence. The other men also spoke little. In the growing heat of the day, they had nodded off. Their heads lolled with the motion of the cart. They were oblivious to the flies that hovered around their faces. They were making up for the hard days of travel from Johor to Selangor.

Ngao held on to the reins of the cart, his mind busy. He had to find some way to escape the clutches of Chow and perhaps even Eng Kim. They had not been bad to him; he just did not want to be involved with opium. No one seemed to be able to understand his concern. Opium was so widespread and so entrenched because the government was involved in it that they thought he was just being awkward. He felt he could not trust anyone to take him seriously, not even Eng Kim in whom his friend Cheng had had such faith. Perhaps, he was being unfair. His future boss had not put him to work yet and had still to tell him what he would be doing. Once again he wondered if he could ever be free? Most of his wages went to repaying his debts. After the months of hard work he had saved very little, nowhere near enough to buy his freedom.

What would Cheng say at times like this, he wondered. His friend's advice to take one thing at a time came immediately to mind. I must not get ahead of myself. I will just have to finish this task of prospecting for tin and do well by Chow, thought Ngao. I must make sure that he does not begrudge my leaving his employ. I cannot afford to make an enemy of him. I must not give an impression that I am disloyal.

The bullock cart rolled forward along the track flanked on one side by the river and on the other by towering virgin jungle. At times, he had to alight and slash away the tall grasses and bushes. The men in the cart were dead to the world. The heat grew intense, and the sun's rays reflected brightly from the running river. Finally, Ngao pulled on the reins and the cart came to a halt. They had arrived at a spot where the torrent was quite strong, but the river was still shallow, shallow enough for them to wade in and pan for tin ore. *Dulang* washing, the locals called it. He woke the men up and jumped down from the cart. "Hong! Lok!" he called, "You have to show us how to pan for ore. I will mark out several sites at random. We will wash out the soil to see how much tin ore there is. We have about six other sites to investigate."

Chapter 21

IN HEONG YOOK's household, the tension of the past year or so had mainly dissipated and peace reigned once more. Heong Yook was happy with her husband's efforts and success in extracting a promise from Edward Grime to secure a passage for Shao Peng. She was still not clear about the mechanics and details of how it would be done; she understood that under the circumstances it was difficult to plan. China remained at war with Britain although the English continued to trade and preside in the treaty ports of Canton as well as Honam. English vessels, particularly the new steamers that Wan Fook had spoken so much about, continued to ply Chinese waters. Faster and more efficient than Chinese junks, she was told they would be better to carry her beloved Shao Peng to her father. She was not in a hurry. The letter from Ngao indicated that he needed time to settle and make good before he could send for his daughter. She would relish what time she had with her niece.

She retrieved the letter she had received that morning. She opened it almost reverently, smoothing out the creases and folds. Through the letter bearer, she had learnt of the complex postal system that had been created to connect those who had travelled to Singapore and Malaya with their families in China. With wide-eyed horror she learnt of the fees that were charged for remitting money, a hefty ten percent of the value of the remittance itself! She learnt about merchant syndicates and their increasing monopoly of the postal system.

"I must tell Ngao not to send money home. How will he be able to save enough to start anew in Malaya if he remits money to us and pays such high fees?" she asked herself. She smiled, a satisfied smile that played on her lips and lit up her eyes. She thought of what she had learned about the outside world. "Malaya!" she said to herself, "I didn't even know it existed. Through Ngao's eyes I am seeing a whole new world."

She turned back to the letter and read on. Her eyes glittered with excitement. She felt she was part of Ngao's adventure into this new world in *Nanyang*.

My Esteemed Aunt,

I hope you and Uncle are well. How is Shao Peng? I long to see her. Has she grown much taller? Does she remember me? I hope I will be able to have her with me soon. I am so happy and grateful to hear that it will be possible to get her a passage when the time comes. It is a day I look forward to and build my hopes around. There is not a day that I do not think of Hua and Shao Peng.

I am now in a place they call Ulu Klang. It is in Selangor, on the west coast of Malaya but north of Johor. There are no pepper plantations here. The Chinese population grows by the minute in this area. They come to work in the tin mines. The Malay rulers invited thousands of them to come and work the mines for which they charge a fee. I was told that there are some twenty thousand Chinese in this state spread out between Ulu Klang, Lukut and a place called Ampang. My boss, Mr Chow sent me to this place to prospect. I have now completed the job and next week I go to work for someone called Lim Eng Kim. You have met him. He is a close relative of my friend Cheng. He has taken over my remaining debts.

Heoong Yook placed the sheaf of papers down. So the man who had delivered her first letter to Ngao was not an ordinary messenger. She wondered why he had not said more and regretted she had mistaken him for a letter bearer. She sighed, took up the letter again and continued reading

I like what I have seen of the country and the local people. It is warm and the climate is not unlike that of Yulin. I love the greenness, the ease in which things grow and flourish. Life here is still wild and untamed. Many die from the shivering disease and deaths caused by tigers are not uncommon. Fights between different Chinese dialect groups led by the societies to which they belong are frequent and vicious.

The societies are what we call 'hui' in Guangzhou although they are practised differently here. The two biggest are the Ghee Hin and the Hai San. I belong to the Hai

*San. Different rival Malay rulers back different societies
or perhaps it is the other way around. It seems impossible
not to belong to one. I was more or less compelled to join up
the day I landed in Singapore. In truth they offer someone
like me great support, but I am terrified of their harsh
laws. So far, I have been able to avoid these 'wars'. I have
to confess that I am still mystified by the workings of these
societies. Their membership is not only based on dialect but
is subdivided further by clans. I met one man who was a
member of three different societies. These societies are all-
powerful and control large parts of trade. They even collect
taxes on behalf of the Malay rulers.*

*I have learned to speak the native language –
Malay – while in Johor. I practise with the locals in the
village near our camp. They are very welcoming and
I go to them most evenings after work. I can't write or
read Malay, but even being able to speak it has been
of great advantage. I am learning English, something
that I started with Cheng my friend before he died. He
worked as an interpreter in Canton. I have learnt now
that it was a form of pidgin English that people are not
familiar with in Malaya. There is a serious movement
amongst some of the Malay chiefs to establish English
schools because some have studied in England. There
are also some well-established Chinese merchants who
have also schooled in England and are clamouring for
more English schools in the country. These Chinese
merchants, mainly from Penang and Malacca are not
recent migrants like us. Many of them have married
local women. I met such a man in Johor. They have
been here for hundreds of years and have done well.*

Aunty Heong Yook, I hope to prosper like them. Their success has given me such hope. You have always encouraged me to study and I am very grateful for this. It might be my way forward because most of the new Chinese migrants do not read or write.

Please tell Shao Peng I love and miss her. I wish I could see her now and that she was here with me. But sadly, I am still not in a position to send for her. Tell her I will send for her as soon as I can.

Your obedient nephew, Ngao

Heong Yook wiped a tear from her eye. Her heart filled with pride. This letter was a letter of hope so different from the previous ones she had received. She went in search of Shao Peng to share the news.

Chapter 22

SELANGOR
(A SENSE OF BELONGING)

NGAO WALKED ALONE through the Chinese settlement towards the Malay village. His fellow companions had all left for Johor a week ago en route to Singapore. They would be presenting his report to Chow on his behalf. He hoped he had done enough to earn the man's goodwill.

He took his time, stopping every now and then to look into alleyways and the dim interior of the shops. He was not expected at Raja Abdullah's house until mid-day where he would also meet up with Eng Kim his new boss. He sniffed the damp hot air. The pot pourri of scents made him think of Beiliu. Stalls of incense and joss sticks stood next to a butcher's stand. Poultry lay on chopping boards, their skin plucked free of feathers and goose pimpled under the hot sun. Chunks of meat lay next to them exuding a ferrous smell of flesh and blood. At another stall, bamboo caskets containing dumplings were piled high on steamers. All around him was the customary hustle and bustle of people vying desperately to earn a living. Wide-brimmed coolie hats dominated the scene. If anything, there were even more people than just over two weeks ago when he had first seen the settlement. No wonder Eng Kim wanted a slice of this business.

He thought of his home in Yulin. One would see no strangers for days on end. The sound of the hill consisted only of the wind and the whispering of trees interspersed with bird song. My Hua would not have liked this settlement, he thought to himself. She preferred the quiet of the countryside. Immediately, he felt a lump in his throat. Hua was no more, he reminded himself. He felt a renewed sense of desolation, so strong that he had to stop in the middle of the street. His lips quivered. He did not know how long his sense of loss would remain with him.

Resolutely, he pushed Hua out of his mind. He forced himself to take an interest in the scene around him. Everywhere he turned, he saw his own countrymen. The local people did not venture here. It was similar to what he had observed in Singapore, the segregation of the different races and the minimal interaction between them. He had asked his foreman why this was. Lee Sik had merely replied it was a good thing because it avoided clashes between them. The foreman had, however, volunteered one interesting detail: interactions between Malays and Chinese, according to him, were confined mainly to Malay rulers and Chinese entrepreneurs. There the relationships were strong and close. He did not explain why.

Perhaps, this meeting with Raja Abdullah and Eng Kim would tell him more about how things worked. As things stood now, Ngao felt he was passing from one world into another whenever he walked from the Chinese settlement to the Malay village.

He left the shop houses behind him and walked on towards the *kampong*. Gradually a sense of space and an aura of leisure replaced the energetic vitality he had experienced just moments earlier. He could hear the sounds of insects broken every now and then by the shrill laughter of children playing in the muddy ground. They were oblivious to the dirt and heat; they ran barefoot kicking and splashing in the puddles. An old lady wearing a brightly coloured sarong tied round her chest smiled, revealing gums stained red by the betel nuts she was chewing. She spat. A red glob stained the soil. Like a child, she pointed to the gaudy flowers painted on her sarong. Ngao returned her smile. "*Cantek!* Beautiful!" he said.

A little boy ran up to him and touched his arm. "She is my *nenek*, grandmother," he said pointing to the old lady who continued her toothless smile. "Bapa! Father!" he pointed to a man sitting cross-legged under the tree with his sarong hitched up over knobbly knees.

Ngao smiled and allowed the boy to lead him to his father. At once a little crowd gathered around him. Ngao exchanged greetings and chatted with them before continuing on his way. He passed more houses. The fervent buying and selling he had seen in the new settlement did not exist here. Life followed a more measured pace. Suddenly in the midst of the languid atmosphere, he saw a man hurtling across the path some ten feet ahead of him. It was Eng Kim. His short thin frame was unmistakable. Ngao accelerated his pace and half ran to catch him up.

Eng Kim heard the heavy footsteps in pursuit of him and slowed down. When he saw it was Ngao, he broke into a warm smile. His eyes crinkled. "*Ahhh!*" he said. "Already you want to catch up with me even on your first day of work."

Ngao was uncertain if he was being teased by his new boss and made no reply. He had caught up and was walking alongside Eng Kim. Now mindful of what was said, he dropped a couple of paces back.

"You did well. Mr Chow was very pleased," said Eng Kim beckoning him forward. "He said he had never seen such initiative. He was delighted with the extra information you gave him on the quality of the tin ore and the different ways of extracting it. He was greatly impressed by your estimates of their costs."

Ngao smiled with relief. "I did not wish to part on bad terms. You warned me that loyalty counts. The extra work I did was to prevent any bad feelings between you and him. I wanted to assure him that although I would not be working for him in the future, I still did my best while in his employ."

Eng Kim smiled. "Good thinking," he said.

"Moreover," continued Ngao, "I heard from the other miners that the yield using the Malay method of digging vertical shafts and sluicing has been declining. I thought he should know. I also thought he would want to know that better alternative techniques exist. A few Chinese miners have successfully opened up extensive pits allowing them to follow the ore deposits. "

"Well, it is in his hands now," replied Eng Kim philosophically. "He has released you. My interest is not in mining. I wish to supply miners with everything they need. I have great plans for here."

Ngao's face fell. He dreaded to be told that opium would be among the things supplied. He opened his mouth to ask, even to protest. He did not get far for Eng Kim silenced him with a look so fierce that Ngao had to drop his gaze. Gone was the affable face that Eng Kim normally presented.

"I will be dealing with food provisions; especially rice," said Eng Kim stiffly. "My business will not include opium. You need to have more trust," he chided in a controlled voice that nevertheless contained more than a hint of anger. "You came to me because you did not want to be involved in the opium trade. It would hardly be right of me to put you straight back into an activity that you have run from. I saw your face. Your distrust is an insult," he said through gritted teeth. He did not deign to give Ngao so much as another glance. "I will overlook it this time because of Cheng. But remember, if you were ever to doubt me again, I think you should go elsewhere."

Mortified, Ngao bowed his head in shame. He felt terrible. How could he distrust Eng Kim after all he had done for him?

"Well, we'll put this behind us. Let me say one final word about opium in this state. The Malay chiefs hold its trade, not the British, not the Chinese; at least not at the moment. So beware of what you say. It is time. Let us go up to see Raja Abdullah."

A FEAST WAS laid out on a mat of woven red and yellow straw. A huge tureen of rice cooked in turmeric and coconut milk took centre place. Laid all round it were platters and dishes of meat and vegetables. Ngao looked on in wonder. He had never seen food with such rich colours. Strange exotic aromas of spices assailed his senses and teased his taste buds. His mouth watered and he turned questioningly to Eng Kim.

"Curries!" whispered Eng Kim. "*La!* They are very spicy hot! Take small amounts."

They sat cross-legged in a circle on a large mat around the display of food, knees touching knees. The atmosphere was informal. Ngao could hardly believe he was invited to the feast. He looked at his shabby clothes. At least, he did not have to wear his worn out shoes in the house. Everyone was barefoot. He looked around him and saw the bare feet of women hurrying past with more food. He looked quickly away worried that he would be accused of rudeness, recalling the slippered feet of Chinese women and particularly the tiny bound feet of the higher born ladies. Such a display of bare feet in public would be considered improper, even lewd.

"*Sila makan!* Please eat!" invited their host, Raja Abdullah. "We'll talk after we have eaten." He ladled a creamy mustard-coloured sauce onto the pile of rice on the banana leaf that served as a plate in front of him. With his right hand he moulded the rice into the sauce and placed it in his mouth. He followed with another handful of chicken meat. His fingers grew slick with oil and sauce. His face flushed with enjoyment. "*Sila!*" he repeated waving his hand expansively over the food in front of him. "We use our fingers, they are the best cutlery. We don't have chopsticks. I can't use them anyway. Use only your right hand, of course!" He stopped to laugh. "Left hands are for different things," he said with a wink.

Nonplussed, Ngao looked around to see what the others were doing.

Raja Abdullah saw his hesitance. "You need spoons?" he asked Ngao teasingly. "You can have them if you feel more comfortable. I prefer my fingers and banana leaves to plates or bowls for that matter. "

Ngao shook his head, smiled and following the example of the Raja, dipped his hand into a finger bowl to wash. He took a spoonful of the curry and moulded the rice into the pieces of meat and sauce. He placed the resulting mound of food into his mouth. The impact was immediate. Tears streamed from his eyes and he broke out in a sweat. His tongue burned and his ears turned a bright red.

Raja Abdullah laughed. "*Sedap?* Delicious?" he asked delighted at Ngao's discomfort. "Try this," he suggested, pointing to a plate of fish with a red sauce. "Cooked in chillies and tamarind!" His eyes, the colour of liquid toffee, twinkled in amusement, defying Ngao to decline.

Eng Kim looked on glad not to be in the limelight. He had experienced the dishes before and was glad not to be under scrutiny. He fiddled with the food in front of him, careful to leave most of the sauce aside, and eating only tiny morsels of the meat and fish. Someone had once confided that twenty or so chillies were ground up to make the paste for that one dish alone!

Cornered, Ngao gamely heaped a spoonful of the fish and sauce on his banana leaf. He could smell the spicy heat emanating from them. His fingers tingled as they once more moulded the rice into the sauce. He took a deep breath and popped the ball of food into his mouth. Again his eyes streamed. His lips burned and tingled. He reached out for the tumbler of water, took a big gulp and pronounced, "*Sedap!*" Something akin to respect glinted in Raja Abdullah's eye and Eng Kim gave a voluble sigh of relief.

"Good man!" Abdullah said to Eng Kim, his fingers, still moist with the sauce, pointing at Ngao.

As the last dish was cleared away, the light-hearted atmosphere that had held sway in the room disappeared.

"So!" exclaimed Raja Abdullah, his eyebrows raised a fraction, a smile still on his face. He left that single word hanging in the air, expectant, incomplete. He did not wish to open up a discussion that he knew would involve a loss of face and show too much keenness. Eng Kim took the one syllable as a cue to speak. "You sent me a message saying you would like a loan of $35,000 to open up your own mine and that you will need Chinese labour," he said coming straight to the point. "We can supply both. In return, I would like the sole concession to supply food to the workers. I shall import rice from Siam where I have a contact. I would also like some land in return."

Ngao repeated Eng Kim's statement in Malay, modifying the directness of the Chinese language with flowery and respectful overtones. Raja Abdullah listened intently; his face initially stern and shocked in response to Eng Kim's matter-of-fact voice became mollified.

Questions, answers, counter arguments and proposals went back and forth with Ngao smoothing out the edges. They discussed the location of the Raja's mine, the size of the Chinese labour force needed, the repayment of the loan and the interest charged. By late afternoon, an agreement was finally reached. Raja Abdullah was pleased. Eng Kim too looked satisfied.

"Shall I write down the agreement and you can take it to Singapore to have it translated officially into Malay?" Ngao asked Eng Kim. "Then the Raja will be able to read the agreement in Malay and verify the terms, and you will have the Chinese version."

"What a good idea!" said Eng Kim. "Tell him."

Raja Abdullah was delighted with the proposal. "Too many agreements reached in discussions fall apart later if they are not written in black and white." He pointed to his own head, "The brain can forget!" He was well pleased for he had not thought of it.

He looked round the room as though in search of something. His eyes fell on a young girl carrying a tray of drinks. "Here," he said waving an arm carelessly towards her, "take Rohani. She will go home with you and help you keep house. A present from me."

"Please! It is not necessary," pleaded Ngao. He was shocked. Embarrassed he looked to the girl to see if she had heard. She had her eyes down and merely stood still as though in waiting for a decision on her fate. All he could see were her long lashes laid like a fan on her flushed dusky cheeks. Was she shamed by it all, by her helplessness? Ngao was upset for her and again repeated that it would not be necessary for him to be so rewarded.

Ignoring Ngao's protests, Raja Abdullah was already bellowing for the girl. "I will not hear of it. She is a present from me," he beamed with satisfaction. "Take her and use her as you wish. She will cook, clean, do anything for you."

He turned fiercely to address the girl who had come forward soft-footed, head bowed low. "See that you obey him! Hear me!"

"Thank him," whispered Eng Kim to Ngao. He had guessed what had been exchanged. "Do not offend him by refusing his gift of thanks."

ONCE OUT OF the house, Ngao turned to Eng Kim. "What shall I do? I have no place for the girl. We can't put her up in the settlement," he said pointing to the sprawling medley of lean-to's and huts. "It would not be suitable. The accommodation is for men." He looked at the young girl behind him. She was a pretty girl about 18 years old. He had noticed her earlier because of her shy winsome smile. She had said nothing so far. She still kept her eyes down. Ngao followed her eyes and saw her bare feet. "I won't be able to clothe and feed her," he added lamely, embarrassed by her bare feet there for all to see.

"Well, you will have to let her stay with you in the temporary hut you are occupying now. When you move to Ampang where the new tin mines will be, we will find you more suitable accommodation. You cannot on any account return her to the Raja. At best he would feel insulted; worst he might think she had failed to please you and take it out on her."

Ngao looked doubtful. He could already picture what his aunt would say and worse still, what Hua would think if she was looking over him. "I really do not need a maid, a woman," he protested.

"You are no longer a coolie. Remember that," ordered Eng Kim. "From today, I am appointing you as my representative in Selangor. I am very impressed with what you did today."

He placed an arm around the young man. He had not expected Ngao's linguistic skill and silently thanked his kinsman Cheng for having brought him to his attention. He had not quite believed it when he was told that Ngao had mastered Malay.

"You must think of the future," he continued. "You might well need a woman to look after you eventually. Continue to do well by me and you will soon be free of your debts. As from now I am increasing your wages to reflect your increased responsibilities. You will not receive them as hard cash. Instead your debts will be repaid at a faster rate. Once they are repaid your wages will be your own and you will be free to do what ever you like with them.

Ngao shook his head. He was still not willing to assume responsibility for the girl.

"Come, come. Consider it done. I'll cover the cost of her maintenance until you can take over," said Eng Kim.

That night, Ngao slept once more out in the open, giving over the one room in the hut to Rohani.

Chapter 23

BEILIU CITY

IN THE SOUTHERN provinces of China, the Taiping Rebellion took a new turn. Fighting between factions of the rebellion intensified after its leader Hong Xiu Quan killed his former ally Yang along with his entire family. Hong's already weak support from the middle class dwindled further. They rebelled against his extreme rules on separation of the sexes and his relentless attempt to uproot Confucianism. Gradually, the landed gentry and the middle class, even those who had supported him initially, sided with the government forces. Yet, despite his weakened power, Hong, helped by a cousin, succeeded in taking over Hangzhou and Suchou. So the balance of the war waxed and waned; the killing and suffering raged on.

The people of Beiliu adjusted to these changes; their major concern remained a lack of food. Belts had to be tightened and the choice of what to eat modified. Vegetarian versions of chicken meat made with soya appeared. Foods became saltier and more intense in taste to liven up taste buds. In the Ong household, fermented bean curds with added chilly spices were eaten instead of fish and meat. Pickled turnips replaced fresh leafy vegetables and boiled rice was rationed to once a week. Watery gruel became their mainstay. Life continued.

Heong Yook grew even more grateful to Mui as time passed. Only she continued to be unafraid to search the city for food, risking her life to get provisions for the household. When Wan Fook, fresh from his confrontation with the Englishman Grime, told her that he suspected Mui's role in Hua's demise, Heong Yook's confidence in the maid wavered. She felt repugnance when he told her how Mui had giggled when Grime said he thought Hua was a virgin. She started watching her like a hawk hoping to find an excuse to get rid of her. It proved to be impossible. Shao Peng was completely attached to Mui. Months passed. Reluctantly. Heong Yook reconciled herself that Mui was there to stay. While she behaved coarsely and was prone to bicker with the cook, she was totally loyal to the little girl and the household. She was, Heong Yook concluded, a product of her circumstances, a survivor who had acted badly in the past simply to survive. She was not intrinsically evil.

THE MORNING BEGAN like every other. In the city, fighting continued like an unstoppable tide. Within the barracaded Ong household, a semblance of normality continued. Shao Peng after finishing her studies was with Mui in the courtyard.

She had grown and her once thin frame had filled out. She was on her knees bent over a game of five pebbles. Two fat plaits of hair hung down her back, skimming her bottom.

"I've got it," she yelled looking up with triumphant joy in her eyes. "I can do it! Watch!" She grabbed the five pebbles with one hand and then threw them up in the air catching them on the back of the hand. One slid off, leaving four. Unfazed, she threw the other four up in the air, snatched the fallen pebble and still managed to catch the other pebbles before they hit the ground. "Watch me!" she insisted, her hand flipping and throwing.

From within, one of the servants shouted. "Mui! Mui! The messenger is here. He has a letter. Come and get it!"

Shao Peng let the pebbles fall with a clatter on the ground. "From father! It must be a letter from father," she cried. "Wait! I am coming." She ran ahead leaving Mui huffing and puffing in pursuit.

❀ ❀ ❀

In the sitting room, Heong Yook sat with the letter in her hand. She motioned her charge to calm down.

"Open it, read it," cried Shao Peng, still unable to contain her excitement, her eyes bright with curiosity.

"Well sit down and I'll read to you." With deliberate slowness Heong Yook opened the letter, smoothing the creases of each fold, taking her time. A smile played at the corner of her mouth. She was teasing Shao Peng, refusing to read until her charge stayed still and raising an eyebrow now and then, when Shao Peng, full of impatience, urged her to hurry.

My Esteemed Aunt Heong Yook,

I hope this letter finds you and Uncle well. How is Shao Peng? Every day that passes brings us closer to the day when I can send for her. It has taken much longer than I had expected. I hope your contact is still in agreement to help bring her to me. From all accounts, the petitions to lift the Imperial Government's restriction on women migrants have not been successful but you have promised that you have found a way. I know Aunty that you do not promise lightly.

In a few more months my debt to my boss will be fully repaid. I will be free. This means that I will be able to start saving for a business of my own. I am so excited. Soon I can send for my daughter. The day cannot come fast enough. I have not seen her for two years. I hope she still remembers and recognises me.

I have moved to an area called Ampang. The discovery of tin deposits here has led to an influx of Chinese labourers to mine the ore. Raja Abdullah – one of the local leaders I referred to in an earlier letter – has been very active encouraging Chinese to open up tin mines. Only they, he believed, are brave or foolhardy enough to venture into the area.

When tin was first discovered in Ampang, almost all the Chinese labour sent in died of pestilence and disease. Despite this thousands of them have continued to flood in as a result of the encouragement of the Raja. The Raja himself has opened up a mine of his own. My boss Lim Eng Kim recruits the labour for this as well as other mines. The local people are not keen on the work. We are on very good terms with the Raja and it is likely he will entrust our company to collect taxes from the miners on his behalf. A disagreement has sprung up between Raja Abdullah and one of his kinsmen and the Raja is unlikely to give the task to his own people.

There is frequent fighting between the different branches of the local nobility and they call upon the Chinese societies to back them up. Imagine Aunty! The two biggest societies, the Ghee Hin and Hai San, are already at each other's throats; they need no further encouragement. I try not to be involved. They call me the 'pen pusher' but I do more than just the administration. Eng Kim has put me in charge of sourcing provisions for the miners who live in the new settlements that have sprung up in the Klang Valley. We bring in rice from Siam, which is to the north of us. The local farmers grow only enough for themselves..

Aunty I have such plans for the future. I hope to start a factory producing noodles and soya sauce. There is a big market for it. I remember when I was a small boy in your house, Cook always made her own noodles. Would you asg her for the recipe? If you could write her instructions down, I will experiment with them. It will be exciting to produce it on my own.

Meantime I am still trying to learn English. It is more difficult than Malay. I am trying to do it properly by learning to write as well as read it. Unfortunately I am not making much progress. We have no English schools and, unlike Singapore, not many English people. You see, the British do not control this part of the country. As a result I have very little opportunity to speak. I have been told this will change soon. The British are also coming to mine tin in Selangor. I have some hopes that missionary schools like those in Singapore will be established. The Sultan of Johor was educated by Christian missionaries and has started a school with a western curriculum in Johor. Perhaps, one will also be built here.

Malaya must sound very wild and war-torn to you. I have learned to live with it just like you must have adjusted to the ever-raging wars in China. One thing is certain. Everyone here wants to do well and works very hard to achieve it. Despite all the fighting and quarrels, tin is produced and business flourishes!

Please tell Shao Peng I miss her. I have now a proper house. It is not big but adequate. I also have a helper, a Malay girl, bestowed on me by the Raja. She would probably help to look after Shao Peng when she comes. It will not be long.

My best wishes to you and Uncle.

Your loving and respectful nephew, Ngao

Heong Yook looked at the smudges around the last paragraph, particularly around the word 'helper' and pondered. She kept her uneasiness to herself and smiled at Shao Ping. "Did you understand all of that?" she asked the young girl.

"Not all. I don't understand the bit about the fighting, the taxes and ... and ... the ... the uninteresting parts."

Heong Yook smiled amused. "What then do you understand?"

"That soon father will send for me," she cried clapping her hands. She stopped suddenly. "Who is the lady who will look after me?" Shao Peng asked.

❀ ❀ ❀

WAN FOOK WAS in his study reading when Heong Yook came in with the letter clutched in one hand. She felt a moment of tenderness seeing her husband absorbed over his books. Since their reconciliation he had become his old self once again. He devoted his time to his studies. Despite the battles fought in the streets between government forces and the rebels, and despite the attacks launched by foreigners on the waterfront, work in the pottery had resumed. Work came in fits and starts but it was better than before. They had even managed to export a little.

"I am worried," she said waving the letter. "Ngao seems to be doing well but he mentions that he has a woman with him now, a native woman he calls his helper. What can he mean? Do you think he is involved with her?" she asked with a frown on her face.

"Does it matter?" asked Wan Fook. "Hua is dead, almost two years now. What do you expect him to do?"

"She is not Chinese!" exclaimed Heong Yook. "Will Shao Peng have to call her mother?"

"Aren't you getting ahead of yourself? Come, let me read the letter." He took the letter from her and read quickly. "I would not see too much into it if I were you," he advised. "She could be the cook. Anyway, you should not meddle. It is none of your business."

Chapter 24

AMPANG

NGAO PAUSED AT the bottom of the stairway leading up to his house and looked up. The house followed the style of Malay buildings where the first floor was raised on stilts. He was glad that he had decided to build it that way. During the monsoon, the rains were fast and furious. Flooding was common. He had been through such a storm since moving in. The water had lapped and swirled round the supporting pillars while he took shelter on the upper floor.

He placed one hand on the banister and ran his fingers gently along the wood, feeling the texture and the warmth of the grain. At times like this, he could hardly believe his change of fortune. His heart sang and with it he felt a renewed sense of gratitude to Eng Kim. It would have been impossible without his help.

The house was modest unlike the other residences of the wealthy and successful. For Ngao it was all he desired. His very first house! He counted himself fortunate to have been able to build it in this part of the town, some distance away from the confluence of rivers Klang and Gombak where thousands of Chinese migrants congregated and away from the makeshift mining camps in Ampang. He had pleaded for the house to be built there citing the danger for Rohani if they were to stay in the Chinese settlement. "Should something happen to her," he had warned, "battles will be fought between the Malays and Chinese." And his employer had agreed. Behind his plea, he was also mindful that Shao Peng would soon be with him. He needed a safe place for his daughter.

He climbed the stairs onto a small portico and then went into the house, shedding his shoes as he went in. His heart quickened expectantly. A meal had been laid out. He lifted the colourful woven conical food cover and smiled. He remembered his first taste of curries at Raja Abdullah's house and his mouth tingled with expectation. Strange that the spicy heat that once brought him to tears was something he now looked forward to. He wished Rohani would sit and eat with him. It would be so much better than eating on his own.

He sat down. The house was so quiet all he could hear were the sounds of geckoes and insects. They seemed to accentuate its emptiness. Impulsively he got up and walked to the back of the house and descended the back stairway. He crossed the short patch of grass to the outhouse that was the kitchen. A smell of cooking drifted towards him. It was sweet, unfamiliar. He moved towards it. "Rohani," he called softly.

She was standing in front of the stove stirring something dense and the colour of caramel. He saw the bend of her head and the wisps of hair around the nape of her neck. They had escaped from the ponytail she had tied high on her head and now swayed softly with her motion. She blew softly upwards to dispel a lock of black hair that had fallen over her eyes, her lips pursed with the lower one pulled forward to direct her breath. She was so intent she did not hear him come into the kitchen nor did she expect him. He never came to this part of the house. It was her domain. Her bedroom was next to the kitchen.

"Rohani?" he called again.

She dropped the ladle with a clatter. "Master! I did not hear you. Did you need something? I have already laid out your lunch."

"Come and eat with me, there is so much food."

"I'll eat when you have finished. I can't eat with you," she replied dropping her eyes.

He realised at that moment that she reminded him of Hua, especially those large expressive brown eyes. They were not almond shaped like Hua's but exuded warmth just like hers. They were shy now and focused on the floor. But he had seen how mischievous they could be at times. When he first pronounced her name she had doubled up in laughter. "No! Rohani!" she said, rolling the *rrr*, her lips parted to reveal perfectly even teeth, "Not Lohani!" He had tried to explain to her that in Chinese, the sound 'r' did not exist. She did not believe him and for days after he had practised rolling his *rrrs*.

"Why?" he asked. He did not understand why he was doing this but he persisted. He did not even know what made him come to the kitchen to ask her to eat with him in the first place. He was puzzled by his own action and a sharp pang of guilt hit him. Would Hua mind?

"No Master, you eat please. The food will be cold."

"Why don't you talk to me and tell me about your family while I eat. I do not like to eat on my own. You know I am not a *towgay*, 'boss man'. I am like you; I am here to work."

"Master, I'll come up in a minute. I have to finish this," she insisted indicating the pot. "*Kaya*, coconut jam, for breakfast. *Manis! Sedap! Buat dengan telor dan santan!* It is sweet! Very good, made with lots of eggs and coconut cream!" She broke into a smile. Her dusky skin glowed from the heat of the stove and tendrils of hair clung to her face. He had noticed her quickness to smile and was gladdened by it.

Reluctantly he returned to the house, shedding his shoes once more as he stepped into the cool wooden floor of the interior. He sat and ate, using his fingers as he had been taught. He would have preferred to eat with chopsticks but he deferred to the custom of the locals when at home for he did not wish to hurt her feelings. He ate slowly, marvelling at how he had adapted to the Malay way of living. Perhaps the Raja had been cannier than he thought when he insisted on presenting Rohani to him. With Rohani, he had not only changed his way of eating, he also spoke Malay so much so that he even thought in Malay in the process. He washed his hands in the finger bowl and went out to the balcony. Would Shao Peng like it here, he wondered. Would she get on with Rohani? This was vital. There were few women around for his daughter to befriend.

He heard the soft patter of bare feet and recognising the sound, turned around. Rohani had just placed a glass of water on the table and was clearing the dishes. Her slight frame moved gracefully around the table. The ankle length wrap that she called a *sarong* accentuated her movements. He found his eyes drawn to her. Once more he was struck by how much she reminded him of Hua, not so much in looks, but how she carried herself. Perhaps he was imagining these similarities. With a shock, he realised that he had grown very fond of the girl and could not imagine living here without her. He looked away quickly, troubled by his feelings. He felt guilty.

"Rohani," he said gravely, "my daughter will be coming to join me soon, perhaps in a few months' time. Do think you will be able to look after her? Her mother is no longer with us."

"Of course I can look after her. I have many brothers and sisters. I am used to it. I looked after them until I was sent to Raja Abdullah," she replied. "It would be nice to have her here Master. Nice for you and also for me." Her delight was apparent in her huge smile.

Ngao heaved a sigh of relief. "I will write to my aunt now. She is looking after my little girl."

That evening he went to see Eng Kim.

ENG KIM'S HOUSE was not far from Ngao's. Set well back from the road, it was a replica of the British mansions in Singapore. He was proud of the wealth and success he had achieved within the short time he had established himself in the Klang Valley. This was his second home. His main house and office remained in Singapore where his principal wife resided.

The evening air was balmy, infused with the heavy perfume exuded by the frangipane trees that lined the pebbled driveway. Ngao breathed deeply and walked quickly towards the house. The sound of his footsteps echoed in the silence. Eng Kim had invited him for a quiet dinner. Ngao dug into his pocket and felt for the letter he had written that afternoon. He would ask

Eng Kim to help send it to his aunt. He would also have to discuss his latest proposition with him.

"YOUR PROPOSAL TO bring your daughter over is commendable. I feel though it might also be foolish. How are you going to look after her?" asked Eng Kim. "And you must know that the conditions for travel are horrendous. You have made that journey yourself. How could you subject her to that?"

They had just finished their dinner. Eng Kim's secondary wives had retreated to the sitting room and the two men were left out on the balcony. The night air was cool. A full moon had risen casting its silvery light over the trees and plants in the garden.

"Rohani will look after her when I work. I will also find her a teacher," replied Ngao.

"There is really no need for her to study. She will marry well because she would be a rarity if you succeed in bringing her here. There are not enough Chinese women," said Eng Kim. "Why do you wish to fill her head with education?" He was amused and thought it a nonsensical idea.

"You might be right. Still, I would like her to learn just as I did. It has stood me in good stead."

Ngao ignored the frown that appeared on Eng Kim's face. His boss clearly disagreed with his views. "As for the journey," he continued quickly to avoid a discussion of the advantages and disadvantages of education for girls, "I worry and fret about it all the time. In fact, I have written a letter to my aunt to ask for more details on the travel arrangements made for

Shao Peng. I hope you will help send it on for me when you get to Singapore."

"Are you sure your aunt could arrange your daughter's travel?" asked Eng Kim taking the letter.

"My aunt seems confident. Until now, I had no idea when I might be able to send for her so I had not asked for any details of the travel plan. The situation was fluid and all that I worried about was whether the Chinese government would allow it. With my own house and my debt almost repaid, I think now would be the right time to ask for details."

"I suppose in a way you are in luck. In the past month emigration laws for Chinese women have been relaxed. Mind you," Eng Kim said wagging his finger, "it is still considered immoral and socially unacceptable for women to travel overseas. You should take that into account. Despite the relaxation of the laws, few respectable women have left China. Provisions to transport them over are, I would say, non-existent."

Ngao ignored Eng Kim's pessimistic comments; he felt it was a ploy to discourage him from bringing his daughter over. He felt sure that his aunt would succeed in getting Shao Peng to him. She had seemed so confident. His eyes strayed to the interior of the house where Eng Kim's two secondary wives were sitting together. How did he manage to have so many? Did they come from China and if so, how did they get here?

Eng Kim followed his gaze and grinned. "I know what you wish to ask. Your eyes betray your thoughts. So I will spare you the embarrassment. I will tell you. My two wives seated over there, the ones you have just been staring at, are from China. A few years back, a terrible quarrel between different factions broke out in Amoy. My two wives are sisters. They fled on a fishing boat with their mother from Amoy to Singapore. I brought them up here to keep the peace with my first wife in Singapore who is local born, a *Nyonya*. Her family is from Malacca and has been here for centuries. Her great-great-grandfather from Swatow married a Malay woman."

Ngao had not expected such a frank disclosure.

"Their circumstance," said Eng Kim gesturing towards the two sisters, "is exceptional, thanks to their fishermen relatives. They are the lucky ones. Many others are less so. Some have been brought here by deceit. Some were kidnapped and forced over. Many were innocent young girls. A fortunate few were married off on arrival to wealthy Chinese men. But others were less blessed and have been forced into prostitution." Eng Kim shrugged his shoulders, "My heart goes out to them. Still, you would not want Shao Peng to be herded with them when travelling here."

Eng Kim sighed. He was clearly in a talkative mood. He suspected Ngao had an ulterior reason for his interest in his two wives.

"Are you thinking of remarrying?" he asked. "There is no reason why one should only think of Chinese women. Many men have taken up with local ladies." He glanced at Ngao for his reaction from the corner of his eye. "I know of several important English merchants in Singapore who have such relationships." This time he looked directly at Ngao for any giveaway signs. He was intrigued and wondered how Ngao got on with Rohani.

"Thank you for sharing your story with me," said Ngao somewhat formally. He had heard enough. He could guess where his boss was steering the conversation. He felt embarrassed with the confidence his boss had divulged and was not keen to answer his questions. He got up abruptly, almost toppling his chair in his haste. "I have urgent matters to attend to and have to leave now," he said.

If Eng Kim had thought he might elicit Ngao's confidence in return for sharing his own he was wrong. He lingered on the balcony after Ngao left the house. He was not convinced that Ngao should bring his daughter to Selangor. He thought of the danger and the hardship. The journey would certainly be terrible unless the aunt came up with some astounding idea. It might, however, be good for Ngao. Ever since he met him, the man had been planning and longing for the day when he could be reunited with his child. It would certainly help ease his loneliness. His eyes glimmered. He wondered again about Ngao's relationship with Rohani. There was no reaction from Ngao when he mentioned the possibility of a Malay wife. "*Ahhh,*" he said letting out a long sigh. "A good lad! Keeps it to himself."

Chapter 25

SHAMIAN AND BEILIU

THE SHELVES WERE empty. Crates of books lined the floor. At one corner, a cupboard stood bereft of its belongings, its door swinging despondently on creaking hinges, opening and closing, opening and closing. The room would soon be cleared completely. All signs of his occupancy would be wiped away.

Edward Grime walked to the window. He watched the junks, ships and steamers in the port. Some distance away, a number of smaller Chinese junks hovered around a large ship flying the British flag. Jardine Matheson! Probably off-loading opium to the Chinese junks. He looked away, unwilling to witness a transaction he despised.

His days in Shamian Island, in fact in China, would soon be over. After the fire in Canton they had moved temporarily to Honam before coming here to Shamian. He had never quite got over the move. He felt isolated. He did not feel connected with China as he did when he lived in the foreign enclave in Canton. Moreover, with the East India Company now nationalised and India brought directly under the Crown, he felt his position had become somewhat untenable. It was time to leave and return to England. His heart was not in his job. By leaving, he would at least not be involved any longer with the handling of ill-gotten opium money for the purchase of tea. Perhaps his return to England would give him a new perspective and he might see the Opium war as some others evidently did.

He sighed and shrugged his shoulders to relieve the tension in his neck, moving his head from side to side. He did not know how his family would receive the news. He was not even sure if he could fit into the English way of life after being away so long. He should visit the new colonies on the way home, he decided. Singapore has been placed directly under the British Crown and there were also the other two Straits Settlements, Penang and Malacca. Perhaps, they would be interesting postings.

He moved closer to the window and looked down on the street below. It stretched from one end of the small man-made island to the other, skirting around buildings that had been erected following the unrest in the Canton foreign enclave. There were few signs that this was part of China. No wonder, he thought. The British held four fifths of the island with the French holding the remaining fifth. They controlled one of the two bridges that linked it to the mainland. The other was under the French. They were cut off completely from the mainland. Heavily guarded, few Chinese were allowed on the island. It was considered safer but at what cost. They would never get to know the Chinese people. He had never agreed with many of his compatriots who see the Chinese as a barbaric and obstreperous race.

He went to the other end of the room. He felt like a caged animal pacing within confines he had created himself. He had grown to love Canton. His secret sojourns in the city opened up a world that he admired and loved. He felt that if his fellow officers had been allowed the same opportunity they too would see China in a different light. The fault lay with his own country as much as with the Chinese with their draconian restrictions on foreigners and insistence on their superiority.

His footsteps rang hollow in the empty room as he paced up and down. How could he get word to Wan Fook that he would be leaving? How could he explain that once he left, it would be difficult to carry out his promise to secrete the little girl out of China to her father? He had made the promise in good faith. So far they had not called for his help. He had waited and waited but he could not wait forever. Unbidden, his sense of guilt rose to haunt him. He must try to help them, he told himself, to atone for the wrong he had done.

IN THE HOUSEHOLD of Heong Yook and Wan Fook, excitement reigned. The messenger from Singapore had left. Heong Yook sat with her hands resting on her knees, the letter clasped between her fingers. Wan Fook occupied the seat next to the tea table. Both of them had their eyes on Shao Peng who was jumping up and down for joy.

Heong Yoke folded the letter she had just read out loud. She pressed it against her chest. She felt a pang of pain. She was taken aback by Shao Peng's delight when she was told that she would soon be leaving to join her father. She caught her husband's eye. He must have noticed her sadness. She mustered a smile. Of course, Shao Peng was delighted. Why shouldn't she? But how I shall miss her, Heong Yook thought. I have grown so used to having her around. My day has become structured around her activities. With a rush of emotion, she reached out and caught hold of the little girl and held her close. She would not get to see her anymore once she had gone, she realised, pressing her nose to Shao Peng's hair. From over Shao Peng's head, she saw her husband looking at her intently. She released Shao Peng.

"You and I have to talk," said Wan Fook. "I have to see the Englishman. I have been keeping track of him through the Merchants' Guild. He has moved to Shamian Island. It is not so easy to go there. Both bridges leading to it are heavily guarded."

"You are not thinking of sending her right now are you?" asked Heong Yook. Her mouth turned dry at the thought. "Ngao asked only for the travel arrangements we have in mind. Can we not just find these out from the Englishman and write to Ngao about it? He might not agree to them. He seems worried about the conditions of travel."

"Of course he is worried. The journey will not be easy to say the least."

Wan Fook got up. He had not told his wife of the stories he had heard from men who had made the journey, of the deaths, sickness and hardships. To maintain a sense of tranquillity and wellbeing, a cocoon for his family, he had even ceased all talk of politics and war. It was enough having to cope with the Taiping rebellion in the streets.

He looked at his wife. She had been so happy since Shao Peng joined them. He could not find the courage to tell her that China had finally ceded to the Anglo-French demands to open more treaty ports, to legalise the importation of opium and to allow foreign legations in Peking. In fact he had kept from her all news of the Tientsin Treaties. It was a shame he did not wish to voice to his family. Likewise he did not mention that, almost immediately, China had abrogated the terms by refusing to allow foreign delegations in Peking. War had once again resumed. This might make travelling even more dangerous. It was best that she knew as little as possible.

"I know I was the one who said we should help Shao Peng go to her father. But ... but now it is time for her to leave, I feel so, so sad. She is so dear to me," cried Heong Yook unaware of all that was going on in her husband's mind.

"I know, I know. You have to let her go though," comforted her husband placing an arm around her shoulder. Even as he spoke, he fretted. "Would it be safe for Shao Peng to travel?" he wondered.

WAN FOOK STEPPED into the *Co-Hong*, the Merchants Guild, in Canton. The building looked slightly the worse for wear from the outside. The walls were dilapidated. Streaks of dirt marked them and in places, the pink walls had been defaced with posters and graffiti. Inside, however, the place was still a hive of activity; despite all that was happening, business continued. He cornered Tan, his contact and friend in the Guild. It was Tan who kept him informed of Grime. After a lengthy exchange of greetings, Wan Fook was impatient to ask the question uppermost in his mind deferring only for the sake of politeness. He asked instead as a prelude how business was.

"*Bu cuo!* Not bad," replied Tan in Mandarin, giving his friend a sheepish grin. "Considering the circumstances," he added.

"Do our ships still travel to *Nanyang,* the south-eastern countries?" Wan asked finally seizing his chance.

'Of course," replied Tan incredulous that Wan Fook should even ask such a question. "The demand for Chinese workers is still on the rise; we send thousands of people to *Nanyang* every month. Singapore, the Malay countries, Indonesia and Siam are all clamouring for our labour just as much as our men are crying out to leave China to earn money to maintain their families here. Times are so hard but you know that."

"Can the boats travel in peace? Is it safe now that we have another war with the foreigners over this blasted opium trade?

"It does not affect travel very much. Foreign ships do not attack boats carrying labour that they themselves seek. Anyway, the battles have shifted further north to Tientsin. They are now bombarding the forts in the Hai River, just south of Tientsin. Canton is temporarily reprieved. The battle is not at sea; it has moved on land."

Wan Fook sighed with relief. "You remember the Englishman, Edward Grime, the one you have so kindly kept an eye on for me? I would like to see him. Can we arrange that?"

"Mmmm! There have been lots of changes since we last spoke. I heard he might be leaving. He is a good man, one of the few who seems to care about us. He was the protégé of the previous British Superintendent of Trade, George Robinson. Sadly Robinson was dismissed for trying to stop opium from being smuggled into the country. Their association has weakened Grime's standing. This together with the dismantling of the British East India Company might be why he is leaving."

"Then I need to see him immediately," said Wan Fook, his face grey with concern. "Please, help me."

"It will be difficult. It is a very awkward time for him to consort with Chinese, so I do not know if he will see you. Apparently, this week the Anglo-French delegation sent to Peking to discuss the terms of peace was ambushed, tortured and killed," warned Tan.

"Please try. It is a personal matter and has nothing to do with opium or matters of state," pleaded Wan Fook. "I'll wait here if you will send word to him."

❀ ❀ ❀

"HURRY!" SHOUTED WAN FOOK the minute he arrived home from Shamian after seeing Edward Grime. "We don't have a moment to spare. The Englishman is leaving in two days time and I have to take Shao Peng to him. The journey will take a day."

Wild-eyed, Wan Fook was gesticulating to his wife and Mui as he related his meeting with Grime. "He is returning to England but intends to stop en route in Singapore. He will take Shao Peng himself, if we can get her to him in time. There is no way round it because once he has left China, there will be no one to bring her to her father. The boats carrying labour are not options we can consider. It would be too rough and moreover, we have no one we can trust."

Heong Yook was speechless. So soon! Her eyes welled up with tears that streamed down her face.

"Wife, say something! I am as upset as you. I wish he had given us more notice, told us sooner that he is leaving China, so we could think more clearly. He said that it was as sudden for him as it is for us."

"Can you trust him?" interrupted Mui.

Wan Fook looked at her with dislike. Unlike his wife, he maintained his suspicion of Mui. "Did I ask you?" He growled. He gave her a cutting look meant to put her in her place.

"She has a point," said Heong Yook. Her lips quivered. She brushed away her tears brusquely using her sleeves.

"Tan says that he is an honourable man. What is the alternative? He is the only one who can do it. We have to dress her as a boy and he will take her as his page."

They stood looking at each other, each with their own thoughts.

"So do we let her go with him?" he demanded finally. He had hurried all the way from Shamian to Beiliu with barely a stop to eat or drink and he was in a highly excitable state. "Or do you wish to smuggle her onto a boat with the coolies and risk her being abducted and sold?" he asked in the same loud tone. "With him, the journey will be better. And at least, we know enough about him to hold him to ransom. He will put in writing his agreement with us so that we will have proof he has taken her. I have asked Tan to be our witness."

He waited for Heong Yook to reply. He became impatient. He had to leave for Shamian and time was not on their side. "Come, we have to decide," he insisted. "Or do we keep her here with us?"

Heong Yook sobbed. The slow trickle of tears became a torrent. She covered her eyes; her breath came in rasps. She, who had always shown strength and restraint, broke down completely. She had placed all her hopes on Shao Peng. She had lost her son. She had no children to whom she could give her love. That place they called Malaya seemed so unreal, so distant. She would never see Shao Peng again. But she had promised Ngao. Then, with the same fortitude she had shown in the past, she stopped sobbing.

"Mui, go to my cupboard. In the bottom drawer, you will see some boy's clothes. They belonged to my son when he was a child. Bring them to me."

Wan Fook came to her and took her hand. He led her to a chair and sat her down. Reaching out to the teapot nestled in the tea box, he poured out a cup of tea for her. He had never done this before. Custom would not permit him as the man of the house, the head in the family to serve his wife tea. He did it ceremoniously with both hands on the fragile teacup and handed it to her. Mui looked on in astonishment. Her hand flew to her mouth.

"*Qing he!* Please drink," he said quietly in Mandarin to his wife. He didn't want Mui to eavesdrop on his deference to his wife. Heong Yook took the cup and drank deeply.

"We won't have time to answer Ngao's queries on travel arrangements," said Wan Fook. "But I shall write and tell him why we had to make such a quick decision. I will give the letter to Shao Peng to carry to her father."

"Please write down Eng Kim's address and the new address that Ngao gave us. Give a copy each to Shao Peng and Grime. And, write our address for both of them as well."

Heong Yook voice shook. "I ... I would like to have some time with Shao Peng while Mui alters her clothes and you write the letter."

"We will have to leave soon. We don't have much time," cautioned Wan Fook.

"I know," she replied.

❀ ❀ ❀

SHAO PENG WAS asleep in bed, curled into a tight ball clasping a bolster to her chest. She had untied her plaits and her hair was spread out on the white pillow. One leg was thrown over the *meen lap*, the silk duvet that Heong Yook had lovingly embroidered with chrysanthemum flowers. Heong Yook lowered herself on the bed and leaned over. "Wake up!" she whispered in Shao Peng's ear. "Wake up!"

"Shao Peng sat up. "What's wrong? Is it morning?" she asked, blurry-eyed.

"We have to get ready. You will leave as soon as we have packed your things. An Englishman will take you to your father. His name is Edward Grime. He is waiting and Uncle Wan Fook will take you to him."

"You mean right now?" asked Shao Peng sliding off the bed. Her eyes were alert and round with excitement.

"Yes, as soon as everything is ready."

"Are you coming with me?" asked Shao Peng, suddenly afraid.

"No! I can't come with you. Women are ... are ... not allowed and for this reason we have to dress you as a boy. On no account should you reveal that you are a girl. Only the Englishman knows. It will be dangerous if you let slip you are a girl. Do you understand?"

The little girl nodded.

Heong Yook's eyes filled with tears even as she tried to put on a cheerful face. She reached out to hug the little girl. "Don't cry," Shao Peng said solemnly. "I shall come back to see you when I grow up. I promise."

Her aunt released her. "I have to shave your head leaving only the hair at the back to plat into a queue. I can't bear it. Your beautiful hair!" she cried.

"No! Don't do that," cried Mui entering the room with her arm full of clothes for Shao Peng. "The journey is long. Who will shave her head during the journey? It will just grow back. Can't we just tie her hair into a pigtail and put this black cloth cap on top of her head to cover it? No one would know unless she takes it off."

"I won't take it off," promised Shao Peng. "Please don't shave my head. I'll even sleep with the cap on."

"Promise me that you will study hard when you are with your father. Remember to write. I shall write to you. I have sewn our address and some money into the seams of your tunic. Take care of it and do not tell anyone. Yes, before I forget, there is also the recipe for making noodles." Heong Yook lips quivered and tears rolled freely down her cheeks.

"I will be fine," comforted Shao Peng with a brave face. "I can take care of myself. Is the Englishman nice?" she asked. She paled. Suddenly the full weight of the situation hit her. She was afraid. Time had softened her memories of the time when she was seized from her home and forcefully taken by strangers. They now returned with force. She was going with someone she had never met before. She burst into tears.

"I ... I hope so," replied her aunt. "I sincerely hope so." She clasped Shao Peng tight, not wanting to let her go.

"Of course you will be fine. You will go in a big steamship," interrupted Wan Fook walking into the room. "It is a new invention and I am told more comfortable than junks. It will be an adventure." He narrowed his eyes and shook his head. "Don't alarm her," his eyes seemed to say.

Holding the girl close to her, Heong Yook held her husband's eyes. "You have to make the Englishman swear that he'll take good care of her," she mimed. "I shall not forgive myself, nor you, if something were to happen to her."

Chapter 26

SELANGOR

THE FIELD WAS cleared of the trees the men had felled. A huge open space stood where there was once impregnable virgin forest. A sharp tang of wood shavings filled the air. Farther to the east was the river. Ngao could see water bouncing off the rocks as the river flowed fast and furious downstream. Froth formed and disappeared. He turned round to face the adjacent mining camp. His shoes squelched. Puddles of water were everywhere. The storm had turned the clearing into a quagmire that the sun was only just beginning to dry out. His cotton tunic clung to him and his legs with their rolled up cotton trousers were splattered with mud. Dribbles of blood covered both legs. Leeches!

He made his way to the river and climbed up a small slope. From this vantage point he could see the crowded campsite with its sea of bobbing heads, black and sleek; some with queues, some without but all of them male. The camp was seething with activity. More and more people had been brought in to work in the mines. As soon as the migrant labour arrived they were put to work. No time was set aside to build houses. The immediate result was a medley of odd buildings hastily assembled. Over time, the increasing numbers and their needs had spun off other business activities. Carpenters brought in initially to build *palongs*, the wooden sluices for the mines, turned their hands to constructing houses. Sturdier buildings began to appear among the lean-tos and odd-shaped huts. Laundrettes strung their clotheslines along pathways. Tunics and trousers fluttered in the breeze. There were food stores and eateries; a stall here and a stall there. Men carried baskets of food on the ends of poles. They walked the streets advertising their wares and hollering for custom.

Gradually a town was in the making. He was excited. He could picture the shops and houses that would be built on the land they had cleared. They needed to work fast because the consignments of rice would soon outgrow the stores they had on the campsite. He ran nimbly down the slope, ignoring the soft plopping of the leeches that had gorged on him. His palms were rough and stinging from the day's work. He had worked shoulder to shoulder with his men. Two more months and he would be free of debt. He would work for Eng Kim as a free man! Soon he would be able to send for Shao Peng. He was impatient to know his aunt's travelling arrangements for his daughter.

He left the men in the field to draw out the boundaries of the buildings. He had no part in this, Eng Kim having employed a builder. He had to go to Raja Abdullah. He had been summoned once again. He wondered what it was about. He hurried, quickening his steps to almost a run.

❀ ❀ ❀

LIGHT SEEPED INTO the room through the open windows brightening up the dark interior with its wooden floors and walls. Waving absent-mindedly to a chair of polished wood, Raja Abdullah invited him to be seated. Ngao noticed that he was preoccupied and clearly agitated; his face was sombre and a frown made two deep lines between his brows.

"*Terima kasih!* Thank you," replied Ngao, declining the chair. "I'll stand, if I may. I came immediately from the camp. I was told it was urgent and I have not changed into clean clothes. *Minta maaf!* Please excuse me!" Conscious of the mud on his clothes and mindful that he might still have leeches on him, he looked down at his bare calves.

"That is the least of my worries. I would think it strange indeed if you were to come straight from the field dressed in clean clothes. I do not stand on ceremony here in this house. It would be different at the Sultan's residence," said Raja Abdullah. He pointed to his own dress, a loose top tucked into a pair of calf length trousers with a short sarong wrapped over it. Tucked into his belt was a *kris*, a short dagger with a serrated edge. His hand went to the kris, and with a swift deft movement he unshielded it. He held it up and looked at it contemplatively. The blade glinted in the light.

"I have an urgent problem," he said, "that must be removed before it gets worse." He glowered at Ngao and for a moment, Ngao panicked.

"My nephew Raja Mahdi is here in Klang," continued the Raja. "He has brought several chests of opium to sell and has refused to pay even the small tax I levied on it. I have had enough of his insolence." His eyes glittered as he slammed the hilt of his kris into his other palm. "He has been a thorn in my side ever since my father-in-law, his grandfather, died. He complains that the stipend I pay him is too small and dares to demand more! My spies tell me he is gathering forces against me. I need your help to build up my defence."

Ngao tried to keep calm. Opium! Once again that dreaded evil raised its head. All manner of thoughts raced through his mind. "My men are labourers," he blurted. "They are not trained in warfare. We are in the midst of building a town. Eng Kim is not here. I can't make any decision without his consent."

Ngao bowed his head and waited for the avalanche of abuse he thought would surely come. When it came, he almost jumped, so loud was the Raja.

"Are you telling me you are not going to help me out? You ... you are here because I gave you the opportunity to be so. Make no mistake! I can easily cancel your permit."

Abdullah glared at Ngao. He bristled with rage. Ngao saw how he held the kris, the knuckles red with the strain exerted on them. Ngao thought of the loan that had been given to the Raja in return for the permission to supply labour for the mines and food to the people. It was a permit that had been paid for many times. It would not be worth his skin to mention such details nor had he authority to do so. Only Eng Kim might choose to do so and he was not here. He thought quickly.

"We are better used as a source of supplies for your fighters. If this is a long drawn out battle, you will need a reliable source of food for your troops and we can provide that."

"My immediate need is a troop of fighters," bellowed Abdullah. His forces were stretched. Ever since the death of his father-in-law the Sultan, there had been fighting and rivalry between contenders for the throne. His father-in-law had not appointed an heir. According to custom, the son of the official royal wife should take the throne, but he was young and powerless against his older brothers, the children of the Sultan's concubines. Raja Abdullah had joined in the fray by backing another son-in-law to the throne. The battle for power had stretched his resources to the hilt.

"Tell me how I can do it? How I can get the reinforcements I need?" Raja Abdullah growled.

"The only way is to bring outside forces. There is one recent arrival amongst the Chinese who is already fast making a name for himself. He is Yap Ah Loy, a Fei Chew Hakka. I have heard he is a wonderful strategist and very brave. He belongs to the *Hai San* society. Ask him," suggested Ngao in desperation.

Raja Abdullah's eyes lit up. He had also heard of the man. He went to Ngao and grasped him by the shoulders. "Then I charge you to bring him to me. I knew you would come up with a solution."

Ngao was speechless. He did not know Yap Ah Loy. He only knew of him and his bravery.

❀ ❀ ❀

IT WAS NIGHTFALL when Ngao returned home. His heart was heavy. Just when everything was falling into place, the unexpected turned up and threatened to undo the peace and prosperity he hoped to build. Would this place ever be safe for Shao Peng, he wondered. There were always battles and fights.

It is the same in China he comforted himself. Yet he knew instinctively that something had changed; the warring between the different Malay factions had intensified. In neighbouring Perak, a mining campsite and an adjacent township had been torched.

He climbed up the stairs to the portico of the house. He opened the door. The kerosene lamp cast a yellow glow in the interior. Rohani was seated under the lamp sewing. Her hand flew deftly drawing the cotton from the garment and then weaving the needle back into it. He watched her fingers work, her head bowed low. She had not heard him. A row of neat stitches appeared on the cloth. She tied a flat knot and then, raising the garment to her lips, bit through the thread. Since that day when he went to the kitchen to speak to her, he had kept away. He spoke only on matters relating to the household or ordinary impersonal things such as the weather. He closed the door. The sound caused her to start. She gathered her sewing and got to her feet.

"I didn't hear you," she exclaimed.

"No matter. I tried to be very quiet because you seemed so absorbed in your work. I have to leave very early in the morning. I won't eat before I leave."

"Oh!" she replied. "Shall I prepare something for you to take along? I'll do it now. I have laid out food on the table for this evening. I'll come up to clear once you've finished."

"Don't go. Stay and talk to me."

❀ ❀ ❀

IT WAS LATE afternoon the following day before Ngao reached Lukut. He came upon it abruptly, rising from the surrounding dense jungle. A single tarmacked street separated two rows of Chinese shophouses; built of bricks and with tiled roofs. Farther away from the town was the river. Along the riverbanks were godowns and warehouses. Ngao was surprised at the orderliness of the town. He had not expected the tarmacked road. It was what he envisaged for the township and shophouses that he was building in Selangor.

"So it is possible," he whispered to himself almost in awe. It was not a dream but something that could be achieved.

He stopped a passer-by to ask for the way to Yap Ah Loy. They pointed towards a road that branched off from the main street to the left of him. The road rose gently and then sloped down to a small hamlet. Three houses nestled in front of the deep jungle with the towering trees behind them providing a rich backdrop of forest green. To one side of the group of houses, was a small pond. A flock of chickens and ducks pecked and waddled unattended. Further on, pigs – hundreds of them – grunted and pushed behind an enclosed pen.

He was excited. Ngao had heard a lot about the man and was eager to meet him. Yap Ah Loy had arrived in Malaya about two years before Ngao, but he had already made his mark. Starting as a mining coolie, he moved on to become a shop assistant, a cook and now a dealer in tin and pigs. He sold pigs to the tin mines and bought tin for sale to metal merchants. His business extended far beyond Lukut where he had first started. Ngao would like to be able to follow in his steps.

"Look for the house with a red door," the passer-by had said. Ngao spotted the house some distance away. He stopped. A man was walking from it towards him. He was of medium height. Even from afar, Ngao could see that there were no traces of fat on him, just compact muscle. The man was taking big strides towards Ngao. As he got closer, Ngao could see a scar above his eyebrows, shaped like the character *ren*, and his skin, tanned the colour of toast, was pulled taut against his skull accentuating his high cheekbones. His eyes, small, dark and steady like steel, locked onto Ngao's as he approached.

"You come to see me?" the man asked.

"Are you Yap Ah Loy?" countered Ngao. He was mystified how news of his arrival in Lukut could have reached the man so quickly.

The man nodded. "And you?" he asked.

Ngao introduced himself. "I come from Raja Abdullah. He sent me here. He needs help. I mentioned your name to him."

Yap smiled, his teeth a flash of white against his brown skin. "You mentioned me? I don't know why. You had better come to my house." He turned and led the way. Ngao felt himself responding to his easy manner and, for a moment, his tension lightened.

Once in the house, Ngao looked around quickly. The furnishings in the room were spartan. There was nothing remotely grandiose. Everything was basic, plain and functional like the man himself: a table, some chairs and, towards the back, an altar with joss sticks. Their spirals of smoke filled the hot air with a heavy scent.

"So why does Raja Abdullah need help?" asked Yap, his gaze unwavering as he sat down.

"He needs to raise an army against his nephew, Raja Mahdi, and to control the warring factions of his father-in-law's family. He has thrown his support behind Raja Samad, his brother-in-law, who is hoping to become the Sultan. He expects the fighting to escalate in the months, even days, to come."

"What about you? Why don't you help him?"

Ngao took a deep breath; he was nervous. "I can't help him," he said. "My boss is in Singapore. He has left me in charge of his coolies in Selangor. But we are not fighters and I am sure my boss is not interested in taking sides. He just wants to get on with business. I thought of you."

"Me? Why?"

"I have heard of your exploits. You hold the Malay title of *panglima* or warrior in Lukut. It is not a title lightly given. Will you help him?"

"In what way?"

"The Raja needs men, guns and ammunitions," replied Ngao. "We can't give him any of these."

Ngao felt the intensity of the man's eyes as he took measure of him. Ngao braced himself and returned the gaze and held it.

"If Raja Samad becomes Sultan, you will be richly rewarded," added Ngao.

"Why should I trust you?" asked Yap after a palpable silence.

"No reason. You could check us out. I know, however, that Raja Abdullah will be grateful for the help. He is the administrator for the Klang River, an area rich with tin. He is dynamic and is one of the few Malay nobility who has successfully mined the Gombak and Ampang area using Chinese labour."

Ngao took a deep breath. He could see that the man was unconvinced. "What I can do for the cause," added Ngao, "is ensure the supply of food to the troops, including your men if you join in the foray."

"What do you want out of this?" asked Yap with a smile. It relaxed the tautness of his face and brought a crinkle to his eye.

"Nothing except..."

"Ahhh!" exclaimed Yap with a laugh. He raised his hand and jabbed his index finger in the air. "Always there is this exception. Tell me what."

"We are building a little township of houses near where the Klang and Gombak rivers meet. We would like this area to be protected. With protection, the supplies of food would not be hindered."

"I shall give the Raja my answer and inform you in a few days. I have to consult with my own people."

Yap stood up. Ngao knew that the meeting had ended. He too got up and made ready to leave.

"One piece of advice," said Yap to Ngao's departing back. "In life, one has to take a stand. There can be no advancement for those who stand at the side."

Chapter 27

THE SEA WAS as smooth as glass, a great expanse of blue broken by froths of white where the waves gently lapped the sides of the steamer. Grime stood waiting to disembark. Shao Peng, a cap on her head and a thick pigtail hanging down her back stood next to him. She looked up. He glanced down and gave a brief nod. "*Deng yi deng!* Wait!" he mumbled in Mandarin. "You have to be patient," he added in English. "And hold on to your belongings."

Shao Peng clutched tightly the cloth bag that held her change of clothes. A wind picked up speed. Quickly she jammed her black skull cloth cap even more snugly on her head. Holding it tight she looked around in wonder.

There were godowns and warehouses all along the river. Junks and all manner of small boats crowded the river mouth.

On shore, carts drawn by horses competed for space with rickshaws and those drawn by buffalos. A row of colourful shophouses lined a hill further up river. People jostled against each other. Chinese, Arabs, English and Indians, people she had never seen before. Their voices carried by the wind formed a medley of exotic tones that clashed and blended and clashed.

"Is this Singapore?" she asked peering into the distance, anxious to see her father.

"Yes! This is it," Edward Grime answered.

"Is my father here? Will he meet us?"

"Probably not. Your aunt had no time to send him notice of your arrival unless by some miracle she managed to find someone able to deliver a letter faster than our travel here. I doubt it," he replied looking down at Shao Peng.

He was struck afresh by how much she resembled her mother. The proximity of the girl had awakened in him memories that he had wanted to push aside. He had not expected his brief encounter to lead to such a series of events and certainly not someone's death. He could do nothing to undo what he had done. He could only do what he was asked and he had kept his promise. He had looked after the little girl and even taught her the rudiments of the English language. Once he found Eng Kim, he would leave her with him. Her father should come from wherever he was to collect her. His responsibilities would end. Impulsively, he reached out and ruffled her cap.

She ducked and held on even tighter to it. "Don't touch me," she said spiritedly with a scowl on her face.

He smiled. The month's journey had changed her from a timid girl with tears that were never far away to a spirited child who answered back and stood her ground. She slept in his tiny dressing room rolled up in a quilt on the floor. He could not let her out of his sight for fear of discovery. People generally accepted it because she was purportedly his pageboy. To keep her occupied when he was out and about, he made her stay in the cabin to learn the alphabets and simple words. He had never seen anyone so diligent. She would painstakingly copy them, head bent low, lips pursed in concentration. She could repeat them after each session of learning. "Not a problem," she had said cheekily when he got to know her better. "*Hen rong yi*, very easy compared to Chinese," she volunteered with a mischievous grin on her face.

They made their way down the gangway to the jetty. "Keep close," Grime commanded as they went in search of a carriage, elbowing their way through the throng of people crowded around the jetty. Shao Peng could hardly see the sky for the people pressed against her. All she saw when she looked up was a canopy of woven hats providing saucer-like shades. The air was dense with an assortment of unidentifiable smells. She sneezed and bumped into the person in front of her. Quickly she held on tightly to her belongings and cap. At times, she was tempted to relinquish one or the other to hold on to Grime's hand. They pushed and jostled until they came out into the open. "At last," cried Grime. "What a confounded place. The congestion is worst than Canton!"

"Take us to this address," he instructed the driver of a horse-drawn carriage, pushing a piece of paper into his hands. He lifted Shao Peng onto the seat of the open carriage and then clambered up beside her.

"We are going to this man Eng Kim. Your father works for him. You will know him because your aunt told me he once came to the house."

She stared blankly at Grime. She could not remember. She did not want to be left with yet another stranger. Her lips trembled.

"I shall leave you with him. He will then contact your father who will come to collect you by and by," said Grime blithely, unaware of his charge's sudden silence. He leaned over to point to a sight. When he turned around to speak to her once more, he saw her face pinched with fear.

"Come on you little goat," he said punching his fist playfully into her upper arm. She remained glum. He could see she was holding back her tears. "Here, take this," he said slipping a piece of paper into her hand, pretending not to care. "It is my address in Singapore. You can contact me there if you need to." He rummaged into his pocket and came up with a handful of coins. "This might be useful if you need to find me. I am sure everything will be fine and you will not come to that." He looked away unwilling to see her so upset. Despite his reservation, he had grown fond of her. They sat in silence while the carriage rolled onward carrying them into Chinatown.

Before long they stopped in front of the Soo Temple with its pink and pale green walls and rooftop emblazoned with magnificent dragons. Grime lifted her down and instructed the driver to wait for him.

"He has an office in this temple. Come, let's go to see him."

They threaded their way across the temple courtyard and into the musty, incense-filled hall with the cauldron of joss sticks, keenly aware of being 'watched'; the painted eyes of the Goddess of Mercy and the Warrior God seemed to follow their every movement. A priest, his head shaven clean except for the shadows of blue at the side, passed by. Grime stopped him to ask for Eng Kim. The priest gestured towards the back, his hand motioning Grime to walk ahead and then to veer to the left. Then he hastily bowed and moved away, all the time throwing curious glances at the white man with the Chinese boy. No European had visited before and he wondered if Grime could have lost his way being so far from the European settlement.

THE ROOM GRIME had been directed to was empty. Scrolls lined the wall. Stacks of documents lay on the table together with a pen brush, an ink block and an abacus. Eng Kim was nowhere to be seen.

Grime had not expected this. He should have, he realised. He had just assumed that Eng Kim would be found at the address he had been given and all he had to do was to hand over the girl. A gong sounded, then the chimes of a bell, followed by the chanting of prayers. Through the doorway he could see a file of monks with prayer beads praying, their feet shuffling forward in step like a caterpillar with many legs. It was not the time to ask them questions. What should he do? He could not just leave her.

"Come," he said, laying his hand gently on her back. "Let's get back to the carriage. The driver might be able to help."

They found the driver dozing in the open carriage. His head under the wide coolie hat lolled and jerked. Loud snores punctuated with grunts came from his slack open mouth. Flies hovered round him, occasionally resting on to his cheeks. He brushed them away and went back to sleep; his head continued its random lolling and jerking.

"Wake up man!" cried Grime, jumping onto the carriage seat. He shook the man's shoulders. "Do you know where Lim

Eng Kim lives? Can you find out? He keeps an office in this temple, or at least did."

Awakened rudely, the driver gaped at Grime. Foggy with sleep, he could not understand his accent. Shao Peng interceded and repeated Grime's words.

"Tell him, we will give him extra if he finds Eng Kim's home for us. Someone must know. It is not such a big place," added Grime desperate to believe that Eng Kim could be found. He did not, however, quite believe his own bravado. His friend Michael Bowe had written to say that the most recent census showed there were over fifty thousand Chinese living in Singapore and they formed sixty-two per cent of its population.

The man's eyes lit up. "*Ho! Ho!* Yes! Yes! I find Mr Lim Eng Kim." With a spur of his whip he got the horses to turn around. He reined them in. The horses stopped. Without another word, the driver jumped down from the carriage and went back inside the temple. Within moments he was back again. "I find him. Temple clerk tells me he go home."

"Where is home?" asked Grime wondering how the driver had managed to get the information so quickly when they could not find even anyone to speak to.

"Northbridge Road!"

"MY HUSBAND IS not here," said the lady in sing-song English. She narrowed her eyes and examined her visitors with suspicion. "He has left for Selangor."

"When will he be back?" asked Grime taking an instant dislike to her. She was rude and petulant. She shrugged. "I don't know. He didn't say. Always he leaves me for long periods without a word to say when he might return. So how would I know?"

She made no attempt to invite them in. He found this strange in view of what Michael had written in his letters. "The natives are always gentle and friendly and the naturalised Chinese who have settled in the land and adopted the native customs are similarly welcoming. In fact they are our biggest supporters and speak good English, some of their men having studied in England."

"Certainly no sign of friendliness here," he muttered *sotto voce*, concealing his sentiment with a broad smile. "This little boy's father works for your husband. I am looking for him and your husband is the link. May I leave the boy with you? When your husband returns, perhaps he could arrange for him to be collected by his father?"

"No, I am afraid not. I can't help you. You must leave now." She took a step back ready to close the door after them and glared at Shao Peng. The little girl cowered.

Grime stared in disbelief, stunned by her rudeness. He was not used to such treatment after being in Canton where his words were hung upon by all and sundry. He had no choice, however, but to leave. He had no official status in Singapore. He was without a job. He felt her eyes on his departing back. Then just as he stepped out, he heard her mutter in Cantonese. "*Sooi chai ngan hai ngo loh gong ge!* That jinx must be my husband's love child. Why else would he want to leave him here? I am not so easily fooled!"

Once out in the sunshine, Grime threw back his head and laughed. The driver, who was waiting with a smile on his lips in anticipation of the reward promised him, was elated. Grime shook his head. "*Mm heong si.* Not here."

"I find him! I find him for you," cried the driver disappointed.

"It is late. Take us to this address," said Grime. "I am staying with a friend. Bring me news of Eng Kim's whereabouts tomorrow and I will reward you."

Shao Peng had become very quiet. Her stomach rumbled with hunger and she was very tired. He placed his hand on her arm and squeezed it gently. "I'm sorry it is taking so long. We will eat and rest. You are coming with me to a friend's house in the Esplanade. He is not there but his caretaker knows we are coming. We will be looked after and tomorrow we shall try to find your father."

Chapter 28

GRIME WOKE UP to the sound of birds outside his window. For a moment he lay dazed, uncertain of his whereabouts. He swung his legs over the bed and touched solid unmoving floorboards. Of course, he was on dry land, in Singapore. He had arrived at this splendid mansion on the Esplanade late in the afternoon. He was impressed with the houses in the European cantonment, the plush gardens and orderly surroundings. It was a complete contrast to the cramped double-storey terrace houses that served as both shops and residences in Chinatown.

He walked to the tall elegant window and threw open the shutters. Sunlight streamed in and a light breeze lifted the muslin curtains. He leaned his elbows on the window ledge and stuck his head out of the window. Bougainvilleas with their bright deep fuchsia petals twisted and climbed from the ground to form a thick carpet that covered the wall. On the angsenna tree in the middle of the lawn, parrots with bright blue and red plumes completely overshadowed the dull brown sparrows pecking the ground.

He pulled on his clothes quickly and went out of the bedroom. Almost instantly, a servant was by his side.

"Sir, breakfast is served on the veranda. Please come." Padding quietly with bare feet, the servant led the way along the hallway, around the gallery and down the wide stairways to the ground floor. "This way, sir," he bade walking through the eastern side of the house, past the dining room and out into a sunlit veranda. A long table, covered with a starched white tablecloth, was laid out for breakfast. A resplendent basket of tropical fruits stood next to the teapot. Further along the table were a rack of toasts, a dish of boiled eggs, their brown pearly shells half covered with a white linen cloth, fried kidneys, scrambled eggs and a dish of butter, somewhat softened by the heat of the day. Shao Peng was already seated. Next to her was a lady who surely must be the mistress of the house. When he had arrived yesterday with the letter of invitation from Michael Bowe the servant had shown him immediately to his rooms. Even supper was served in his room. He had met no one and beyond being told that his friend was not in, a fact he already knew, the servant had said little.

"Good morning," said Grime bowing to the lady.

She inclined her head slightly and smiled indicating the seat next to Shao Peng. "I am Janidah. Did you sleep well?" she asked. Only the slight lilt in her pronunciation betrayed what would otherwise have been perfect English.

"Wonderfully! I woke up late. I hope he did not bother you," said Grime placing his hand on Shao Peng's head. He realised he was staring; he averted his eyes and sat down. Michael did not warn him that he had a wife and one who was not English. He had merely said that he would be away when Grime arrived and that he should make himself at home. Her features were delicate and finely etched. He wondered about her origins. Arab, perhaps or could it be a mixture of Malay and Arab ancestry. There was after all a significant Arab community on the island.

"He? Or shall we call her she?" asked Janidah directing her wide gaze at him, totally unaware of his thoughts. "Such a pretty girl. May I give her a change of clothes? She is the same size as my daughter. My children have gone out with their *amah* to the market. They will be back soon."

Temporarily non-plussed at being discovered in the subterfuge, Grime smiled sheepishly. "We had to pass her off as a boy on the ship for her safety. It was so kind of you Madam to take her, I mean both of us, at such short notice. When will Michael be back?"

"Not for a while. He is in England. Perhaps you will see him there. He has returned home to his wife and family." She took a slice of bread and buttered it for Shao Peng. "Try this," she said to her before pulling off the skullcap. "You don't need this anymore and we will give you a good wash later." She smiled and continued with her breakfast.

Grime could only stare. Had he misheard, he wondered? But she said it with no affectation or embarrassment. The tone was totally matter of fact. If Michael had gone back to his wife, then who was Janidah? He had met Michael when he was a student and had only renewed their acquaintance through exchanges of letters in the past year. In these exchanges they had spoken mainly of work. He had assumed when Michael told him he could stay at his place while in Singapore, that he was on his own like Grime had been in Canton. Then when he saw Janidah, he assumed Michael had neglected to tell him he had a wife. It would seem not.

He saw Shao Peng push the slice of bread surreptitiously under her plate. She looked at him appealingly with a slight shake of her head. She mouthed silently that she didn't like it. She had not eaten butter before and found the taste and smell of it completely alien and uninviting. He reached over and popped the bread onto his plate. Janidah saw.

"It is okay," Janidah said. "Take something else. I too couldn't eat a breakfast like this before. When you come to my house, you can have rice for breakfast. The servants insist that you would prefer an English breakfast and have served up dishes that Michael likes." She looked up and saw the perplexity on Grime's face. "My house is in this compound. I don't live in the main house. I have my own quarters over there," she pointed to a bungalow situated to the rear. When Michael has official guests I do not join in these events. With friends, it is an entirely different matter."

"What an honour for us!" exclaimed Grime, hiding his discomfort with a smile. He could not think of anything else to say. They continued their breakfast speaking little except for the odd comment on the sights of the city and weather. He was not a prude and he was not judgmental. He wished he had a similar arrangement in Canton. He reflected on his abortive attempt to form a relationship. The situation in China was different. There, Chinese restrictions against foreigners would have made it impossible to have such an open liaison.

After breakfast Grime asked for directions to the Governor's office.

"Take the carriage," Janidah said. "The driver knows. Michael goes there often."

"Thank you Madam. You are most hospitable. I shall not be long." He turned to Shao Peng. "*Liu zai zhe er deng wo*, stay here and wait for me. I have to find Eng Kim's whereabouts and also your father's. The driver from yesterday might come back with news and you will have to be here to speak to him."

"I don't want to stay here. I want to come with you," wailed Shao Peng, slipping out of her chair. She grabbed Grime's hand. She did not understand what was said during breakfast and was frightened in the new surroundings. She feared Grime would leave her.

"It's okay," said Janidah placing an arm around her. "Don't be afraid. Look my children are back!"

Shao Peng did not understand her but she saw children, a boy and a girl of her age running towards them. "Look! Look! We have a little puppy," they cried.

Janidah looked at Grime and with a motion of her head indicated that he should take the opportunity to leave. Shao Peng was totally captivated with the puppy. The children immediately took turns to cuddle it.

"Shao Peng," said Grime, "I shall be back soon." She did not hear him.

A TARMACKED ROAD cut across the town flanked by a network of smaller roads. Across the river stood the Town Hall, Government offices with well-trimmed lawns, and a Cathedral. On the outer edges of the centre, building work was underway. Scores of men slaved under the sun. Their dark brown bodies gleamed as they hacked and dug. The ground was a runnel of turned up soil.

"Indian convicts brought over specifically to build," explained Orfeur Cavenagh to Grime. "Look over there. That will be the site for the fort. The street lamps you see burn coconut oil; soon they will be replaced by gas lamps." The Governor pointed to the various sights as he spoke, proud of his achievements.

The two men were on the opposite side of the river looking on. Behind them stood an imposing row of fine buildings.

"You will not find the same situation were you to cross over to the Malay Peninsula. We do not have much control there except for Penang and Malacca which, like Singapore, are under British rule. We call them the Straits Settlements. It is a pity, because the Malay states have considerable potential. Crops grow easily and, of course, there is tin. Yes, those lands are of great interest to me personally, particularly Perak and Selangor."

"So who administers them?" asked Grime. "I am not familiar with how these parts are governed."

"Malay chieftains; they have various titles and ranks from rajas to temenggongs to sultans. Utterly charming people but quarrelsome. They are forever squabbling. They have the most antiquated inheritance laws. A long war is almost inevitable after the death of each chief as they fight for the succession. That is where I think we could come in. At the moment, the chieftains enlist the help of Chinese labourers. Good fighters though they are, they do not have the organised machinery of a government behind them. We have that. We acquired Penang because the Sultan of Kedah asked for help against his enemies from the bordering lands of Siam and Burma. It is more than likely we will be asked for help again."

"So, we might still see the extension of British power in Malaya," surmised Grime. "Certainly, what has been done here is most impressive."

"*Ahhh!* Don't quote me. It is only my personal view. As far as the Colonial office back home is concerned, we are to avoid interfering. That said, thank you for your observations on Singapore. We have worked hard and I am very fortunate to have the backing of locals. It was not always like this. When I first came there was a lot of friction between the merchants and the British administration. They disliked intensely being regulated by rules set in India. Now that the East India Company is no more, I have made sure that I consult and cooperate with the local people."

"Sir, coming back to the matter on which we spoke earlier. Would it be possible for me to go over to Selangor to deliver the little girl to her father? I cannot wait here indefinitely for Eng Kim. I do not know how long it will be before he returns. His wife has been most unhelpful."

"I know of him. He is quite a prominent Chinese businessman with strong contacts with Chow See Kok, to whom we have given the opium license. The reaction of his Singapore wife is understandable. He has, I believe, a second or even third family over in Selangor. Unfortunately, now might not be a good time to go to Selangor with the child. The Malay rulers are at war. The Chinese are involved. Hundreds, some say thousands, have died in the fighting. The chances of being ambushed are high."

"I have to leave for England soon. So what do you suggest?"

"Send a letter to Eng Kim and the father. Get them to come and collect her. We can help you with that. How long do you have here? When is your passage?"

"In a fortnight's time."

Cavenagh turned to look at his guest. "Have you considered a post here?" he asked.

"It did cross my mind."

"Well think about it. There are lots of opportunities. I'll put in a good word."

"Thank you. I will definitely consider it."

Chapter 29

NGAO GOT DOWN from the cart. Taking hold of the bridle, he led the horse into the jungle. The wheels of the cart creaked under the weight of the gunny bags of rice. The animal was nervous. It resisted, swinging its head from side to side, neighing and refusing to budge. The dense undergrowth made passage difficult and the thorns on the jungle vines had cut into its flanks.

Ngao drew out his machete and slashed to clear a way. The blade flashed brightly when it caught the sun. The sinews of his arms strained and bulged with the combined effort of urging the animal forward and clearing the way. He had no choice if he was to get supplies to Yap and his men. It was too dangerous to take the road. He would be ambushed.

The news was not good. Many of Yap's men had been badly wounded. Word that a Malay chieftain had beheaded Shin Kap, the Chinese leader of Sungai Ujong, made everyone afraid. Yap, they deemed, was a marked man. No one was willing to deliver provisions to him. Ngao was left to do it himself. After all, he was the one who made the commitment.

The cart lurched forward, bumping over roots that lay like thick manacles over the jungle floor. Each movement was an effort. Ngao paused briefly to strip off his tunic top. He wiped the sweat pouring off him and threw the tattered garment on to the cart. Thin traces of blood dribbled down his arms and back. Man and horse continued slowly forward, pausing now and then to recover from their exertions. Gradually the sun was no longer overhead; it had shifted to the west and the rays seeping through the foliage had dimmed. Soon it would be dark.

Without warning, gunshots rang out. One after another they came in rapid succession. They were followed by fearful screams of pain. Ngao crouched down instantly. The animal was spooked by the noises. It neighed and despite the weight of the cart reared on its front legs, desperate to escape. Ngao caught the reins and held on to them tightly to control the frightened beast. Some distance away where just moments ago, there had been only the forest, men, hundreds of them, emerged. Ngao could feel his heart pumping. He crouched deeper into the bush. Ahead he could see a clearing with a few huts. A woosh of light sparked fast and furious! Flames leapt throwing a thousand fizzling glitters into the sky. Fire! In the light, he saw a man running towards him, limping and hopping. It was Yap. He was clasping a hand to his thigh. Blood streamed down from it. Still he pressed forward. Ngao shouted, "Here! This way!" Yap turned and saw him and started limping in his direction. Ngao ran to meet him. He took him under his arm and half carried him to the cart. No one followed for they were distracted by the mayhem of the fire, the screams of men dying and gunshots.

"Go. Leave me," said Yap. "I have lost too much blood," pointing to the gunshot wound on his thigh. "I will be a hindrance. Just leave me here. We have been routed. They attacked the huts where we were sleeping. The family that housed us have all been killed."

"No! I'll carry you. We'll leave the cart here. They probably do not know you are alive. No one seems to be coming this way. They probably think that with the gunshots and the fire, everyone in the huts is dead."

Ngao lifted Yap into his arms and ran, staggering like a drunk under his burden. Then they were enveloped in the dense night of the jungle.

RAYS OF LIGHT filtered through the jungle canopy. Yap groaned. His bloodless lips were parched and flecked with white. Ngao lifted the injured man's head and dribbled water from a leaf onto his lips. They had no supplies at all. "Leave me," urged Yap. "You have done what you can. If I live I will remember this deed.

"Stay here." Ngao rose to his feet. "I will see if I can get help. Don't move. I will be back."

Ngao walked eastwards. His movements were slow and laboured. Every limb ached with the effort. His shoes were falling apart. He stopped, tore pieces of cloth from his trouser leg and bound them back together. About a mile on he heard noises, voices. He crept forward, hunched low. He saw a road, then people. He hid behind a bush. Further back from the main road were houses and then the jungle. He looked to his right, attracted by the sound of flowing water. It was a river. His heart leapt. Beyond a corpse some distance away, he could see *palongs*, tin mines. With luck, he might find people with whom he had traded and supplied food, people whom he knew and could trust. He waited, crouched low and out of sight, to see if he could recognise any of the faces. No one! He felt his calves straining. Then he spotted a man approaching. A man he had dealt with before; a man who had come regularly to his shop in Ampang over the past year and one sympathetic to their cause. He stood up and called, half running towards him. He stumbled several times.

"Help!" Ngao pleaded. "Come with me. It is Yap. He is wounded."

The man came forward and grasped him. "Show me the way," he said.

Ngao led the way re-tracing his steps through the jungle to where he had left Yap Ah Loy. They found him delirious, stretched out under a tree. He had lost a lot of blood and the opened wound was beginning to fester. Gently they carried him back to the village.

❀ ❀ ❀

ON THE THIRD morning after their rescue, Ngao went to see Yap Ah Loy. Despite his injuries and loss of blood, the man showed remarkable resilience and was sitting up. He had just eaten and was still holding a rice bowl. He placed the empty bowl quickly on the wooden table by his bed. He beckoned Ngao over.

"I am grateful to you for saving me. I shall remember it. This is a setback but do not fear. I will regroup and our war will continue until the last drop of blood has been vindicated." His eyes shone bright. Ngao was astonished by the energy in them. "I have lost over five hundred men," his eyes clouded with tears, "and everyone of them will be avenged."

"I did what any one would do in my position," said Ngao. "Now I have come to say goodbye. I must return home. I have matters to attend to. We are making good progress with the building and I need to be there. Besides, I am expecting another consignment of rice, vital as we have exhausted the last shipment, and a very important letter from China."

Witnessing the fighting had heightened his anxiety for Shao Peng. Was it too early for him to think of bringing her to live with him? He needed to send a letter to his aunt to delay Shao Peng's departure. He vacillated between wanting to have her with him and the wish to keep her safe.

Yap nodded. "Go! Thank you again. I will be fine. My men are loyal," pointing to the five bodyguards outside. "We are waiting for reinforcements. I will return to Lukut where we will re-assemble."

Chapter 30

CASTING THE HOE aside, Rohani wiped her forehead with the corner of her blouse. The ground was prepared. The soil, freshly dug, was moist and loose. She picked up the hoe again and quickly piled the soil up in a line. Before long she had four lines of piled up soil. Ngao had taught her that this was the best way to plant the spinach. She dipped into the pouch hung from her waist and took out a handful of seeds. Squatting down, she carefully placed one seed at a time into the raised soil, pushing it firmly into the moist dark earth with her index finger. Soon two rows were planted, sufficient to feed themselves and perhaps have some left over to barter in the market.

From an adjoining pouch hanging from her waist she took out another handful of seeds. These were larger and darker. Bitter gourd. Strange, she thought, that washed and dried they were brown yet they were bright red when fresh. She did not understand why Ngao liked it. The gourd itself was pretty enough. Long and fat, riddled with curly ridges that formed a lovely pattern on its pale green skin. She had not eaten nor cooked it until one day Ngao had brought the gourd back, proclaiming its virtues as a vegetable. One bite and she vowed she would never be able to eat it. Ngao, however, loved the bitterness and so she was sowing it. Soon one row was planted. The plants would eventually need support because they grow into tall vines; for now it was sufficient for the seeds to germinate and get established.

She smiled. The last row of plants will be mine, she thought. She took short lengths of bamboos and stuck them into the ground. At the base of each rod, she sprinkled a few chilly seeds. He was beginning to like the heat from chillies. Strange, she now thought of her master as Ngao. He had insisted she call him by his name and gradually she relented. She found the name strange. It tripped her tongue. Saying his name aloud, she enjoyed the strangeness of the sound that went right to the back of her throat and out again, like *ow* with *ng* sound to the front. She missed him. He had been away for almost a week and she had heard no news.

Rohani stepped back to admire her work. Leaving the tools beside the plot, she took a bucket and carefully watered the newly sown seeds. Once finished, she went back to the house. The previous day she had cut coconut palm leaves and left them to dry, strung between the pillars that supported the house. She now fetched the dried fronds and with great care placed them over the planted seeds. That, Ngao had said, would protect them from birds and the scorching sun. He had shown her how to pare the fronds down to a manageable size.

Thinking of him made her fret. Why was there no word from him? She had been to Raja Abdullah's house to ask the other servants for news of the war and particularly of Ngao. They told her of the fighting. She had not realised that since her last visit a week ago, Raja Abdullah had fled and died in exile and his son, Raja Ismail, had taken over. It made her skin crawl to hear of the atrocities committed, the violence. Still they had nothing to report about Ngao. Was he caught in the middle of it? She shivered. She was alone in the house and frightened.

Gathering her tools she quickly made her way back to the kitchen. He had told her about his daughter, Shao Peng. She conjured up an image of a little girl. She imagined her bright eyes, how she wore her hair tied into bunches on either side of her ears and the dimple in her cheeks. Poor girl! To lose her mother at such a young age! She wondered what Ngao's wife had looked like. Did he miss her still? She closed her eyes and felt a strange silence enclose her. It seemed as though the air reverberated with a dull low humming sound ... of emptiness. She missed her family, her sisters and brothers; she missed her master Ngao. He filled the house with his presence. Her heart quickened with the thought of him. She remembered his smile. It gave her something to look forward each day.

She went from the kitchen into her room. Delving into a cupboard, she took out her sewing basket and a pile of garments. "I'll attend to these in the portico," she said to herself. "When he comes back, he'll find at least all his clothes mended."

Balancing the basket on one hip, and with the garments firmly under the other arm, she mounted the back stairway to the house. She stopped mid-way up. The sound of wheels churning and horse hooves filled the air. She went back down the stairway and ran to the front garden. She could hardly see for the dust that had been churned up.

"Is Ngao in?" bellowed the man driving a horse cart. "Do you understand me?" he said emerging from the storm of dust to tower over her. "Ah a native!"

Rohani observed his face, the pale skin, the bushy eyebrows and beneath them eyes the colour of the sky. She shrunk back, frightened by the eyes. Instinctively she clutched her basket tight against her body bringing the other arm filled with garments tightly across her chest.

"*Jangan takut!* Don't be afraid!" he said breaking into Malay. "I am looking for Ngao. His daughter has arrived and she is in Singapore. We would like him to come and collect her."

She was speechless. She had never seen such a man before. So tall! So huge! He must be at least one foot taller than most men.

"Here! Take this," he said pushing a piece of paper into her hand. "She is at this address. Tell him to come quick. *Chepat!*" Without another word, he spun round, jumped onto the carriage and sped away leaving once again a trail of dust and wheel marks.

Only then did she find her voice. She screamed. It was neither of fear nor of sadness. It was a sound of relief; relief from pent-up emotions. She felt encased by the silence of the house and all around her and she was anxious about Ngao's absence. She had expected the worst when she saw the white man. She thought that he had come to tell her that Ngao was wounded, even dead, that was until he spoke. With her arms full and the letter clutched in her hand, she ran to the back of the house and sat down heavily on the bottom rung of the stairway. Shao Peng is here, she thought. She said the name aloud, practising the words '*Shao Peng*'.

❀ ❀ ❀

THE NIGHT OWL hooted. It was dark except for the flood of light coming from the open windows of the upper floor of the house. Ngao stood for a moment looking up at the window, bathed in the yellow light of the kerosene lamp. Then slowly he walked up the stairs to the house. He pushed open the door. He saw Rohani by the window, sewing. She jumped up and ran to him. Without thinking he opened his arms wide and she went into them, nestling into his chest. They held each other for a long time. No words were spoken. The silence embraced them like a warm cocoon. Reluctantly they separated, his hand lingering on the small of her back. She bowed her head embarrassed by her show of affection.

"Rohani," he whispered.

She looked up and only then saw the bruises and cuts on his face and body.

"What happened?" She touched his face and his neck; her face was filled with concern. "Who did this?"

"It's nothing. Just scratches. Many were really wounded and even more lost their lives. I was not involved in the fighting. I was only delivering supplies."

"Wait here. I'll bring some ointment and dressing."

"What now?" he asked himself after she had gone. He had not planned it. His arms just swept her to him when he saw her running to him, her eyes shinning with gladness and welcome. Could it be love? Warmth seeped through his body. He could still feel the softness of her body pressed against him. And he felt a longing, a longing so strong, that he had to clench his fist and bite his lip. What about Hua, he wondered? Instantly he felt guilty. How could he explain to his daughter when she arrived, that there was another woman in his life now?

"What's wrong?" Rohani asked when she returned. She could see that his mood had changed. He had not heard her coming in, so engrossed was he in his thoughts. He was cradling his face with both his hands, bent over.

"Nothing. I was just thinking."

"A letter for you. An Englishman brought it this afternoon. He said that Shao Peng is in Singapore, at this address. He asked you go to collect her."

He took the piece of paper. His hands shook. He was overjoyed. Then his joy turned abruptly to confusion. Why didn't his aunt warn him? Was this a trick? Who would play such a trick? He turned deathly pale. All the worries he had about safety for Shao Peng resurfaced and came to a head. They were no longer just abstract thoughts; they were real problems he had to confront. She was here. How could he keep her safe?

"I have to go," he said rising to his feet.

"But you have hardly rested and eaten?"

He didn't answer. It was as though she was not there. He hurried out of the room without a backward glance. She heard him running down the stairway and out into the garden. Then there was silence again. Slowly she sat down, the ointment and bandages still in her hands. She blushed, a stain that spread from her neck to her cheeks and ears. She could feel the warmth of them. Was she mistaken about his feelings for her?

"WILL YOU PLEASE let me have some men to guard my house?" asked Ngao.

Eng Kim was on his terrace, sitting on a rattan chair, legs crossed and relaxed, enjoying the cool night air when a maidservant showed Ngao in. Breathing hard, Ngao launched immediately into an explanation.

"I have left Rohani alone and I am afraid that it is no longer safe to do so. I have just come back from the outlying battleground near Lukut. The situation has worsened."

"Calm down! Calm down! Why this urgency? She is always on her own when you leave for work so what's the difference?" Eng Kim set aside the cup of jasmine tea he was nursing in his hand and waved Ngao to a seat.

Ngao took a deep breath. "My daughter is in Singapore. I have to get to her. I have to leave immediately. She must be frightened on her own in a strange country. That will mean leaving Rohani for an even longer time alone in the house."

"You said you were worried about your maid's safety. Aren't you worried about your daughter's? Do you still wish to bring her here right in the middle of what you call an escalating war? I won't say I told you so. I had warned you not to send for her."

"That is why I asked for your help, for guards. I meant them not only for Rohani, but also for my daugher of course." He knew he was rambling; he was not making a clear case for himself. He sensed his boss's disapproval and winced at the thought that he had given the impression that he had been more concerned about Rohani than Shao Peng. It was not so but to protest would make things worst.

Ngao looked over to the sitting room where Eng Kim's two wives were seated. They were embroidering a piece of blue silk between them. He could see the shape of a phoenix with wings spread in flight emerging on the silk. The women were smiling and talking, oblivious to the urgent conversation between the men. The scene was so tranquil and normal that it was surreal. Soon it will not be like this but if Eng Kim was going to keep his women here, surely it should also be safe enough for Shao Peng and Rohani if he had some guards to watch over them. His eyes lingered on the women wanting to say what was on his mind. He could not find his voice to say it aloud to his boss. He could not speak because he himself was not fully convinced of the arguments he had posed in favour of bringing Shao Peng over to this war-torn area. The fatigue of the past weeks was beginning to catch up on him. His head reeled.

Eng Kim followed the direction of his gaze. He saw the exhaustion on Ngao's face, the troubled eyes, and how his lips, normally smiling and cheerful, had lost that upward quirk. He had worked him hard and Ngao, in turn, had been unfailing in his effort. He was single-minded in his pursuit to be a free man and to save enough for his daughter. He was loyal, innovative and intelligent. For that Eng Kim could not spare him. He could not allow him to go to Singapore at this juncture. Soon the battles would recommence. Raja Ismail, keen to revenge his father, had specifically mentioned that he wanted Ngao to be around. They needed someone with knowledge of the supply lines, someone willing to put himself in danger. Ngao had become too important, too indispensable to be allowed to leave. Moreover, he needed him to oversee the completion of the building of the stores.

"My wives, those two sisters you see over there. They are staying on. I have asked them to go to Singapore; they refuse. They would rather take the consequence and the risks of staying here than join my first wife. Such is the relationships between the women in my household. If I could persuade them to leave I would. They maintain that life for them would be impossible if they were to go to Singapore. I believe them. The last time they visited my first wife, they ended having pots and pans thrown at them."

The shadows in Ngao's eyes deepened. There! He had his answer. It was not safe. The women were here not because it was safe but for other reasons.

"Shao Peng is waiting for me," insisted Ngao, "and I have to go to Singapore even if I was eventually to decide not to bring her back here."

Eng Kim rose to his feet and walked to the window. He looked out into the darkness. The moon had lit up the branches and lengthened their shadows on the ground. A cat meowed and the light breeze set the leaves rustling. "I hear what you are saying and I sympathise with your feelings. Only I can't let you leave just when all your work over the past year is coming to fruition," Eng Kim said softly.

"You don't understand. I have to. She is only a child." Ngao rose to his feet.

"Wait! Let me make you a proposition." Eng Kim did not turn around. He sensed Ngao's presence behind him. He just didn't want to see the anguish in his face. "I'll ask the Raja for some men to take Rohani to Singapore. She can collect your daughter and they could stay together in my house in Singapore. They would be safe there. When things settle down they can return here."

The argument that both women would be safer in Singapore could not be refuted. Much as he wished to convince himself that his daughter could be safe in Selangor, Ngao had doubts. He was torn.

Eng Kim sensed his indecision. He turned round and walked towards Ngao. He placed both hands on the young man's shoulders. "The war is not going to last forever. You'll have both of them back soon," he said persuasively. "The next battle will be big. Yap is gaining strength by the minute. See the building work through and our stores in the new township opened and then we'll talk about it."

"No! We will not just talk about it. Once it is safe, I will fetch them. I shall be free by then."

Ngao's eyes glittered with a ferocity that had never been seen before. He realised that despite Eng Kim's benevolence, he would always place his business interests before Ngao's wellbeing. He was stung by the suggestion "We'll talk about it". This would be the last time. For now, he agreed that it was not safe for Shao Peng and Rohani to be here in the midst of an escalating war amongst the Malay chieftains, a war in which he had become involved. He feared, however, there would always be some reasons for not having his daughter here. He would have to determine his own path and fate. Like Eng Kim, he had to place his family first.

Chapter 31

SINGAPORE

"SO HAVE YOU given any thought about staying on?" Cavenagh asked as he poured out a large measure of whisky into the glass and handed it to Grime. Taking another glass, he poured a shot of the amber-coloured liquor for himself.

"It is not a bad place to be. We need someone like you. None of us speak Chinese and they make up the bulk of the population. The system here is begging for reform. Not least is the coolie trade. You know from your Canton experience, how corrupt the system is and how the coolies are exploited. They come as labourers and are practically enslaved thereafter. With your knowledge of Chinese you can help. I am sure we can do something to vet their contractual agreements and discharge those who have repaid their passage fare. Most of them intend to return to China. They remain here, trapped under appalling conditions only because they are ignorant of their rights. Very few can read and write."

Grime swirled the drink in his glass watching the golden liquid rise and fall against the side. The last four days had opened his eyes and ears. He agreed with Cavenagh. There was a lot to be done, a lot that he could do. He witnessed first hand the corruption in the Courts made possible because of the way the documents were translated or not translated as the case might be. He smiled as he recalled the Chinese translation for Europeans: *fan gui!* Western devils! And the English: *hong mo gui!* Red haired devils!

"The conditions of the women who came are no better," Cavenagh continued interrupting his thoughts. "They are massively outnumbered by the men and have been used abominably. So far, we as a government have done little to help. I am ashamed to admit that a few Chinese businessmen have done more than we in the years we have held this island. Last month they set up a care home for women. It is time we did something. I would like to support their effort and see this as an area you might take on."

Cavenagh looked expectantly at the young man before him. "So! What do you think? Do you think you can help?" He took a gulp of his drink, his eyes still on him.

Grime finished his drink and placed the glass down on the cabinet. His thoughts were racing. He did not know if he should be so frank about his views to someone he had just met. He wished Michael were with him. On all accounts, the Governor was a good man, much liked by the people for his warm-heartedness. He decided to take the plunge.

"On the way from Portsmouth to Canton, that is when I first took up my post in China, our ship stopped at Calcutta.

I had the opportunity to see the poppy fields. I was shocked. Every farmer growing wheat previously had been, I was told, forcefully persuaded by the East India Company to grow opium. The peasants there were hungry and indebted, yet they were made to grow poppies instead of food: plants that were subsequently left to rot in the field once the sap had been removed from the seed pods, plants that polluted the rivers and destroyed the soil. In China, we have forced the drug into the country waging wars on her to do so. I am ashamed. I am ashamed of my part in all this; my passive resistance has stood for nothing. Of course I want to do something to help the people we have caused so much pain. In fact, I had long thought that Singapore would be an interesting posting. But I have a problem. My being so far away from home has destroyed my marriage. My wife has accused me of being obsessed with all things Oriental. If I don't return this trip, my marriage will be over. Her last letter was little short of vitriolic."

Cavenagh had heard tales of Grime's problem in Canton. He was too much of a *Chink* lover, some said. It did not bother him. What he saw was a good man, a passionate man. He could not, would not comment on Grime's concern over the opium trade, but he felt he could offer some guidance on his personal problems.

"From an older man to a younger one, may I suggest that you ask yourself one question?" Cavenagh said. "Is it a marriage that you wish to save? If it is, then you should go home. If it is not, then it would be another matter."

Grime had not expected this. "Do I want to go home? Do I want to return to my wife?" he asked himself. These were not easy questions for him to answer. He had studiously avoided them even though he realised that they were the right ones to address in order to make the right choice.

"Michael, your friend, was standing at that very spot where you are standing when he asked himself those questions. Michael is not coming back," said Cavenagh, his face serious. "You probably do not know this. He has returned to England for good. He made that decision in this room. He has passed the running of the business to his Chinese partner, a trustworthy chap who has so far carried out to the letter all that was entrusted to him."

Grime was shocked. "What about Janidah? What about his children with her? Or the house she is staying. What will happen to them?"

"She is well provided for. She will have the bungalow on the estate. She knows. The main house will be eventually sold; until then, she has use of it if she wishes."

"Is that not cruel?" Grime protested even though, as he asked the question, he recalled he too was prepared to go that same route himself. Had he succeeded in establishing a relationship with Hua in China, he would probably also have to decide on whether to return to his wife or stay with his oriental mistress. It could swing both ways and either decisions would be cruel.

Cavenagh's eyebrow rose and his eyes glimmered with amusement at the question.

"Sorry. I overstep. I should not judge," apologised Grime. "It is not my business. However, you are right. The crux of the matter is to examine my own feelings with regard to my marriage. I will take my leave now. You will have my answer very soon."

❀ ❀ ❀

WITH CAVENAGH'S WORDS still ringing in his ears, Grime returned to Michael's house. He stepped into the hallway. Somehow it felt empty. The silence that greeted him left him with the feeling that the soul had left the house. The walls were bare. A closer look revealed the ring marks of picture frames, darkened smudges on pristine walls. Strange he had not noticed it before: the empty spaces where furniture might have been and the relatively few servants in a place that would normally have required many more. Michael had truly left.

"Sir, wait here please," said the servant who had opened the door. "Ma'am said to call her when you come back."

"Where is the little Chinese girl, Shao Peng?"

"Sir! You wait here," the servant insisted. "I bring Ma'am. Not my fault! Not my fault! I know nothing!" He was already half way out of the hallway. His footsteps echoed through the house. Within minutes, he returned with Janidah.

"Where were you?" she asked breathlessly. Her long hair was loose and flowing and she had not bothered to put on any shoes. He had observed her shoeless on many occasions when she thought she was on her own. "They came. They took Shao Peng away. I could not stop them because they brought a letter from Shao Peng's father." She placed both hands to her face. "Shao Peng cried and cried. She didn't want to leave. I couldn't stop them."

"Who are they?"

"Two men, a Malay and a Chinese, and a young Malay woman. They explained that they come from the father. The woman called Rohani is to be Shao Peng's carer. She didn't say a word. She was young and looked scared. They have taken Shao Peng to Mr Lim Eng Kim's house, the man you visited last week. They thanked you for bringing her to Singapore. They will care for her now, they said."

❀ ❀ ❀

THE ROOM WAS small, airless and dim. The only light came from a tiny window situated high up the wall. A wooden cupboard stood between two bunk beds placed against opposite walls. Shao Peng sat on one. Rohani occupied the other.

"I wish you did not come for me. Why can't my father come instead? Why did they leave me here with you?" cried Shao Peng in Chinese. "You don't even understand a word I say," sobbed the little girl. In frustration, she snatched a pillow off the bed and threw it at Rohani. Then with a loud wail, she threw herself on the bed and buried her head into the mattress.

"*Jangan menangis!* Don't cry!" said Rohani in Malay. She attempted to wipe away the girl's tears and cradle her.

"Go away! I don't know you. I want my father. I want my uncle Grime." She pushed Rohani away flailing her arms and legs. "They don't want us here. That woman with the painted eyebrows! She hates us."

Rohani looked on in despair. She did not understand what Shao Peng was saying, but it was not difficult to see she was unhappy. She had been rudely snatched from the big house and put in a place where she was unwanted, where they were both unwanted.

The lady they called Mrs Lim did not mince her words even when she knew I understood them. "*Tak tahu malu gadis nakai. Saya tak mahu anda disini!* Shameless hussy! I don't want you here!"

She had even screamed at the men who brought them. She scolded Rohani and Shao Peng, sprinkling her words with "*benchi*, hate, *suami gila,* my husband is mad. Finally, sobbing uncontrollably, she had asked the servants to show them into this room, situated between the kitchen and the toilet at the back of the house. The men had given her an ultimatum. Take the woman and child or they would report to Mr Lim. He would cut off her maintenance, they threatened. It was, they said, first and foremost Mr Lim's house.

Rohani tried once more to take Shao Peng into her arms.

"I don't want you. Go away!" Shao Peng hit out and caught Rohani in the face. She stopped alarmed that she had actually hit her, the only one who had been kind to her: a big patch of red showed where her hand had connected. Sorry for her action, she immediately caught Rohani's hands. "Didn't mean it. I didn't mean it," she cried. Rohani took her in her arms and rocked. Over and over again they rocked forward and back until Shao Peng calmed down. They said nothing because they did not understand each other. They understood, however, they were both in the same plight.

Finally, Rohani released her and using her hands beckoned her to follow. Rohani sniffed exaggeratedly and mimed with a stirring action and then fingers to the mouth that there was food. "*Makanan! Mari!* They crept out of the room to the adjoining kitchen.

On a charcoal stove, a big red clay pot was simmering. Steam rose from it sending out cooking smells. Shao Peng's stomach rumbled with hunger. She stepped forward, hands reached out. *Smack!* Someone clipped her across the side of her head. Startled, she turned round, her ear still ringing.

"Heh! No stealing. This is for dinner. If you want to eat

you have to help. Madam said that you are not guests. You have to work your way. I am the cook," said the man shooing them away. He was dressed in loose black cotton trousers and a white top. His hair, tied up in a queue, hung like a fat black rope down his back. "You speak Hainanese?" he asked Shao Peng hopefully. "I'm Ah Tong, from Hainan."

They couldn't grasp what he was saying and in exasperation he pointed to a pestle and mortar. "Ma'am eats lots lots chilly. You take this," he indicated a pile of chillies and using a pounding motion, waved Rohani over.

Under his watchful eyes, Rohani took a low wooden stool and indicated that Shao Peng should sit on the floor next to her. She showed her how to slice the chillies into two and take out the seeds. They worked quickly and before long they had a bowl of clean deseeded chillies. Rohani dropped a handful at a time into the mortar. She pounded with the pestle until they became a mush. Then she spooned them into a bowl and dropped more chillies into the mortar repeating the process until all the chillies were pounded.

"*Cuci tangan*. Wash your hands," she said to Shao Peng motioning and rubbing her own. "*Pedas!* Hot!" she said, pointing to her eyes. "Don't touch."

The cook beamed delighted to be spared a task that he hated. "Good! Good! There! Eat." He handed them two steaming bowls of rice from a pot "After eat, you help me other things," he said wagging his fingers at them. He walked over and dished out a bowl of vegetables. "Eat!" he repeated. "After, peel those," pointing to a basket piled high with red shallots. Then with a cheerful smile, he walked over and pinched Shao Peng's cheek. "Who are you? Why my Madam hates you so much?"

Neither Shao Peng nor Rohani understood him. With fingers burning from the sting of the chillies they tucked into their food.

By the time they went to bed, they had peeled and thinly sliced hundreds of shallots and peeled and diced an equal number of garlics. Their eyes stung from the fumes of the shallots. From her bed, Rohani could hear Shao Peng sobbing. She went over and slipped in next to Shao Peng and put her arms around her. *"Shhh Shhh!"* she comforted and kissed the girl. Quietly she sang a nursery tune. Shao Peng quietened listening to the song; to words she did not comprehend yet found soothing. Eventually she fell asleep.

"How do I rescue Shao Peng from that most unpleasant woman?" asked Grime. He had hurried back to Cavenagh's residence. "I am sure she wished to have nothing to do with her."

"As I understand it, you were entrusted by the aunt to bring her here and hand the child over to her father. You have a letter to this effect. The men who came to Michael's house had a letter from the father requesting that she be handed over to them and be brought to Mrs Lim Eng Kim's house. If the letter the men carried is genuine, I am afraid you have little say in the matter. You have done your job."

"I have not seen the letter. I was here with you. It could be *bona fide*, on the other hand it might not be. What if the men have taken her somewhere else?" The mere thought sent shivers up his spine. The last thing he wanted was for Shao Peng to have the same fate as her mother. "We have to go to Mrs Lim's house to verify."

Cavenagh grew pensive. "We cannot march to Mrs Lim house and make accusations. Perhaps we should try to find out if the child is with Mrs Lim in a more circumspect manner. Through the servants grapevine."

Grime nodded. "Can we do it now? Do you think we could find the men who took her? I would dearly like to see the letter."

"Stay here. I'll call my houseboy. He is the most talkative man I have ever met. He knows everything that goes on in the island. I do not know how he finds time to work." Cavenagh rang a bell. Within minutes a diminutive man, no taller than five feet, arrived.

"Sir! You call me? I come quickee quickee." Ah See bobbed his head up and down, a smile on his face ever ready to please his master.

"Do you know anybody in Mr Lim Eng Kim's household in Northbridge Road?"

"Yes Master. I know the cook, Ah Tong. He and I from same village in Hainan. We came same boat, same time. We muchee good friends."

"Well could you ask him if a little girl called Shao Peng has arrived in Mr Lim's house? Could you do it now? This evening."

Ah See's face froze. His eyes darted from left to right. How did his master know about the girl? How did he know that Ah Tong was here, in the kitchen, in this very house?

"Well," said Cavenagh who was, in fact, not aware that Ah Tong was in the house, "what are you waiting for? Go! Find out."

"Yes sir. I talk to him. I ask him." Ah See left and returned almost immediately. He knew the answer to the question. Tong had already told him.

"Sir, girl in Mrs Lim's house."

Chapter 32

THE DOOR SQUEAKED open a fraction and a manservant peered out from behind it. His eyes, narrow and almost bare of eyelashes, glared at the callers. Within an instant his disdainful expression disappeared. He recognised the visitors. Englishmen! Englishmen of distinction! The younger one had come the other day. Now, resplendently dressed in a deep blue velvet waistcoat and a snow-white cravat, he looked different. And the older gentleman; everyone knew him. Who could fail to recognise no less a person than the Governor of Singapore?

The manservant opened the door immediately; bowing low, he bobbed his head up and down.

"Is Mrs Lim in?" asked Grime.

The manservant quivered. He bobbed again and invited them in. Then he turned and ran into the house leaving the bemused Grime and Cavenagh in the hallway.

From the kitchen, Rohani could hear him shouting. A woman's voice responded in Malay. "*Siapa datang?* Who is calling?" Then a commotion, followed by a hasty muffled exchange, and then the clacking of wooden clogs. The sounds grew louder and louder and then stopped.

Rohani hurried with Shao Peng in tow out of the kitchen into the dinning room. Barefoot, they crept on tiptoe to the door leading from the dining room to the hallway. They peeped out from behind the door. The hallway, with its dark rosewood stools set around a small round marble table in the middle, opened to the left into the dining room and to the right to the sitting room. She saw Mrs Lim. She had her back towards them. Rohani placed a finger to her lips and, with an almost imperceptible shake of her head, warned Shao Peng not to speak. They leaned forward their heads almost touching the door to listen to the conversation.

"No we will not stay. Thank you. All we want is the little girl. We wish to collect her and return her directly to her father," said Grime. "These are the letters from her aunt in China entrusting her to my care."

He spoke slowly and deliberately. He saw the glimmer of gladness followed by shadows of doubt on Mrs Lim's face. Her eyes vacillated with uncertainty. He realised, however, that he had already made headway. She had not refused outright like she did previously and he knew from Cavenagh's houseboy that the woman did not want Shao Peng. She was hesitating only out of fear of her husband. He turned to glance at Cavenagh, appealing to him for support.

"You have my word that I will clear the matter with your husband. I know him, so rest assured," said Cavenagh, "I will send him a letter to explain. I promise that the girl will be well cared for."

"She is the daughter of one of your husband's employees and has no direct relationship with your husband," Grime assured her. He stopped. A slight movement to his left made him glanced in the direction of the door there. He saw two pairs of anxious eyes looking out from behind it. He recognised the long almond eyes with the thick dark lashes as those of Shao Peng. Quickly he turned back to Mrs Lim. "I bear no grievance," he said. "We will overlook whatever misunderstanding that might have existed."

From behind the door, Rohani could hear a sharp exhalation of breath from Mrs Lim. She saw how the lady's body visibly relaxed. Then she saw the lady nod her consent. Rohani grabbed hold of Shao Peng, all the while pressing her finger to her lips to mime silence. Still they could not suppress their gladness, they smiled, a wide lip smile that transformed their faces. It took all of Rohani's effort to stop Shao Peng from rushing out.

Relieved she would no longer be responsible for Shao Peng and glad of the assurance that she was not her husband's love child, Mrs Lim spoke for the first time. "Take them. Today if you wish. As long as you guarantee that you take responsibility and will explain to my husband."

Chapter 33

THE CARRIAGE ROLLED forward. Shao Peng sitting by Edward Grime clung to his hand for the entire duration of the trip back to Janidah's house. She chatted brightly, all her tears wiped from her face. Every now and then, she would turn to Rohani and smile, her cheeks crunched up showing her little white teeth. "I told you that he would look for me," she said to Rohani in Chinese. Although Rohani did not understand her words, she understood the sentiment. It was all too obvious; the joy in the little girl's eyes and the way she held on to the English gentleman's hand. The feelings were obviously reciprocated by the gentleman. He looked fondly at the girl and patted her head every now and then. Hastily Rohani looked away, not wishing to be seen watching them.

"We have to learn Malay if we want Rohani to understand us," said Grime to his charge. "This might be our priority while we wait for your father. With both Janidah and Rohani and the children as your teachers, you have no excuse not to be fluent."

"When is father coming?" asked Shao Peng. She was worried. She was afraid she would not recognise him. In the early days, she was able to conjure up an image of him; with time that image had faded. While she could recall some of the things they did together she found it harder and harder to remember his face. Her mother's face was clearer. When she thought of Hua she could still recall how she sat by the doorway sewing, the way she would sing while she cooked and the little quirk of her lips when she was happy. Yet even these memories were becoming more distant. In her disturbed sleep of the past few nights, she had started calling out for her aunt Heong Yook. Worst still, she had also called out for Uncle Edward. She felt guilty.

"Soon," replied Grime observing how quiet his charge had become. "He'll come as quickly as he can."

The motion of the carriage and the steady tapping of the horse's hooves began to have a soporific effect on Shao Peng. She was tired from the excitement and emotions of the past couple of days. As the carriage swayed and rolled, her eyes began to flutter and then close. Rohani got up and put her arm protectively round Shao Peng. Soon the carriage was filled with the soft sound of Shao Peng's sleep and the churning of the wheels.

❀ ❀ ❀

"No Master. I'll tell Mistress Janidah. You please wait there," said the servant pointing to a room beyond the entrance. "She'll come shortly."

"Wouldn't it be more convenient if I went to her instead? Her house is only a hundred yards from here. Surely it would be impolite of me to summon her here?" Edward did not comprehend why his suggestion to visit Janidah should cause such a furore. Why was this man so adamant that he should send for Janidah instead? He was almost hysterical with the vigorous shaking of his head.

"No! No! Better she come here."

"Is it a social practice that I am impeaching if I go to visit her?" wondered Grime perplexed at the fuss. Before he could ask, the man had hurried away. Grime looked at the departing back. It must be a local custom so it was best to do as he was told, he decided. He walked into what might be called a drawing room, the one to which the man had directed him earlier. He had never been in it before.

He sat down in an armchair. He ran his hands lightly over the upholstery feeling its smooth and thick texture. The opulence and richness of the room was almost over powering after the spartan furnishings of his own rooms in the factories in Canton. The drapes with their embossed gold trimmings that hung from the tall windows were testament to it. It was almost not in character with the Michael he knew from university days and certainly different from the other rooms in the house. Perhaps this was a side of his friend's nature he did not know. He would not be surprised at anything after stumbling upon the existence of Janidah. He sighed. Life changed people. There was no right or wrong. He shrugged. He had grown too cynical. Perhaps he needed to be if he were to remain in the Orient.

He heard someone approaching and got up immediately. Janidah entered the room. He felt awkward and embarrassed.

It was the first time he had been alone with her. Previously there was always someone with them. He felt he had to apologise for his intrusion and make clear he was not the one who had sent for her.

She waved her hand gaily. "I have explained. This is not my house. It is Michael's. I hardly ever enter this drawing room. It is mainly reserved for important guests. You are his guests and it is quite right that I come to you instead of you to me." She laughed a throaty gurgle coming from deep, her head thrown back and her eyes bright. "What would people say if they saw a man come to my house at night? Phew!" She passed her hand exaggeratedly over her forehead. "Anyway, this house will soon be on the market. He is selling it."

She looked away quickly. He could see a glimmer of tears. He realised with a flash that behind her jubilant and cheerful appearance was another side of her, a side that was hurting. "Are you alright?" he asked.

"What do you think?" she responded with a fierceness that took him by surprise. She whipped round to face him squarely; her hands clenched. "Of course, I am not alright. I am sick of pretending. How can I be alright when he has left me, when even the servants define what I can and cannot do? Michael is not to blame. He explained right from the start of our relationship. He did not lie. I knew this is how it would end. I lied to myself, thinking and hoping for the impossible. I am the one who is at fault. I betrayed myself."

"I am so sorry to encroach on your privacy at this most inconvenient and unfortunate time. I did not know. Shall I leave?"

"No! Stay! You are a guest and I have had the strictest of instruction to play hostess." She softened her voice when she saw his discomfort. "I am sorry. That was an unbecoming outburst. I do not know what came over me. It is just the attitude of the servants since Michael left. I am not as badly treated as I make myself out to be. I am well provided for. And I would like you to stay. Please," she said looking up directly into his eyes beseeching him. Her voice was almost a whisper. "I will be most embarrassed if you were to leave after my outburst. Moreover, I hear that you have succeeded in bringing Shao Peng back and, not only that, her companion a pretty Malay woman as well. Where are they?"

"They are here. That was why I wanted to speak to you." Grime could see that she was genuinely mortified and wanted to change the subject to safer ground. "Would you mind if they stayed here. I have not asked Michael. I will write to him. However, I would like to consult you first."

"Of course," she smiled. "Don't bother to write. It will take months for your letter to reach him and his reply to arrive here. If the house is sold and they still need shelter I can always put them up. I know what it is like to be homeless."

He stared, slightly flabbergasted by her change of mood but aware of the effort it must have taken of her to control her true feelings and to place others first before herself.

She sat down and gazed up at him. "When I first met Michael I was very young. My mother had just died and I was sent out to work. I worked here, you know, as a maid. The rest is history. Michael taught me to read and speak properly. He gave me everything. I do not want to give you the wrong impression." Her voice was business-like, disarmingly honest and with no hint of the earlier emotion.

"Thank you, thank you for telling me. Thank you for your generosity. I hope we will not need to intrude on it for too long."

"Is there anything else I can do to help?"

He pondered, uncertain if he should ask for more.

"I have the time and I would like to do something useful," she urged.

"Could you speak to Rohani; ask her who she is and why she is here? We can't talk to her; she speaks only Malay."

"Of course. Perhaps I should teach Shao Peng some Malay so she can communicate with her. She learns fast. In the few hours spent with my children, she has already picked up some words."

He thanked her. She blushed still embarrassed by her earlier outburst. He saw the pretty flush of colours in her cheeks and wondered how his friend could have beared to leave her.

"Shall I introduce them? They are on the veranda," he said.

WEEKS WENT BY.

It was late in the day. The trees and flowering bushes threw long shadows over the lawn. The pending sale of the mansion had brought the sales agents to the house. They had come to draw up the boundaries of what would constitute the main estate to be sold and what would be Janidah's. Until then, the grounds of one had run seamlessly into the other.

They were in the garden. Rohani sat cross-legged on the grass. Shao Peng was busy playing a game of hide and seek with the children. Having mastered her numbers in Malay, she was busy counting while the others ran to hide behind bushes. Janidah paid little attention to the play. The surveyors distracted her as they tramped round the grounds with their markers. Try as she did, she could not help but feel sad. She felt deserted, lonely and ostracised. Since Michael left, the servants in the main house had made her feel an outsider when she visited. Perhaps she was over-sensitive. She leaned further back in her chair and looked across to Rohani. She saw in her what she had been when she first came to this household. She was fifteen then. Now at twenty-eight she felt old. She should not complain. She had no right to feel hurt. What would she have been if not for Michael? Yet, she wished that their relationship had been more and that he had not returned to his home country. Of course he had a wife and she had more right to him, still ... She sighed. She wondered how his life was in England.

The men continued marking the boundaries. Janidah looked on helplessly. She saw how her garden would shrink to little more than a verge. A small road would be built to lead directly to her house, she was told. She would no longer be able to use the estate's driveway. She smiled. What did it matter? She could not maintain a large garden anyway. She turned to survey her house. She had not done badly. If she was in *kampong glam* her house, if she had one, would be an attap-thatched wooden affair on stilts, with just one tiny room that would serve as kitchen, dining, sitting and bedroom. Toilet facilities would be an outhouse and bathing would be from the river or well. She grew up in such a house. Now her house was of brick with four bedrooms, a sitting room and a separate dining room and kitchen. She sensed Rohani observing her and once more cast her eyes in her direction.

Rohani had explained her circumstances. She spoke highly of Shao Peng's father. Janidah could sense that she had stronger feelings than just those of a loyal servant for a master. The way Rohani's face softened and her colour deepened when she spoke his name were a giveaway. Perhaps she would fare better with this Chinese man than she had with Michael. Perhaps he would even marry her. She must help her by teaching Shao Peng Malay so that at least they would be able to speak to each other. Shao Peng, she thought, would prove to be Rohani's key to her boss's heart. She had wondered at the Chinese Malay alliances she saw around her in Singapore. Were they loosely structured relationships like hers with Michael? Michael did not take up Islam and he would have to if they were to be betrothed officially. The term marriage was so loosely used on the island and in the hinterland of Malaya. She shrugged. She did not place much store on these customs and rules. It was not important as long as Rohani did not mind. She grew pensive as she thought of her own situation and what she had become.

The men gathered up their tools. They had left markers all around her compound. She tried not to look at them. She got up. It was time to prepare. Tonight they were dining at the main house.

"Rohani," she said. "*Bawa Shao Peng balik rumah besar.* Take Shao Peng back to the main house. Bathe her. She badly needs a bath and a change of clothes before dinner. We will join Mr Grime later in the evening."

"But I have always bathed myself," protested Shao Peng when Rohani fetched her.

"Let Rohani help you. She will do a better job. Your hair badly needs washing and it is far too long for you to do it properly," Janidah explained.

❀ ❀ ❀

"THERE SHOULDN'T BE any problem if you are sure that is what you want," said Cavenagh. "I have spoken to Michael's partner who he left in charge of his business in Singapore. Your letter to Michael will be on its way to England tomorrow. Until you receive Michael's reply, you will have to deal with the partner. He is a good Chinaman, honest and open in his dealings. You won't have problems with him."

"Thank you sir. And here is another letter that I hope you will send. It is urgent. It is to my wife. I have written to her of my decision to stay on in Singapore. She won't like it. And I dread what she will say." Grime handed the envelope to Cavenagh. It was bulky.

"You have thought it over carefully, I presume," Cavenagh said. "I am happy to have you here, more than happy. Even so you need to weigh up your personal circumstances. Bridges are hard to build from afar, especially when you tell me she is so unhappy having you abroad."

"I have. I have been away too long. In the beginning I missed her dearly and she me. However, just as her letters to me have grown colder, my feelings for her have also waned. These past nights I have re-read all her letters over the past year. Her demand that I return seems more obligatory rhetoric on her part and less to do with missing me. I fully sympathise with her. I have placed my career before her. I am to blame. With the new legislation she should be able to divorce me. If she does, I will not contest it. I have treated her badly."

Cavenagh looked questioningly at Grime.

"I am referring to the 1857 Act. For the first time women can sue for divorce in a civil court without requiring a private Act of Parliament to be passed."

Cavenagh placed his hand on Grime's shoulders; he squeezed it gently. "I make no judgement. I shall have this sent. Remember do not be afraid to change your mind if you feel that you have not made the right decision."

He went to his bureau and poured out two small tumblers of whisky. "Here's to you! And here's to your new life!"

Grime drank it down with a gulp. They stood looking out of the tall window towards the harbour. It was a clear day with just a hint of clouds on the horizon. The river was, as usual, crowded with vessels of all sizes, colours and origins; sampans nudged against fishing *perahus*, passenger boats lay next to canopied boats selling and carting goods. Steamers and ships flying the flags of European nations sailed next to Chinese junks. On the riverbank overlooking all this maritime traffic stood European-style warehouses and Chinese shophouses. Further inland the rooftops of Buddhist temples, mosques, Hindu places of worships and josshouses roughly demarcated the city's ethnicity. Grime drew a deep breath. "To a new life," he repeated holding his glass up.

BACK IN MICHAEL Bowe's mansion, Rohani was preparing the bath. She looked with amazement at her surroundings. Every room was magnificent, even this bathroom with its black and white tiled floors and thick fluffy towels. The Raja's house was nothing in comparison. She knelt down and poured a kettle of hot water into the bath. Then carefully placing the kettle to one side she emptied a big bucket of cold water into it. "*Mmm, baik*. This should be about right. *Mari*," she said waving Shao Peng to her. She stood next to the bath and rubbed her arms and legs to demonstrate before announcing *mandi*! Bath! Then demonstrating that Shao Peng should stand still on the floor to enable water to be sluiced over her, she dipped a bucket into the water and waited.

Shao Peng pulled a towel off the rack and stuffing it into her mouth doubled up and laughed. *"Bu shi! Bu shi!"* she cried in Mandarin. "I go into the bath, like this," she demonstrated, dropping her towel and climbing into the bath.

"Don't! The water will be dirty!" cried Rohani in alarm. To no avail, Shao Peng had already submerged herself into the water and deftly taking a piece of soap had begun to scrub. Soon the water was filled with soapsuds. Rohani laughed. Who but a little girl would go into a bath, scrub and then rinse in the same dirty water? She shook her head and wagged her finger to indicate that it was the wrong thing to do. Shao Peng just laughed.

"*Shi! Shi!* Yes! Yes! Janidah told me this is how people in the main house bathe. It is fun!" Shao Peng grinned splashing water at Rohani. Soon the floor was wet and the bath water a greyish brown from the dirt on the girl's arms and legs.

Rohani ran out of the bathroom with a bucket and caught the attention of a servant passing. She spoke in Malay to ask urgently if she could have more water. "I need it to rinse the little girl of soapsuds. She has stepped into the bath instead of staying outside it. The bath water is now dirty."

The servant flashed her a look that implied that it was Rohani who was stupid. She shouted rudely in Malay, "*Tak apa!* Never mind, you can dry her straight out of the bath. You need not rinse her again. They do it that way. She is right. Otherwise you will flood the house. *Yeong yeong yeh do mn sik! Chun do sei! San ba mui!* Know nothing! Stupid! From the jungle!" The latter said in Cantonese.

Red faced, Rohani returned to the bathroom and closed the door. She felt a fool. She was supposed to look after Shao Peng yet she had managed not to anything right. She could not communicate with her. She was in awe of the house and terrified of the Englishman, that tall big man. And who would think that you rinsed in dirty water, she asked herself once again. She had failed Ngao. She wished she were back in her master's house, in familiar surroundings. Despite the grandeur and comfort, she still preferred her own hard wooden bed and straw mat. She missed the routine of running the house. Here she had no one to talk to. She was lonely. There was only Mistress Janidah and, while kind, she seemed so preoccupied. Most of all she missed her master. How she wished he were here.

Shao Peng saw Rohani's distress. The loud derisive laughter and string of ridicule shouted aloud by the passing servant had caught her ear. She stepped out of the bath and, wrapping herself in a towel, went up to Rohani and put her arms round her. Rohani dropped the bucket and squatted down. She held the little girl and kissed her on her forehead. They didn't speak. They didn't need to.

guest might like to try some instead of roast beef and Yorkshire pudding. The Hainanese cook was particularly proud of his Yorkshire pudding. Today, however, there were neither dark looks nor mutterings from the servants. They went about their tasks quietly, almost meekly like they did when Master Bowe was around. Even Janidah noticed the change. She had raised an eyebrow when a servant drew back a chair for her, a practice they had conveniently forgotten following the departure of Michael Bowe.

It was a Sunday. They had finished lunch. The children had scrambled off to play hopscotch and five stones. Rohani went with them. Janidah leaned back on her chair and closed her eyes. She wore her hair down with a flower tucked behind one ear. The children had strung together a chain of red hibiscus and insisted she wore it round her neck. The bright flaming red garland cast a pink glow on her dusky neck. Grime was intensely aware of her presence, the fullness of her lips and the glow in her cheeks with that strange tantalising colour of golden nutmeg.

Her eyes fluttered open. "Is anything wrong?" she asked noting how he was looking at her. Her heart sank; she saw how serious he looked. Was he going to leave and return to England, she wondered?

She took a quick look around the room. The servants were hovering in the background finding excuses to stay. They wanted to hear from the Englishman what they had already heard through the grapevine. They moved slowly, their feet dragging each step ever so quietly. Not a sound came from their movements. Suddenly they had so many things to attend to at the table, a glass to be removed, a stain to be wiped, water to be poured, cutlery to be put in place and aligned.

Chapter 34

The muslin curtains in the dining room lifted gently with the sea breeze. The room was empty. They had all congregated on the open veranda, a practice introduced by Janidah and welcomed by Grime. Despite the muttering of the servants and their dark looks, breakfast and lunch were always served on the veranda unless it rained. The servants moaned when they laid the table each day. "No class! So dusty! So hot!" They complained about the informality of the arrangement, how the children were allowed to leave the table to play in the garden and their messiness. They blamed it all on Janidah whom they viewed as an upstart. They looked askance when the Chinese girl suggested that Rohani sat with her. How dare she, they thought. They grumbled, pursing their lips in disapproval when asked to serve local Malay food because the English

"Perhaps Madam I should tell you. I had originally planned to do so next week. I think it is only right that I tell you now instead," said Grime. He spoke gently, aware that he had made Janidah anxious by his staring. She was gripping the arms of her chair and leaning forward; her eyes were intent on him. It could not be easy for her not knowing what will happen from one day to the next, Grime thought. He cleared his throat. "I have put in a bid for this house. I heard yesterday that I have won the bid. Tomorrow, I will sign the deed."

Janidah half rose from her chair and then sat down again, her hand flew to her mouth. She had not expected this. An audible release of breath came from the servants. They wanted to know their fate. Would they go with the house to this Englishman who had such different ways from Master Bowe? They did not move, their activity suspended for the moment. Their ears pricked up in the hope to hear more.

"You are not returning to England?" she asked, her voice weak and incredulous.

"No! I am staying on and will be working here with the Governor for the moment and then..." He paused to look at her. Her eyes were still wide with surprise. "You don't mind do you that I am buying the house? You can have access to it just as before, if you wish. In fact, I will remove all the markers the estate agents have placed round your garden. There is really no need for them."

Her lips trembled. After days and nights of worry this was more than she could have hoped or prayed for.

"I will make the transition as painless as I can," said Grime, worried that she disapproved. "You are welcome if you wish to use the house. I am out during the day anyway except for the weekends. The children can come and play whenever they wish."

"Thank you," she said. She placed her hands in his; she could feel the warmth of them. "I can't tell you how relieved I am that it is you who will be the owner. I will not take advantage of your kindness. Once the contract is exchanged, I will not come here unless invited." She smiled, withdrawing her hands from his grasp. "But for now, I am still part of the house and you are Michael's guest and hence, in a way, mine." Her eyes twinkled with mischief.

"I would like to reciprocate that kindness and generosity," he returned gallantly,

They heard a flurry and smiled. The servants had left the veranda. They had gone to report the events in the kitchen.

Chapter 35

SELANGOR

THE WOUNDED AND dead lay scattered on the riverbank and their blood soaked into the soil turning it red. Around the corpses flies hovered and in the skies buzzards circled, their wings spread out wide, waiting, waiting for an opportune moment.

In the river a boat floated, its deck riddled with bullets and cannon shots. Filled with provisions and commanded by Ngao, the boat had been on its way to the warehouse when they were attacked. The attack came from the hill, from Raja Mahdi's Fort, the enemy's stronghold. A cannon shot was quickly followed by gunshots. A whole section of the boat was blasted sending a shower of wood splinters into the air. Ngao standing at the stern had jumped clear into the river. Shielded by the boat he escaped; others were less fortunate. Some fell overboard to be picked off one by one by snipers. The dead hung from the sides of the boat, their heads dipping into the water, bobbing, bobbing as though in merriment while everywhere blood flowed.

On the riverbank, the army of Yap's men had fared little better. Its prime task was to guard and protect the boat but it was soon cut down. Cannons were fired straight into its midst. Boom! Boom! Boom! And men fell like toy soldiers, piling one on top of the other. The earth opened up into big craters. Cheers and shouts of jubilation from the fort were answered by the mournful cries of dying men from the riverbank. The air was thick with smoke. The acrid smell of gunpowder mingled with the ferrous odour of blood.

Ngao dived deep into the water and swam as fast as he could. He hardly dared to surface for breath. He felt his lungs bursting and his arms strained to their limits. With a final release of strength, he pushed forward and up, his legs kicking strongly. Gulping for air, he turned to survey the carnage. The side of the boat had finally broken free from the keel completely. A body slipped into the water. It floated like a log. Ngao turned away and swam, stroke after stroke, moving further and further away. A tree loomed ahead of him on the riverbank, its roots reaching out in the water like the tentacles of an octopus. He grasped one and hauled himself on to land. He lay gasping for air and then he ran. He ran as if on fire into the refuge of the jungle.

❀ ❀ ❀

"You have to take the Fort. Otherwise, I cannot get supplies to Raja Abdullah's son, Raja Ismail," said Ngao.

He was in Lukut. It had taken him two days of walking to reach the town. His feet were cut and sore. His arms and legs were a mass of bruises and covered with insect bites. He had eaten little during his time in the jungle. Roots dug out from the ground, wild fruits and rainwater were his mainstay. By the time he reached the outskirts of the town, he could hardly walk. It was Yap's men patrolling the area who found him sprawled on the ground, exhausted and delirious with fever.

Ngao looked round the room. It was packed. During the course of the week, more and more men had arrived; lean, sinewy, burnt brown, they were men ready to place their lives at stake, men to be feared. Yap Ah Loy rose from his seat.

"You have heard him," he shouted arms raised high, his fingers pointing at Ngao. "Raja Ismail's men are starving and their morale is low. We have to help them. As Ngao said, the position of the Fort has given the enemy a strategic advantage. With their guns and cannons sited on the hill, and pointed at our boats, our men are sitting ducks."

He looked at each and every one in the room. "We have to change this. We must take the Fort. We will take it. We will avenge all those who have died for this cause. Let the river and the land be drenched with the enemy's blood!"

The men cheered. Yap Ah Loy raised his arms once again and pummelled the air to urge them on. His eyes glowed with power and savage intensity.

The men jumped from their seats infected by his fervour. "Yes! Yes! We will wipe them from the face of the earth!" They roared their support, "Lead us on. Lead us on!"

"When we win," Yap continued opening his arms wide and his voice growing fiercer and louder, "you will have the land. You have nothing to fear for your families. I promise you I will compensate every family's loss handsomely. Give me the head of a leader and I will give you this," he cried, thrusting a fistful of money into the air.

Cheers erupted in the room. The men were fired up. For months they had suffered reversals. For months they had lain low. For months they were told to be patient. "Let the enemy be deluded into thinking that we are defeated," they were instructed. They complied, honing their martial skills, their gunnery and weapons, sitting, waiting, impatient. Not any more, they were going on the offensive. It would not be just a matter of guarding and protecting their own territory or their provisions. It would be a fight to the end. No quarter would be given. The uproar rose to a peak; many of the men had relatives who had been massacred.

"Go! Rest! Eat! We will leave soon."

Yap then turned to Ngao. "Come with me, I want to hear the full details of the battle again. I want you to point out on this map the enemy positions, the lie of the land, and the slope of the hill; even the density of the forest. Every detail is essential."

A WEEK LATER three battalions of Yap's men armed with cannons, guns, bamboo rockets, knives and daggers entered the jungle. They took different routes: one to the west of the Fort, one to the east and the other to the north. Scouts were sent ahead to reconnoitre the ground. Throughout their journey the three battalions maintained contact through scouts on horses. When they reached the base of the hill, they burrowed in and built stockades of bamboo and lashed tree trunks together with rattan. Sharpened spikes of bamboo were attached to the top of the stockades. Beyond the walls, they dug pits and filled them with pointed stakes.

When all was completed, they took up their positions and waited for nightfall, for the signal to attack. Men were sent up the hill. They scrambled up and then they took out one by one the guards, a knife into a neck, a slit throat, a slash with a *parang*. They moved quickly to disarm and dispense with the guards manning the cannon. Jubilant from their successive victories, the men defending the Fort were relaxed and unsuspecting. Yap's battalions at the base stood tense waiting for the signal. Finally it came, a flash of light. It lit up the sky. They fired in unison sending cannon balls from all directions into the walls of the Fort. Bamboo rockets followed, their sharp ends burrowing deep into flesh on contact. The enemy returned fire, but confused, they directed it towards the southern approach to the fort. Yap had anticipated this and had stayed clear of the south. He had expected it because the supply boats always came from that direction travelling upriver towards the warehouse. Ngao had told him of the battle and described in detail the artillery attack.

The battle dragged on. Hours passed. Suddenly there was silence. Yap's battalion ceased fire to rest and to regroup. Men were despatched to relieve the weary and the wounded and to carry away the dead. Food supplies were replenished. Revived, his force resumed the battle. It raged on for days. On the eighth day, a white flag appeared on the Fort. It was hoisted up over the archway. Starved of supplies, and with dwindling numbers and ammunitions the Fort could hold out no longer. Yap's men marched in and took it over.

❀ ❀ ❀

NEWS OF THE victory reached Ngao and Eng Kim. They were outside the row of shophouses watching their final completion. The remaining bamboo scaffolding was being dismantled and workmen had begun painting the shophouses. Men, barechested in rolled-up black trousers tied at the waist, hurried by with brushes and brooms while others loaded remaining stones and debris on to bullock carts to be taken away.

"I don't imagine that the fighting will end," said Ngao.

"No! There will be a lull, a temporary peace before it starts all over again," answered Eng Kim. "So many issues and quarrels remain unsettled. It is no longer just a war between the rajas, there is also the contentious issue of who will eventually succeed and become the leader of all the Chinese settlers in Kuala Lumpur. Already people are jostling for power."

A silence settled over the two men. Both were in deep thought. Their concerns took them in different directions. The war would have different implications for them.

"Surely it will be Yap Ah Loy," ventured Ngao.

Eng Kim made no reply as he continued staring ahead at the buildings. Then he glanced questioningly at Ngao throwing the question back at his assistant. "What makes you so sure?"

"I suppose that was a silly statement," admitted Ngao. "It will not be so easy with the challenge posed by his rival. I hear that Chong Chong is bent on fighting Yap."

"Do you wonder? It must come as a shock to Chong Chong to see himself losing out to someone who was formerly his employee," replied Eng Kim. "Yap, in the early days, was his cook!"

"Well, we will have to make the best use of the lull and build up our supplies. Whether it be peace or war, food is one essential commodity that will be in demand."

Ngao turned to look at his boss. Eng Kim was still staring at the shop houses. Ngao wondered if he should bring up the subject. He decided that there would never be a better time. "Today," he said, his words rolling off his tongue slowly and hesitantly, "today is the last day of my bondage. My debt to you has been fully repaid."

Eng Kim turned to face Ngao. "Yes! You are no longer in my debt although you have never been my bondman in the true sense of the word. I have treated you like the son I never had. And you have been loyal, hard working and faithful."

Ngao swallowed hard in an effort to quell his emotions. "I know and I am grateful. At times I have doubted you. You have proved me wrong." His mind went back to the near quarrel between them when Eng Kim stopped him from bringing Shao Peng to Selangor. He had suspected Eng Kim of ulterior motives. He regretted his outburst. It proved to be good advice.

Each man wanted to say so much to the other; they could not for fear of embarrassment. Shows of emotion and affection had never featured in the upbringing of either of them. In the case of Eng Kim, it was because he came from a traditional Confucianist family. Ngao could not bring himself to reveal his feelings because no one, with the exception of his aunt, had shown him any open affection since he was a child. So they stood side by side, each with so much to say to the other but each constrained to say very little. They looked at the shops they had built together and the sense of pride and connection between them grew.

After a while, Eng Kim pointed to a corner shop house. "That could be yours at a price. It would place you again in my debt. Would you dare take it up?" Eng Kim feared losing Ngao.

"Would I still be working for you?" Ngao's thoughts went back to the early days when he went to Eng Kim for help. There was little he could say that could really express his gratitude. He sensed the older man's reluctance to sever their connection completely.

"Yes! You would be working for me," replied Eng Kim. No inkling of the excitement that bubbled in him was evident in his face. It was smooth and devoid of any expression.

"Will I be able to run the shop as a separate enterprise?"

"We can work something out."

"I plan to leave soon for Singapore to bring Shao Peng and Rohani back."

"Are you sure?" A shadow appeared briefly on Eng Kim's open face.

Ngao nodded. "There will never be an optimum time. I think I should take the risk."

"Very well," said Eng Kim, "I shall stay here until your return. Do not take long."

It was time, Eng Kim felt, to release the rein on his protégé.

Chapter 36

SINGAPORE

THE STATEROOM IN Governor House was packed with dinner guests. Aside from British officers, many prominent Chinese merchants and representatives from the various ethnic groups attended. All were dressed in their colourful finery. Black skull caps worn on top of black sleek heads and pigtails contrasted with bright turbans and gold embossed headgear made of kerchiefs stiffened and tied to have two over-lapping corners standing jauntily above the brow. A semblance of the comfortable mixing of people in the early days of the island presided. In those times distinctions in class, colour and race counted for little. As the years went by, this cordial atmosphere had all but dissipated until Governor Cavenagh's attempt to encourage its return. Even so, the evening's assembly was a relatively rare event; the island had gradually become even more polarised on ethnic lines. Europeans formed clubs of their own, bringing English sports such as cricket and swimming into their midst. They soon became a binding cohesive force for the English community. The segregation of races extended even to commerce. Despite their importance in trade, the Chinese withdrew from the Chamber of Commerce, turning it into a European affair. For this evening, however, everyone was convivial. The room was filled with cigar smoke and the intoxicating aroma of whisky and brandy.

Grime stood with a glass in hand surrounded by people of all creeds with their own idiosyncratic renditions of English. He noted, however, that some spoke excellently and he would have been hard put to tell that they were not English had he not been able to see them. Inevitably the conversation veered toward the subject of the worsening situation in the Malayan states of Perak, Selangor and Negri Sembilan and the civil war in Pahang.

"The British administration must do something. The fighting there has implications for all of us in Singapore," said a merchant. "The bitter rivalry in those Malay states has spread to the heart of our commerce."

"Of course. What do you expect?" another merchant butted in. "I am totally behind you on the need for the British to be involved. In order to protect trade here, couldn't the British administration intervene? The fighting has disrupted mining and our trade in tin is being badly damaged."

"I am afraid it is out of the question," said an officer. "Her Majesty's Government will not intervene in native affairs. If merchants wish to engage in commerce in those barbaric places, then it is up to them. They should not expect any help from the British administration. These are not my words; I am just repeating our instructions," he added hastily when he saw the raised brows and disbelief on the faces round him.

Grime was absorbed in the conversations. He hoped to distil from them the views of the people and the British administration. The complexity of the opposing interests, both on the island and beyond needed to be carefully analysed if he was to help sort out the problems. A hand tugged at his sleeve. A manservant, no higher than his shoulder had appeared at his side and was calling him with some urgency. His pigtail swung as he turned to point to the door before hastening away. Grime followed him.

"A message from your house. Quickee! Quickee! Go home. Say girl's father here. Come fetch girl? Wants muchee thank you," the manservant said breathlessly once they reached the door.

Grime stopped mid-stride. He had been anticipating this day. He did not wish to meet Shao Peng's father. The guilt he felt over Hua's death had eased with all the excitement and newness of Singapore. Yet it never went and had only been momentarily buried. His face turned white. How could he excuse himself? Cavenagh was striding towards him.

"So he's here. I heard. You should go and meet him. We'll excuse you. We know how important it is for you to hand over your charge safely. Go! We'll meet tomorrow," said Cavenagh.

❀ ❀ ❀

THE HOUSE WAS fully lit when his carriage turned into the driveway. Light flooded out from the windows illuminating the surrounds. Grime stopped the carriage and got out, his shoes crunched on the gravel driveway, making sounds that seemed too loud to his ears. He had passed another carriage parked at a discrete distance away from the main gate when he turned in. It was a simple affair like the passenger carts in Chinatown. It must be Ngao's. He must have thought it inappropriate to bring it into the estate and left it outside.

Grime walked towards the main door. A servant, hearing his approach, rushed out to greet him, lamp in hand. Nervous, Grime took a deep breath. He wiped his hands surreptitiously on his trousers. They were damp with perspiration. It had to be done. With luck the whole handover would be done quickly. He was sorry to see Shao Peng go. He was fond of her. But this was not uppermost in his mind. What bothered him was meeting Ngao.

"Master! They are in the sitting room."

Grime acknowledged the information with a grim quirk of his lips and went in. Janidah was seated, legs crossed, in an armchair; everyone else was standing. Next to Shao Peng was a man, well built and tall for a Chinese. Beneath the loose tunic with the Chinese collar, he could see the arms of a man used to hard labour. He caught the man's eyes appraising him. They were sharp, intelligent and openly curious. He was not the bowing, scraping labourer intent to please. With a start he realised that Ngao was already walking towards him.

Ngao stopped in front of Grime. He put two hands up in a close clasp and bowed slightly, the traditional Chinese formal greeting. "*Xie xie!* Thank you! I am indebted to you for bringing my daughter and looking after her." Ngao looked up and into Grime's eyes and wondered at the apprehension there.

Grime could not hold the clear gaze of the man before him. He bowed quickly in return. "*Bing bu!* Not at all," he replied in Mandarin, strongly aware that Ngao was educated because he had not thanked him in dialect. He did it in Mandarin, the language of scholars and officials. He should not have been surprised. Shao Peng had already told him of her father's prowess with the pen.

While marvelling at Grime's linguistic skill, Ngao could not understand why the Englishman seemed so uncomfortable. He looked from Grime to his daughter. She was all smiles and was already running towards the man. With a jolt he realised that his daughter was fond of the Englishman. She had not run to Ngao when he arrived; in fact she had been shy.

"Uncle Edward, my father," she said dragging Grime's hand and thrusting it into Ngao's. "Shake his hand father," she said, "the English do that in greeting."

Ngao withdrew it quickly embarrassed by his daughter's forwardness, while Grime dropped Ngao's hand like hot coal. "You don't have to thank me. Wait here. I have a letter for you from your aunt. She gave it to Shao Peng. I kept it for safety. Are you planning to leave to night?"

"Tomorrow. I leave Singapore tomorrow," Ngao replied. Was there a slight edge in Grime's voice, Ngao wondered? Was he anxious for us to leave?

"Wait here. I'll get the letter." Without pausing for a reply, Grime walked quickly out of the room leaving Ngao puzzled.

Shao Peng looked disconcerted. "Is Uncle angry?" she asked, her eyes round with disappointment.

"Of course not," replied Janidah as she went over to put her arms around Shao Peng. She too had observed Grime's reserve, even coldness. He was certainly not his usual relaxed, hospitable self. She felt she had to make up for it. "Have you a place to stay for the night?" she asked Ngao. "Would you like to..." But before she could finish her sentence, Grime was back in the room waving the letter.

"Here it is. I hope you have a good and safe journey." He hardly looked at Ngao. Instead he turned away abruptly to speak to Shao Peng. Her anxious eyes pulled at his heartstrings. He bent down and took both her hands in his and squeezed them gently. "I shall miss you, my pet. Write to me, won't you?"

She dropped his hands and buried her face into his lap and sobbed. Ngao looked on. Grime, his arms still round Shao Peng, reluctantly raised his head and mimed, "I am sorry. She is tired."

Janidah hurried over and gently disentangled Shao Peng's firm hold on Grime. Rohani, hitherto silent also rushed over and placed her arm around her Shao Peng. "*Shhh,*" she said soothingly.

"Come, your father will be hurt," said Grime, his face still close to Shao Peng.

Ngao stood ashen-faced. He had not expected it: the long years of waiting for his daughter only to find her so attached to someone else.

"She was so looking forward to seeing you," Rohani said to Ngao. "She is just tired from the excitement; she is upset and fearful of yet another change. I have felt the same these past months so I can understand her."

"Of course," said Ngao. He went over to Shao Peng, squatted down so that he had to look up to her. He placed a palm on her cheek and then gently stroked it. "Everything will be fine," and then kissing her on her cheeks, whispered, "our house will eventually be as beautiful as this one. It is not grand now; we will make it beautiful together." He stood up and holding Shao Peng's hand in his, bade Grime goodbye, thanking him once again. "*Wo de jia shi ni de.* My humble house will be yours. You are welcome any day. We owe you a great debt and it will be remembered."

Grime could only nod in response. He wanted to confess there and then that it was not magnanimity on his part. It was his attempt to atone for his part in Hua's death. Words failed him. He reached out and shook Ngao by the hand.

From behind, Janidah looked on. She saw the emotions that crossed Grime's face and wondered. She waited until Grime left the room, and then hurried out of the house.

"Stop!" she called after Ngao and his family. "Let Rohani and Shao Peng stay with me for the night. When we were waiting for Mr Grime to return, you said that your lodgings in Chinatown would not be suitable for them because the quarters are mainly for men. Leave them here with me. Come back for them tomorrow. Come through there," she said pointing to a back gate.

IT WAS STILL dark when Ngao returned the next morning. Stopping his cart near the main gate, he tethered the horse to a post and went in through the back gate. It squeaked open; the metal hinges were wet with the morning dew. He threaded quietly along the pathway Janidah had shown him. His steps made soft scrunching sounds on the wet grass leaving shadow memories of where he walked. The dawn light was beginning to send the darkness into retreat. He could see better now, the lawn with the maze in the centre, the fountain and the rose garden. The bungalow was set well back from the mansion. He quickened his pace.

Rohani was waiting just outside the main doorway of the house. She ran to him, gathering her sarong to her until it was hitched over her knee, her face filled with happiness. They had had no opportunity to speak the previous night. Now on their own, they felt just as tongue-tied. They stood awkwardly, shyly and then he hugged her to him, His heart filled over and he could hear hers beating against him. He had so much he wanted to say, to ask ... but that would have to wait. He wanted to leave immediately. Reluctantly he relinquished his hold.

"Shao Peng?" he enquired for she was nowhere to be seen.

"Still sleeping. I'll wake her up now. She is fully dressed to go. She slept in her daywear. I have been up most of the night. Mistress Janidah asked me to pack some food for the travel. Everything is ready. She said it would be absolutely fine if we wish to leave without saying goodbye again. She said it might make it easier for Shao Peng."

"Then let's do it."

Within minutes Rohani was back again with Shao Peng and a bag. Ngao lowered himself and took hold of Shao Peng's face. He pushed away the wisps of hair that had come undone from her plaits and gently tucked them behind her ears. "Everything will be good from now on," he said. Then he held her close. He looked up and met Rohani's eyes; she smiled. It was not in her mind, he did care for her.

From up on the upper floor of the mansion, Grime saw the three figures walking away across the lawn and then through the back gate. Shao Peng was in the middle with her father and Rohani on either side of her. He heard the gate clang shut. He lingered by the window. He had not slept. His mind had gone over and over again the past and the recent momentous decisions he had made. Today is the end, and the start of a new chapter in all our lives, he thought.

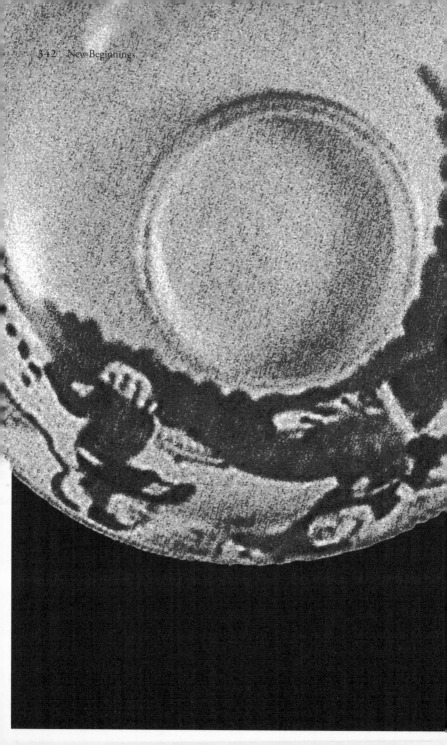

Part
Two

Selangor

1868

Chapter 37

SHAO PENG PICKED up a piece of wood. Bits of broken splinters came off in her fingers. The ground was littered: parts of a roof's thatching lay wet and partly buried in the soil; wooden planks were washed to one side and piled high; pots, broken bowls and plates lay in puddles of brown water. A blanket lay sodden next to a tangle of clothing and a comb poked irrelevantly from the soil. Further ahead of her the river Klang roared, its water tumbling with ferocious velocity, spitting its fury onto the riverbanks. The water cascaded violently at a steep bend and beneath it, in the pool, more debris collected.

Nearly eighteen, she had grown into a tall slim girl. Her black hair still plaited into two thick gleaming plaits hung on either side of her reaching down to her budding bosom. She swirled her head impatiently to fling the plaits to the back then bent over to examine an ornament embedded in the wet earth.

"Shao Peng," cried Rohani striding towards her. Behind her at a discreet distance away were two guards, burly men with loose jackets and rolled up trousers. She held the bottom ends of her sarong up revealing the streaks of mud that covered her calves. "*Hujan!* It might rain again anytime. We have to get back quickly to the house. Your father might come home early. I think he has something special to tell us. Then what would he say if you were not at home? Quick! Come. You are wet through." She tucked an arm through Shao Peng's.

Rohani was the shorter of the two. From the back they might be mistaken for sisters except that Rohani was darker. She had grown plumper and with her new status had taken to wearing her hair up instead of letting it fall loose. Unlike the Chinese *sam foo* Shao Peng wore, she continued to wear her Malay sarong and bijou top fastened together at the front with decorative pins. Shao Peng squeezed her arm affectionately.

"And who is wet?" she teased tugging gently at Rohani's sarong. It squelched with water and clung to her buttocks. "Anyway what does father want to tell us?"

"You'll see when we get back. You shouldn't wander off to the river on your own. You know your father disapproves. It is not safe. You should have at least asked those two to go with you," waving at the two men behind them.

"It is safe. The flood has already receded and I was curious to see the damage it has done. Father was so worried about his warehouses and the store and spoke so much of the storms that I had to see for myself. I didn't go very far. We are only minutes away from the house."

"Girls don't go wandering on their own. Your father worries about you. It is far better for you to stay at home with me."

"I don't like to be confined to the house. I get bored," said Shao Peng.

"I thought we were going to cook together this afternoon," said Rohani squeezing Shao Peng's arm affectionately. "You were going to show me the things you learnt to cook in your aunt's place. We were going to adapt them to local ingredients. Your father loves chillies now and has to have them in all his food. I hope to spice up his Chinese meals." She beamed with pride. "You know he couldn't eat chillies before."

"*Mmm!* Don't rely on me. I confess I don't remember much about the cooking I did when I was little. I was only six or seven. I have written to aunty Heong Yook and perhaps in the next letter she'll let me know."

Shao Peng took a plait of her hair and nervously twiddled it between her index and third finger. "She sounded really sad in her last letter. She said that nothing had changed. China is impoverished. Corruption has become even more rife."

"Ooo! *Kepala sakit!* My head gets all muddled up when I hear you and your father talk about China."

They reached home. The ground was muddy and the path to the house was riddled with puddles. A young sapling had snapped and many of the flowering bushes were battered. Petals and leaves lay scattered on the ground, wind blown and yellowed with soggy decay.

"First the fires and now floods," said Shao Peng. She looked at the house with fresh respect. It had withstood both calamities that had swept the whole settlement. Her father had rebuilt the house in bricks, and replaced the thatched roof with tiles. It had also grown in size over the years with extensions added on to the side and to the back of it. They were so absorbed looking at the house that they did not hear the approaching footsteps.

"Yes, it is fortunate that we have tiled roofs. The house would not have withstood the wind and deluge we have had over the past few weeks and certainly not the fires of six months ago," said Ngao coming up right behind them. Beside him, holding his hand, was a little boy of about four years.

"Mummy! Mummy!" the boy cried relinquishing Ngao's hand and rushing over to Rohani. She turned and swept him into her arms, kissing his cheek before hitching him up on to her hips.

"Siew Loong, you are too big to be carried. Come, get down," said Ngao with mock firmness; his voice, indulgent and soft with love, belied the sternness he tried to muster on his face.

"No! No!" squealed the little boy. He nuzzled against his mother's neck and clung even harder to her. Clamping his two sturdy little legs tight round her waist, he bounced up and down, banging his bottom on Rohani's hip.

"Rohani, put him down. Be careful or you will get a bad back. You spoil him," Ngao said with a smile. There was no sting in the chastisement and Rohani knew it. She continued holding the boy and he did not stop bouncing up and down on her hip.

Shao Peng sidled up to her father and leaned her head on his shoulder. She felt left out at times like this when all attention was on Siew Loong. She could understand why her brother was the focus of attention. He was adorable with lightly wavy hair, so unlike her dead straight locks. Above all he had the most beautiful eyes, large dark brown eyes. So unlike mine, she thought. And of course, he was a boy and boys are always important in a Chinese household. Hadn't her aunt warned her? Ngao absent-mindedly placed his arm around his daughter unaware of her thoughts.

"So how has your day been?" he asked her.

"*Bu cuo!* Not too bad!" she replied in Mandarin and then switched to Malay to include Rohani in the conversation. "I studied. I practised my calligraphy and did some maths and then I went..." She stopped. Rohani was making signs with her eyes and Shao Peng realised that Rohani was warning her not to tell her father about her trip to the river. "And then I went to look for Ro..." She stopped again. Her father wanted her to call Rohani mother. "She has loved and looked after you so well," Ngao had said many a time. Yet, much as she liked, even loved Rohani, she could not bring herself to do so and she had on the whole managed to avoid calling her anything in the presence of her father. Rohani did not mind and had said so herself.

Ngao dropped his arms. A grimace of annoyance flashed across his face. He forced a smile. He felt his skin stretched in protest as he quirked his lips. "Maths?" he asked. "Why do you need to learn Maths?"

"Aunty Heong Yook says that it is vital to learn maths, at least the basics of addition, subtraction, multiplication. I have been practising on the abacus and..."

"Sometimes Shao Peng you drive me mad with your incessant quoting of Aunt Heong Yook. Why would you need to add, subtract and multiply? You are not going into business are you? I am certainly not having you in the stores," said her father, his irritation rising to the surface. He glared at her from the corner of his eye. He looked away. Increasingly, he found he could not look at Shao Peng without feeling a deep pang. She was the spitting image of Hua. He did not wish to be reminded of his first wife.

Rohani tried to diffuse the tension. "So what were you going to tell us?" she asked her husband brightly.

Ngao fought to stem his emotions. He knew he was unjust and his anger had nothing to do with Shao Peng. After all, he was the one who had initially encouraged her to study. Over time, he began to be persuaded that excessive learning might not be such a good thing for his daughter. She took no interest whatsoever in what his boss and mentor had pressed on him as essential attributes of a good wife. Both Hua and Rohani loved cooking; Shao Peng would have nothing to do with any domestic pursuits. He placed his arm around her again and gave her a gentle pat in an attempt to diffuse his harsh words. Her shoulders were tense. Stung by his remark she clenched her fist until her nails bit into her palms. She fought back her tears. Her face was stony.

Ngao dropped his arm. "I am going to Singapore," he replied. "It has been many years since we were there. So what do you think if you and I went together?" he asked Shao Peng. "I have some business to do over there and while I am working you might like to visit Janidah, the kind lady who housed you." He forced himself to look at Shao Peng. "Perhaps you would get to meet your English friend."

"What about ... Siew Loong?"

"He'll stay here with his mother. It would be too difficult to look after all of you. It will be just you and me and we will leave in a couple of days. The journey might be dangerous so you will have to dress as a boy. The Raja has promised to send some men to protect us. After all I am going on his behalf."

Shao Peng's initial excitement vanished. So Siew Loong was not going because it might be too dangerous. He does not care if I am in danger, she thought.

❀ ❀ ❀

DISCARDING THE TWO men who normally accompanied him for security, Ngao left the house immediately after lunch. Except for Siew Loong's chatter and Rohani's light-hearted responses, it had been a tense meal. Shao Peng could not be drawn into the conversation. He had looked at her overtly many times through the meal. He was struck at how like her mother she was. Even her manners and expressions reminded him of Hua. The difference was that Shao Peng was stubborn; perhaps all that learning had made it worse. Hua had always been quiet and pliant. He recalled his last sight of Hua before he left for Beiliu city to look for work; her beautiful oval face and her calm, quiet eyes still haunted him. He caught his breath. He had been thinking of Hua a lot in the past few months. For some time now he had been successful in setting thoughts of her aside. Now they invaded him, tortured him.

He forced himself to think of something else, to conjure up a different image. He knew he must avoid at all cost thoughts of how she was in her last days. His mind, however, could not be controlled. It twisted and meandered until he was once again at that painful point. He pulled the rein of the horse and his cart came to a stop. He had to deal with the devil within him.

He left his horse and cart at the path and walked over to a fallen log. He sat down, burying his face in his palms. He knew from past experience that he had to sit out these dark moments. The dampness of the log seeped through his cotton trousers; he did not care. He ran his fingers through his hair, rubbing his scalp in an attempt to wipe out all thoughts. Images of Hua had come repeatedly to torment him ever since Shao Peng told him that her mother had been sent away with a bondmaid called Mui to Canton. So Hua had not been with Shao Peng when she died. He had assumed his daughter was with her mother all the time because he had believed that his aunt would have told him if it were otherwise. Critically, Hua was not ill when she left for Canton. So why and how did she die?

In the early years he had not asked Shao Peng about her mother; he did not wish to distress her and he accepted the little his aunt told him. He was happy that at last he had his daughter with him. Later, as the years went by, snippets of information began to be revealed. He learnt that the place where they were both held was a house of ill-repute but it was not really a surprise. Although Shao Peng seemed unaware when she told him of what went on in that place, he had long suspected it. In fact if he were to search his heart, he probably knew it from the beginning. He had pushed it to the back of his mind. There had been so little time to think. The mere struggle for survival in the early years helped him cast out all dark thoughts so that the images of his first wife and daughter when they came were of a kind that provided him with a reason for living. Then when he married Rohani and Siew Loong was born, his attention became focused on them.

Shao Peng's unexpected revelations brought all the bad memories crashing back. He wrote to his aunt Heong Yook asking for more details of Hua's death only to receive evasive replies. He grew exasperated with the answers. He had then asked someone to look up Mui. From him he learned all the tawdry details of the house in Canton where Hua had been sent on her own, without Shao Peng, and from that moment on Ngao was tortured. He wished he had not pursued the matter. Until then he had been able to make believe that Hua was merely on the brink of prostitution, and had somehow escaped this fate, sequestered in the house where he had tried to find her. His belief was now shattered.

Unreasonably he became angry with Hua. When he considered her predicament in a rational way, he knew she was a victim, but, at times like this, he was not rational. His desire to preserve the image of her on a pedestal had been rudely shaken. He realised that if he had rescued her, she would not have been abused. So at times, he was full of self-recrimination. He imagined the men with whom she had been obliged to consort. He wanted revenge. His inability to do anything frustrated him. Beyond details of the Canton house of ill-repute, he had made no headway in his search for further information. He grew angry with his aunt Heong Yook, his only link with the past during his early days in Malaya. So the dark thoughts grew and festered in his mind. He vowed that Shao Peng would never suffer such a fate. He would protect her at all cost.

Ngao took a deep breath, then another and yet another. He grew calmer. His rational self returned. His moment of bleakness subsided. He returned to the cart and resumed his journey through Ampang to Kuala Lumpur.

As the cart rolled forward, a relative sense of wellbeing returned. The countryside had changed beyond recognition. Proper houses had replaced the sheds and lean-tos of the mining campsites. A road system now existed. It was a far cry from the early days when eighty-seven Chinese men came to the area to mine only to have sixty-nine of them die from disease. It was just jungle then. Not any more. His mood lightened further. He should not look to the past. He should look to the future, a future he was helping to build in this beautiful country; a country that had captured his imagination and which he loved.

The horses trotted on taking him towards the commercial centre of the Chinatown just minutes away from the original Chinese trading post where the rivers Gombak and Klang meet. *Kuala Lumpur* they called it now; *kuala* meaning mouth and *lumpur* for muddy. He stopped in front of a row of shophouses. He looked at the cladding, the intricate workmanship of the artisans brought over from China. His chest filled with pride. Going to Singapore and seeing my old mentor Eng Kim will be good, he thought. I will make it up to Shao Peng. I have not been kind to her. I will make it up to Rohani who has stood by me.

SHAO PENG SAT huddled in her room by her desk. She had bolted to her room with her father's words still ringing in her ears. A light breeze blew in caressing her skin with a damp coldness. She shivered. The temperature had dropped since the floods. She looked out of the window. Rohani with Siew Loong in hand was overseeing the clearance of the garden. A small army of men were sweeping away the debris left from the floods. She could hear the swishing of the long bristles of paddy stalks. Suddenly Siew Loong broke free weaving between the brooms while Rohani ran after him. The garden was filled with laughter and merriment.

She turned back to her letter. She felt so alone. She took up a brush to write but she could not pen her thoughts to her aunt. How could she tell her aunt that her father seemed indifferent to her? Perhaps if her aunt came she would not feel as lonely. It was wishful thinking. That would be difficult if not impossible. Was it, she wondered? She sat up straight, her eyes alert. It was not impossible! Her eyes lit up; she smiled. She heard her father say that the restriction on women leaving China had long been lifted and although initially few women had taken advantage of it, last year the number of women coming from China had increased. Uncle Eng Kim had explained that it was because many Chinese men no longer saw themselves as transients. With their decision to stay the women followed. She became excited. Perhaps Uncle Edward could help. She had not seen him since that day in Singapore and he had not maintained contact. She had heard talk of him though and often thought of him. She had devoured whatever information came her way and had kept it close to her heart. Her smile stretched into a grin. The trip to Singapore would not be bad at all. She picked up her pen brush and diligently started writing to her aunt.

Chapter 38

SINGAPORE

FROM HIS OFFICE Edward Grime looked out across the Singapore River to the prosperous commercial sector of the west bank. Cavenagh had left. His words on his departure still rang in Grime's ears. He recalled his friend's hurt, his disbelief that the British Colonial Office had appointed someone to replace him without even informing him of the decision. "After all that I have done," Cavenagh had said, his face red with anger, embarrassment and incredulity. "I have no choice. I will not stay another day."

Grime studied the surrounding buildings on both sides of the riverbank: Fort Canning, St. Andrew's Cathedral, the court and the town hall followed by the peripheral government offices that formed part of the Empress Place government buildings. They housed the newly established administration of the Government. Further out near Commercial Square, was land reclaimed from the sea. All carried the imprint of his friend's influence and effort. No wonder he was upset.

The new appointment had been precipitated by the decision to make Singapore a colony. The decision had taken both Cavenagh and Grime by surprise. Singapore had always resented being administered from India, first by the East India Company and then by the Indian offices of the British Crown in Calcutta. Although Cavenagh was appointed from the Office in Calcutta, his skilful administration had reduced the resentment down to just a pocketful of English merchants. So it was generally thought that his post was secure and that the idea of Singapore becoming a colony in its own right had been shelved. Moreover, the Crown's stipulation that Singapore must pay for its own civil and military defences before becoming a colony was thought to be sufficient deterrent to it ever becoming one.

How wrong they were, thought Grime, turning from the window to address the empty room. They did not foresee the change of heart in the War Office. They did not anticipate that the island would be considered as a possible alternative to Hong Kong to house the British force. He sighed and walked back to his desk. He sat down. "So here we are, a crown colony under a Governor appointed by the Crown's Colonial Office in London no less. And my friend, Cavenagh, the last of the 'Indian Governors' appointed from Calcutta gone."

Grime rifled through the papers on his desk: petition after petition all testifying to the unease that had arisen in Singapore following the transfer of authority. The fact that the fate of Singapore was tied irrevocably with the Malay states could not be denied. Yet no new directions on how to tackle the warring states in the Peninsula had been issued. It seemed the Singapore Administration would still have to sit on its hands. The Colonial Office in London had no intention of intervening. Secretly, Grime was in accord with the new Governor, Sir Harry St George Ord that something had to be done. His mind wandered to the pending visit of a delegation from Kuala Lumpur. His secretary had penned it in his diary. No doubt they would be asking for help to resolve the troubles in the Malay Peninsula. He flicked over to the entries. He sat back with a jolt. Amongst the list of names was one called Ngao.

THE CARRIAGE DREW to a halt at Eng Kim's house. The horses were weary. Dust covered their bodies like a sprinkling of talcum over their black and brown flanks. They neighed, shaking their manes and stamping their hoofs impatiently. Ngao and Shao Peng descended from the carriage. Her black cotton trousers clung to her after sitting cramped in the carriage. She shook them free from her legs. She reached up to fasten her skullcap. It was strange to be masquerading as a young man again.

Eng Kim was at the door to welcome them. Ngao went up to him with Shao Peng in tow. He clasped the older man's hand warmly and was rewarded with a firm shake and pat on his shoulder. Their relationship had evolved and moved on. Eng Kim regarded Ngao as an equal and indeed he was; Ngao was no longer in his employ.

"*Ahhh!* Shao Peng!" cried Eng Kim with a broad smile. He stroked his grey beard and whiskers, which he had allowed to grow to reach some three inches below his chin. "You make a fine looking young gentleman. So how was the journey? Any trouble?" he asked turning to Ngao.

"Good! No trouble. By taking a long detour we were able to avoid the dangerous areas. For that I have to thank Yap. He sent out scouts before we left and provided us with an escort of fighters."

They entered the house into the hallway. Ngao had never been to the house before; Shao Peng had. She remembered it vividly. She did not want to be there. She reached instinctively for her father's arm. Unaware of anything amiss he brushed it away and told her to go into the sitting room reducing her once more to a mere child. He was preoccupied and did not notice her distress. His eyes were on Eng Kim.

"So from what I gather the rivalry has not ceased. The fighting has just paused while the sides regroup," said Eng Kim.

"Yes, the cease fire was only temporary. After his defeat Raja Mahdi succeeded in appealing to the Sumatrans. His army is now reinforced. He has dug in at the mouth of the Selangor River and is proving to be a nuisance for the movement of tin. Since Raja Abdullah's death, the Sultan has given the responsibility of administering Selangor to Tengku Kudin, his new son-in-law. We are supporting him. He is from Kedah and he is the one who has to face Mahdi. Tengku Kudin has sent me here to gauge the feelings of the British Government. He says he needs their help. Although he has the backing of Yap Ah Loy he says it is insufficient."

"The fighting has gone on for far too long. It has taken its toll. You look tired my friend," commented Eng Kim, observing the shadows under Ngao's eyes, "you should look after yourself." The Ngao he had once known with his smooth tanned face and dark brows was no more. The Ngao before him now was a mature, solid man. His brows were still bushy and his eyes vibrant and alert. Underneath this exterior, Eng Kim could discern sadness. He wondered why. Ngao should be happy, he thought. He is reunited with his daughter; he has a son, a Malay wife and a flourishing food business that has grown irrespective of the fluctuations in the tin market. In fact, just the other day Kam the pepper merchant from Johor told him that his daughter, married with two boys, was still hankering after Ngao and perhaps it would have been better if he had married her off to him. Moreover, thought Eng Kim putting himself in the place of Ngao, if it were only a matter of women, there was no reason for sadness; there were many more to choose from now that they were allowed to leave China.

Ngao was unaware of his friend's thoughts. He dropped his voice to a whisper, and glanced over to see if Shao Peng was within hearing. She was moving listlessly in the sitting room.

"We have a lull now and there has been no fighting," he said. "Everyone is preoccupied with the damage caused by the floods. Soon I am afraid there will be renewed warring between the Malay chiefs and obviously this will involve the different Chinese factions. I fear this time, the situation will be even worse. Kapitan Liu has died. With his death, tension between the Chinese factions has also increased. We are now not talking about mere jostling of power. As we had anticipated, Yap Ah Loy has been appointed to succeed Liu and to govern the Chinese community in Kuala Lumpur. Tengku Kudin supports this. Liu's relatives, however, oppose it and are up in arms. And Chong Chong, long a rival of Yap, has stepped in to lead them."

"I fear for my family," continued Ngao. "I have brought Shao Peng to Singapore with the intention of leaving her here for the moment. She is too self-willed and independent; she sometimes goes off on her own despite my warnings. It is not safe for her in Selangor."

"You are welcome to leave her here with me. Have you told her? What about Rohani and Siew Loong?"

Ngao shook his head. "I have not said anything to Shao Peng. Rohani will stay with me. She won't leave my side. She is adamant. Siew Loong will obviously have to stay with his mother."

Eng Kim wondered if his friend was telling him everything. Surely, he must put Siew Loong's safety above the rest of his family? After all he was the male heir. If any one was to be sent away for safety, surely it should be him.

Ngao could see the scepticism in Eng Kim's face. "Rohani listens to what I say. She would not go wandering off on her own like Shao Peng does. Kudin and Yap have promised me some men to guard the house. So for the moment, my wife and son stay with me. If things change for the worst, I may have to send them here as well."

"What about Kuala Lumpur, Yap's domain?"

"The situation is fluid. The town is prosperous," he said recalling the new shophouses, "but you never know how long it will last. Chong has thrown in his lot with Raja Mahdi and his ally Raja Mashor. Yap is with Raja Abdullah's son, Raja Ismail, and Tengku Kudin, the sultan's son-in-law. So you can understand my concerns. You recall how many times we have built only to have to rebuild again?"

"Of course! That is why I moved back with my other wives to Singapore despite their protests," replied Eng Kim.

❀ ❀ ❀

SHAO PENG, HER hands clasped behind her back, wandered around the sitting room without any enthusiasm. She remembered the room; she had stolen into it with Rohani. It was unchanged: the lacquered panels on the wall, the black elm console and the carved chairs with their ivory and mother of pearl inlays and spindly legs. She wondered if Eng Kim knew how she and Rohani had been treated when she was briefly here as a child. She had never mentioned it to her father and, as far as she knew, Rohani had not either. Rohani had told her that no good would come from offending Eng Kim, her father's boss at that time. Moreover, Uncle Grime had promised not to tell on Mrs Lim and Shao Peng had respected his wish.

She wandered over to the console. She hoped that they would not stay long. She was looking forward to seeing Uncle Grime and Janidah. She glanced out to the hallway where her father was still talking with Eng Kim. She wished she could change out of her man's clothing. She did not want Janidah and Uncle Grime to see her in them. She drummed her fingers with impatience on the console, coming to a rest at a tall celadon vase placed on a carved rose wood stand. Absent-mindedly, she stroked the smooth cool sides of the vase. She looked at her reflection on its shinning surface. There was someone behind her! She turned round and looked straight into the eyes of Mrs Lim. She must have come into the room through the dining room door. They were the same hard eyes, unchanged except for the lines round them. They were cold and unwelcoming. Instantly, Shao Peng reverted to her child-self. She recoiled, withdrawing her hands from the vase and almost knocked it down. "I'm sorry," she said. Her words fell empty. Mrs Lim had already left the room.

Shao Peng went quickly out of the sitting room to her father. "Shall we go now? Shall we visit Janidah?"

"Don't you want to stay for dinner? Surely both of you are staying with us for the night?" Eng Kim looked up in surprise.

"Don't be rude," said Ngao frowning at his daughter. "Please forgive her. Of course we will stay for dinner and thank you for having us."

Shao Peng nodded numbly. "Sorry," she mumbled, embarrassed.

"I will have the servants get your luggage and prepare a bath. Go and rest. We will see you later," said Eng Kim.

❀ ❀ ❀

THEY HAD SAID goodnight to their hosts after dinner. Ngao saw his daughter to her bedroom. As she was about to go in, he reached out and stopped her. Shao Peng turned in surprise.

"You embarrassed me," he said his hand still on the door, staying it. "You didn't say a word even when Mrs Lim asked after you? Why? You are too old to sulk. I do not know what got into you; to behave so ungraciously when our hosts have been so kind."

Shao Peng could not answer. She did not know what to say; how to explain her intense dislike of Mrs Lim and her conviction that the questions did not reflect any true interest in her.

"I have to tell you this now," Ngao said sternly. "You might have to stay here in Singapore. I have discussed this with uncle

Eng Kim and he has kindly agreed to have you. So make sure you behave. Don't let me down."

Shao Peng caught hold of his forearm. "No! Please, I can't stay here. I just can't. Mrs Lim does not like me, hates me even. You never said you would leave me here. You said it was a trip to see Janidah and uncle Grime. You lied to me."

He shook off her hand. "Get a hold of yourself. How do you know she hates you? Why would she hate you?"

"Ask Uncle Grime. Ask Janidah. Ask Rohani. Please, please don't leave me here."

"I will ask them. I am leaving you in Singapore for your own safety. The whole of Selangor is becoming too dangerous. We expect a full-scale civil war. The fights we have had up to now would be considered mere skirmishes compared with what lies ahead. You will not be safe at home."

"What about Rohani and Siew Loong. Why can they stay with you and not me?"

Ngao look at his daughter, the spitting image of Hua. It was not her fault that she reminded him of Hua. He thought that a separation would do both of them some good. She would be safer in Singapore and it would give him much needed time to sort himself out. "I'm sorry. Let's talk about it tomorrow. We are both tired." He turned away vowing to write one last time to his aunt Heong Yook for answers.

Shao Peng's heart sank. She went into her room, closed the door and, flinging her slippers to the floor, climbed on to her bed. She drew her knees up to her chest and curled into a tight ball. She had to do something. She could not, would not, stay in this house.

Chapter 39

"WILL YOU BE alright?" Ngao asked his daughter as she got down from the carriage. It was mid morning. They had arrived at Edward Grime's mansion. Ngao was on his way to the Government House where he and one of Tengku Kudin's men were to meet with officials. He had sent a messenger the previous night to Janidah to enquire if it would be convenient for Shao Peng to visit and had received a warm invitation immediately.

"Of course," said Shao Peng smiling for the first time since their arrival in Singapore.

"I'll come back as soon as I have finished my business."

"Don't worry, I shall be fine. There!" she said, "I have company already." She heard someone calling her. She turned round excitedly to see a lady approaching them. For a fraction of a second, she did not recognise her, then she was in her arms. How could she forget? It was Janidah. Once she got over the shock, Janidah looked like she did those many years ago; perhaps slightly plumper. They held each other close for a moment before moving apart.

"How are you?" they said at the same time and broke into laughter.

"*Baigaimana anda telah berkembang!* How you have grown! You are even taller than me," exclaimed Janidah in Malay.

"Where are...?"

"My children are in England. They are visiting their father." Janidah turned to Ngao. "*Minta maaf! Selamat datang.* Please excuse me for my rudeness. Welcome. Come in, come in," she said extending her arm inviting the two of them in.

"Thank you for having Shao Peng. I am sorry I have to leave now. I have an appointment at Government House. I will come back later and collect her."

"Come for dinner. We will be expecting you." invited Janidah.

"You are kind ... I must not impose on you," Ngao replied awkwardly.

"No problem at all. I will expect you," Janidah said firmly. She was not going to take 'no' for an answer.

"So how are things?" asked Janidah once Ngao had left. She led the way into the shady interior of the house. The black and white tiled floors were cool and inviting. "Let me have a better look at you," Janidah said turning Shao Peng round to face her.

She marvelled at the symmetry of the oval face, the widely spaced eyes and the clear, clear skin. She patted the cheeks. The child's plump round face was gone. "Don't they allow you out in the sun?" she asked bemused by Shao Peng's colouring. It was as light as light could be.

"Father is quite strict. He says it is not safe. He prefers me to stay in-doors and rarely agrees to my going out unless accompanied."

"Really? I suppose he has a point. I heard that the place is still lawless."

"I do venture out when I can. I don't see why I have to stay at home all the time while Rohani and Siew Loong are free to wander and play in the garden. He seems to have different rules for me."

Janidah tucked her arm around Shao Peng's, sensing the resentment in her voice. "*Ahhh*, Rohani! She has married your father I assume." Janidah held Shao Peng's gaze for a while searching for the truth; she was interested because of her own situation. "Doesn't she take your side?"

"We get along fine. She tries but father will hear none of it. Rohani has been good and kind to me. Father married her some five years ago and I have a brother, Siew Loong who I just mentioned."

"Well, well," said Janidah. So her predictions came true. "Was it a big wedding presided over by an Imam?"

Shao Peng lowered her voice conspiratorially, drawn to Janidah immediately and reminded of her time with her when she first arrived in Singapore. It brought back such wonderful memories. She had freedom then. "I don't remember; I don't actually know what happened. There was a small celebration. We don't have much of a family here. Father has not changed his name or become a Muslim if that is what you want to know," said Shao Peng. She stopped; her hand flew to her lips. "I am sorry. I shouldn't have said that. My father says that my tongue runs away with me.

Janidah looked sideways at her guest. "Rohani is a lovely girl. I am glad she is happily settled. When you see her, send her my love. Come let us sit down." She guided Shao Peng to an armchair and sat down herself, sinking deeply into the cushions. She leaned back and allowed herself time to observe her young guest. Still a child, be it in a young woman's body, that someone – perhaps the father – is so intent to hide from the world, she thought. They must have kept her completely secluded and isolated.

Shao Peng looked curiously at her surroundings. The house was somehow different from before. The old grand furniture had almost all gone replaced by pieces she did not recognise. She did not know much about western-style houses having only seen this one. To her inexperienced eyes, she thought it looked wonderful. Everything seemed so comfortable, like the armchair, she was sitting on. You could sink and relax into it and fall asleep if you were tired. She imagined curling up in the sofa. It would be bliss and quite different from the furnishings she had left behind this morning. She fiddled with the frog buttons on her *sam foo* top. She was glad that she was at least not wearing her man's outfit today. She looked longingly at Janidah's hair and dress. She was wearing it loose like she did before. Janidah caught her staring.

"You are not going to tell me that I have grown old are you?" she teased, the smile crinkling up the corners of her eyes.

Shao Peng shook her head vigorously. "No! I was just admiring your hair."

"I know I am dressed somewhat incongruously, as they say," replied Janidah. "The western ladies always have their hair up. I often wear western clothes but I don't put up my hair when I am at home. If you like I can dress your hair for you," she said amused by her earnest young guest.

Poor girl she thought. She needs some pampering. She is becoming a young woman yet from the look of her clothes no one has paid much attention to her grooming. Those thick plaits are too severe. Her hairstyle has not changed from the time when she was a child staying with me. They do nothing for her beautiful face.

"That would be nice though I would have to plait it back before my father returns," replied Shao Peng, excited at the prospect.

"So what do you wish to do first, hair or ...?" Janidah asked, pretending not to hear. "We have the whole day before us."

"May I visit your house first? I only have vague recollections of it."

"It is not used much now. I live in the main house ... with Uncle Grime."

"Have you married him?" Shao Peng asked, her eyes wide with surprise. She was agog with curiosity and thrilled to be addressed as a young adult. She moved closer, shifting her chair forward so that it almost touched Janidah's.

"Sort of. I am more married to him than I was with Michael, my children's father. Edward, Uncle Grime, is now divorced and I hope we will be married properly eventually." She sighed. "This is not the kind of conversation that a young lady should be having. What would your father say," she exclaimed, rolling her eyes in feigned horror to cover the tinge of regret that threatened to bubble up in her; Grime had still not proposed.

Shao Peng's face fell. "You are the only one who speaks to me as an adult. Rohani is preoccupied with Siew Loong and I don't think my father loves me anymore."

"Nonsense! Why do you say that?" Janidah was intrigued. There was such an air of mystery about the man. In fact, Ngao was not the only one who was mystifying so was Edward. She still remembered his reaction to Ngao when he came to collect Shao Peng. He was quiet and withdrawn for days after they left. Was it because of Shao Peng? Did he miss her or was it because of Ngao? She had never been able to prise any information out of him.

"Father wants to leave me with Uncle Eng Kim. He says it is not safe for me to be in Kuala Lumpur. I won't stay there. I just won't." Shao Peng's face was flushed and there was a catch in her voice when she continued. "Mrs Lim hates me although she pretends to be ever so kind when people are around." She leaned over and caught hold of Janidah's hands. "Please tell my father what happened. He wouldn't believe me if I told him myself. I have left it too long." Shao Peng dropped her hands. "Perhaps I can stay here?" she asked shyly.

Janidah did not answer at once. "Perhaps," she said finally. "I'll have to ask Edward. If you stay here, what would you wish to do? You need to have something to occupy you."

"I would like to study. When I was with my aunt Heong Yook in China, she insisted that I learn. I have been writing to her and she continues to encourage me to do so. I have studied on my own. I am bored, though. I know most of the books by heart. Aunty Heong Yook sent me some new ones, all of which I have read. We have such a paltry selection in Kuala Lumpur. There are no bookstores; no one seems interested. Rohani doesn't care about books. My father does not approve."

"I wonder why," said Janidah surprised. "He is a learned man himself."

"I think it is Uncle Eng Kim's influence. Father, who had initially encouraged me to learn, seems to have changed his mind and now sides with him. Although he is very nice, he feels that education makes women too ambitious and dissatisfied." Shao Peng stood up and mimicked Eng Kim stroking his beard and shaking his head sagely. "There is no need for girls to learn! What they need is a good marriage."

"Well, we'll see about that," exclaimed Janidah clutching her sides, laughter spilling out of her. "Uncle Grime tells me titbits of gossip and talk in his circle. One British officer has reportedly said he is disgusted with the ignorance of local born Chinese *peranakan* women. If only your uncle Eng Kim can hear what is being said. There has been some movement to improve their wellbeing. We have at least two schools for girls. A missionary school, started by an English woman Maria Dyer, has been going for a while and now we have a Chinese girls school established by a Hokkien gentleman, Huay Kuan. It follows a Chinese curriculum."

"So I could go to one of them?" Shao Peng almost jumped up from her chair in her excitement.

"Not so fast. We haven't even established whether you can stay with us so don't build up your hopes. And we do not know if the schools will take adult students. Now let me do something about your hair." Taking a braid of Shao Peng's hair, she began uncoiling it. The braid unravelled into a sleek sheen of black silk. "Much better," commented Janidah fluffing out the long tresses until they hung loose down Shao Peng's back. "Now let's look at your dress. Come with me," she said rising to her feet.

❀ ❀ ❀

GOVERNMENT HOUSE WAS an imposing white villa with arched ways flanked by pillars and long tall windows with white wooden shutters. Ngao and Raja Suleiman were shown into a reception room and asked to wait. Left to their devices the two men wandered round the room admiring its tall ceilings, majestic doorways and windows. A portrait of Queen Victoria adorned one wall. Severe, disapproving even, with her hair pulled back neatly into a coil at the nape of her neck, she gazed haughtily down at them. In her grey high-collared bodice with a hint of lace around the throat and voluminous skirt, Ngao could not associate her with the lush tropical grounds that surrounded the building. He turned to see Raja Suleiman standing next to him. He too was staring at the portrait.

"I hope they have an interpreter or at least send someone who speaks Malay," said Suleiman nervously. He had been asked by Tengku Kudin to accompany Ngao to make sure things went to plan. He had never been to Singapore before.

"I am sure they will. I am told we will not be seeing Governor Ord. He is in England at the moment. I once knew of a man called Edward Grime, during the time of Governor Cavenagh. He is still here. Perhaps we will see him instead. Eng Kim was not very helpful when I asked him about Mr Grime. Since his retirement Eng Kim seems disinterested in all matters except his birds," said Ngao. He omitted to tell his associate that he had been at Grime's house that very morning although he did not see him. He did not know how the day's discussion would work out and did not want to reveal too much about his association with Grime. Moreover, it might not be Grime who they would see. He could have asked Janidah, but he had shied away from that. It seemed inappropriate somehow. He did not wish her to feel that he was trying to use her to lobby for Grime's support.

"Not only birds. Eng Kim's time is taken up in keeping peace in his household," laughed Suleiman.

"Mr Edward Grime!" The announcement took them both by surprise so engrossed were they in their discussion. They turned. Ngao smiled. He was pleased. Although his meeting with Grime many years ago had been abrupt, he nevertheless had felt an affinity for the man. He owed Grime for bringing his daughter to him and looking after her so well. Shao Peng had nothing but praise for him. He hoped the connection would help with what he had come to do.

"*Ngao xian sheng!* Mr Ngao!" said Grime slipping into Mandarin. He turned to acknowledge Raja Suleiman. "Come, let us go into my office," he said striding off.

Inviting them to take a seat, Grime sat down behind his desk, a heavy mahogany table with a green leather top. After the initial surprise of seeing Ngao's name on the list, he had pulled himself together. He reassured himself that the entire affair in the past should be water under the bridge. If Ngao had any suspicion, he'd had more than ample time to raise it. Heong Yook, the aunt had kept her side of the bargain and he, Grime, had also done all that was asked of him. Yet he did not find it totally comfortable to sit before Ngao. He saw the confidence and, yes, prosperity of the man, if that was the appropriate word to use 'Prosperity' was an important measure in Singapore where social ranking was by wealth and wealth alone.

"So!" Grime said letting the word hang in the air for a moment. "We have your petition from Tengku Kudin," he said indicating the papers in front of him. He looked from Ngao to Suleiman. "Is there anything you wish to add or clarify?" he asked.

Seated opposite, Ngao returned the appraisal. He saw that Grime's hair was still thick and how the sideburns framed his face. They were speckled with grey, lending him an air of distinction. He looked comfortable in his own skin, different from when Ngao last saw him.

"Tengku Kudin has asked us to represent him. He needs the support of the British Government against Raja Mahdi if he was to settle the escalating war in Selangor, a war that is already hampering the supply of tin to Singapore, as I am sure you are aware. His enemy's army has been reinforced by the defection of one of Tengku Kudin's warriors, Syed Mashur. They are menacing the Sultan's land and at sea they have pirated and attacked commercial vessels. We need to isolate and weed them out. We cannot accomplish this without Britain's help."

Grime got up from behind his desk and walked to the window. "Merchants in the Straits Settlements too have asked the Crown to intervene to stop the escalation of feuds among the Malay chiefs and within Chinese factions," he said with his back towards the two men. He turned around. "Just yesterday," he continued, "we received a delegation from Penang with another such petition. I am also well aware that Singapore's trade is being damaged by the disruption to tin supplies, but, as we have explained time and time again, the Malay states, of which Selangor is one, are not ruled by us. Therefore they are not our concern. We cannot intervene between the warring factions."

Grime had delivered a similar message to another Malay state previously. While privately he, as well as the rest of the administration in Singapore, believed that Britain should intervene, the Colonial Office in London remained adamantly against it.

"Sir," said Ngao swivelling around in his chair to face Grime. "You are no doubt aware of the war in Perak. I hear a rumour that the fighting factions are considering appealing for help from another third party if assistance is not forthcoming from Britain. In Selangor, we are discussing a similar possibility."

Grime walked quickly back to his desk and sat down. "And who might this third party be?"

"Germany," answered Ngao. He glanced quickly at Suleiman and caught the man's surprise. "Germany," he repeated confidently. He was sure that if Germany were not interested, it surely would be if Tengku Kudin were to approach the ambassador.

A palpable silence followed. Ngao knew he had scored.

"I will take this up with Governor Ord. He is discussing these issues at this very moment in London." Grime got up. "I will see you out," he said. They walked to the door. Grime extended his hand and took Ngao's in his while Suleiman looked on marvelling at the way the two men seemed to know each other. He set it aside to tell Tengku Kudin. Still gripping Ngao's hand in his, Grime asked, "And how is Shao Peng?"

Ngao smiled. "Shao Peng is at this moment with *Puan* Janidah. Yesterday evening I asked if my daughter could visit her. This morning I dropped her off just outside your residence. I hope you have no objection. It is the only way to her house. *Puan* Janidah was waiting for us. She has kindly invited us for dinner." He was not quite sure about the relationship between Grime and Janidah. In a small island like Singapore, rumours abounded particularly when they concerned affairs between a local person and an expatriate of high office. He chose to feign ignorance.

Grime did not allow his surprise to show. Janidah had not mentioned it to him. She had always been somewhat of a maverick. That was part of her charm: her unexpectedness, her warmth. In any case he felt sufficiently at ease. The morning's discussion had confirmed there was no undercurrent of animosity. He felt ready to face his inner demons. He smiled, "Then, we will meet this evening."

"EDWARD SHOULD BE back soon. Do take a seat," said Janidah waving Ngao to an armchair. "Tell me! Do you like Shao Peng's hair?"

Shao Peng shrunk back in her seat in alarm. She did not want her father to notice her. Despite her protest Janidah had insisted that she left her hair loose. It cascaded down her back like shimmering silk. At least, I succeeded in getting back to my high collared Chinese dress, thought Shao Peng.

Ngao glanced at Shao Peng and quickly looked away. The grown young woman next to him looked nothing like the young girl he left this morning. What have they done? His eyes drew once more to his daughter. Even the same dress sat somehow differently on her body from this morning. It showed more of her. His decision to keep her with Eng Kim was right.

"So what do you think?" insisted Janidah noting his grimness. "She is prettier when she wears it loose, is she not?"

"Umm ... perhaps. I prefer if she would plait it. In our culture, women do not wear their hair loose. It is considered improper. Only husbands are entitled to see them so ... dressed and, of course, the maids who attend to them. It is quite inappropriate." He glanced sharply at his daughter.

Janidah refrained from reminding him that Rohani also wore it loose when she last saw her.

"I'll braid it," said Shao Peng. With her face bright red she went off. Tears threatened.

"It is not Shao Peng's fault. It is mine. We were just fooling around. You have a very pretty daughter and you should be proud." Her eyes lingered on Shao Peng's departing back, noting how she drooped her shoulders as though in defeat and shame.

"Thank you," he said somewhat stiffly. "I prefer that she concerns herself with more serious things."

"Such as studying and improving herself you mean? You speak so many languages and Shao Peng shows a similar flair. Wouldn't it be wonderful if she could also be fluent in English?" Janidah smiled enthusiastically.

"Of course," replied Ngao. He reflected on his attempt to master English. He now had some knowledge of it and wished he had the time to master it. However, before he could elaborate on his reply, Janidah was already speaking.

"Well then, there are two girl schools in Singapore that would meet her needs; one teaches English and the other teaches Chinese. I will be more than happy to make some arrangements. I have just found out today that there are special classes for older girls. If you agree she can stay with me." Janidah had thought that it was an opportune time to intervene. The past hour convinced her that Shao Peng was miserable. I can always tackle Edward afterwards, she thought, changing her earlier position of first asking him.

"Please father," said Shao Peng coming into the room. "Please."

Ngao did not wish to have an argument in front of his hostess. "We'll talk about it," he said. His face, however, was unrelenting.

"Talk about what?" asked Grime coming into the room. He looked from Janidah to Ngao. Then his eyes fell on Shao Peng. The thumping in his heart soared. He could not believe the likeness.

Shao Peng was already walking towards him. He felt his knees weaken; he almost buckled. He reached out and held on to the back of a chair. Everyone was looking at him. Janidah got up and took his arm. "Are you all right? You look like death," she said.

"Fine! I am fine, just a sharp pain in my knee. It's gone now." He mustered a smile. "Shao Peng," he said. He took her outstretched hands. He could feel a shiver run up his spine.

"Uncle Grime. Would you have recognised me if no one had said anything?" she asked.

"Of course I would, my dear. How are you?" He did not wait for an answer. He was already turning away to address Ngao leaving Shao Peng embarrassed and feeling foolish. Janidah looked on with a puzzled frown. Again, she thought. He is behaving strangely again. Why?

❀ ❀ ❀

THE GUESTS HAD LEFT. They were in the bedroom. Outside the night sky was a sullen inky black. Once the eye became accustomed to the darkness, the bare outline of the shifting shapes of trees could be detected in the starlight. It was quiet. From time to time, an owl hooted and a flutter of wings set the leaves shuffling in the trees. The windows were thrown open allowing a slight damp breeze to blow in. The servants had turned down the bed and drawn the mosquito netting leaving the shutters ajar. It was too hot and humid to have them closed. Janidah was brushing her hair. The gas lamp cast a soft glow all round her. She was pleased with her reflection.

"Edward," she said over her shoulders, her voice breaking the still silence. He was in the dressing room. "Do you not think that Shao Peng is a little beauty?"

"I didn't notice," he replied.

"How could you not?" She got up, her brush in hand and strolled over to the dressing room. She leaned on the doorway.

"I am rather tired," he said squeezing past her. "I shall sleep in the other bedroom." He did not wish to discuss Shao Peng. He wanted to shut her image away.

"Her father plans to leave her in Singapore because of the chaos in Selangor. I have asked her to stay with us."

"What?" He spun around and walked towards her. "We didn't discuss this. I don't want her here."

"I thought you would be delighted. You adored her when she was a child. What has changed?"

He sat down heavily on a stool at the end of the bed, his face was drained of colour.

"What's wrong?" She bent over to touch his cheek. He brushed it aside.

"At times you are totally ... totally impossible..." He tousled his hair roughly, frustration, anger, guilt all mingled in one. "I can't have her here. I can't face her day in, day out. I ... I ..." His voice rose and then broke. Hua's face flashed before him and with it, Shao Peng's. In his mind eye they seemed to be one and the same, forever intertwined. The guilt he had so successfully suppressed bubbled up with ferocity. His inner demons were not tamed after all!

"You behaved most strangely with her father before and now with her. What is wrong? Please tell me."

He told her. The need to unburden and confess was overwhelming. He told her in a voice so low, it was barely audible. He left nothing out. She listened in silence without interrupting once. She knelt down.

"You were young, on your own, without your wife," she said. "It is difficult for young men to be celibate for years on end."

She held his face with both her hands and very gently, pushed away the lock of hair that had fallen over his forehead.

"You cannot undo what you have done. What you can do is make up for it. Helping Shao Peng would be the best thing you could do. It is dangerous for her to return to Selangor and you certainly would not wish her to be kidnapped, a real possibility in the lawless, highly anarchic situation there. She would be really miserable if she had to stay with Eng Kim's wife. You rescued her before. Remember? You must remember how that dreadful woman treated her?"

She got up and sat next to him, her arms around his shoulders. She bent close to his ear. "I don't think badly of you. I have seen the good in you. You have treated me well. Forgive yourself. Just do what is right now."

❀ ❀ ❀

SHAO PENG AND her father were in Eng Kim's house waiting for their host's return from the temple.

"I am not sure she is a good influence on you," said Ngao to his daughter. His suspicion that Janidah and Grime were together had been borne out. He was not quite sure if he approved. It was not his concern except if his daughter were to be involved.

"Please, I promise I will not do anything that would bring you shame. I will be happier there and I am sure that Uncle Grime, who looked after me so well when I was small, will make sure I do not do anything wrong," pleaded Shao Peng.

Ngao's eyes rested on his daughter for a second then he looked away. He was not only worried about Shao Peng's behaviour but of the men who saw her. Janidah was right, he thought, my daughter is a young woman now and beautiful like her mother. His heart contracted with pain whenever he thought of his first wife. He did not know why because he was very happy with Rohani. He loved her. He thought of her gentle ways, her lovely face; he was a lucky man and yet he continued to...

"Father did you hear me. Please let me stay with Uncle Grime."

He silenced her with a withering glance. He got up and walked to the lacquered screen. He ran his finger on the panel depicting the three figures, *Xingfu, Fanrong* and *Changshou*, representing happiness, prosperity and longevity. Grime is a good man, reliable, he thought. If Shao Peng were to be fruitfully occupied, perhaps it would work. She would certainly be safer in his residence than even in Eng Kim's house. Although Singapore was much safer than Kuala Lumpur, sporadic outbreaks of violence still occurred between the various Chinese factions in Chinatown. New mercenaries arriving in Singapore from China on their way to the hinterland of the Malay Peninsula also posed problems. That said Grime was not Chinese; much as he respected and trusted him he was still a *gweilo*, a foreigner with foreign ways. He was not sure he wanted his daughter to adopt such ways. And would Janidah be a good example? He hesitated.

"Papa..." she pleaded, sliding from her seat to her knees.

"I will consider it. I will speak to Uncle Eng Kim."

✿ ✿ ✿

"I AM NOT offended. I suppose it might be better for Shao Peng," said Eng Kim. He was glad because he could not tolerate another night of his wife's nagging. She obviously did not wish to have the girl and it was far better that it came from Ngao himself. He sighed. He was getting old, too old for the incessant domestic squabbles. He wanted to rid himself of all his troubles and give his full attention to his songbirds. Even his other two wives did not interest him as much. With the agreement that he would divide his time equally between them, a sort of peace had reigned between the women, that was until last night, when he told his first wife about the plan for Shao Peng to stay.

Eng Kim took a sip of his tea, savouring the aroma appreciatively, his lips hovering above the porcelain teacup. Steam rose and settled on his moustache. He raised his eyebrow and looked at Ngao; his eyes with a speculative gleam in them. "Would you like to take over my tin mines in Selangor?"

The invitation came from nowhere and took Ngao completely by surprise. His mind raced ahead considering what it would mean. He was elated. He had toyed with the idea of going into the industry in the past. Then he was strapped for cash. He was not any more. "Should I?" he asked himself. Suddenly a doubt crept in and his earlier elation dwindled.

"I don't have an heir. I am getting old and I do not wish to be embroiled any more in the endless round of fighting in Selangor," explained Eng Kim. "I am fed up with going up country. By now you know the tin business and you are on the spot in Selangor. I am not. We could easily come to an arrangement."

Ngao rose to his feet. He was overwhelmed by the offer. There was, however, a snag. He could not take it without telling Eng Kim his deepest worry. He owed that much to his mentor, the man who had given him a lifeline when he first started.

"Don't think I am not grateful for all that you have done for me and for giving me this opportunity. Before you pursue this offer, there is something you should know." Ngao sat down again. He leaned forward, resting his elbows on his thighs. "I do not know if I am of the right frame of mind at this time to take on the mines and do well by them. If I take them over I want to make a success of it and not fail you."

"What is the problem?" asked Eng Kim.

"I ... I am not myself. At times, I have dark thoughts. When this happens, I can't focus."

"I have noticed you seem unhappy at times," remarked Eng Kim. "Why don't you tell me about it? That is if you wish to."

Ngao could not bear to look Eng Kim in the eye. Instead he looked at his hands. He hesitated. Eng Kim had been like a father to him. If he could not speak to him, then to whom could he turn? Yet still he wavered. It would mean revealing so much of himself and the circumstances of his first wife's death, circumstances that no one knew. Would his confession create future problems for Shao Peng? Would it reduce her chance of a good marriage if it became known that her mother had died a prostitute? In this male dominated society a woman still had to prove her virtue to her in-laws on the marriage night. He had to be circumspect in what he said.

"Don't worry. What you tell me will remain in this room," assured Eng Kim.

"You swear by it?" asked Ngao.

Eng Kim nodded. "As the Heavenly God would bear witness."

"I am tortured by thoughts of my wife Hua's final days. I feel my aunt is hiding something from me. I have written to her again for answers. I plan to go back to China, to Canton, to where Hua was taken by force, to find out for myself. I do not know how long I'll be away. For that reason alone, this might not be the right time to take over your tin mines." His voice broke. There was so much anguish in his face that Eng Kim wanted to reach out and place an arm around him, like a father to a son. He refrained.

"And what good will that do?" he asked instead. "You have a new life, a new beginning. What good will digging up the past do for anyone? Why not let Hua rest in peace?"

"I can't bear the thought of her being violated, another person touching her, it turns my insides. My Hua was as pure as snow." He wept. He wept uncontrollably; great racking sobs, his shoulders shook and his breath came in rasps. This was the first time he had really let himself go, the first time he had spoken of his deepest thoughts. It made him nauseous to think of his wife with another man. At the same time he felt ashamed because he had let Hua down by leaving her on her own. He had failed to rescue her. Revulsion, shame, and anger took turns chasing his thoughts and pulling him in different directions.

It seemed like hours before he stopped sobbing. He was utterly spent. Eng Kim poured him a cup of tea. "There is too much at stake here for you to abandon everything to go back to China. You might lose everything while you are away. Tengku Kudin and Yap Ah Loy need you here. If you go, they will find another person to replace you. Let me try to write to your aunt. As one older person to another I can speak with more weight. I will also make some enquiries for you. Why didn't you come to me earlier?"

"Shame, for Hua and for me. I couldn't face the fact that she died in a brothel, that she had become a prostitute. I was small-minded to be so tortured and jealous when she was a victim. I was ashamed of my small mindedness."

"Go and rest. Leave it with me and let me try to find out more before you make any precipitous decisions. Remember your daughter is as much affected as you and she needs you."

"She reminds me too much of Hua."

"You should channel that to recall all the good memories and to banish the bad ones. Hua has left herself to you in her daughter."

Ngao nodded. The tears had liberated him, a weight seemed to have been lifted. He bade his mentor good night. Before going to bed, he stopped outside Shao Peng's room. He knocked and went in. She lay huddled in bed, looking vulnerable and lost. He saw her as the child he loved, not an unwanted reminder of Hua. She was someone who would forever link him to his past. His eyes were opened. He sat down beside her. He told her that she could stay with Grime. He told her how much he loved her. Then he held her for a long time. "I'll come back for you," he promised.

Chapter 40

BEILIU CITY

THE ROOM WAS almost bare. A table, a chair with a missing leg and a broken stool were all that remained in the main reception hall. Of the different rooms, only the study was left intact. Wan Fook, Heong Yook, the old retainer and the cook, had locked themselves in it when the looters came. The mob had smashed the front portal and forced their way into the house, pulling down the screen that stood behind the main entrance. They ransacked every room, running from one to the other, gathering all they could carry before bolting off. Like a typhoon they swept away just as quickly as they had swept in, leaving behind irreparable damage. Nothing was sacred. The ancestral tablet had been carelessly flung to the floor in the looters' hurry to carry away the altar table. All that was left were broken shards of granite stone. In the kitchen, the cupboard was bare. An eerie silence presided as the household tiptoed around clearing up the mess.

They were not the only ones to have suffered. Other households on the road had experienced a similar fate. Hunger drove people to do bad things, Heong Yook thought. She sat down; she was tired. She could not walk around nor bend down to clear the debris easily. Her feet hurt so. She needed a rest and then she would start again. All the servants had left, bar the cook and the old retainer. Mui was long gone; she went soon after Shao Peng left. She could never get on with the cook and, after one particularly gruelling episode and exchange of acrimonious words, she packed her bag and left. Slowly one after another, Heong Yook had freed the bondmaids and servants who had been part of her family. Times were changing and with it, people.

Wan Fook came in and sat beside her. She regarded her husband with affection. He too had changed. His hair had greyed completely. He looked careworn as though the whole nation's woes sat on his shoulders. Hua's death and his unwitting role in it, China's defeat and the ransacking of the Emperor's summer palace by western forces had already shaken him to the core, as had the huge indemnities China was forced to pay. But they were nothing compared to the effect of China's enforced legalisation of opium imports into the country. He took it personally. He had already lost his son to opium. Now he was seeing even more young men fall victim to the drug. "What hope or future do we have?" he had asked the evening they received news of their son's death. He had died alone in a far off provincial town in Fukien; his shrunken, emaciated body cremated by strangers. Wan Fook had wept; his lineage had been obliterated.

"I have checked the pottery," said Wan Fook aware of Heong Yook's eyes on him and thinking that his wife was worried about it. The pottery still provided them with a small income. "It has miraculously escaped the looting, probably because they knew they would not find any food there. We will be fine," he comforted her. "We do not need much furniture; we are not many."

"How long will all this turmoil go on for?" asked Heong Yook. She thought of what the house had been and compared it to what it had become. She was seized with despair and desperation.

He shrugged his shoulders. "It might be with us for years to come. We are squeezed on all sides. Foreigners want our land. Empress Dowager Cixi, that usurper, is corrupt and is completely out of touch with the people. Every day we see more and more people turning to banditry. The Taiping Rebellion might be over but a new wave of anarchy reigns. We never learn despite the millions of people killed during the rebellion. What hope do we have?"

"Not banditry," she replied rising from her chair with some difficulty and making her way to the kitchen. Her voice was weary, tinged also with bitterness. "They are banding together to strike at the foreign powers and to rebel against the Qing government. I don't blame them. A day will come where the Qing dynasty is no more and a new form of government will take over. We don't need another imperial emperor. Perhaps what we need is rule by the people for the people."

Wan Fook followed Heong Yook, holding her by the elbow, as she made her way to the southern buildings. They walked into the kitchen, an area he had never visited in his heyday. It was the territory of his servants. How things had changed; first Heong Yook ventured into it and now even he.

The cook was moving slowly retrieving pieces of broken ceramics. Bowls were smashed into useless fragments. A pot lay on its side, its contents spilled out into a congealed mess. A looter must have eaten some of the contents. A spoon licked clean lay next to it. Chicken feathers rose like a cloud of dust as she rummaged through the debris. "Our one chicken, my precious little thing. Gone!" she lamented.

"Is there any rice left at all?" he asked.

"I'll check," she replied. She walked with a slow wobbly gait to a small adjoining room, shifting her weight from side to side. The pain in her arthritic ankle was excruciating. She lifted a cloth covering the low wooden plank platform that served as her bed. Underneath it was a small ceramic pot. She bent over and pulled it out. Uncovering the wooden lid, she dipped her hand in and brought out a fistful of rice. She allowed the grains to slip through her fingers back into the urn before covering and pushing it once more under the bed. Carefully, she lowered the cloth. "We have enough for a few days if we cook a watery rice congee."

Wan Fook walked over to her and placed a hand on her shoulder. He patted it warmly before turning away. "Well done for hiding the rice."

The cook almost jumped in shock with that one contact. She was moved that the master had touched her in such a friendly way and gratified by his praise. Of late she had become disgruntled with her lot when her nephews and uncles talked about the mass movement against the middle class and rich. No, she thought, the family she serves were not that kind of people.

Oblivious to the cook's reaction, Wan Fook laughed, a dry bitter laugh. "We certainly will not be demanding 150 dishes to be prepared for each meal like Empress Cixi. And we will certainly not be eating with golden chopsticks or drinking from jade wine cups." Taking hold of Heong Yook's elbow, he led her out of the kitchen and into the walkway that linked the different buildings.

"Cook's family are among those who have become bandits," Heong Yook whispered, "so be careful what you say. They have ensconced themselves in the hills. I didn't realise the depth of people's anger, ordinary people: farmers, traders and labourers. I didn't realise there was so much nationalistic and anti-foreign feelings. I thought it was only the gentry, the educated people who are expressing dissatisfaction."

"The indemnities that China has to pay to the foreign powers touch us all," said Wan Fook. "Cixi passes all of the penalties on to us while continuing to squander the nation's wealth on herself."

"In cook's village the anger is not just over the taxes they pay toward the indemnities. They are unhappy that so many foreign priests have been allowed into the country. Christian missionaries have taken over the temple in her village."

Wan Fook shook his head in sorrow. "What do you expect now that China has to allow foreigners to travel freely within its borders? It is one of the terms of the treaties forced on us. An increase in the number of Christian missionaries is inevitable."

"Cook says the villagers are angry at the special privileges given to the missionaries. Foreign priests, she says, have taken land from the villagers and deem themselves to be above Chinese laws. She admits that not the entire village is of the same mind, for there are those who have adopted the new religion. They are defending the Christian priests, while others are up in arms against them. So the villagers are turning on themselves as well."

She lowered her voice and whispered into her husband's ears. "I heard her say that some of the villagers are planning to attack the temple to reclaim it. I fear this will again bring the wrath of the English and French forces on us."

They reached the study. "What shall we do?" she asked her husband.

"Nothing," he replied, "as far as the cook's village is concerned. We can't go to the authorities to inform on them. Moreover who can we trust to tell?" He paused at the entrance to his study and said, "What we have to do is perhaps think of ourselves and what we should do."

She went ahead of him into the study and made her way to the chest of drawers. She retrieved three letters. "Here read these. They arrived together. One is from Shao Peng asking us to join them. The other is from Ngao. Again he asks for more details of Hua's death. Even after all these years. I have not told him and he is tortured by it. I wanted to spare him. He is so persistent. Now he is threatening to go to Canton to find out for himself. I know he is angry with me."

"And the third letter?" asked Wan Fook.

"From Eng Kim. He urges us to tell Ngao everything to give him peace of mind."

"Will you tell Ngao?"

"No!" she said. "He worshipped Hua. He will take it badly."

"Do you want to go to *Nanyang* Malaya? I know you miss Shao Peng," he asked.

"Yes I miss Shao Peng," she paused, and then shook her head, "but no, I won't go." Heong Yook gazed into the distance a faraway look in her eyes. She saw through the open door the courtyard and, beyond it, on the opposite side, the western room. Despite the damage done and the bareness of the place, this house was her world. "What about you?" she asked her husband.

"I am too old to leave and start anew. My place is here. I will try in my small way to make this a better place to live. I cannot forsake China."

She reached out and touched his hand. "My place is with you." She laughed. "Who would want me?" she asked pointing to her feet.

He threaded his fingers around hers and squeezed them. She was gladdened by the decision. At least she was freed from worrying about the matter. They had made up their minds.

"While I do not wish to tell Ngao the truth I have to respond to his persistent questioning. I do not know what to say," she said.

"You have to tell him that she took her own life. You can't just ignore his questions. Tell him she did it to protect her virtue. Tell him that they failed to prostitute her. Don't let him know that she was raped. I am a man, I know. It will help Ngao. Do not tell him about the Englishman. He has done us a great service. He has helped bring Shao Peng to her father and from all accounts has looked after her well. What is more we gave our promise to him."

"So we should not tell him the whole truth like Eng Kim urges?" At times she felt like capitulating to Ngao's questions. She was beginning to be worn down by his persistence.

"It will do more harm than good. It will not give him any peace of mind to be indebted to someone who violated his wife and indirectly caused her death."

Heong Yook sighed. How strange it was to discuss saving a man, a *fan gui,* a European devil. Her husband was right. She would take his advice and write accordingly, not because of the *fan gui* but for the sake of Ngao and Shao Peng.

Chapter 41

THE BABY WAS crying. Rohani quickly hitched her top up and gently guided the baby to her nipple. The crying subsided. The baby grunted with contentment, his lips clamped round the dark centre of her swollen breast. Rohani raised her eyes and met Ngao's. He smiled. His heart swelled with happiness. He turned to Siew Loong. "Your sister will be back soon," he said. He reached out to tousle his son's dark hair. Across the table, the baby gurgled. Ngao sat himself down on the wooden stool by the table. His mind drifted to the events of the past years.

Six years had passed since he left Shao Peng in Singapore. During those turbulent years the civil war in Selangor escalated to such levels that no one believed it could come to an end. The victory finally achieved by Tengku Kudin and Yap Ah Loy was far from straightforward. Raja Mahdi with the support of Syed

Mashor and Yap's arch enemy Chong Chong had repeatedly attacked Kuala Lumpur with Chong Chong mounting the attack from Ampang. Ngao remembered Chong's force of some 2500 men arriving in Ampang and the horror he felt to find his house and family endangered. He had chosen that very location because he thought it safe and far away from the epicentre of conflict. That was then. With the escalation of the civil war, nowhere was safe.

Ngao and his family had fled with nothing more than the clothes on their backs to his store in Kuala Lumpur, the very place he had previously sought to avoid. At least, it had Yap's force defending it and he, himself, could play a part in protecting the town. He knew by then his previous resolve not to be involved was unrealistic. It was fight or die.

Each day, he and his family and all the town residents waited anxiously for news of the fighting. He remembered the joy and jubilation when news arrived of Yap's victory. His success in the early years in getting re-enforcements from the rajas of Damansara and Ulu Klang were greeted with elation and celebrated by the townspeople. Ngao remembered how he had jumped with relief with the rest of them when he heard that Yap had succeeded in attacking Chong from the rear, overturning his strategy of surrounding Kuala Lumpur. Yap had brought in reinforcements from Singapore and had routed Chong's force. A few months later Chong launched a counter attack; again Yap intercepted him. Chong lost hundreds, some said, thousands of men. Under the sweltering heat of the sun, the smell of blood and decaying corpses had filled the air with such a stench that men choked and retched. Ngao remembered barring the doors and closing the windows to stop the foul air from infiltrating into the shop. Rohani and Siew Loong had hidden behind the sacks and boxes in the rear of the house while he ventured out with others to help barricade the town and to retrieve the wounded. Clouds of flies rose in the air as they searched for kin and friends.

Chong and Syed Mashor fled only to reappear within months. They had not given up. They gathered a new force and launched another attack, this time from Ulu Selangor. Yet once more, Yap succeeded in outmanoeuvring and routing Chong's men.

Then, a year later the tide turned against Yap Ah Loy. Syed Mashor once again surrounded Kuala Lumpur, starving the town of supplies. Ngao's eyes swam with tears at the memory: the killing, the suffering, the starvation and above all the treachery that had caused it all. Tengku Kudin had sent one of his men to bring provisions to Yap's men and the town. He was also supposed to bring reinforcements. In the midst of battle, he switched sides. Yap was outnumbered by ten to one and betrayed. Ngao remembered the day vividly. They were forced to abandon the town. They had no alternative: it was that or risk being massacred. They ran. Ngao with Siew Loong in his arms and Rohani heavy with child followed Yap and his retreating force. Mahsor's men pursued them. The massacre began. One thousand seven hundred of Yap's men died.

Ngao could feel the emotion rising in his chest as he recalled tripping over the dead, men falling all round him as he and his family ran. It was a miracle they escaped; yet the knowledge that many others were less fortunate filled him even now with remorse. He looked up somehow aware that Rohani was looking at him.

"What are you thinking about?" she asked.

"Do you remember the time we fled to Klang, to Tengku Kudin?

She nodded. "*Jangan,* Don't. I don't want to be reminded of it," she said, tears forming in her own eyes. She felt the pain in her abdomen as though it was still fresh. Her arm went round her baby protectively.

"We lost everything. Kapitan Yap lost two-thirds of his men. Do you remember how distraught he was?" he continued. "Yet within two months, he had raised sufficient troops, sending for men from China, to launch a counter attack. He recaptured Kuala Lumpur. Do you remember how the town people came to welcome us?"

"*Shhh!* Don't think about it anymore," she said rocking the baby in her arm.

"What I want to say is we too can rise from our present situation. We can regain what we have lost. When Shao Peng comes home, we will be a complete family again. We'll start again."

"*Tak apa.* It does not matter," Rohani whispered. "It really does not matter. They are just material things. As long as we are all together and alive."

Ngao brushed his eyes with his sleeves. He was lucky that his family had survived. Still he regretted the loss: the loss of life and the destruction of Kuala Lumpur. He also regretted his own losses. He looked around the room they were in; it was tiny with walls that had been scarred and ravaged. When Shao Peng returns, he would take her to see their old house or what remained of it. Then she would understand why he had left her in Singapore. Hua would have approved. He sensed Rohani's eyes on him. He went to her and, dropping down on his knees, took her and the baby in his arms. Hua would also approve of

Rohani. He was sure of it. Rohani had been unfailing in her believe in him. He loved her unreservedly. His inner demons had been laid to rest.

❀ ❀ ❀

IT WAS A day like any other day. Shao Peng got up from the breakfast table and walked out to the veranda. She lifted her face to the sun and felt her skin tingle with its heat. A light sea breeze blew, lifting a strand of her hair up and away from her face. Quickly she drew her hair into a bunch and twirled it into a neat coil. Digging deep into the pocket of her pinafore, she drew out a hairpin and carelessly secured her hair. She had taken to wearing a dress with a pinafore. She looked at her stocking feet shod in shoes that were far too heavy and hot. Should she take them off like Janidah did, she wondered. Impulsively she took her shoes off. She walked out on to lawn carrying them in her hand and made her way to the Angsenna tree. It was in full bloom, its brilliant yellow flowers all but covered the leaves. The branches provided welcome shade from the fiery sun above.

She sat down on the grass, delved into her pocket and took out the letter that had been delivered that morning. It had arrived after Uncle Grime had left for the office taking Janidah with him. She was going to drop him off on her way to the ladies' coffee morning. Shao Peng smiled. No doubt she would assail them with a hilarious account of the morning's event. Janidah was always able to see the lighter side of things, a wonderful companion for someone like me, she thought. A shadow crossed her face. At times she felt almost like an orphan.

She had not seen her father for six years. He had not been back to Singapore since he left her there. Uncle Grime had explained that it was impossible for her father to visit. Uncle Eng Kim had been to see her several times and confirmed what had been said. It seemed unreal that it should be so bad in the hinterland of the Malay states and so tranquil here. She looked across to the house with its white clad walls and the deep cool verandas. Bougainvilleas nodded their heads riotously splashing their vibrant colours on the wall. She tore open the letter and read quickly and hungrily, her eyes following the columns of characters.

She let out a squeal. She got up, picked up her skirt and ran back into the house. "I have to pack," she yelled to the wind. Her voice echoed across the lawn. The gardener turned in astonishment and the cook came hurrying from the backyard to see what had caused the commotion. She laughed and waved to them and hitching her skirt up ran into the house and up the stairway leaving her shoes behind under the tree.

Once in her room, she sat down and retrieved the letter to read it once more. She was not unhappy here. Far from it she had enjoyed herself. True to their word, Janidah and Uncle Grime had spared no effort in getting her the education she had been promised. She studied Chinese and learnt English. Uncle Eng Kim was always somewhat baffled when she told him about her studies but her aunt Heong Yook was delighted.

She re-read the letter and let it flutter to the ground. "I can go home," she whispered. "I'll see my father, Rohani and Siew Loong. I'll also see my new baby brother, Siew Wong." She grew excited. What would she find? Her father had warned her that she would be shocked to see the changes that had taken place. Would they see her as changed? She walked to the mirror. The image that stared back was as familiar to her as the palms of her hands: oval face, jet-black hair and dark brown eyes. She thought nothing of them. Instinctively, she touched her hair. The coil had come undone. Her father would not like it. She thought of the time when Janidah had tried to impress upon him to let her wear it loose. Slowly, she undressed, peeling off her pinafore, her dress and the underlay of petticoats. She would have to get use to wearing her Chinese clothes again.

Her disquiet grew. Would her father too raise the question of marriage like Uncle Eng Kim? In her father's absence, Eng Kim had suggested to Uncle Grime, that perhaps he ought to be thinking about Shao Peng's future. She was getting old and should be married. "*Loh koo poh hai ho koo tok*, a spinster is one plagued with loneliness," she had heard him say in Cantonese. "If I had my way I would have married her off years ago. There were umpteen eligible young Chinese men who would have married her then. Now..." he shook his head with regret, "it might be too late. At twenty-four, she is too old!"

She sat on her bed, her early excitement somewhat abated. Her hand went to the side table beside the bed. Slowly, almost reverently she picked up a small dance card. She placed it to her lips. She recalled the ball, her first. She went because Janidah had forbade her to remain in her room while the ball was held downstairs in the reception. She had not danced; she didn't know how. Yet he had written his name down. "I'll come and sit with you," he had said. She closed her eyes. She could see him even now; his face with eyes the colour of the deep ocean, so different from her own. She had to look up to him when they spoke for she reached only up to his shoulders. From below, she heard Janidah's voice. She jumped up and ran down light as a deer, her feet skimming over the steps. She would talk to Janidah.

"Of course your father won't force you to marry," Janidah replied at once. She laughed and pooh-poohed the idea, flopping down on the sofa. Patting the seat next to her, she said, "We'll miss you. You must write and now that things are more settled over there, you will be able to visit us. Promise," she said. "We'll make arrangements for your travel once Edward returns." Impulsively, Janidah drew Shao Peng close to her. "We'll miss you," she whispered against her ear.

THE SUN FILLED every nook and cranny of the store with light. They had cleared and scoured it. Sacks of rice and other dried provisions stood in a corner and some of the shelves were filled. The store was once more open for business. Already it was beginning to look like it had before.

Ngao walked nervously from one end of the shop to the other. He had woken at the crack of dawn. Shao Peng was due to arrive any time with Mr Grime. He was immensely grateful to the man for not only caring for his daughter but also bringing her back. "He has a heart as big as an ox," he had said to Rohani. "I do not know how to repay his kindness. For certainly nothing is safer than travelling with the protection of the British Government. I am happy that at long last after a decade of lobbying for their help to arbitrate amongst the warring Malay factions, the British have agreed to appoint a British Resident to advise the Sultan."

Ngao shifted a sack of rice and fidgeted with a crate beside it. Any minute now, he thought. His throat was dry. He had been looking forward to this moment. He had missed his daughter. Nothing could take away his happiness at having his entire family with him, not even the devastation of a large part of his business. For devastation it was. The mines he had acquired from Eng Kim were completely flooded and the machinery destroyed. He had lost his entire labour force. The noodle factory was razed to the ground. Restarting would be a long haul. He forced himself away from these thoughts. If I have the will, I will find the way, he thought. He looked around his diminished store and spoke out loud, "I will fill this again and even my next store. I have done it before and I can do it again."

Someone clapped. Ngao turned around. In the doorway, framed against the light, stood a young woman. She ran to him and within seconds her arms were around him.

"Papa," she cried pressing her face to his. It was wet with tears. She had been standing at the doorway looking at her father, seeing the sadness in his face and the nervous way he was re-arranging the sacks and crates. During the journey she had seen the destruction in the surrounding countryside and the town. She almost jumped out of her carriage to help the people toiling in the sun with tears streaming from their eyes. Everything she had known six years ago had been destroyed. She had seen the town flooded and burned before but never destruction on a scale like this. She felt ashamed of her worries for herself. They were insignificant, nothing compared to what her father and the rest of the family must have gone through.

Slowly, tentatively Ngao placed his arms round the young woman. "Shao Peng," he said tenderly. After a while he placed her at arms length to look at her. His heart leapt. She was the splitting image of Hua. This time his heart was filled with gladness. She was Hua's gift to him. He had done right by Shao Peng by sending her away, away from the chaos that had befallen them. She was safe. He looked across and saw Edward Grime. He nodded in acknowledgement and mouthed, "*Xie xie*, thank you."

Ngao beckoned Rohani. She was holding the baby in one arm and Siew Loong with the other hand. Shao Peng turned. She rushed to them before they could reach her and embraced all three. "I missed all of you."

"*Saya juga*. And I you," cried Rohani.

Grime smiled. He too felt at peace. He had done the best he could. He had said his farewell to Shao Peng. It was time to let go of his guilt. Without waiting for Ngao, he walked out of the store accompanied by the young cadet he had brought with him, the cadet who would be staying on in Selangor to support the new British Advisor to Sultan Samad of Selangor. He had seen how the young man looked at Shao Peng and she at him.

Epilogue

BACKGROUND

"As the confidence of his countrymen in Yap Ah Loy is great, if not implicit, so is his stake in the country superior to that of all others, and from this fact I conclude that the government may rely upon him to use his influence for law and order, and that his past loyalty and successful administration of the District entrusted to him would seem to entitle him to consideration and a careful hearing of his views on matters affecting the well-being of the Chinese population in general and in Kuala Lumpur in particular. It is his (Yap's) perseverance alone, I believe, (that) has kept the Chinese in the country."

—FRANK SWETTENHAM
(first Resident General of the Federated Malay States)

YAP AH LOY is widely credited as the founder of modern Kuala Lumpur, the capital city of Malaysia. He was born in 1837 in Tam Shui village in Guangdong, China. He was a Hakka. He came to Malaya in 1854 at the age of seventeen as a coolie and took up various jobs. He rose from being a tin mine labourer, a shop assistant, a cook, a handy man, a pig keeper, a *panglima* (Malay for warrior) to become finally *Kapitan China* of Kuala Lumpur. The term *Kapitan China* was used to refer to a Chinese leader who had the powers equivalent to a Malay chief, including the power to make laws and pronounce death penalties. His leadership had to be confirmed by the Sultan of the state

Yap Ah Loy became the third Kapitan China of Kuala Lumpur, succeeding Liu Ngim Kong, in 1868. His leadership was confirmed and endorsed by the Sultan of Selangor, Sultan Samad, in whose state Kuala Lumpur was situated. Liu Ngim Kong's relatives were unhappy with the appointment. Supported by Chong Chong, who had been one of Yap Ah Loy's early employers, they took up arms against Yap.

In 1866, even prior to Yap's appointment, Selangor was in a state of civil war. The conflict arose because of a dispute over the succession to Sultan Muhammad who died in 1857 without appointing an heir to the throne. The two main opponents were Raja Abdullah, son-in-law of the deceased, and Raja Mahdi, the grandson of the deceased and son of the former ruler of Klang. Raja Abdullah supported the appointment of Raja Samad, the nephew of the late Sultan Muhammad, as the Sultan of Selangor. When Raja Samad became the Sultan of Selangor, he saw Raja Mahdi's continued refusal to remit revenues to him as a grievous affront. The Sultan appointed Tengku Kudin as his Viceroy to deal with Raja Mahdi. Tengku Kudin worked with Raja Abdullah and after Raja Abdullah died, his son Raja Ismail, against Raja Mahdi. Yap Ah Loy became a staunch supporter of Tengku Kudin.

Into this fray came Syed Mashor, a Borneo-born fighter. Originally under Tengku Kudin, he subsequently switched his allegiance to Raja Mahdi.

The Selangor civil war hence was divided into two camps: Sultan Samad, Raja Abdullah, Tengku Kudin and Yap Ah Loy on one side; and Raja Mahdi, Syed Mashor and Chong Chong opposing them.

The civil war began in 1866 and lasted until 1874.

Up until 1874, British involvement in the Selangor wars was largely peripheral. Britain ruled the Straits Settlements comprising Singapore, Penang and Malacca. The policy of the Colonial Office in London was not to intervene in the warring states in the Malay Peninsula. There were, however, several occasions when they deviated from this policy of non-intervention.

In 1871, pirates attacked a Chinese merchant ship from Penang. The British authorities traced the piracy to Raja Mahdi and forcefully drove him out of Kuala Selangor. Following this J.W.W. Birch, Singapore's colonial secretary, formally acknowledged Tengku Kudin's position as Viceroy to Sultan Samad in Selangor.

In November 1873, another case of piracy in the waters off Selangor provoked a further extension of British influence. Governor Andrew Clarke of the Straits Settlements persuaded Sultan Samad to accept a British Advisor. In August 1874, Frank Swetternham was sent in the interim to live at the Sultan's royal capital of Langat as Assistant Resident until the arrival of the British Resident. In 1875, the following year James Guthries Davidson was officially appointed as British Resident of Selangor and Selangor became a British Protectorate. In 1876, Captain Bloomfield Douglas succeeded JG Davidson as

British Resident. In September 1882 Frank Swettenham, who had in the interim moved to other Malay states distinguishing himself as a member of the Commission for the Pacification of Larut following the Perak Wars, replaced him.

After the civil war, Yap Ah Loy undertook the reconstruction of Kuala Lumpur. He brought in fresh labour from around the Malay Peninsula and China to rebuild the city and restart the tin mines. He imported supplies for its reconstruction, borrowing money for the purpose. In this, he was fortunate to have the sponsorship of the British Resident J.G. Davidson. He encouraged Malay farmers to grow paddy to reduce reliance on imports from abroad. He established law and order, built a prison, and established Kuala Lumpur as a centre of commerce in Selangor. Fire frequently broke out in Kuala Lumpur because the buildings were made mainly of wood and attap. In 1881, after the town was burnt down, he started a brickworks just outside to rebuild the town. This area is now known as Brickfields. He also devised and constructed a road system connecting the town with the main mining areas and laid out the streets of Kuala Lumpur. Petaling Street, as it is known today was the site of his tapioca mill which gave rise to the Chinese name, *Chee Cheong Kai*, for the street. He contributed to the founding of the first Chinese school in Kuala Lumpur and took an active part in the development of its pupils. Yap Ah Loy died on 15 April 1885 at the age of forty-eight.

Kapitans China of Kuala Lumpur:
- Hiu Siew 1858–1861
- Liu Ngim Kong 1862–1868
- Yap Ah Loy 1868–1885
- Yap Ah Shak 1885–1889
- Yap Kwan Seng 1889–1902

About the Author

CHAN LING YAP (or Yap Chan Ling when in Asia) was born in Kuala Lumpur. She was educated in Malaysia and subsequently in England where she obtained a PhD in Economics. She lectured at the University of Malaya before joining the United Nations Food and Agriculture Organization in Rome where she worked for nearly two decades. She now lives in the UK with her husband and family. *New Beginnings* is her third novel. For more information visit www.chanlingyap.com.

Also by Chan Ling Yap

SWEET OFFERINGS
ISBN: 978-981-4328-44-9
Set in the late 1930s and 1960s, this is the story of Mei Yin, a young Chinese girl from an impoverished family. Her destiny is shaped when she is sent to Kuala Lumpur to become the companion of the tyrannical and bitter Su Hei who is looking for a suitable wife for her son Ming Kong ... and ultimately a grandson and heir to the family dynasty.

Sweet Offerings is not just a fictional story of the events that ripped one family apart, but a taste of Malaysia's historical, political and cultural changes during its transition from colonial rule to independence and beyond.

BITTER-SWEET HARVEST
ISBN: 978-981-4351-68-3
Set in a Malaysia emerging from the outbreak of racial conflict in 1969, *Bitter-Sweet Harvest* tells of the difficulties and tensions of a marriage between a Malay Muslim and a Chinese Christian. Atmospheric, dramatic, action-packed and intriguing, this novel is peppered with local flavour evoking the heat, colours and sounds of Southeast Asia. Prepare to be taken on a spell-binding journey through contrasting cultures: from the learned spires of Oxford in England to the east coast of Peninsula Malaysia; from vibrant Singapore to Catholic Rome and developing Indonesia.